W

"The writing duo that makes up Ashleigh Raine really did an outstanding job on Lover's Talisman. They found an intriguing combination of action, science fiction, magic, and suspense. ... This is a multi-layered adventure that has something for everyone. I highly recommend this book; it is a fun filled roller coaster ride with laughter and nail biting suspense. Overall rating: 5 hearts." - *Sara Sawyer*

"LOVER'S TALISMAN is a fun and thrilling paranormal romance that will keep you reading late into the night. Ms. Raine's unique humor will have you laughing out loud... If you like laughter with your loving and enjoy a good paranormal, this one is not to be missed." – *Nicole LaFolle, Sensual Romance Reviews*

Discover for yourself why readers can't get enough of the multiple-award-winning publisher Ellora's Cave. Whether you prefer e-books or paperbacks, be sure to visit EC on the web at www.ellorascave.com for an erotic reading experience that will leave you breathless.

www.ellorascave.com

Ellora's Cave Publishing, Inc.
PO Box 787
Hudson, OH 44236-0787

ISBN # 1-84360-558-9

Lover's Talisman, 2003.
ALL RIGHTS RESERVED
Ellora's Cave Publishing, Inc.
© Lover's Talisman, Ashleigh Raine, 2003.

This book may not be reproduced in whole or in part without author and publisher permission.

Ashleigh Raine edited by Briana St. James.
Cover art by Jason Stoddard.

Warning: The following material contains strong sexual content meant for mature readers. *LOVER'S TALISMAN* has been rated NC-17, erotic, by a minimum of three independent reviewers. We strongly suggest storing this book in a place where young readers not meant to view it are unlikely to happen upon it. That said, enjoy…

LOVER'S TALISMAN

Written by

ASHLEIGH RAINE

Dedication

To our hubbies for understanding late nights, dirty houses and high phone bills.

To Bree for holding her breath in a good way, Allie for showing us where LT really started, and MamaZ for loving Freeze as much as we do.

To Wendy for bringing us Harmony.

And to those who've been with us from the very beginning. We'll be loving you forever.

Prologue

A steady balance
Truth and Darkness
The forces equal
Preventing chaos or epiphany

Where water caresses sand
A leader who walks in shadows
A fighter in Truth's war
Will find a destined love
Her untouched strength from birth will rise
And alter the path of time

To create a new beginning
In life as well as war
The balance will be shifted
Light will shine through darkness' door

But more than one may change the fates
And chaos may surprise
Light can be extinguished
And shadows won't survive

    Black eyes sparked as they memorized the words written in blood and tears on the parchment. This interpretation of Fate's whimsy was twisted in nature, but honest. Fire flashed from strong fingers and the prophecy crumbled to ash. Perfect white teeth gleamed in a dark smile.

The game of destiny had just begun.

Chapter One

Sure, it was Stephan's duty as a Shadow Walker to rid the city of demon mayhem, but this had gotten boring. And old. Things had to change and change immediately. Hadn't he sacrificed enough yet? His patience was absolutely spent.

"I'm gonna rip your fuckin' head off if you don't put that down."

The Crayken demon snarled, told him to fuck off in his native tongue, and took off running. For a brief moment Stephan thought about letting the little bugger go, but his constitution wouldn't let him. Talisman Bay was his town. No demon havoc of any kind was allowed.

Stephan caught up quickly. The ugly runt couldn't scramble fast enough. He grabbed its shoulder and spun it around to face him. "Get the fuck outta here."

"But I'm just trying to make an honest living," the Crayken whined, looking up at him. Stephan towered over the coward by almost two feet.

"There's nothing honest about what you're doing. I asked you to leave. I'm not gonna ask again." Stephan strode straight for him as the tattoo-covered demon retreated backward into an alley.

"Don't come any closer or I'll kill you."

Stephan just shook his head at the pipsqueak.

"You, kill me?" Stephan crossed his hands over his chest and laughed darkly as he continued. "You think you're hard enough? Then bring it on." Stephan dodged the cinderblock as it whizzed past his head. Then he lunged at the infuriated imp.

The brawl was expertly quick. As much as Stephan didn't like fighting beings smaller than he was, he really needed—wanted—to rip something's head off. As luck would have it, that was the only way to kill a Crayken demon. At least clean up would be easy. Without their heads, they turned to dust. Stephan scattered the demon remains with his boot and continued on his way.

Then his eyes discovered something much prettier than any Crayken demon.

He watched the woman from the shadows, a grim smile on his face.

The distant streetlights illuminated her pale skin, adding a life to it that wasn't really there. Full scarlet lips were the only true color in her face. She was damn sexy, an alluring mix of sensuality and innocence.

Too bad he had to kill her.

She relaxed against the wall outside of Talisman Bay's only strip club, *Silver Twilight*, wearing a thin cotton sun dress and not much else. No one else seemed to wonder why she wasn't chilled by the cool sea breeze. No one else knew what she really was. And no one else would become her prey.

Stephan stepped from the shadows and approached the club, becoming just another hapless victim in her eyes. She ran her tongue over her lips, making them seem even redder…fuller, and with practiced skill, her brown eyes welled with tears. In this little drama, it was time for his line.

"You okay? Can I help you with anything?" Stephan played his role to perfection, injecting each word with the right mix of concern and desire. He caught a quick flash of victory in her eyes before she became the victim again.

She stepped forward, placing one small hand on his arm. "I was on a date…things went bad. I—" Here she broke and let a few select tears roll down her cheeks. "I had to make a quick getaway, and I left my purse behind. I don't have any money, no cell phone…"

"Can I take you somewhere?" Stephan hurried the show along. There was only one conclusion and he didn't need to draw it out.

She smiled up at him, the tears magically disappearing from her eyes. And some men actually fell for this? Stephan shook his head at man's weakness for good pussy. She frowned at him, and he smiled at her, repairing the damage his actions had caused.

"Sorry, just wondering how anyone could treat you badly." Stephan held back his laugh. That line played well into her fantasies and her smile grew. "Here, I'm parked behind the club. I'll drive you somewhere." He held out his arm and she took it, and they stepped together into the darkness of the alley between the buildings.

He was ready when it happened. She tripped and he caught her against him, letting her cling tightly to him. Eyes flashed desire and she stood taller and kissed him, her tongue immediately darting into his mouth.

He kissed her back, the adrenaline pulsing through him. She tasted like sweet wine, not blood. He must have been her first chosen this night.

He quickly pulled his mouth away, surprising her as she didn't have time to hide her red eyes or elongated teeth.

He shrugged. "Sorry, babe. I don't fuck vampires." He struck out quickly, the stake sinking deep before she had a chance to retreat. She collapsed at his feet, no longer a danger to the men of Talisman Bay.

It wasn't as easy as the TV shows portrayed it. Vampires didn't burst into clouds of dust when they were staked. The only thing that would turn a vampire to ashes was fire or sun...neither of which were an option at this point. And he couldn't exactly leave her body in they alley for someone else to stumble upon.

He threw her body over his shoulder—thankful she was a lightweight—and climbed on top of the dumpster. The ladder to the roof of *Silver Twilight* was about four feet away. He tightened his hold on her body, stepped to the edge of the dumpster, and jumped, catching the ladder with one arm. Quickly, he adjusted the body, and using both arms, pulled himself up the ladder far enough for his feet to grab purchase.

Within minutes he'd reached the roof and laid out her body. The early morning sun would destroy all remnants of this vampire. One more killer off the streets.

Stephan smirked as he climbed back down the ladder and dropped the ten feet to the ground. He and the rest of the Shadow Walkers were the biggest killers in Talisman Bay, but they did it for the good of the town.

Stephan made a right at the corner, smiling and nodding at the people exiting *Silver Twilight*—people who had no idea that he kept their city a safe and pleasant place to live. The duality of his nature made him want to laugh, but not a jolly laugh, more the laugh of the clinically insane.

Music pounded out through the open doors of the club. Stephan started to walk by, to continue with his patrolling but he found himself stepping inside without a second thought.

He walked into *Silver Twilight,* his worn jeans and black leather jacket mirroring the shadows in the corners where it seemed life ceased to exist. He exchanged friendly greetings and shook hands with a man he recognized from the Chamber of Commerce, but he didn't linger. The pounding music momentarily drew his attention to the stage where girls in various stages of dress and undress accepted money from the drunken patrons. His gaze slowly wandered over the crowd, watching for anyone or anything that seemed out of place. Nothing seemed unusual but old habits die hard so he moved to a table in a back corner. There, no one could approach him unseen.

So this was the place that his friends had been fighting over patrolling. Funny how they could be entertained by a few nude women and think it was just the greatest thing in the world. He didn't really know what the hell he was doing here. He hadn't actually been inside *Silver Twilight* since before...well, before everything had changed.

He and his brother were looking for some fun, and they had snuck in on his 20th birthday — just weeks before his life had been irrevocably altered. They were hot heads desperate to get laid and with the over-exuberance and arrogance of youth they had thought that the women would flock to them. Well, the women had flocked, taken their money and walked away laughing. Leaving Stephan and Marlin embarrassed, horny and sadly alone. Stephan chuckled at the memory. Everything had seemed so dire then. Shit. That was nothing.

Stephan ordered a beer from a woman whose face was plastered with enough make-up to keep Revlon in business for the next decade. She smiled and flirted with him but her tired eyes and hunched shoulders told the real story. Another lost soul. This town seemed to collect them. She returned moments later with a cold beer in a warm glass. He paid her with a hundred dollar bill and told her to keep the change. The light returned to her eyes for a moment but then she closed back up and tucked the bill into her bra.

Today was the anniversary of when he and his friends' lives had completely changed. He lifted his glass in a silent mock toast. None of his friends had made reference to it at the patrol meeting that night, but Stephan knew that they were all thinking about it.

Twelve years ago, their friend, David, had betrayed them in the worst way possible. Sure, they'd ended up cheating death, but the ultimatum offered made them essentially sacrifice their lives anyway. Not in death, but service.

Stephan never saw David again. He'd just disappeared from their lives as quickly as he'd appeared. Their friendship had only been about six months, but it had been incredibly close...or so he'd thought. Rumor had it David had killed himself. It was certainly possible. David always had problems trying to deal with his less than perfect life. Stephan gritted his teeth in heartfelt frustration. He'd never learned what made David turn on them — and that was what bothered him the most.

His thoughts wandered further into the betrayal, anguish and sacrifice that had created his twisted adult life. Stephan chugged down the last of his beer and motioned for the waitress to bring him another. This was going to be another long night of painful memories.

The lights changed on the stage and a hush went over the crowd of drunken men surrounding it. Stephan sat up to scope out the audience, prepared for anything. Something was about to happen, he could feel it.

The rowdy mass began to surge forward. The bouncers had to remove a few particularly amorous guys who were getting too close to the stage. Mist began pumping from the edges of the runway as the stage went dark. A haunting Celtic melody filled the room as a single spotlight lit the stage entrance.

Unexpected chills ran up and down Stephan's spine as a woman stepped on stage, dressed from head to toe in filmy, flowing silver. He forgot about his beer as she danced slowly, sensually to the music, moving in and out of the mist that surrounded her body. The fabric shimmered and glistened, displaying tantalizing glimpses of the smooth white flesh underneath. The deep blush of her nipples peeked through the fabric, and a dusky patch of hair was visible between her legs. She was a natural brunette…his favorite. His cock stirred to life for the first time since walking into the club. He was familiar with magic, and she definitely held some type of power over her audience. So this was the reason his fellow Shadow Walkers were fighting about who would get the coveted Sector 32 this evening.

As intrigued as he was by her dance and obvious sexual attributes, it was her eyes that entranced him as he watched. Their deep silver blue depths were full of bitterness and hatred as she glowered at the men surrounding her. He wondered how it was possible that the men didn't notice her disdain as she danced along them on the runway, collecting fistfuls of money from all the eager patrons.

As the music sped up, her movements quickened to match the rhythm, the dance becoming one of lust and hate, frustration and fire. The lights on stage flashed over her body, now devoid of the silky fabric. What had only been hinted at before was shown in all its glory and Stephan swallowed hard in awe. Her breasts were exquisite and obviously real—the only kind he liked—and his hands itched to feel their weight in his palms. His mouth watered, his tongue aching to slip inside her pussy and taste her femininity.

His cock was rock hard, straining against the front of his jeans as thoughts of fucking this woman for days on end ran rampant through his mind. He wanted to watch her eyes as he thrust himself inside her, hear her moans as he brought her to climax after climax. He lifted his beer and swallowed deeply, trying to free himself from the images filling his mind.

She flowed with the music, clad in nothing but mist and light. As she sensually swayed and danced, her eyes continued to study the crowd, meeting each man's gaze for a moment. He recognized the look of a predator facing down its prey. No, wait. That wasn't quite it. It was closer to the look of a victim facing down her attacker. And no one seemed to care. They all just wanted a piece of her.

When her eyes connected with his, a surge of electrical energy shot down his spine. There was a deep fire behind the ice of her stare. In her dance, her hands seemed to gracefully reach out for him. Everything moved in slow motion as they looked at each other; Stephan unable to turn away. The shock passed as the moment ended and she continued to scour the audience, swaying and curving her beautiful body as if to tease him. Stephan knew then that it was hardly over.

For the brief moment she had met his eyes, he swore he'd never felt such passion. But yet, she had continued on. Obviously, she'd seen him, just no more than any other man in the audience, but for the first time in his life, he wanted to be seen, consequences be damned.

The music sped up even faster as she began to spin round and round, arms out to the side, long golden brown hair flowing out around her, for a moment looking as though she was flying free. Then the music crashed to a halt as she fell to the floor, her hair and the mist covering her body as the lights dimmed and faded out. An instant later the lights came back on but she was gone. The stage returned to normal as several girls resumed their bump and grind routine.

Stephan came out of his daze to discover that he was now standing, having crossed halfway to the stage during the mystery woman's dance. He took a mental inventory of what had just transpired. A woman had actually stirred a part of him he'd closed off long ago and now that she had disappeared, he felt as though part of him had gone with her. He blinked hard a few times. What the hell was wrong with him?

He had always considered his constitution ironclad enough to resist being enchanted by a woman. He snarled discontentedly. This night had infuriated him. A partial grin swept across his face. This night had also invigorated him. It was good to know that fighting demons hadn't completely hardened him. He sighed. *Back to work, damn it. You will never get close enough to melt her ice. You can't have her fire. Your duty forbids it.*

The group of men that had been closest to the stage pushed through the crowd back toward the bar.

"She was checking me out. She only had eyes for me, man," a tall middle-aged man boasted to his friend.

"She only had eyes for the money in your hand," his large friend laughed, slapping his friend on the back. "Mariah never gives a damn what you look like, as long as you come bearing large presidents."

"I'd love to get in there," the shortest of the three replied as he ordered another beer. "She could probably fuck all night long and not even break a sweat. Her tits, her legs—God, the whole damn package." He stopped for a moment and wiped the sweat from his brow. "I'm going to lose it just thinking about her. I should take her home with me tonight. I'd give her a ride to remember."

The three men laughed and punched each other. "To Mariah!" the large man cried, holding his beer in the air. "Without the thought of her, I would never be able to get it up for my wife."

The three men continued their loud, crude cheers as Stephan turned away from them. He kept his agitation in check and knew that if he stayed any longer, he would not be able to avoid doing some serious damage to three men who didn't quite deserve the wrath of a Shadow Walker. He could just see the newspaper article now. *Talisman Bay's most successful businessman involved in brawl at strip club.* Not the type of attention he could afford to attract. He swallowed his anger and left in search of another demon to take it out on. This was Talisman Bay after all, there was bound to be one around the next corner.

* * * * *

"As always you were stunning, darling." Monte wrapped a robe around Mariah's shoulders and followed her back to her dressing room. "I love your new routine. Fire and ice and magic and lust. You know how to bring in the crowds." He began massaging her shoulders as she sat down at her dressing table. Mariah leaned back into him and smiled.

"I love your hands, Monte. If you ever decide to leave Lewis, don't forget how much I love you."

"Honey, you really need to find a man of your own kind." He smiled happily at her in the mirror. "I like dick as much as you should." Monte picked up a hairbrush and began combing it through Mariah's hair. The rhythmic pull relaxed Mariah even further and she closed her eyes and sighed contentedly.

"No lectures tonight please, Monte. You know how I feel about men—you excluded of course." Mariah sat up and began counting the money she had pulled in during her routine. "I don't need a man in my life. I make enough money to support myself, I have friends and I have a vibrator. Why would I complicate things with a relationship?" She smiled up at Monte and tucked the money into her purse before moving to the sink where she began to remove her stage make-up.

Diesel, one of *Silver Twilight's* elite bodyguards, walked into the room, his muscular arms overflowing with flowers and other assorted trinkets. "Too bad you can't get money for all these as well, huh?" He smiled as he laid the gifts on the counter near the sink.

"I don't know why you bother bringing this stuff to her. She'll just throw it away like she always does." Monte picked up a bouquet and smelled the roses.

"I dunno either. I guess I feel bad for the guys who think they're gonna get somewhere or something." Diesel placed a protective hand on Mariah's shoulder as he turned to head back out the way he came.

"Y'know, Diesel, if you ever change your mind about me, I know that Lewis wouldn't mind a threesome." Monte grinned lasciviously at Diesel and wiggled his eyebrows, drawing a much-needed laugh from Mariah.

"Sorry, Monte, but I still don't like dick. I'll let you know, though, if I ever change my mind." Diesel grinned as he walked out of the room.

"If he didn't work here, I'd say you should give him a go." Monte moved behind Mariah at the sink and continued playing with her hair.

"I already tried."

Monte gasped in pretend outrage and lightly tugged her hair. "And you never told me? Do tell. Now. No excuses…please tell me you at least fucked him? I *must* know how luscious his cock is." Monte shivered in ecstasy and Mariah giggled.

"It was about a year ago, I guess. We wanted to keep it quiet because you know how quickly gossip can fly around this place." Mariah raised an eyebrow and met Monte's reflection in the mirror. He was wearing his most innocent expression.

Mariah laughed again. "Oh, please! You know you're the gossip queen."

"That's not all I'm queen of, but you've already heard my naughty girl stories. I want to know every dirty detail about your date with Diesel and maybe I'll forgive you for not telling me earlier." He pouted and leaned against the sink.

"Okay, okay. We spent the day together. He picked me up on his bike and we rode up the coast. We ate at this great little restaurant overlooking the water. And we talked. It was nice. He's a great guy." Mariah stopped in her storytelling and smiled up at Monte. "Can you hand me my T-shirt and sweats?"

Monte glared at her, grabbed them and held them out of reach. "And?"

"He drove me home and walked me to my door." Mariah stood up, snatched her clothes and began to change.

"And...Mariah, you *cannot* leave the story there."

Mariah couldn't help it, she had to tease Monte. She gave him a coquettish grin as she spoke. "Diesel put those large hands of his on my hips. I could feel the heat of his fingertips against my ass, practically burning through my jeans."

"Oh, God...Tell me every detail!" Monte's eyes closed on a moan and Mariah swallowed her giggle.

"I just knew what was going to happen next. He kissed me..." Mariah paused, relishing the expression of awe on Monte's face, "...and we both started laughing." Monte's eyes blinked open and his mouth gaped. "He realized that he felt like he needed to protect me from himself. He couldn't get past our work relationship. And, as hot as he is, I couldn't either. So we hugged and he left. And he's a great friend. End of story."

Monte shook his head and sighed. "Such a waste. You couldn't have just fucked him once to tell me about it?"

Mariah laughed again. Her date with Diesel was one of her favorite memories. "Well, you and I both know that the only good men are gay." She sweetly grinned at him. "I'm going to take tomorrow off, okay sweetie? Twyla has a big meeting with a jewelry distributor and since I know she is going to nail the account, I want to take her out to celebrate." She held out a deep blue and silver bead drop necklace. "Look at her newest design, isn't it gorgeous? She puts spells on each one — protection, love, self-enhancement and tons of other things. The distributors will love these!" Mariah turned back to the mirror and fastened the necklace.

"So, what spell did she put on yours?"

Mariah grabbed her purse and kissed Monte before waggling her fingers and heading toward the door. "A protection spell, of course! To save me from all the evil men in this world."

* * * * *

"SHIT!" Stephan expertly ducked the fire spewing from the mouth of a very unhappy L'Fail demon. L'Fails' lives were simple. They dimension hopped, set fires and made a quick escape. Fortunately for the owner of the flower shop next to where they were fighting, Stephan had shown up before the demon could start the fire. Now he just had to permanently stop him.

The charred smell emanating from the hairy, reddish brown beast brought back memories Stephan would prefer not to think about. He hated fire — the smell of burning wood, the crackling sound as it devoured whatever was in its path. He grimaced and blocked the images from his mind. This was business, not personal.

As Stephan expertly ducked another fire burst, he rummaged through his pockets for something he could use to distract the demon. As much as he would like to just jump the demon and slice its throat, he would need something to debilitate it first. The beast's coarse hair covered an extremely thick hide. He'd need something sharp and hard to kill it. Before

Stephan could react properly, the yellow-eyed demon rushed him. Together they flew through the window of the flower shop.

Stephan hit the ground inside and deftly rolled to his feet. Glass rained from his clothes and crunched beneath his boots as he spun to face the L'Fail. It charged once more. This time Stephan was prepared. He crouched low as the next blast of flame shot from the beast's mouth. With lightning speed and strength borne from years of fighting vicious creatures like this, he brought his knee into direct contact with the demon's genitalia.

The beast faltered just long enough for Stephan to regain his edge. Attached to the wall next to him was a sink with a hose. Knowing it would damage the demon worse than the shards of glass had, he grabbed the hose, turned it on and aimed directly for the L'Fail's charred face. The demon roared, the inhuman sound of pain echoing in the enclosed space. Stephan took possession of the pressure hose with one hand as he continued to spray the infuriated beast. Quickly, he drew his hunting knife from his jacket. Several hard strokes into melting demon hide and it was over.

Stephan stepped away from the half-melted bleeding mess on the floor, taking a moment to catch his breath. The demon was not overly large, but it would be heavy. He shook his head in disgust. He was going to need help disposing this one. He opened up his telepathic mind link and clicked-in to Ryan.

You available, Ryan?

Yeah, boss? Whatcha need? Ryan responded in his usual laid-back way.

I need clean-up help in Sector 27. The flower shop on the corner of Hayden and Third. I've got a heavy L'Fail that wouldn't play nice.

Be right there. Jake just got back, I'll drag him along too. Ryan made to click-out but Stephan interrupted the disconnect with a quick burst of thought.

I gotta finish patrolling this sector and make sure our friend was playing solo tonight. You think you two can handle this clean-up?

Jake's gonna bitch and moan but we'll be fine. Let us know if you need anything else. Ryan clicked-out.

The ability to click-in to his friends had come in handy many times since they had begun patrolling. As convenient as cell phones were to some people, they just weren't effective in the middle of battle. A quick burst of thought was all that was needed to bring the rest of the Shadow Walkers help in times of trouble. It was one of the few totally positive perks of being a Shadow Walker.

Stephan circled the body once more and then washed off his knife in the sink. L'Fails didn't come to Talisman Bay very often. He wanted to make sure there weren't any others as well. And tonight, he had a seemingly insatiable need to annihilate demon flesh.

As he was leaving, Stephan felt something crunch under his boots. He picked up a bouquet of flowers that had fallen to the floor when they'd crashed through the window. He looked at the damaged blossoms and shook glass off the fragile petals. It had been years since he had given anyone flowers. He didn't have time to date, and he knew that it was a bad idea to introduce someone else into the violence of his daily world. But that didn't stop him from wanting it.

He growled and threw the flowers back to the floor. No use thinking about what he couldn't allow himself to have. He climbed out the window, leaving the idea of love and flowers behind him in sacrifice.

* * * * *

The walk home was her favorite time of night. A light chill filled the air, a comfort after the stifling warmth of the club. Mariah took a deep breath, filling her lungs with the fresh ocean air. The darkness scared some people, but for her it was refreshing. It calmed her down, relaxed her after the intensity she put into her dancing.

Her new routine was powerful and had drawn in a large crowd—more than the usual lowlifes that frequented *Silver Twilight*. The extra draw was great on the pocketbook, but it was also emotionally draining. She put everything into her dancing; all the pain and anguish, desire and betrayal she had felt in her life made its way into a routine at one time or another. Whatever it was she did worked, but it also meant constantly reliving a past she wished she could forget.

Mariah paused for a moment and peered over her shoulder, sure that she heard more than just her footsteps echoing around her. No one was there. She reached into her purse and pulled out her pepper spray just in case her eyes were betraying her. It wasn't a gun, but it had convinced a few overenthusiastic wannabe suitors that she wasn't interested in anything they had to offer.

She kept walking, this time at a more brisk pace. There it was again! This time she knew she wasn't imagining things. She peeked over her shoulder again and still didn't see anything, but wasn't going to wait around for an introduction. Turning back around, she began to jog, and ran directly into a wall. At least, it felt like a wall but the two hands on her shoulders made her think that her first assessment was probably incorrect. Startled, she tried to back away but the hands were locked in a vise like grip on her shoulders.

Prepared to fight, she looked up into the ugliest face she had ever seen. Huge, silver ringed ears poked through dark hair, cut as though with a lawnmower. Thick, coarse hair grew over plump lips that didn't quite cover a mouthful of crooked teeth. Mariah's gaze dropped lower. The man had breasts. Breasts! It wasn't a man! She was in the grip of a tall Amazon-like woman. Mariah couldn't stop her jaw from dropping. This was just too strange. Was she on candid camera or something?

The woman peered down at her surprised expression and grimaced. Or maybe it was a smile, she couldn't be to sure.

"Whoops. Silly me. Not looking where I'm going. Sorry." Mariah pasted on a fake-friendly smile. "Now if you could just let me go..." Mariah's smile faded and her voice trailed off as the woman leaned over to inspect her more closely. The woman's leather corset encased bazookas practically smothered her and Mariah tried to step away from the potentially dangerous boobs. One huge hand left her shoulder and grasped Mariah's ponytail, her fingers fondling the length of Mariah's hair.

This was beyond absurd. What did this woman want...the name of her hairdresser or something? "Let go of my hair!" Mariah tried to jerk away again. When that proved impossible she aimed the pepper spray up into the Amazon woman's face. "Leave me alone, you crazy bitch!"

Mariah cried out when her ponytail was used as a leash and she was wrenched tightly against the Amazon's dangerous boobs, the pepper spray swiftly slapped away. With a quickness that startled even herself, Mariah punched the woman with all her might and heard something crack as her fist made solid contact with her attacker's jaw. Mariah hoped it wasn't her own bones cracking, although the pain in her knuckles made her think it likely. The woman let out an inhuman roar and lifted Mariah into the air, throwing her headfirst at the wall just feet from where they stood. There was no time to prepare for the intense pain and darkness that immediately followed.

* * * * *

After many years of patrolling, Stephan's instincts had sharpened significantly. When something unfortunate was happening nearby, his heart rate increased and adrenaline coursed rapidly through his veins. Such sensation was assaulting him now with an unusually urgent intensity. Intuition at peak, Stephan picked up his pace. Whatever was out there was going to put up a big fight. And oh how he welcomed it.

The roaring sound filling the air would have most people turning and fleeing, reliving the sound in their nightmares for years to come. Stephan bolted around the corner toward the sound, arriving in time to see a small female body hitting a wall and crumpling to the ground. The muscle bound attacker knelt next to the body, its huge hands circling the neck of the unmoving woman, black hair hanging down almost like a curtain over the victim.

"Get your filthy hands away from her. Don't even think about it." Stephan stepped out of the shadows and strode toward the creature. It glanced up at his approach and he groaned in frustration as he shook his head. He knew this demon personally and had hoped never to make its acquaintance again.

Losfun demons were androgynous creatures always on the lookout for a possible mating specimen. The demons couldn't mate with themselves or others of their kind, so they required a host subject for sperm or ovum donation. It wasn't a pleasant task for anyone chosen, but for a human female, the results were most often fatal. The creature froze, but did not look up to meet Stephan's rage.

"Asfar. Last time, I told you to seek your pleasures elsewhere. This time, I don't feel like playin'."

"Mmmmm, Stephan." Asfar purred as she faced him and stood up, then smiled as she approached him. Her green eyes looked as though they were devouring him. "A tastier human male I have never come across in all my travels. Are you sure I can't convince you to change your mind about my previous proposition? Although the woman I just met has spark and fire in her, you have a dark side I think we could both enjoy exploring."

Asfar began circling Stephan, one large yet eerily graceful hand lightly tracing a finger over his back and chest. He ignored her hand as he sized Asfar up, trying to determine if she'd leave peacefully this time as well. She was hardly a threat—at least not to him. The woman on the ground hadn't faired so well. As Asfar's hand dropped lower and caressed him through his pants, Stephan forcefully removed her wandering fingers and stepped away.

"Not gonna happen." He glared into her pupil-less green eyes. "When did your foreplay start including bashing someone's head in?"

Stephan approached the fragile looking woman crumpled at the base of the dirty wall. His abhorrence quickly mounted as he realized that the dancer, Mariah, was Asfar's victim. It appeared that the back of her head had been smashed in. He didn't see any brain matter mixed with the blood pooling beneath her head, but he still had to hurry, or she would die. He knelt down next to the pale skinned beauty and felt for her pulse. The beat was slow and weak beneath his fingertips. He hated to move her, but knew that was the only option so he leaned down and scooped her into his arms.

Asfar crept toward Stephan, a pout contorting her face. "You deny me both you and the woman? You can't do that to me. You owe me something for my troubles."

Stephan looked calculatingly at the woman in his arms and the creature blocking his departure. He scrambled for something to say. Asfar could be defeated without difficulty, but there was no time for games while Mariah slowly bled to death. He quickly fabricated a lie that would hopefully deter the demon.

"Actually, you can't have either of us. Our souls were joined using the ancient texts of those with the knowledge of Eternity. Not even you can separate us. I am hers and she is mine." Stephan stepped around the frowning Asfar, moving as fast as he dared. If Asfar challenged his impromptu claim on the woman he could lose her. And that wasn't something he would let happen.

* * * * *

"FIERO! Get here now! I need your help!" Stephan burst into the living area below *Rare and Unusual Imports* and gently placed Mariah on the sofa. Her chest slowly rose and fell but she still hadn't regained consciousness. He surveyed the room, waiting before calling out again.

"NOW, FIERO! There's no time!" The room shimmered in front of him and the ghostly apparition of Fiero appeared, a serious expression marring his generally easygoing demeanor.

"What the hell did you do this time, Stephan? The Sacred Order is in an uproar over something. I kept hearing them say your name, but no one's told me exactly what's up. You got yourself knee deep in some more shit again, didn't you?" Fiero's form had solidified within moments of his appearance. He stepped around the sofa and peered down at the unmoving woman lying there. "Then again, I should have known it had something to do with a woman. Wait, you brought someone here? What the hell were you thinking?"

"She's hurt, pretty bad. She was slammed into a wall by a Losfun during an attempted mating ritual." Stephan chose not to react to Fiero's question. He had trouble admitting that he'd actually brought an outsider to their compound below *Rare and Unusual Imports*. For security reasons, it wasn't allowed. In fact, Stephan was the one who made that rule in the first place.

"I can see that. She's going to have one hell of a headache when she wakes up, but at least she won't be dead." Fiero placed both hands over the wound and quietly spoke a few words. A green light flickered from his fingertips and began circling her head. He removed his hands and stepped away, letting the healing light do its work.

"Who is she?"

Stephan picked up her purse and opened her wallet. "Well, her ID says she's Mariah Andrea DeSilva..."

"And you know her how?"

"She's a dancer at *Silver Twilight*."

Fiero looked at Stephan, one eyebrow raised. "I could see Marlin or Dusty going for a dancer, but you...well, hey, I'm proud of you." Fiero grinned as Stephan glared in response.

"Fuck off. She's not mine. I'm just doing my job."

"Your job doesn't include bringing people here for healing."

"Yeah, well, it doesn't include letting people die, either." The forceful tone in Stephan's voice kept Fiero from continuing that line of conversation.

"So, what the hell did you do to piss off The Order?" Fiero repeated his earlier question.

"I dunno. All I've been doing is kicking demon ass as usual."

"Well, you set something in motion tonight that got them in an uproar. I hope you didn't do anything like giving Cheerios to any more Blorey demons. It took forever for The Order to forgive you for that one. They had to apologize in person for your…uh…mistake and pay to have all of the Bloreys's fifth arms removed after the Cheerio dust created the mutation."

"Well, The Order started letting me delegate tour guide duty after that, didn't they?"

"Just watch your back and be careful." Stephan nodded his head. Fiero was pretty tight with the Sacred Order so if he was giving him a warning, it probably was rather serious.

The green light circling Mariah's wound flared brightly and then disappeared. Stephan returned to her side and examined the wound. Blood still matted the hair around where it had been, but the skin appeared fresh and new. He walked to the sink in the kitchen, filled a bowl with warm water and grabbed a soft cloth. Returning to Mariah, he gently wiped the blood from her head and face. No need for her to wonder where all the blood had come from.

"She'll be waking up soon." Stephan looked up as Fiero stepped away. "I'm gonna get more info about what's going on. I'll let you know. 'Til then, stay out of trouble, will ya?" Fiero shimmered and disappeared. Stephan's attention returned to his patient as her fist slammed into his eye.

Chapter Two

Mariah heard the sound of male voices as she returned from her unplanned trip to the land of the unconscious. She had a headache that surpassed all of her past hangovers combined, but considering how hard she must have hit that wall, she was just glad to be alive. Although not knowing where she was or whom she was with kept her from immediately celebrating.

She opened her eyes a tiny sliver to see one man kneeling near her, his attention drawn to something on the other side of the couch where she lay. A male voice spoke from somewhere on the other side of the room.

"She'll be waking up soon."

Mariah tensed. Who the hell were these people and why was she here? And where was here for that matter? Two men and her lying injured on a couch. Definitely not the type of situation she wanted to be in. From bazooka woman to a gang rape. Oh yeah, she was having a *great* night. Her gut told her to get away as quickly as possible. It felt as though the other man had exited and she waited to see if the man next to her would leave as well. Not likely. As he turned toward her she reacted instinctively and punched him in the face.

"Damn it!" The man stumbled backward as Mariah leapt to her feet, ignoring the pain in her head—and now her hand—as she moved. Her heart beat frantically and her mind raced, trying to determine the best way to evade this man. There was a closed door, but she would have to somehow get around the man standing between her and the apparent exit.

Mariah met his hazel eyes, her hands clenched in fists at her sides. Her heart continued its rapid flutter, but this time it seemed to be reacting to the sheer magnitude of this man's presence. He was gorgeous, dressed in leather and denim, and although there was definitely something dark about him, her instincts didn't scream at her to get away from him.

Hello. Note to brain. Now is not the time to drool. She shook her head, vanquishing those betraying thoughts. Her instincts about men had been proven wrong before. *Just get out of here, Mariah. Don't be a dumbass!*

Too late. Her breath caught in her throat as he graced her with a face-splitting grin. Anger took over…and she ignored the heat in her cunt his grin caused.

"Oh, this is fun for you, is it? You enjoy hurting people smaller than you?"

"Whoa, chill out. I *helped* you." He crossed his arms over his chest…his very nice chest. "Look, you got jumped pretty hard. I only brought you here to make sure you were okay. And you're fine now. Hey, you can leave whenever you want." He stepped back, his arms raised in a gesture of truce.

He seemed to be telling the truth—or at least her body hoped he was telling the truth. God, it had been so long since her body had responded this way to a man…what the hell was her body thinking going all achy now?

She shook her head and grimaced at both the ache and that she actually wanted to thank this man by slamming him against the wall and fucking him until she passed out…which, considering the pain in her head, would take all of five minutes. It was time to leave before she did something she'd regret.

She bent to retrieve her purse from the floor next to the sofa. As she stood up another wave of pain rocketed through her head and she groaned, grabbing her head as she lost her balance and fell forward.

Before she could catch herself, she found herself cradled in the man's arms. Her body reacted instinctually to his touch, nipples beading and moisture flooding her pussy.

Damn those instincts!

"Let go of me!" She struggled against him and her bad instincts. She didn't know where she was or whom she was with. She would *not* be stupid and let her body rule the moment. Last time she'd done that she'd almost paid with her life.

He gently set her back on her feet. "You should take it easy for awhile. You took a big hit on the head."

"That had better be all that I got." *Hello, bitch alert!* Mariah watched him as she stepped backward toward the door, silently cursing her big mouth. All of her thoughts were in turmoil. Her body was attracted to this man, while her heart and mind reminded her of past mistakes. Fear was her voice. "What the hell happened tonight? Where am I and why am I here? If this is some type of sick game you like to play—"

His eyes lit up in anger. "Now you just hold on a damn second. I'm the good guy here. I rescued you. That's what I do…um…did."

Mariah swallowed. Okay, maybe being a bitch wasn't the smartest thing when appearances made her believe this man was telling the truth. Her best bet was just to get out of there, go home, and forget this night ever occurred.

She reached the doorway, her hand poised on the knob when he spoke.

"Hey, is there anything else you need? Something else I can do for you? Seriously."

Mariah stared back at him, studying his features, but didn't reply. She remained in the doorway, prepared to flee if necessary.

He smiled. "Hey, my name is Stephan—Stephan Rashleigh. This…" he gestured to the room around him. "This is where I work."

He paused, his eyes an open invitation she wanted to accept. But she'd gone down that path before, and it only led to pain and heartbreak.

He continued, his smile faltering. "So, do you need anything? Can I take you somewhere?"

"Just leave me alone," she said softly as she turned and exited the room.

* * * * *

Stephan waited until he heard her footsteps reach the top of the stairs and the sound of the back door closing behind her. After what happened to her tonight there was no way in hell he was going to let her walk home alone. But she didn't need to know he was there.

He followed her in silence and shadows, rationalizing that he was just doing his job, that she was just another Talisman Bay citizen to be protected in the night. But he had never been able to lie to himself. He wanted this woman. From the first notes of the Celtic melody she had danced to, something about her had crept into his blood, into his very soul.

Shit! He was waxing poetic over a stripper who obviously hated men. It was time for a trip to Polgara where he could indulge in some hard fucking with his favorite, very willing Pleasure goddess.

Or maybe another fight would leach the lust out of his system. Stephan noticed another figure walking in the shadows across the street, following Mariah on her trip home. The figure appeared to be a human male, but at this distance he couldn't be too certain. He watched as Mariah entered a house. She was safe, now he could attack.

He stalked across the street, staying out of the light from the street lamps. The figure had disappeared down a cross street, but Stephan needed this fight…needed to know who was following Mariah home. If she was in future danger, well, he could be there for her. He rounded the corner, just glimpsing the figure as it disappeared again into the shadows. His blood thrummed as he ran, hands fisted, prepared to fight. Seconds before he attacked, the figure turned, gun aimed at Stephan's head. He ducked and swore.

"Shit, Marlin! What the hell are you doing here?"

"Fuck! I could say the same thing about you. You tryin' to get shot?"

The brothers watched each other as the adrenaline continued to pump through their veins. Marlin pocketed his gun, a cocky grin widening his face.

"I saw that fine-assed woman walking by herself in my sector. Figured if she needed a rescue, her gratitude would be sweet. You figured the same, huh?"

Stephan wanted to knock the grin off his brother's face. Marlin fucked a different woman every night. He was good looking and knew it. Considering his track record, if Marlin decided he wanted to fuck Mariah, he would probably succeed.

"You're too late. I already rescued her once tonight. She's mine. End of discussion. Go to Polgara if you wanna get laid. Keep your cock away from her." Stephan turned away but not before he saw the shock cross Marlin's face. Good. It was about time someone told Marlin he couldn't get what he wanted. Hopefully Marlin wouldn't take that as a challenge.

* * * * *

Mariah couldn't stifle her sigh of relief when she closed and locked the door of the house she shared with Twyla. Her head throbbed, she smelled like a sewer and she probably looked like a traffic accident. All she wanted was a hot bath and a dozen uninterrupted hours of sleep.

"What the hell happened to you?"

Mariah jumped and turned to see Twyla approaching her from her office — or as she affectionately called it "that damn bead room."

"Oh my God! Are you okay? Is that blood? Do you need a doctor?" Twyla nearly tripped over the couch in her haste to get to Mariah.

"I'm fine, just tired and sore. I just need to go to bed."

"No, you need some TLC. Let me look at you." She grabbed Mariah and led her toward the sofa.

Mariah grumbled but she let Twyla take her to the sofa, knowing it was easier to acquiesce now and let Twyla baby her.

"Do I really look that bad?"

Twyla grabbed and picked at Mariah's torn clothing. "You look like Bruce Willis at the end of Die Hard."

"1, 2, or 3?"

"Hmmm... I think probably 1."

"Oh good, I still have my hair then."

"Smart ass."

Mariah grinned at Twyla as she settled deeper into the sofa. "Really, I'm fine."

"So, you gonna tell me what happened or am I gonna have to keep you up all night playing twenty questions?"

"Definitely twenty questions." Twyla glared at Mariah. "Okay! Okay! Well, the thing is I don't really remember everything. I was walking home and I was attacked by a woman—"

"By a woman!?" Twyla uttered in disbelief as she threw up her hands and went into the bathroom. "She think you took her man or something?"

"I don't think that was it. It was like she was sizing me up. But she never said anything to me. And she was huge—like seven feet tall at least. Damn! She had a grip the WWF would drool over."

"Geesh, then you're lucky you got away." Twyla returned with a few wet towels and some bandages.

"Well, I didn't. Not really. I tried to get away and I punched her really hard after she grabbed me so she threw me into the wall. Then nothing until I woke up in a room with a guy leaning over me."

"You need to start carrying a gun again. You were a real good shot with it."

"I don't like guns. That's why I got rid of it."

"Oh yeah, and getting beaten up is better?"

"Okay, okay. Point made. I'll think about it." Mariah sighed deeply.

Twyla leaned closer to Mariah, her face a mask of concern and worry. "Sweetie, are you sure you're okay? You weren't raped..." Twyla studied Mariah's eyes, as she gently began wiping her face. Mariah smiled to cover her grimace. Her head still throbbed with a loud salsa rhythm.

"No! At least, I don't think so. No, I would know if I was. This guy, he told me that he saved me. He said that he just wanted to make sure I was okay." Mariah stared off into space, trying to remember everything that had occurred. Her memories were mired in fog, slipping out of her grasp even as she spoke of them. The accompanying throb of her headache didn't help her recollections either. "Everything else is a blur."

"And you're sure he didn't hurt you? 'Cuz if he even so much as gave you a dirty look, I swear I'll hunt down the bastard and teach him that it's not nice to fuck with women smaller than he is." Twyla hesitated and looked Mariah over. "You're okay? You're sure?"

"I'm sure." Mariah paused again and gave Twyla a bewildered smile. "He seemed nice."

"Nice?" Twyla laughed. "You must have hit your head pretty damn hard if you are calling a man *nice*. So, was he hot? You need a nice, hot man in your life." Twyla grinned as she studied Mariah's face. Then she gently scrubbed another little spot.

"I don't need a man in my life."

"You can't let what happened with Michael—"

"I don't need a man in my life!" Mariah repeated with force.

"Okay, but you still didn't answer my second question. Was he good looking?"

"I didn't notice."

"Liar! You so noticed! So, how hot was he?"

Mariah couldn't help but grin. "He was 'Jose's Ultra Spicy Salsa not even featured on the menu because we can't afford the lawsuits' hot. Dark brown hair, lightly tanned skin, intense hazel eyes. One of those tall, dark, serious and mysterious types."

"Oh, and you didn't try to do him right then? You are one crazy chickie, y'know! That's okay. I'll go personally thank him for saving your life."

Mariah felt a twinge of jealousy at the thought of Twyla showing Stephan her gratitude. There wasn't a straight man in Talisman Bay that would turn down that offer. Twyla liked to describe herself as "not bad to look at" but the truth was that she often stopped traffic. She wore her black hair short and spiky, which just enhanced the appeal of her dark brown eyes. And she was the only person Mariah knew that could get away with wearing anything—including a potato sack—and still look heart stopping sexy. If Mariah didn't love her so much, she'd be compelled to kill her. So why shouldn't she let Twyla go after Stephan? It wasn't like she was ever going to see him again.

"He works in that import shop on the pier—"

"Oh my God! You met one of THOSE hotties? Oh, I've seen them around. There's a whole group of 'em that own that shop. Once that store opened, this whole town started to clean up 'cuz they ran the riffraff off the pier. Every one of those fine-assed men defines sex! Girl, you have done a serious disservice to me by not fucking him and then telling me all about it. Oh my God!" Twyla continued to stare at Mariah in shock. She leaned back into the sofa, her face a study in disbelief. "I can't believe you didn't do him when you had the chance. Do you know how many women would kill someone to get rescued by one of those guys? Do you realize how much those guys are worth? They are Talisman Bay's most eligible, most rich, most handsome bachelors! I understand your indifference for most men, but to pass up on one of those guys? You can now be declared legally insane!"

"Are you done chastising me for not being a slut like you?" Mariah grinned at Twyla.

"Not a slut. I just really, really enjoy having wild sex with hot men—like most normal single hot-blooded women do."

"Ouch."

Twyla patted Mariah's hand. "Look, sweetie, I know you've had bad luck—" She held up a hand, stopping Mariah's protest. "You just need to get back on your feet, or more appropriately, flat on your back with a man." Mariah snickered. "I'm not saying you should fall in love, or find a relationship or any of that bullshit. Just fuck a man. Sex is the best part of man/woman relations. And, from what I've heard about the guys who run that shop, it would be a great lay."

Mariah snorted. "Well, I have been rather horny lately."

It was Twyla's turn to snort. "No kidding. You really need to get a quieter vibrator, my dear. That thing purrs through the walls."

"Twyla!"

She just laughed in reply.

"All right. All right. I'll *think* about going to thank him tomorrow. And if I do I'll wear something slutty and act like you."

Twyla grinned crookedly. "Sounds like a plan. And bring back details."

Mariah just shook her head. She couldn't believe what she was thinking about doing.

Twyla reached over and patted Mariah's neckline and upper chest.

"You should have been wearing the necklace I made for you. The protection spell could have helped you."

Mariah grabbed at her neck. "I was wearing the necklace. I put it on as I was leaving *Silver Twilight*. Damn, it must have fallen off when I was attacked. I'm sorry."

Twyla hugged Mariah. "I don't give a damn about the necklace. You're more important. I'll make you another one, and I'll put a stronger protection spell as well as a don't lose it spell on it."

Mariah laughed and hugged Twyla back. "Thank you. Wait! You have that meeting in the morning with that distributor. Why aren't you in bed?"

Twyla groaned in frustration. "I was working on a new design and I just couldn't get it to work right. Sometimes I wonder why I do this to myself. I should just go get a job working at the *Taco Shack* with Jose and his hot sauce."

"Are you kidding? They'd never put up with you." Mariah grinned as Twyla stuck out her tongue. "You're going to do great tomorrow. I'm taking you out to celebrate you winning the account. How does *Dante's* sound?"

"Sounds extremely expensive. Why don't you wait to make sure I get it?"

"Because you will get it, and if you don't, then you have to pay."

"Ha! You're on!"

Mariah slowly stood up and groaned as she felt the effects of the past few hours spreading over her body. "I'm going to go soak in the tub. I'll see you tomorrow night to celebrate." Mariah climbed the stairs to her room, the idea of a hot bath the only thing keeping her from sitting right down on the stairs and falling asleep.

Okay, maybe the idea of a hot bath wasn't the only thing keeping her awake. Her mind swirled with images from that night. Stephan was an incredibly attractive man, and from what Twyla had told her, he was also safe. She could break her celibacy streak and say goodbye without looking back. Her cunt began a merciless throbbing and she could feel moisture dampening her panties. Yeah, it would be nice to use something other than her hand and a vibrator to ease that ache.

Mariah turned on the light in the bathroom and avoided the mirror, intending to prepare her bath first. She turned the water on hot to boiling, added large amounts of bath oil, and then turned to study herself in the mirror. She grimaced at her reflection. Twyla had been wiping all sorts of stuff, but there was still so much more. She wasn't about to win any beauty contests this evening.

Mariah examined what was left of the blood streaks on her face. Where had the blood come from? She fingered her scalp and couldn't feel any large lumps or cuts. Her whole head throbbed but she couldn't find one particular space that hurt worse than the others. What the hell had happened to her and where had the blood come from?

The steam rising from the tub convinced her to leave the questions for later. She removed her clothing and gingerly stepped into the tub, moaning in appreciation as the water covered her sore body.

She closed her eyes and leaned back, spreading her legs as wide as the tub would allow her. The hot water caressed her, teased her, arousing her even more. Using both hands, she cupped her breasts, rolling her nipples between her thumbs and forefingers just the way she liked. Her nipples beaded into hard pebbles and an electric jolt shot to her cunt. She let out a soft sigh.

One hand slid slowly down her body, enjoying the slick feel of bath oil over skin. Her hand parted the already swollen folds between her legs. Her pussy was releasing a moisture of its own, and easily welcomed the two fingers she thrust inside. She let out a quiet moan as her cunt welcomed the invasion, muscles clasping and releasing.

Her other hand left her breast and trailed to her demanding clit. Mariah was moments from orgasm, as she slowly circled the protruding nub. Her breath came in panting gasps as she circled her clit faster, fingers thrusting in and out of her dripping pussy, bringing her closer to the precipice. Her mind sought an anchor in the maelstrom as her body spun out of control, and her mind flashed on intense hazel eyes and a body encased in denim and leather. She swallowed a shout as she came hard, her cunt pulsing around her fingers, her clit almost bursting with the pleasure.

Oh yeah, it was definitely time to get fucked.

* * * * *

It seemed like only a few minutes passed between when Mariah climbed into bed and when the blaring of the phone woke her up. It was light outside, but still much earlier than she wanted to be awake. She fumbled for the phone on her bedside table, knocking over her newest mystery novel and several unlit candles. She finally grabbed it on the fourth ring just as the answering machine picked up.

"Shit!" Mariah cursed to herself. The answering machine was ancient. It didn't turn off. The person calling wouldn't be able to hear Mariah over the machine message. She could go downstairs to find out who called or she could just go back to sleep and check the machine later. She started to climb out of bed and almost screamed when the aches and pains assaulted her all at once. The message would have to wait.

* * * * *

Several hours later Mariah managed to pull herself out of bed. She still ached all over, but it was more of a subtle pain now. After two Advils and a shower, Mariah almost felt like her old self. She stared at herself in the mirror, surprised to find that there were no obvious marks on her anywhere.

The ring of the phone shifted her attention reminding Mariah that she had a message she needed to listen to. She vaulted over her bed, excited that the pain in her body was practically non-existent. Advil was now her new best friend.

"Hello?"

"Hey Mariah, is Twyla around? She's supposed to be watching the store for me so I can meet Simon for lunch."

Mariah looked at the alarm clock in her room. It was just after noon. Twyla's morning appointment was at eight, so it should have ended by now. *Darla's Boutique* was just off the pier, a quick walk from the restaurant where Twyla was meeting the distributor. And just a few stores away from the import shop where Stephan worked. Her body pleasantly tingled at the thought of what she wanted to do with him, but she quickly pushed it aside.

"I haven't seen her Darla, but let me check downstairs. She could have come in without me hearing. Maybe things didn't go well for her this morning and she forgot. Hold on."

Mariah set the phone down and ran downstairs. The house was quiet and appeared locked up tight. Mariah peeked into Twyla's office and grinned at the mess Twyla worked in. It was amazing she got anything done at all in there. But the office was devoid of Twyla as well.

It wasn't like her to miss a shift at the boutique. Twyla and Darla had become friends and co-workers after she became the first person willing to carry *Twilight's Fancy*, Twyla's line of homemade beaded necklaces. Now Twyla worked there whenever Darla needed time away—and Twyla had never missed a shift. Mariah quickly walked the rest of the house while calling out for her. The house remained quiet and empty, the only sound the echo of her own voice.

Mariah went to pick up the kitchen phone extension when she noticed the answering machine. She hit the play button, hoping it was Twyla explaining away her unusual absence.

"Hello, Twyla? This is Damian with *Fenst Jewelry*. I had us scheduled for a meeting at eight this morning at *Xena's Café*. It's after nine now and I need to leave for another appointment. I'm sorry I missed you and hope we can reschedule. I'm very excited about *Twilight's Fancy* and hope you haven't changed your mind about meeting with us." Damian repeated his phone number twice and then the message ended. Mariah stared in shock at the answering machine, willing it to explain to her what the hell had become of Twyla. Mariah knew that Twyla wouldn't have missed that meeting for anything. Something crazy must have happened.

In a semi-daze, Mariah returned to the phone.

"Darla, there was a message on the machine from the distributor that Twyla was supposed to meet. She didn't make that meeting either. Something isn't right so I'll call you when I get more information. Tell Simon I'm sorry."

"Wow. Okay. Let me know if you need anything. I'll call if Twyla shows up here."

"Thanks, Darla. Keep your fingers crossed that everything's okay."

Mariah hung up the phone and ran up the stairs. She threw her robe on the bed and grabbed her comfort clothes—blue jeans and a hot pink stretch T-shirt. Her hair was a mass of riotous tangles around her face. It would take time to tame the mess so she just finger combed her hair back and used a scrunchie to keep it off her face. She stepped into her sandals and grabbed her purse. Then she just stood there as she realized she had no idea where to look for Twyla. Other than the café, the boutique and home—Twyla's normal hangouts— Mariah didn't know where to start. Especially since Twyla wouldn't have willingly missed today's meeting.

"Just get going, you'll figure it out as you go," Mariah lectured herself as she ran back down the stairs and out the front door. She didn't make it past the porch before it became obvious just how bad things were. Twyla's cherry red convertible 1965 Mustang, lovingly restored and perfectly maintained, was still in the driveway, top down and ready to go. Twyla drove that car everywhere and would have had it with her today. But what unnerved Mariah most was the sight of Twyla's portfolio and carrying case she used for her necklaces lying open on the ground, loose beads and paperwork scattered over the driveway.

Lover's Talisman

Mariah bent to pick up the scattered remnants of Twyla's portfolio. As she got closer to the car, ice-cold fear encompassed her body. Twyla always kept the top up this time of year, to keep the interior in perfect shape. Upon closer inspection, the top wasn't down as Mariah had first thought. The ripped remains torn from their frame fluttered on the opposite side of the car, waving in the wind as though offering themselves for surrender. Mariah stifled a cry. Oh dear God, what had happened to Twyla?

* * * * *

The distant sounds of a shout and crash brought Twyla back to full awareness. She was lying slightly reclined, her body twisted at an awkward angle. Only a sliver of light crept under the opaque fabric covering her eyes. She moved her head, trying to dislodge the blindfold, but the damn thing stayed firm.

A tight rope chafed her wrists and some sort of strapping bound her ankles together. She shifted and pulled, trying to loosen any of her bindings. At least her ankles weren't tied to whatever she was laying on.

Sharp pain burned along her upper left arm and shoulder. She flinched as she recalled how that injury had occurred.

Ready for her presentation, she was carrying her briefcase, necklaces and drawings out to her car. Her arms were full, but she was still walking with a bounce in her step and a swing to her hips, just knowing that she was going to kick some ass and get a deal with the jewelry distributor. She had the ideas and the designs plus an outfit no heterosexual male could take his eyes off of. Her low cut semi-transparent gray blouse, black lace bra and a shorter than short red skirt paired with red 3-inch stiletto heels was her good luck outfit, and she was going to use it for all it was worth.

She had heard a growling sound near her car, and just assumed that the neighbor's dog, Charlie, had gotten out to take his morning piss. Charlie growled at everyone, and then gave them a tongue bath when they acknowledged his call. Twyla didn't have time for the bath and the subsequent shower she would have to take to remove the doggie stench, so she ignored the sound.

The next thing she knew, she was flat on her back, surrounded by everything she had been carrying. Her arm burned as she staggered to sit up, and blood dripped out through the shredded layers of her blouse. She peered up into a face out of her nightmares—glowing red eyes, fangs and a man's body covered in thick hair. He slid closer and she opened her mouth to scream, but his hand—or was it a paw?—covered her mouth. He flung her over his shoulder and began a loping run. The pain in her arm had become unbearable and she slipped into unconsciousness.

Until now.

She tested her bonds again, moving from side to side, desperately trying to loosen them. Nothing happened. She determined that her wrists were tied to whatever she was lying on. She cursed and kept up the rocking motion, gritting her teeth at the pain it caused in her shoulder. There had to be a way to loosen her binding. She didn't know what the hell was going on, but she wouldn't go down without a fight. Especially since the bastard that took her had made her miss her appointment. He would pay for that alone.

At the sound of voices, she instinctively paused, straining to hear what they were saying.

"You fucked up! You grabbed the wrong girl. You will make this right." The voice was deep, demanding immediate respect. Twyla instantly hated the man behind that voice.

"I'm sorry, sir. The necklace carried her scent. It was my mistake. There were two scents on the necklace and I chose incorrectly. I will find the correct one and I will do it immediately."

"I want her here. Tonight. Stephan has found the woman. Time is of the essence. We must move quickly to bring the Shadow Walkers to their knees. Do not fail me again."

There was a pause in the conversation and Twyla continued her struggles. Shit! They had to be looking for Mariah. She was the only other person who had handled the necklace. What kind of trouble had Mariah gotten into?

And what kind of person found someone using their scent? Who the hell were these people?

Twyla paused again when a third voice entered the conversation.

"What should we do with her? I'll kill her if you'd like." That voice was cool and calm, and Twyla believed that he wouldn't hesitate to kill her. She frantically resumed her attack on the binding.

The same deep voice from before answered. "She'll stay alive until we have the other girl. If Ivan can't bring in the other one, we have this one for leverage. Besides, look at the way she struggles. She's feisty. I like that."

Twyla craned her head toward the voice, determined to show the man that she wasn't scared.

Fuck them!

Fuck them all. Those assholes had no idea what she was capable of.

Chapter Three

Mariah made her way along the pier, terror and exhaustion warring inside of her, both hoping to be the first to make her collapse. She had been everywhere, talked to so many people, and still no one had seen Twyla. The sun had ventured so far below the horizon that the time for their celebratory dinner date had long since passed. And there was still no word from her. The fear for her best friend was overwhelming.

An empty bench called out to her aching feet and Mariah willingly collapsed on it, needing a few moments to try to plan her next move. The police hadn't been much help. She'd called them to come to her house after discovering the destruction of Twyla's car. The young officer had been more interested in trying to determine how he recognized her, than in listening to what she had to say. He'd shrugged off the damage to Twyla's car, deciding that Twyla had probably hit a low hanging tree branch and been so upset by the mess that she'd stormed off to cool down. He saw no reason to believe that foul play was involved.

As the officer had stared at her breasts, the light of recognition had finally flashed in his eyes. All pretense of caring for her missing friend became shrouded with propositions. She finally gave up on him and was left with not only her worry for Twyla, but now the added worry that the asshole at the police station knew where she lived.

Now she sat alone on the pier, wishing she could feel the tranquil peace she associated with listening to the roar of the ocean at night. But instead of peace, she felt achingly vulnerable and alone. Warm tears ran down her cheeks. She hadn't cried since the incident with Michael. Twyla had been her savior during that time, filling her days with pep talks and a shoulder to cry on. But, Twyla had also given her the kick in the ass she needed to get over what Michael had done to her. She had to find Twyla—she'd never forgive herself if she didn't bring her home safely.

"You all right? You need something?"

A warm hand settled on her shoulder, and Mariah jumped to her feet, prepared to run. She gazed up into chocolate brown eyes and a smile that could peel the clothes off of most women. His hair was a slightly darker brown than his eyes and his hard body was well showcased in a white T-shirt that clung to his chest, outlining perfect pectoral muscles, and jeans that enhanced his very masculine thighs. She could only assume his ass would fit the rest of his astounding perfection, and was quite glad she couldn't see it so she wouldn't be tempted any further. He was by far the sexiest man she had ever seen—next to Stephan.

Mariah found herself comparing his looks to Stephan's. He was about an inch shorter than Stephan and didn't have the same depth of character upon appearance. The way this man carried himself emanated sex—the kind of sex that would leave a woman begging for another steamy night in his bed. He was the type of man Twyla would eat up.

The smile on the man's face faltered. His eyes sparked with recognition and his smile changed to a cocky grin. "You must be waiting for my brother..."

"Your brother? No, I don't think so." Mariah started to walk away, heading toward the import store. Hopefully Stephan would be there. Although now wasn't the time for her plan of thanks and a fuck, maybe he could help her find Twyla.

She heard the other man following her.

"My brother...Stephan." He paused as Mariah turned back toward him, unable to hide her surprise. It would figure that the two sexiest guys she had seen lately were related.

He laughed, a deep sound that sent a shiver through her body and down to her toes. "I can see that my dear brother didn't mention me. I'm Marlin." He held out his hand and

Mariah surprised herself by taking it. She met his eyes and shivered as he lifted her hand to his lips and kissed her palm. It burned where he touched her.

He continued to stare into her eyes, his lips teasing the sensitive flesh of her palm. She jumped as she felt the tip of his tongue lightly dance between her fingers. She swallowed a moan as the first stirrings of desire flooded through her. Damn, this guy was good. She wouldn't mind getting naked with him.

She stopped her thoughts from going any further. Geesh! Decide to break a celibacy streak and suddenly she wanted to fuck every man she saw. Okay...maybe not every man, but fucking two brothers was even too slutty for her. She smiled to herself. But it didn't hurt to fantasize.

Marlin abruptly pulled away. Mariah's body cried out at the loss of his touch. "C'mon. I'll take you to my brother." He started to walk away and then glanced back at her. His eyes sparkled invitingly. When had she become that easy? He reached out and took her hand. "C'mon. He's just inside the shop."

Mariah went with him, wondering what the hell she was getting herself into and not sure she cared either way. If Stephan couldn't help her, perhaps Marlin would. He didn't have the same assurance as Stephan, but for some reason, she was certain she could trust him.

* * * * *

Stephan punched the bag again, this time harder, causing it to swing back into the wall. He swung out with his left arm, knocked it back. He continued pushing himself, faster and faster, harder and harder. He circled the punching bag, jabbing, kicking, punching, stabbing. Sweat soaked his body and he paused just long enough to remove his T-shirt and wipe the sweat from his eyes before he continued. Dammit! This wasn't working either.

He attacked the bag once more, this time imagining the worst of the creatures he'd ever been up against. Their faces became superimposed on the bag and he killed them again.

There were the Dahken demons, smelly, vicious killers that kept their victims alive while they skinned them. Three of them had pinned him down and taken a good chunk of skin off his back before he got away and proceeded to rip them apart limb by limb.

The Solunen demons, solitary creatures with no respect for any life, not even each other's. They thrived on any kill, the more pain the better. Fiero had spent a while healing him after that fight.

He'd been in some horrible brawls, almost lost his life several times, but he always won. Nothing took him by surprise anymore.

Well, nothing but a beautiful woman with one hell of a right hook.

He smiled at the memory of her passion, anger and obvious strength through her fear. She would be one hell of a fireball in bed.

Stephan frowned and forced those thoughts from his head. He sounded like his brother now, wanting to fuck every hot woman he got near. But that didn't change the fact that he couldn't get Mariah out of his system. There was no way he would allow himself to do anything about his lust for her.

After making sure she got home safe last night, Stephan had immediately left for Polgara. A long fucking session with Lita could usually fix all his ills. That's what Pleasure goddesses were for. It was their duty to bring pleasure to anyone who wanted it. And Lita always knew what he needed.

He cared for Lita, as much as he'd ever cared for any woman, but she didn't make him feel the things he felt after just a few moments with Mariah.

Lita had known something was different, and she'd pulled out all her tricks. Nothing worked. He'd fucked her hard, all night and well into the new day, sharing with her the darkness and violence that had resided in his soul since the day he had become a Shadow Walker. He knew that she could take everything he had and probably more. Lita had orgasmed several times but he remained erect, unable to bring himself to climax.

After her sixth orgasm, she rolled him over, taking his cock into her mouth. Her tongue was probably the most talented part of her very talented body. She ran her tongue up and down his shaft, cleaning her juices off of him. He watched as she took the head into her mouth and started pulling and suckling, putting pressure on his most sensitive areas. His whole body tensed, preparing for release. He wanted this—no, he needed this. Her tongue darted into the small hole at the top, tasting and teasing. He moaned and closed his eyes. This was killing him. Why wouldn't his body let him come?

When he reopened his eyes, he saw Lita, and something about the way her hair fell over her face reminded him of Mariah. The color was the same and the way it fell over her naked breasts, just brushing the nipples, stimulating them. He remembered Mariah dancing, her hair flying out around her and then settling on her breasts.

At that moment Lita took his entire cock into her mouth. The mental image of Mariah coupled with Lita's mouth brought him over the top and he shouted out his release. Lita continued sucking and swallowing, bringing him continuous pleasure until he was empty. She removed her mouth from his now tired cock and crawled up his body, kissing him. He tasted both of them on her lips. Damn! Nobody treated him as good as Lita. It was too bad he desired something more.

"You've met someone, haven't you?" She paused, smiling, a knowing look in her eyes. "Someone has finally caused your heart to beat with love." She met his gaze as she straddled him, rubbing her wet heat against his cock, which was slowly renewing its interest. Lita continued rubbing him with her wet pussy, undulating in a circular motion, her body in tune with what both of them desired.

Lita arched her neck back and purred. He loved to watch her in the throes of passion. As a Pleasure goddess, her body was made for sex.

Stephan brought one hand to her breasts, cupping each one in turn—rolling her nipples between his thumb and forefinger, tugging and massaging. His other hand sought out her clit and began a steady rhythm there. Her unique sexual scent filled his senses, bringing him back to full erection. He was surrounded by the sounds, taste, touch, sight and scent of Lita, although as much as it turned him on, it wasn't what he wanted. He wanted the fire of Mariah. The passion he saw hidden in her eyes while she danced. It pained him to realize that. Lita had always been good to him, but he wouldn't—couldn't—use her anymore.

Her body tensed as she cried out and came violently against his fingers.

When her body stilled she placed her hands on his chest, settling over his heart. "Just be careful, Stephan. I can see that this woman will bring you your greatest joys and your deepest heartache."

He sat up then, reclining on his elbows. "What do you mean, you can 'see'?"

Lita smiled at him fondly, continuing to run her hands over his chest, sorrow in her eyes. "I can 'see' things about those I care about. I have known that this day would be our last together for a very long time. You have found your true heart link—your soulmate. You must go to her, be with her only. Your destiny awaits you, as does my own. But I will miss you."

Lita had settled him back onto the bed and proceeded to straddle him again, taking him deep inside her. This time their loving was slow, a goodbye. They orgasmed together and he held her tight to him until he fell asleep.

He awakened a short time later when she kissed him goodbye, a lone tear falling from one violet eye onto his cheek.

"I will always adore you, Stephan, and will look fondly on our years together, but our paths will no longer cross." He kissed her again, passionately, saying with his kiss the words he couldn't utter.

She'd turned and walked away and he had wondered what he would do without the companionship of his only lover for the past twelve years. She had been his friend, his confidante and he couldn't have asked for a better lover. But at the same time, he knew that he would never feel for her what he could feel for Mariah. And Lita deserved someone who could love her completely, if she could break free of the rules of Polgara and find a love of her own.

Stephan's thoughts came crashing back to the present and he continued pummeling the bag in front of him. The punishment he inflicted on himself and the bag hadn't made him feel any better. It was time to mount up and go find some tangible, grotesque and hopefully killable demons. They were much less predictable fighters than the ones his mind was trying to project onto the damn punching bag. Maybe then the fire inside him would cool.

Stephan turned from the punching bag and saw the beautiful reason for his fire standing in the doorway watching him. His brother stood beside her, touching her, trying to coax her into the room. But Mariah didn't move, as her gaze united with his. He saw the same fire in her eyes that he felt burning inside himself—but he saw sorrow and pain as well. He knew those feelings all too well and wanted to take them away from her if he could.

And perhaps Lita had been right. Maybe Mariah was the one.

* * * * *

Mariah couldn't catch her breath. First, she was kissed on her hand more passionately than she had been kissed anywhere else in years. Then, she was brought into the backroom of *Rare and Unusual Imports* to witness an even more passionate Stephan beating the shit out of an inanimate object.

There was something so primal about watching a man fight. Her body began to heat from the inside out.

His body was amazing. She watched the muscles of his back flex and ripple as he pounded the bag repeatedly. He was perfectly built—lean and muscular. Every synapse in her brain was firing, trying to comprehend what it hadn't been allowed to enjoy for so very long—the body of a gorgeous man. She kept herself in check long enough to make sure she wasn't dreaming about the sight before her. Her breath caught in her throat as he stepped out for a harder shot.

He started kicking the bag, and she was able to see just how amazing an ass Stephan had. She just wanted to watch him for hours—the way the sweat glistened all over his body, how his shorts hung low on his hips. Everything about him was worth making a mental movie of, to play back in her head during those lonely nights with her vibrator.

She could only imagine what it would be like to be fucked by him. A no hold's barred session, where he could unleash that intense passion hidden within. There would be nothing like it.

Mariah's inner temperature skyrocketed and the stirrings of desire that had begun when Marlin had tongued her fingers became a flood of wet heat directly where she wanted him most. Her cunt ached for him, for the something that had been missing from her life for so long. She remembered her bath from the night before, the image of him she'd had before she came, and she blushed. Her nipples hardened beneath her shirt as her body continued to ready itself for fucking.

She wasn't prepared for the look in his eyes when he turned toward her. Their gazes met and Mariah was lost. His hazel eyes were deep and penetrating and seemed to breach the depths of her soul. Her whole body was drawn to him. She had to fight the urge to move toward him, to remove those sinfully low-riding shorts, and to get sweaty with him.

And then he smiled. If she wasn't smitten before...

She had to get a hold of herself! This wasn't about her. This wasn't about getting laid for the first time in over five years. This was about finding Twyla. She could worry about ending her celibacy streak later. Much later. Well...hopefully not too much later.

Marlin's warm chuckle startled Mariah out of her staring contest with Stephan. "Maybe I should leave you two alone."

"Yes...I mean no...I mean..." Mariah felt herself reddening when she noticed the smile widening Stephan's face. When had she turned into a slave for lust? Just because Stephan was watching her the same way she was watching him, just because she wanted to catch the drop of sweat sliding down his chest with her tongue, just because he was the only man who could help her....

And that's what she needed to focus on.

Marlin laughed again. "I'll be around if you need me."

Stephan glared at Marlin's retreating form. Although Marlin's comment had been directed at Stephan, Mariah couldn't help but think he was talking to her as well. Maybe she should ask for both of their help? Two strong bodies were better than one. She almost choked on that thought. Images of being fucked by both brothers simultaneously tumbled through her mind and the relentless throbbing in her pussy demanded immediate gratification. Maybe she really *was* a slut in disguise.

She turned to stop Marlin from leaving as the door closed behind him. She was alone with Stephan. That was the last thing she needed to focus on right now.

"I need your help."

"Okay. What kind of help do you need?" Stephan's smile faded to a look of concern as his heavy breathing began to return to normal. He stepped closer to her and Mariah was enveloped in the scent of him—the smell of a man who knew how to use his body. He was musty, sweaty male—the aroma of good sex on a hot night.

Lover's Talisman

She stifled a moan at the pictures her mind was creating. She was on the verge of climax just from her damn thoughts! Then she flashed back to Twyla's car, her items strewn all over the driveway. She wouldn't, couldn't think about sex when her best friend was missing. What was wrong with her? Although Twyla had been encouraging her to get fucked, and as often as possible, she just couldn't jump right in while her friend was in danger.

Mariah swallowed and forced herself to meet Stephan's eyes. His obvious concern touched her and she realized he deserved an apology for her behavior the previous night. "I owe you both a thank you and an apology for yesterday. I-I..."

"There's no need to thank me. I'm just glad you're okay. You are okay, right?" His hand captured her below her elbow, his thumb rubbing soothing circles on the skin of her inner arm. His touch lent the illusion that everything would be okay, and fanned the desire thrumming through her cunt. She tightened her legs, desperate for some relief. Twyla was right, she really did need a hot man to fuck. She looked forward to Twyla laughing at her and saying, "I told you so." But until then, she would keep her pussy to herself.

"No, I'm fine, really. Better than I thought I should be. But this isn't about me. My best friend, my roommate, she's missing. I think—no, I know—she's in trouble."

* * * * *

She needed a lot more from him than just help. Her body had visually responded to his touch. She was flushed with desire, her mouth slightly parted. It was like she was inviting him deeper into her world. He wanted to kiss her, to hold her and fuck her and wipe the traces of fear from her eyes. His hand slid up her arm to her shoulder and then the side of her neck and jaw, continuously rubbing circles into her skin. She felt so damn good.... He repositioned the discarded shirt to cover his bulging cock. The last thing he wanted was to scare her away by jabbing her with the evidence of his lust. Although he could tell that she wanted him as badly as he wanted her, he wasn't going to take advantage of a desperate female. At least not yet.

"Tell me what happened." He knew how to do this job. He could play the hero, rescue the damsel in distress and then request a favor from the damsel's best friend. All in a night's work.

"She had an important meeting this morning. One she's been waiting awhile for. She never made it." Mariah paused for a moment to still her ragged breathing as tears welled up in her eyes. Stephan used his thumb to wipe away a tear sliding down her cheek. Her silver-blue eyes searched his and a bolt of electricity shot through his heart. At that moment, he was certain. He would do anything within his power to take her pain away. Consequences be damned.

Mariah continued, her voice more ragged than before. "I found her portfolio scattered all over the driveway and the convertible top of her Mustang was ripped through. I don't know what could have happened to her and I don't know what to do. The police were no help…" Mariah reached out her hand and settled it on his chest. The heat of her touch burned him. Her eyes begged and her touch pleaded. "Please, I need your help."

Stephan couldn't deny her anything. Her hand remained on his chest, his hand still cupped her cheek. They were frozen in time, burning with desire and fear and need. He wanted to kiss her, but she appeared so fragile he was afraid he would scare her away. Yet she was also the same woman who had punched him just last night. She was not his usual damsel in distress.

"Let me get some clothes on and you can show me the mangled car and tell me about your friend so I can get a better idea how to help you." Mariah's eyes lit up with a faint spark of hope and she smiled. She was so beautiful. He wanted to see her smile more often. He wanted to hear her laugh and moan and tease and play. "Wait here. I'll be right back."

Stephan pulled away from her, his body immediately missing the physical connection to her. These feelings had cracked open a door in him that he'd long ago slammed shut. But he would be damned if he let her down.

As he dressed, Stephan thought over what she had said. Could Asfar have been seeking revenge against him for taking his prey? The fact that the convertible top was ripped through bothered him. It didn't sound like something Asfar would do. But two roommates being attacked within a twenty-four-hour period was suspicious. He wouldn't be able to tell until he saw the scene, but he had learned long ago that in Talisman Bay, there was no such thing as a coincidence.

* * * * *

"Her beads and paperwork were scattered all over the driveway and yard." Mariah gestured with her arm over the area. Clouds covered the night sky making it difficult for most people to see, but as a Shadow Walker, Stephan was used to seeking out details in little light.

The car caught his attention. It would normally be considered a perfectly restored Mustang, but the mangled top ruined that image. He studied the damage. It looked like it was done with claws. Shit! This *was* some type of demon activity.

He open-clicked-in to his friends. *We've got evidence of some kind of demon attack in the residential neighborhood in Sector 34. Who's closest and available to help verify the sector's clear? I've got a civilian under watch and I need to get her outta the area as soon as possible.*

Sorry, gotta live one here. I'm busy for a while. Ryan immediately clicked-out.

I'm playing tour guide tonight to a group of Tarintulne demons. Give me the word and I'll rush them back to their dimension. I'm with ya if ya need me. Jake's response wasn't unexpected. He hated playing tour guide. *'Sides, I think they're just here for the Kool-Aid anyway. They tell me it's an aphrodisiac where they come from. Who knew?*

Dusty's voice seemed distant. *Umm...I can be there in a bit, but I've got a very...um...appreciative female and—*

Marlin cut in. *Hey, I'm close. Dusty, you with Jeneane?*

Yeah, and if I quit now, she'll never call me again.

Cool, Dusty. Yeah, guys, he really does need to get laid. I'm tired of all the whining. Stephan, I'll be with ya in a few. My sector's pretty quiet.

Dusty grunted out a quick thanks and was gone.

Jake groaned. *If you need more help, just let me know.* He clicked-out as well.

Stephan scowled. The last person he wanted around Mariah was his brother. But her safety was more important.

Same house as last night? Stephan could hear the smile in his brother's voice. Marlin was enjoying this situation way too much.

Yeah. Same house, and hurry. I wanna get her back to the compound until I know what we're dealing with. Stephan clicked-out with Marlin and reached for Mariah.

"We gotta go back to the import store. It's safer there."

Mariah pulled out of his reach. "I need to go inside and check the machine, just to make sure no one has heard from her or that she hasn't been trying to get a hold of me."

Stephan studied the dark house. No lights on—anybody or anything could be hiding inside. While he was certain he could protect her, it would be better to do a thorough perimeter search to see if there were obvious signs of an intruder.

"No. First, I gotta clear the perimeter. After it's clear, then and only then will I determine if it's safe for us to actually enter. Stay close to me." Stephan reached out a hand to her. Mariah looked at his hand for a brief moment before she placed her hand in his. The heat from her touch infused his entire body with warmth and his thoughts immediately turned to sex. This was not a good time for him to get distracted.

"You sound like a commando. 'Clear the perimeter.' 'Safe to enter.' Do you really think we need to do this?" Mariah's voice lowered to a whisper as they approached the back of the house.

"I'm not taking any chances. Anything could be waiting in the shadows." He wished he could say more, make her understand the depth of danger she might be in. But he couldn't. Not without compromising his job and the secrecy of the whole Shadow Walker organization. He'd already done more than he should by having Fiero heal her yesterday, and by bringing her to the compound in the first place. What was it about this woman that made him break his own rules?

"Twyla's missing. This doesn't have anything to do with me, does it?" Mariah paused and Stephan tried to think up an answer that wouldn't scare her. He hadn't yet seen evidence of someone inside her house, but he wasn't going in unprepared. He quickly turned to face Mariah when she dropped his hand. "Oh God! Do you think this has something to do with my attack last night?"

Stephan gazed into her big, blue eyes, glistening with unshed tears. He didn't know what to tell her. It probably did have something to do with last night, but it was obvious to him that she was already feeling guilty and he didn't want to add to that. The last thing he needed was a hysterical terrified woman on his hands.

He pulled her closer to him, placing her head against his chest. One hand settled on her head and stroked her hair while the other rested against her back. She sighed and moved in closer and Stephan noticed how well they fit together. Every moment spent with her convinced him that maybe she really could be his. But he remembered her ice-cold stare from the night before. It had to be a man. Someone must have fucked her up and scared her off men. He'd seen that kind of abuse happen all too often while he was growing up. If he ever met the man that had hurt Mariah, he wouldn't hesitate before killing him.

"I'm not sure what's goin' on, but I won't take any chances with you. We'll find Twyla, I promise." He didn't mention that he was afraid that when they found her, it might already be too late.

* * * * *

Mariah had never before felt this secure. In the middle of her darkened yard, while searching for her best friend, she was completely safe. She wrapped her arms around his waist, luxuriating in his strength. Stephan's breath wafted against the top of her head, and his heart beat steadily beneath her cheek. The soft cotton of his tight black T-shirt felt comforting against her face. She closed her eyes and for a moment let herself enjoy how he made everything feel so right again.

She started to pull away, but not before lightly brushing her lips against his chest. His muscles tightened beneath her hands and she knew that he had felt her kiss. Her gaze returned to his eyes and her breath caught at the desire she saw reflected there. He pulled her back toward him, quickly, fiercely, and ground his mouth to hers.

Mariah's body lit up, an explosion of feeling that set her on fire. She wanted to pull him closer, she wanted to pull away. She wanted to strip naked and fuck him right there against the back wall of the house.

Instead, she kissed him back. She opened her mouth and invited him inside. It had been so long since she had been kissed but she didn't ever remember feeling one down to her toes. He surrounded her, consumed her and she wanted to give him more to take. Her hands found his hair, and she ran her fingers through the short strands in the back. She heard a moan, but wasn't sure if it was his or her own.

He picked her up, turning and pressing her against the house. She wrapped her legs around his waist, grinding her hips against his, desperately wishing their clothes would disappear. One of his hands remained on her ass, crushing her to him, while the other wandered…caressing…touching. His lips traced from her mouth to her neck, which was one giant erogenous zone, and Mariah almost had an orgasm right then. She could feel his cock right against her cunt, the barrier of their jeans an impossible hindrance.

His hand found its way under her shirt, his fingertips just brushing the underside of one breast. She reached between them, running one hand from his chest to his stomach and down to the bulge of his cock. Her hand grasped him through his jeans and his body quaked as he moaned against her neck. She wanted more of him and she wanted it now.

His jeans were button fly. The top button came undone easily and she impatiently reached her hand inside, desperate to feel his cock in her hand. He was molded fire — large, powerful and hot. She wrapped her hand around him, loving the thrill of power it gave her to have him thrusting against her. He moaned again, this time louder. She continued her ministrations, exploring with her fingers what she wanted to actually see and taste.

His hand slid from her breast to her jeans and made quick work of her button and zipper. Mariah spoke a prayer of thanks that she had worn her sexy pink lace panties, and not her comfortable, man-hater, white cotton granny underwear. His fingers brushed over the damp lace stretched over her cunt and she almost cried. It had been so long since anyone's hands but her own had traveled there. One finger slipped under the barricade and rubbed slowly back and forth, spreading her juices over her clit. She whimpered and rocked against his finger. God, she had to have him now, the pain-desire was killing her. If she could just get the last few buttons of his jeans undone…

A shaft of moonlight broke through the clouds overhead, illuminating someone rapidly approaching them. She pushed against Stephan, scrambling to get away, her desire fast turning into fear. This figure, completely covered in dark hair, long fangs dripping, with red glowing eyes, was almost upon them. "Stephan! Run! We have to run!"

Chapter Four

Stephan's mind, heart, and cock were buzzing with lust, so it took him an extra moment to notice Mariah's withdrawal. The fear in her eyes took him completely by surprise, until he realized it wasn't him causing it. He whipped his head around to discover what was scaring her just as he was viciously shoved to the ground.

Fuck!

"Mariah! Run! Now!" Stephan's voice carried over the inhuman growls. He wrestled with his attacker, but the werewolf had the upper hand. Stephan felt a tearing across his chest and the red heat of blood. That was going to hurt when he let it.

Out of the corner of his eye, Stephan saw Mariah dart away. The werewolf noticed the same thing and launched himself off Stephan toward Mariah's retreating figure. Stephan jumped to his feet to follow, but couldn't match the speed of the shape-shifter. Mariah screamed as she was grabbed from behind and tossed over the creature's shoulder. She kicked and fought with a vengeance, but her tiny body was nothing compared to the monster who carried her away. Her nails drew blood as she frantically scratched at the werewolf's back.

Stephan saw red, the rage he kept buried inside flooding furiously to the surface. His woman! He was not going to lose Mariah when he had just found her. His pace quickened to almost inhuman speed to match the werewolf. His heart pounded, his chest throbbed with pain and he didn't give a fuck about anything but getting Mariah to safety and then slowly torturing and killing this creature who would dare try to take her away from him.

Stephan caught up and with a leap, tackled the werewolf, knocking it and Mariah to the ground. He roared his triumph as he pulled the beast from Mariah and began ripping at it with his bare hands, the rage dumping waves of adrenaline into his system.

Marlin raced toward them, the light from a street lamp reflecting off the gun in his hand. Stephan shouted to him.

"Get her out of here!"

Hitting the ground hard, Mariah rolled and skidded to a stop. She hurt, but knew it was nothing bad. Stephan, however, was locked in combative embrace with the creature, blood oozing from deep furrows on his chest. It had to be painful, but he didn't even flinch as he pounded on the monster. The thing fought back, snarling, howling, fangs flashing as he bit and snapped, claws ripping, trying to sink deeply into Stephan's flesh.

Both growled in fury, man and beast, each determined to win and claim her as their prize. She wanted to run, but she couldn't leave Stephan to fight that hairy, growly, scary thing alone—not that she'd know how to help.

What the hell was that thing? It was like something out of a horror movie...or a nightmare...or a nightmare after watching a horror movie. It just didn't make sense. She saw it in front of her, and if she was asked to name what it was she would have to say a werewolf, but werewolves didn't exist. At least an hour ago she didn't think they did.

Someone picked her up, startling her into fighting until she realized it was Marlin carrying her.

"Put me down! We can't leave him here with that thing!"

"He'll be fine. I promise. I gotta get you outta here now." Marlin practically sprinted, acting as though carrying a woman while running wasn't difficult for him, or even unusual.

Mariah peered over Marlin's shoulder and saw Stephan still battling the werewolf. She couldn't handle it if something happened to him.

"Please, go back and help him. I can't...I don't want anything to happen to him."

"He's been in worse stuff before. I'd be back there fighting too if I thought he needed me. He told me to keep you safe." A cocky grin lit up his face and his eyes sparkled with mischief. "Hell, my brother never shares girls with me. This is kinda fun."

Mariah's immediate thought was to deny being Stephan's girl, but the fact that her underwear was still damp from their most recent encounter made her realize that denial would be futile. And she *wanted* to be his. She hadn't felt like this in…well, really, she had never felt like this. At one time she would have said she'd loved Michael, but now that part of her life seemed so distant, the relationship memories blocked with ones of pain, she didn't think it had been love. It was a relationship built on necessity, and ultimately betrayal.

They reached the import store much quicker than Mariah would have thought possible. She remained silent, caught up in a whirlwind of worry and emotions. She didn't understand how much she already cared for Stephan. There seemed to be so much more to him than he let on, but at the same time, he came across as such a strong and honest man. She wasn't afraid of him, just of her deepening attraction to him.

Marlin had said that Stephan had been in worse situations before. What type of man was prepared for situations like that? Who was he really? And what was that thing that attacked her? And why? There had to be an explanation for the strange chaos her life had become.

Marlin still carried her. Mariah hadn't even realized she'd placed her head against his chest, her arms around his neck. There was no denying that Marlin was a very sexual man, but he didn't make her ache inside like Stephan did. Marlin's sexuality emanated from every pore, while Stephan's burned deep inside, waiting for the right moment to explode. She wanted to be the one that he erupted for. Hell, they probably both would have exploded several times by now if they hadn't been interrupted. That memory brought a blush to her cheeks and caused her pussy to begin its merciless throbbing again. Even in the midst of chaos, her body wanted Stephan now. She'd laugh, but it scared her more than it amused her.

Marlin carried her through the backroom of the store, and down a narrow flight of stairs before settling her onto a couch. The room was vaguely familiar, and she realized that it was the same place she had awakened in just twenty-four hours earlier. So much had changed in that time.

Marlin handed her a glass. "Here, drink this, it should soothe you."

Mariah studied the drink, then took a small sniff. It smelled like wine. She took a few sips. "Mmmmm. Thanks. This is great stuff."

"Good. Now let's see about taking care of those scrapes you got there." A warm hand offered comfort as Marlin investigated the damage she'd received when she hit the ground. He pulled a few strands of hair from beneath her fingernails.

"It's really no big deal. I hardly notice it."

"Well, that's good, but I told my brother I'd take care of you, and I'm gonna do that. Wait here. I'm gettin' a few things to make you feel better."

"Really, I'm fine—"

A raised eyebrow was his only response before he turned and exited the room.

Mariah studied her surroundings. This room basically looked like the living room area of a house. She was sitting on the same couch as last night. Its unbelievably baby-soft, creamy beige leather screamed high dollar. Two matching recliners, one on either side, framed a state of the art entertainment system. A modern deco coffee table, lots of gray chrome and glass, was covered with car magazines, dirty plates and empty soda cans. A bachelor pad—a rich bachelor's pad.

The walls of the room were slightly rounded; one side of the room had the door from which they had arrived, and the other side had an archway that lead to what appeared to be a hallway, where Marlin had gone. A kitchen and dining area were on the opposite side of the room from where she sat. There were no other windows or doors.

Something about the room seemed wrong. Hell, everything felt off for her right now. She wanted to know if Stephan was okay, she wanted to know what the hell was going on. She wanted Twyla back and her whole world to go back to normal.

So many questions. Her body ached, her mind spun a web of unanswered questions. She set the now empty glass on the coffee table and sank deeper into the couch, weariness taking over. She closed her eyes for a moment, craving any relief. From a distance, she thought she felt warm hands comforting her, but before she could figure out what was going on she was deeply asleep.

* * * * *

Marlin waited for him upstairs, outside the boundary of the lower rooms.

"You look like shit."

"Fuck you." Stephan glared at Marlin and tried to walk around him. He was sore and tired and pissed as all hell and he didn't need any of Marlin's shit right now.

Marlin stepped in front of him. His first thought was to stride right through him, or maybe throw him against the nearest wall, but good sense prevailed for the moment.

"She's fine. I gave her a little something to help her sleep. I figured it's safer to have her sleeping below stairs, less explaining to do. Anyway, she's got a few scrapes on her arms, a bump on her head. I cleaned her up. She also has some reddening on her neck, her lips were swollen, and her jeans were undone, but somehow I don't think the werewolf was responsible for that."

"Don't—"

"Look, you know I'm all for getting laid. As often as possible. But I can see it in your eyes, this isn't about getting your dick wet. Use her, but don't fall in love—"

Stephan grabbed Marlin by the throat and shoved him up against the wall. The rage from earlier came back and he knew it would be too easy to take it out on his brother. Marlin didn't reciprocate, and other than his obvious desire to take a breath, he remained completely still. Stephan slowly lowered him to the ground.

"Don't fucking tell me what to do with her." He continued past his brother and opened the door to the stairs. The pain from his injuries started affecting him and he slowly descended each step. Opening the door, his eyes immediately sought out Mariah fast asleep on the couch, her long brown hair tousled around her. The feeling of possession washed through him again, overwhelming his already exhausted body.

Marlin's voice echoed behind him. "Remember what happened to Judy. Remember what happened to me."

Stephan didn't move, didn't take his eyes off of Mariah's sleeping form. "It might be too late."

Within moments Fiero appeared. Stephan stumbled from the doorway, staggering in his attempt to stay upright. He didn't admit defeat or pain, but he was fucking sore, the deep furrows in his chest burning, blood still oozing from the wounds. Fiero glared at him and grimaced as Marlin sat down in a recliner.

"It's worse than The Order thought, isn't it? Something's started and you're right in the middle of it." Fiero solidified from apparition to flesh and put an arm around Stephan, leading him to the other recliner. He raised his eyes when he spotted Mariah asleep on the couch.

"I didn't realize that you were offering a discount to frequent visitors here. It was my understanding that this was still a *secret* hideaway and that visitors were to be kept to a minimum—like never."

"Fuck off. She needs protection, Fiero. Somebody's after her, somebody with lots of power. They got her roommate and now they want her too. Until I find out what's going on, this is the only place she's safe."

Fiero placed his hands over the wounds on Stephan's chest. He muttered a few words and green glow lights appeared from his hands, surrounding Stephan. He remained rigid in the chair, eyes focused only on Mariah.

"Stop the healing before it's complete. I want these scars. To remember."

Fiero scowled at him, halting the lights and calling them back within. Crossing his hands over his chest, he glared, demanding an explanation.

"I wasn't paying close enough attention and she could have been hurt because of that. These will remind me." Stephan stood up and removed his ripped shirt, a small cringe the only thing that betrayed the pain he still felt. The deep furrows were gone, replaced with red, puckered skin.

He knelt next to Mariah, his hands lightly tracing her face, then skimming down her body. Standing up quickly he turned to Fiero. "Check her out. Make sure she has no other unseen injuries. I have to go out. Marlin, you stay with her until I come back." With one last glance at Mariah he walked down the hallway toward his room.

Fiero turned to Marlin. "Great. He fucking loves her, doesn't he?"

Marlin kicked back in the recliner. "I hope not."

They both looked at Mariah, her innocence in sleep a far understatement to the havoc she was unknowingly causing.

"Shit..." Fiero mumbled as he approached Mariah. The green lights danced between his fingertips as he chanted the words to release them. They played about the entire length of her body. They paused for a brief moment at her abdomen, flared brightly and disappeared. At least life wasn't going to be boring anymore.

* * * * *

Ivan had failed. He hadn't been able to retrieve Stephan's girl so this one would pay.

Freeze's eyes investigated the sleeping girl tied to the cot. He'd seen her wrestle mercilessly against her bonds for what must have been hours. They had loosened only slightly, but she'd never managed to free herself completely. The knot holding her wrists was magically strengthened, and only a magic-user of his caliber could release it. Watching her struggle stirred many memories. He fully understood what it was to struggle against immovable ties that bind. It sometimes felt as though he'd never really broken free.

With his right hand, he drew his sharpest knife.

It was a shame that she was expendable. The hand not holding the knife ached to touch her, to remind him what goodness felt like. Of its own accord, his left hand caressed her face. She was beautiful.

And powerful.

He pulled his hand away from her face, startled by his discovery. She wasn't a complete innocent. Magic flowed in her veins, deep and strong and mostly untouched. It was too bad Craze had marked her for death.

She stirred gently as he was about to begin.

"Shhh...sweet one." He waved his hand over her face to execute his spell. "Sleep. Find sleep."

The knife felt heavy in his hand as he did what Craze bade him to do.

Chapter Five

Mariah's body was more alive, more on fire than ever before. Electricity, rather than blood, pumped through her veins. Desire coursed through her and she smiled up at the man who made her feel this way. He returned her smile with a wicked grin—the look of a man who knew exactly the way he made her feel.

She licked her lips, watching his eyes follow the trail of her tongue. She could feel his body tense, saw his eyes darken and knew that he wanted her as much as she wanted him. The power in that was exhilarating.

She shifted her body closer, stretching up to her tallest height. Their bodies didn't touch yet, but she could feel the heat emanating from him. Her nipples were erect and demanding to be rubbed up against his chest, but she forbade it for now.

Her tongue darted out again, this time tracing his lips. The only place their bodies touched was where her tongue intimately circled his mouth, slowly, agonizingly slowly, learning and memorizing every molecule of his lips. He moaned, a deep growl, but let her continue uninterrupted. She was in control of this powerful, beautiful man. It took all of her willpower not to beg him to fuck her hard and fast right then. But she wanted more. She wanted everything, every bit of this man engraved in her mind.

A warmth flooded through her stomach and down into her pussy. The ache was so much worse now. Every moment with him was a study in the pain of pleasure. She couldn't prolong it anymore. She had to have his hands, his lips, his tongue, every part of him against her hot flesh.

"Please. Now." The breathy sound barely passed her lips before Stephan disappeared. Mariah blinked her eyes open and let out a moan. It was only a dream. Her body raged. She was so aroused that a good stiff breeze would probably push her over the edge and into one hell of an orgasm. If she didn't get fucked soon…

"Are you okay?"

Bedroom eyes. That's what they were called. Marlin had a set of eyes that demanded sex, reminding you how good it would be anytime you wanted it. He leaned over the back of the couch, assessing her.

Mariah struggled to sit up. A kink in her neck made her cringe as she swung her feet to the floor. "I'm fine. Just a little stiff." *And a lot horny and I'd really like to fuck your brother now, right now, hard, on the floor, on the couch, on the table, against the wall. Hell, I'm so horny, you should join in as well. If I'm going to turn into a monster slut, I might as well indulge all my fantasies.*

"You looked like you were having a bad dream or somethin'. Stephan would kick my ass if I didn't make sure you were all right."

"Stephan! Oh God! Is he okay?" Mariah's lust level dropped to almost zero as she recalled the danger she had left him in.

"He's fine. Just fine. He had to go back out again. Something about checking up on leads about your friend's disappearance. He left me in charge of making you feel at home." Marlin stood up and walked over to the recliner, plopped down into it and kicked his feet up onto the coffee table. A man in his domain.

Mariah remained silent, her thoughts revolving around the fight she'd witnessed.

"You really fell asleep there. I left to get a washcloth and came back to a sleeping beauty."

Mariah almost snorted. "Oh, please. You didn't think that line would really work, did you?" She stood up, trying her best to shake off her thoughts.

Marlin laughed. "Well, it was nicer than me saying I came back to a scene out of Night of the Living Dead."

Mariah started to laugh and then stopped. "Um...speaking of Night of the Living Dead...what was that thing...the uh...creature...monster, whatever, that attacked Stephan and I?" She impatiently tapped her foot, waiting for his response. She could almost see the thoughts swirling through his head. He knew...he knew what it was and he didn't want to tell her.

Marlin shook his head slowly. The mischievous grin that always seemed to hover right below the surface disappeared. He stood up and faced her, taking her hands and leading her back to the sofa. He settled her down and then sat on the coffee table facing her, still holding both of her hands in his.

"There are lots of things in this world...creatures...myths...things that people talk about but don't think are real." Marlin's thumbs stroked the tops of her hands, moving in soothing, reassuring circles. She didn't think he even realized what he was doing. "There is truth behind every story—"

"And a desire behind every action." Stephan stepped into the room, a darkness in his eyes, and Mariah's focus tunnel-visioned until nothing existed but him.

* * * * *

Dammit!

He knew better! He knew what his brother was capable of, and he'd still left Mariah in his company. What the hell had he been thinking?

Stephan looked her over, hair tussled, eyes smoky with desire. Her face was flushed, her nipples taut and erect beneath her shirt, yet another woman to succumb to the charms of his dear brother.

His attention shifted to Marlin. Oddly enough a flash of guilt crossed his features. Marlin removed his hands from Mariah's, then slowly slid them down the front of his jeans before standing up.

"You need to tell her." Marlin met Stephan's stare unflinchingly. Stephan waited, sure there was some gallant act or sexual comment forthcoming. He expected his brother to make a claim, to show Stephan that yet again he could have whatever or whomever he wanted. His fury mounted as he waited, but Marlin remained silent, seemingly waiting for something in return.

"Tell me what?" Mariah stood up, standing between them, but facing toward Stephan. She looked confused and scared, yet determined and sexy as hell. "What do I need to know? Is it about Twyla?" She wrapped her arms around herself, as though holding herself together, but Stephan could see a tremor of fear shoot through her body. "God. Please tell me she's okay."

"I don't know. I honestly don't know. But I'll find her for you. I promise." Stephan couldn't help it, her anguish melted him, and he stepped forward, ready and willing to protect her against all fears real and imagined. Even if she had fallen for his brother, he would still do anything to protect her. He pulled her into his arms and she softened against him, her arms immediately wrapping around him, holding him close. She whimpered and he could feel her sobs wracking through her body. He rocked her close, whispering his vow to her over and over. "I promise…I promise. I'll do anything to help you. I will. I promise."

Stephan met Marlin's eyes over Mariah's head. Marlin quickly turned and stalked away, but not before Stephan saw a flash of envy cross his brother's face. It surprised him, almost scared him that Marlin would be jealous. Marlin protested that love wasn't for him, at least not anymore, that he was happy with one-night stands and hot fucks with his favorite Polgaran, Tresca. Maybe things were about to change for everyone.

Stephan clicked-in to his brother.

Get everyone back here. We've gotta get things going tonight. There's a rescue to plan and research to do. Something big is brewing and I need to know who's behind it.

What about Mariah?

Look, she's in danger because of me. She'll be fine right here for now.

Marlin was silent, but it was obvious to Stephan that his younger brother was judging him for his mistakes. Stephan countered that judgment.

Just trust me.

Marlin clicked-out.

Marlin's hostility made sense. Stephan knew that he had never gotten over Judy. He had been practically inconsolable, restlessly searching; yet he never found a way to bring her back from the dimension a demon had thrown her into. After a full year of continuous hunting, he had learned of her death from the very demon that had taken her. The demon had paid for her loss viciously. And since then Marlin had kept his distance, never allowing love into his life. He was always charming, but never stayed with a woman long enough to make more than a sexual connection.

Yes, maybe they had all learned something from Marlin's loss. Since then, through an unspoken pact, none of them had let themselves fall in love. Or at least none of them would admit it. Their lives entailed too much danger and relationships could get too complicated and painful for all involved.

Stephan brushed his lips over Mariah's hair and continued rocking her to him. His words to Asfar had essentially broken that pact, and now Mariah was paying for his actions. It was his fault, so he would make it right. And when he knew she was safe, when the demons were vanquished and her friend brought home, he'd let her go. In twenty-four hours, she'd crept under his skin, pushed aside the darkness and found the part of him he'd thought incapable of feeling anything but hatred and pain. With her light and magic and pleasure, she'd touched the part of him that most guys would never admit they had. It would kill him to let her go, but he would rather die than let anything ever happen to her.

"C'mon sweetheart. You're totally safe here. I promise. I've got a place you can get some sleep."

Mariah peered up at him, her eyes wide, wet and beautiful. She smiled at him through her tears, and stepped out of his embrace, wiping her eyes with her hand.

"I'm not usually like this you know. All teary-eyed, useless female. It's all just been too much. Twyla's my anchor—my best friend—and not knowing where she is or if she's okay…well, I'm feeling a bit lost." She smiled up at him again. "But you, you and your brother both, you've been so great to me, so helpful and understanding…. After the way I treated you last night I didn't deserve this. Thank you."

He opened his mouth to reply but she placed one hand over his mouth to keep him from speaking. Her fingers were cool against his face. She traced one finger over his lips and then pulled her hand away. He held himself steady, unsure what she was doing but trying to keep his body under control.

It wasn't working.

"Now I need you to answer some questions for me. I know that you and Marlin know more than you're telling me. I want those answers."

Stephan sighed deeply and ran his hands through his hair. He'd known this time would come, but how could he explain everything to her without scaring her away? The Sacred Order wouldn't be happy with him if he told her about the Shadow Walkers and the reasons they existed. What they did, they did in secret. Society wasn't supposed to know about their existence or the existence of dimensional portals and the things that came through them. He hated being forced to hide his life and who he really was.

"Okay, I'll tell you what I can."

"No. Please. I need you to tell me everything."

"Well, there's a lot to tell, and probably a lot more than you wanna know." It was obvious she wasn't going to back down. "All right. Sit down. Here goes." Stephan waited for Mariah to sit before he positioned himself on the couch next to her, not quite touching, but close enough that he could feel her heat. He couldn't help it. He wanted her next to him, wanted the constant temptation having her near him would cause.

"Okay. Where do I start?" How could he shatter what she thought of her world? "That thing that attacked us earlier when we were at your house. It was a werewolf. They exist, as well as vampires, demons and every other creature you've ever imagined or had nightmares about. There's even a whole list of ones you never would've imagined."

Mariah's eyes widened and her jaw fell slightly open as he continued.

"I am..." He paused, trying to find words that wouldn't scare her away. "I didn't think this would be so hard." He looked straight into her eyes to make sure that she was still with him. "I'm a Shadow Walker."

"A what?" Her words were barely audible.

"I keep all those bad things from taking over. I'm serious. That's what I do. But I'm not supposed to talk about it with outsiders. There's all sorts of crazy things around here that I really can't begin to explain. I mean, even right here, right now, we're actually in another dimension."

Mariah laughed nervously. "No, no, no...you had me going for a moment with all the vampires and demons and stuff. I mean I saw you fight and you weren't afraid and your brother wasn't afraid at all—"

"Well, yeah, I fight all those things, but there's also..." How on earth could he make her understand without totally losing her? As her breathing quickened more, he wracked his brain for just the right thing to say and hopefully draw her in to him further. "Okay. We're in what appears to be a basement, right?"

"Yeah?" she agreed cautiously.

"We're in the basement of a store that is on a pier."

"Oh God! There should be waves...the ocean. This doesn't make sense..." Mariah slumped into the couch, her eyes growing larger by the second. He smiled at her reaction. She was following him. He stood up and motioned as if to emphasize.

"The stairway down here is a sort of dimensional portal. Right here is the safest place you can be…. And no matter what, you're completely safe with me, too." A shock hit his heart. It wasn't like him to say things that specific. Sure he'd protect any woman, but to promise to protect her through thick and thin was something he never thought he would hear himself utter.

She must have felt his sincerity.

She stood up and brought herself closer to him again. Then, on tiptoe, brushed her lips over his. He breathed in her words as she spoke them. "Thank you. Thank you for telling me everything. It's crazy, but I believe you." She lingered there, as they both took in each other. Their breathing was heavy…in…out…in…out…. She seemed to be offering herself and he wanted to take the invitation, but he couldn't. He wouldn't. Not now.

He stepped away and spoke barely above a whisper. "I…I do want you, and I want you now. Don't even doubt that. But when I have you, there can't be anything between us…no worries and no time limits." He paused, his cock currently hating him for turning down what she was offering, his mind reminding him that he was doing the right thing. His hand refused to listen to reason and reached out for her, taking her hand in his. "Let me show you your room. It's late, you should sleep."

He walked the short distance down the hallway, leading her to his room. Opening the door, his eyes focused on the bed, visions of her naked and waiting for him there filling his thoughts. He tried to get his cock back in check as he crossed to the dresser and opened a drawer. After sifting past a few ragged and stained shirts, he pulled out a T-shirt and sweats.

"I don't have any girl clothes. Marlin might. These should be real comfortable at least. Or I can go see if Marlin's got something."

"No, this is fine…really. Thank you again."

Lover's Talisman

"Bathroom's in there behind you. Y'know. Shower and stuff." He swallowed hard at the thought of her undressed and wet. It was hard enough to keep his cock from standing at attention. The thought of pleasing her up one side and down the other in that cascade of water was getting unbearable to resist. His duty was to protect her, not join with her. "Y'know, just make yourself at home. Get some good clean rest." He turned to go, knowing that if he stayed much longer he'd have to show her how comfortable the bed was for two.

"Stephan?" Her hand on his arm and the question in her voice stopped him. He turned to face her, knowing he couldn't take much more. "If you change your mind—"

"I've already changed it ten times. You deserve better than that. Long and slow and hot and amazing. We'll only stop when we're ready, not because we have to be somewhere or do something else. I wanna slowly learn every inch of you...lick you, taste you, kiss you, and when you can't take anymore of that, I'll fuck you until neither of us can move."

Before lust could win over logic, he removed her hand from his arm and kissed it and walked out of the room. He could hate himself later for leaving her when they both wanted each other, for not being quite able to tell her just how magical they would be and for being afraid to tell her what he was really feeling for her.

Hell, who was he kidding? He already did.

* * * * *

He'd walked out and left her alone.

Mariah sighed. He'd walked out and left her *horny* and alone. Her mind still reeled from the heat in his eyes and the smooth sexiness of his voice when he'd told her how he wanted to fuck her. They both wanted this, and damn him for having the strength to walk away. She looked at the closed door, hoping if she stared hard enough Stephan would walk back through it, throw her on the bed and fuck her into oblivion.

It didn't happen.

She flopped backwards onto the bed and sighed loud and dramatically. She'd finally decided to take the bull by the horns and get herself well and fucked, and the guy she had chosen was determined to be a gentleman? What type of bad luck did she have?

She thought over what Stephan had told her about himself and what he did. She knew that she should be more surprised, but for some reason it all made sense. If anything could really make sense right now. Mariah had always thought of herself as open-minded and learning that the imagined and fantastical were real was actually kind of neat. Well, it would be if she wasn't right in the middle of it and Twyla wasn't missing.

Stephan was a silent hero. Kind of a superman—a mild mannered successful businessman during the day, demon fighter by night. And damn sexy at everything he did.

She sighed again and rolled onto her side, pulling the pillow against her. Her whole body cried out with the need to be touched by him. Even after all he'd told her, she just wanted him more. After so many years of believing that the perfect man didn't exist, she was actually afraid that she might have found him.

The bed smelled like him. God! She was in his room, lying in his bed! Oh, she just couldn't take anymore! Celibacy was overrated and she'd remedy it soon enough. But until then she'd take a shower and try to calm herself. If that was even possible.

* * * * *

Twyla awakened to the sound of footfalls near her cot. Goose bumps covered her flesh, and it wasn't just from fear. Her nipples were erect underneath her black lace bra and her red silk thong wasn't exactly made for holding in warmth. The wound in her shoulder had calmed to a dull ache.

Lover's Talisman

"Great. First you brutally abduct me. Now you strip me. What's next?" She kept her voice strong, clearly meaning business although she had no idea who she was speaking to.

"Aren't we a little sharp considering your disadvantage?" The voice remained by her side.

"I'm cold. I'm in pain. I'm blindfolded. I'm naked. How does this get worse? Can I be dead yet?" It wasn't good to let her perturbation prevail, but what choice was there? She had started to shiver, and she didn't want to let any weakness show.

A hand gently removed her blindfold.

Ice blue eyes. All she could focus on were his ice blue eyes. They were strong and deep and she wondered how they'd look in the heat of passion. Her shivering stopped. It was replaced with warmth emanating from down below. She didn't need her thong to hold in heat anymore, she was doing just fine producing her own. At this point, she thanked her lucky stars she wasn't dead. Too bad her body didn't recognize the danger she was in…but then again, wasn't that part of the thrill?

He placed a thick blanket over her. She sinfully enjoyed the warmth of his hands as he smoothed the wrinkles from the blanket.

"Well, it is a little cold in here. I figured you might need this." His eyes met hers.

"How thoughtful. You could've brought me some clothing, but then you'd have to untie me, right?"

"As much as I wanna untie you, I just can't." He leaned over her. His eyes would have spoken volumes if she'd known how to read them. She stole a better look at his trim, hard body. He was taller than she had imagined by his voice. Maybe six feet tall. Her favorite, actually. She'd learned that men of that size could easily toss her around in bed as she bent around with them.

"Great. So I get to stay here. Just what I've always wanted. I missed one of the most important meetings of my life for this!"

"Hey, take it easy. Your life just changed." He pulled the blanket up a little further to tuck her in. His eyes lingered on her wounded shoulder. She wasn't sure, but it seemed like there was a particular sparkle about him. Something remained in the back of her mind telling her that this man in particular was going to either be the end of her, or just the beginning. As much as she wanted to be free, she wanted to know more about him.

"Yeah, my life and Mariah's. Who are you? What have you done to her?" Twyla shifted to test her bindings once more. She cringed as her shoulder reminded her that moving was not a good thing.

"Nothing. Yet. You really should relax. There's no sense in getting upset over things you can't control." He smoothed the blanket again. She hated to admit it, but she welcomed his touch. It was warm and firm and infuriatingly reassuring for some reason. "Everyone calls me Freeze. Just relax."

"No. I want out of here. Out of this place. Away from all of this. And I want my best friend unharmed—"

"Or what?" He grinned.

"I don't think that's really the point, do you? Keeping someone against her will is bad enough. You've humiliated me at the same time. I want this day to be over."

"Twyla." He paused as he looked her up and down, his beautiful ice blue eyes softening. "Perhaps I should put the blindfold back on."

She wished he'd never said her name. How did he know her name? It just rolled from his lips like a melody. Her mind and her cunt were in a vicious battle and she didn't understand how or why.

"Whatever. I know I'll find my way out. A girl's gotta make her own way these days. Go ahead. Just one more hurdle for me to sail right on over." She sighed. "By the way, thanks for the blanket."

"Don't mention it." He lingered briefly as he placed his hand over her injured shoulder and then walked out the door.

Lover's Talisman

Recognition finally dawned on her. Freeze's voice was that of the man whom she'd heard coldly say he'd kill her. What an actor.

Twyla tried to get her blood flowing again by shifting positions. Her shoulder no longer hurt. She strained to try to see it through the corner of her eye, to no avail. Instead, she just tried moving all around.

The pain was completely gone. Damn, he'd healed her! She'd heard magic like that was possible, but had never met anyone with enough power and experience to do it.

Twyla assumed that as long as Mariah was still alive, she would be alive. Freeze hadn't killed her yet, although he'd said he would. That alone was reason to celebrate. If that beautiful man she now knew as Freeze hadn't killed her as he'd said he would, everything was still just fine.

As she thought over the events of his visit, she realized that the odd sparkle about him must have been magic. She couldn't really be attracted to him, could she? He must have been using magic all along. That's why she hadn't noticed right away that he'd healed her.

She had to get out of there and back to her beads. She desperately searched her mind for spells of her own. Any little spells she'd made up to put on the necklaces. The man who had just left had a lot of power and it encouraged her to use her own. She marveled at the idea that she really might be truly powerful like she'd always surmised…and not just because she was a woman who liked to take control of her men. She smiled. If her magic didn't work, then she'd use that power she had over men and get Freeze to let her out of there. That could be fun for both of them.

Chapter Six

The water felt fantastic as it ran over Mariah's body in hot waves, stimulating her already aroused flesh. The shower was large enough for several "close friends" to enjoy together. Mariah had arranged the multiple showerheads and was being pelted and massaged from all angles. Next to her grope sessions with Stephan, this shower was the most erotic thing she'd encountered in years. She could certainly get used to it.

Mariah closed her eyes and let her arousal and imagination take over. She had to do something to ease her sexual need. The water hitting her body felt like warm hands caressing and running across her skin. Many hands...four hands. Stephan's and Marlin's hands. She moaned and bit her lip as she imagined them both joining her in the shower, their hard gorgeous bodies entangled with hers. She could finally add names and faces to the men in her favorite ménage fantasy.

Unconsciously, she shifted her hands to her breasts, lifting them, feeling the weight of them in her palms. She squeezed and massaged them, using her thumb and forefinger to lightly tweak each already erect nipple. The pleasure shot through her body, straight to her pussy and her knees shook with the effort of keeping her upright.

She leaned back into the tile, pretending it was Marlin holding her up. Stephan would be in front of her, kissing her mouth. His tongue would devour hers with a practiced skill while Marlin's hands would caress her body. Her hands became his, one staying on her breast, massaging and pulling at her nipple, the other hand teasing the aroused flesh between her legs.

Her fantasy continued, taking over. Stephan kept kissing her, melting all her inhibitions with just his tongue and lips. Her body strained to be united with his. He stepped closer and her hands discovered the muscles of his chest. She tore her mouth from his and ran kisses down his chest, following the path of her hands.

As she slid down Stephan, feeling his muscles tense below her exploring hands, mouth and tongue, Marlin followed her movements with his body still held close. She knelt on the tile floor, with Marlin kneeling behind her. His legs surrounded hers, his erect cock pressing into her lower back.

She rocked against it and Marlin moaned in response, his exhale warm across her neck. His lips found her shoulders and back and his tongue danced across her skin. His hands continued exploring her curves from behind. One hand rested on her lower stomach, fingertips just lightly brushing over her clit. His other hand trailed lower and parted her labia, gently thrusting one finger, then two, inside of her. Her cunt pulsed around his fingers, while his other hand focused on her clit, matching the rhythms they'd aroused in her body. Mariah gasped, barely able to keep herself from collapsing.

Her hands had finally reached Stephan's cock, and she marveled at the hot, hard length in her hand. His whole body emanated unleashed power, and she wanted to feel it all inside of her. She ran her hands up and down his shaft, watching Stephan's face as she did it. His eyes were closed, his teeth clenched. As Marlin's fingers continued moving inside of her, she closed her mouth over Stephan's cock.

Stephan's groan echoed in the shower around them. The water pulsed on the back of her head as she ran her tongue up and down his length, circling the head of his cock before pulling it completely into her mouth where she could feel the head brushing against her throat. She matched her rhythm to that of Marlin's fingers on and in her, all three of them moving in time to their own sexual orchestra. Mariah could feel the urgency building up inside of her, ready to release, fed by Marlin's increased pressure. She arched into his thrusts and cried out around Stephan's cock as her first orgasm washed over her body.

Stephan pulled her to her feet. She trembled all over, the effects of her orgasm still crashing through her body. He pushed her back against the tile, his mouth coming down hard over hers. His body lay flush against hers, his cock pulsing against her belly. She started to place her hands on his ass but he grabbed her arms, holding them with one hand above her head. Removing his mouth from hers, he settled his lips against her ear, growling, "This is about you. If you touch me anymore, I'll lose my patience. And this has to last." His tongue flicked out and ran along her ear, causing shivers to rain over her body. Wetness seeped from her cunt as his words and actions brought her back to full arousal.

She was spun around, her hands braced above her head on the tile wall. Stephan controlled her movements, forcing her to remain still for his pleasure. His large hands moved roughly over her breasts, pulling and pinching as his cock rubbed the cleft of her ass. She thrilled with the thought that he could take her at any moment. She spread her legs wider, offering herself, wanting to feel more of him, all of him in her. Stephan shifted her hips and with one quick thrust buried his cock deeply inside of her dripping cunt. She cried out as he began to rock back and forth inside of her.

She turned her head to her side, and saw Marlin watching them. His eyes were narrowed, his breathing labored as he watched them fucking. Mariah was frozen, unable to move, her eyes locked with Marlin's, her body full of Stephan. Marlin stepped closer, taking possession of her mouth with his own. His tongue swirled through her mouth while Stephan continued thrusting harder and faster into her.

Stephan bit the back of her neck where it met her shoulder and pinched her clit between two fingers. Pain and pleasure shot through her and she screamed into Marlin's mouth. Her body was lit up, on fire. She'd never felt like this and she didn't want it to end. Both men, all hers.

Stephan pulled out of her, separated her from Marlin, turned her around, lifted her up and slammed into her again.

She screamed as he filled her over and over, lifting her legs and placing them around his waist so he could go even deeper. He punished her lips with his, owning her. Their bodies were so close, each thrust of his cock added more burning pressure to her swollen clit.

A look passed between the brothers and Stephan moved, carrying Mariah with him before settling himself with his back against the wall. She held onto his arms as his hands grasped her hips, slowly lifting her up and down. She rode his cock, tightening her muscles to keep him from completely leaving her.

Marlin's hands began rubbing circles on her back. A light floral scent perfumed the air and Mariah turned her head, spying a bottle of opened body oil in a tiled alcove. Marlin's hands continued their ministrations, but they trailed lower until he was smoothing the oil over her ass. She froze, unsure of how to react, when an oiled finger penetrated her anus, slowly slipping inside. His finger eased gently, readying her for complete submission. She relaxed as the pleasure took over. This was what she wanted.

Stephan pulled his cock out of her at the same time Marlin removed his finger and she whimpered as Stephan set her alone on the tile. He smiled at her, the grin she adored. "It's okay. We'll do this right. Trust me."

She nodded. "I do trust you."

"Come here." Stephan's back was still against the wall, and she moved over to him. "Place your hands on either side of me. Yeah, just like that. Now, bend over just slightly at the waist and rest your head against my chest.... Good. That's perfect."

Mariah waited there, open and exposed, scared yet desperate for their combined touch. The scent of oil filled the air once more and Mariah assumed Marlin was rubbing it on his cock.

She moaned when Marlin's hot, oiled cock slid between her ass cheeks. He rubbed the large head in slow circles around her anus, preparing her for his entrance. Mariah's pussy contracted almost violently and a flood of moisture slid down her legs. God, she never would have thought she could want this, but she knew she would die if it didn't happen.

She bent over further, fully offering herself to him, then laughed when he groaned. Marlin accepted her blatant invitation, slowly entering her as no one else ever had before. It hurt, but it was a good hurt. Pain became pleasure as she burned and ached for more, everything they could give her. Mariah gasped as Marlin's cock slid even deeper, finally settling himself completely inside.

"God, you feel so good," Marlin groaned behind her.

Mariah couldn't talk, she could only feel. Stephan's hand had crept down her body, sensually separating her wet folds, making sure she was ready to take him.

"Look at me, baby." Mariah lifted her head from Stephan's chest and met his eyes. He closed the small distance between their bodies and shifted her weight to rest primarily on Marlin's cock. She felt so full, so hot. She didn't know how she could take more, but she wanted it all. Stephan's cock penetrated her vaginal lips and deep into her cunt. All three of them moaned simultaneously.

They both began to rock her, back and forth, in and out, a practiced rhythm that created spirals of pleasure through her body. She clung to Stephan's shoulders, so strong beneath her fingers and Marlin surrounded her from behind, his cock continuing to fill her ass with each stroke. The pleasure was intense, overwhelming. She was cocooned between the two strongest, sexiest men she'd ever met and being fucked hard by both of them, experiencing pleasures she'd never understood. Yet through it all her strongest feeling was that she was safe. Safe because both of them would give their lives for her.

Their movements sped up, bringing her closer to her peak. The pleasure of two cocks inside of her, pulsing and thrusting together, overwhelmed her senses. She tasted the sweat dripping down Stephan's chest and felt Marlin's breath hot on her neck. Everything tightened inside of her. She was full, ready to burst, but not wanting it to end. She knew they were all nearing orgasm and she screamed as the first wave of pure pleasure rocketed through her body. Her toes curled, her pussy throbbed. The pleasure continued as first Stephan and then Marlin slammed into her, their moans echoing around her as they each filled her with their seed.

She trembled as they all collapsed around each other. Her body ached but she still wanted more...so much more.

Mariah slumped to the floor, opening her eyes. She was alone, the fantasy was over. And it was much better than it had ever been. She felt like such a slut, but then she laughed. She could be a slut in her fantasies and no one ever had to know.

She pulled her hand away from her dripping pussy—no semen there. Her legs shook as she stood back up and washed herself off. She had never fantasized quite like that, and even when she had fantasized, she had never before lost control. Even after multiple orgasms, her body still ached for a man's touch, Stephan's touch, his hands, his body. She shivered, turning off the water.

So much for a relaxing shower. Now she wanted Stephan even more.

* * * * *

Stephan approached the meeting room. Mariah still occupied his mind and, apparently, his cock as well. He tried to calm his breathing with one deep exhale as he entered the room. His cock had never been this hard just thinking about a woman. He was electric. If this kept up, he'd need a cold shower. No, a shower of ice cubes.

"So, what's up? What's this all about?" Jake sat on the back of a chair with his feet on the seat.

"Yeah. We gonna patrol tonight or what?" Ryan popped open a can of soda and drank deeply.

"Guess I'll be canceling my date." Dusty grinned as he playfully jabbed Ryan's arm enough to make him spill a bit of soda.

"You're lucky I'm quick." Ryan flexed his bicep as he transferred the soda to his other hand.

"Hey, hey. Come on now, guys. Let the man speak." Marlin's voice rang out louder than the rest of the guys.

"Sorry, I'm late." Fiero appeared out of thin air and took a seat.

"It's all right. We ain't even started yet." Jake grinned.

"You guys done? We need to get started here." Stephan stalled while searching his mind for the reasons he had called the guys together. Mariah was showering just a few walls away. He couldn't help but envision her naked and wet. After seeing her perform at *Silver Twilight*—was that just last night?—every detail of her naked body was imprinted on his memory. Coupling that with the sound of water hitting bare flesh, he was about to burst through his jeans.

"Yeah. What's up? Talk to me, bro." Marlin crossed his arms in front of his chest.

"You boys gotta quit fuckin' around. Some big shit is about to fly. This is serious. Okay? Here's what I know." Stephan took another deep breath and tried to get the visions of Mariah out of his head just for this one moment. He needed order. It was time for business. He scolded himself for letting his mind wander. The scold was only half-hearted. "Wait. Dusty, did you say you actually had a date?"

"Oh, that's cold…" Dusty shook his head as the rest of the guys chuckled. "Man…I'm finally getting somewhere and you guys give me shit. Thanks."

"Naw, Dusty, it's nice to see you happy for a change. You actually comb your hair now." Jake laughed with the rest of the guys.

Marlin gave Stephan a stern look. "You said we gotta plan and research. For what?"

"I hunted down Asfar." Stephan instantly came back to business as the guys began to settle down. "It wasn't easy, but I did get some more information about things." His mind was calming. Then, he heard a loud splash that any person would make while showering. He blinked. Bad move. He envisioned droplets of water falling from Mariah's nipples. "I...uh...he said that someone had a bounty out for any information on a Shadow Walker having a girl."

"But none of us actually have girls." Marlin raised an eyebrow and crossed his arms over his chest.

"Yeah, Jeneane's just a fuck," Dusty clarified.

Fiero raised his palms into the air. "Guys. Will you let the man speak?"

"Well, I did say that Mariah was mine." *And naked in the shower after inviting me into her bed.* Thank goodness for his over-developed self-control. His thoughts were running away with him. "J-just to get Asfar to leave her alone."

"So, now you're keepin' her down here while we all go take out these new baddies, right?" Jake said with a grin as he leaned back in his chair and kicked his feet up onto the table.

"You're sending us to do the dirty work?" Marlin inquired.

"No. We also have to get Mariah's best friend back. Guys...there's a lot to do here." *And I wanna do Mariah right here as well.* Stephan quickly shook his head, trying to remove his mental slideshow of naked and wet Mariah images. It still didn't work. "Fiero, talk to The Order and see what you can find out. There may be one who knows about these kinds of movements. We have to get the jump on this situation and figure out who is doing this and why.

"Dusty, sorry about your date. Imagine making it up to her, though. I need you to hit your old stomping ground and see if the guy at the pawn shop knows anything. Last time I was in there, he was asking me some off the wall questions.

"Jake, you look for anything about Mariah's best friend, Twyla. My guess is that the same person with the bounty requesting information has her, but I have nothing but instinct to base that on. Something about a necklace that Asfar grabbed and Mariah saying something about Twyla working with beads. Just go see what you can find out."

"I get to pass up a date just so I can talk to some old stinky guy and Jake gets to hunt fox?" Dusty raised his arms.

"Yeah. 'Cuz Jake's gonna have to sneak everywhere and steal information. Sorry, you're the ass kicker, not the weasel." Stephan thought of Mariah's bare ass and how nice it would feel to touch it. He smiled at the thought while shifting position to try to find more room for his cock in his unfortunately tight jeans.

"So, next time, I get to hunt fox?" Dusty shook his head.

"Hey, guys...this is big. I mean, just the other day I saw some new freaks in town. They didn't look like the usual harmless type." Ryan chugged the last of his soda.

"And Ryan, you seek out those freaks. Find out where they came from. Whatever's starting, we need to stay on top of it." *Just as I should be on top of Mariah right now.*

"I think I'll just go see what I can do about finding Twyla myself. There might be more clues at the house." Marlin headed toward the door to the stairs. "Don't work too hard, bro."

He planned on working hard. All night long. With Mariah. He took another ragged breath.

Ryan walked over to the weapons cabinet, opened it swiftly and traded a small switchblade for a larger one. He placed the new blade in his jacket as he grinned at Dusty.

"This is bogus." Dusty shook his head.

"I get the fox hunt this time. Ha!" With lightning speed, Jake dodged what would have been a perfectly executed left hook from Dusty.

"Next time, I'll be quicker." Dusty laughed heartily at the astonished look on Jake's face.

"Damn...take it easy, man. You'll get the girl one of these days." Ryan got between Jake and Dusty and put a strong arm around each shoulder.

Stephan stopped trying to deny his thoughts and just let them take over. God, she looked good naked and wet. Soapsuds glistening on her nipples. One hand washing the soft thatch of hair between her legs. She smiled at him so invitingly...

The vision disappeared as Fiero got in his face. "Hello? Stephan? Listen, I'll see what I can find out. There's definitely something brewing. Catch you on the flip side." Fiero disappeared.

The flip side. Stephan paused for a moment as he considered flipping Mariah from side to side, fucking her from every angle.

Stephan glanced at the kitchenette. A few dishes were in the sink and someone had left the bread out. His mind raced. This was the perfect reason to get back in that room with Mariah. He'd make her a snack or something. She probably hadn't eaten much in the past day.

He got straight to work, opening the refrigerator to see what could possibly be used to make a small sandwich. Just something to let her know he was thinking of her without making it look like he'd gone to too much trouble. He also had to hurry before she finished with her shower to avoid the temptation to stay in that room with her.

The fridge was mostly empty. He did manage to locate some strawberry jam and peanut butter in a cupboard. Thank God it was simple to make. If he tried to cook anything he'd probably end up burning the damn compound down because all he could think about was water sliding down her luscious curves.

He threw the sandwich together and headed to her room to drop it off. At that point, he'd do anything to put himself one step closer to that shower with her. As he passed Marlin's room, he decided to dig through Marlin's stuff to see if he had a nightgown or some other girly type of nightwear that Mariah could wear, something that would make her feel more at home.

Marlin had only one nightgown among the various articles he'd accumulated from the fucks of his past. This particular nightgown wasn't anything special, but it would have to do. It was yet another reason to walk through that door. To justify his hot desire to be near Mariah without her clothing.

He listened for a moment outside her door. All he could hear was some pretty vigorous splashing. She must have been trying to clean off all of the grime from the werewolf attack. Sometimes even he felt dirty for days after touching one of those things. But she was really going at it and he wished he was going at it with her.

With quick resolution, he sighed, opened the door and walked in. He went directly to the far side of the bed to put down the sandwich. While turning to toss the nightgown on the foot of the bed, he saw her clothes strewn on the floor. He leaned over to pick up her bra and nearly undid the buttons on his jeans at the thought of touching her. Setting the bra on the bed next to the T-shirt he had given her, he grabbed the rest of her clothes. The light smell of her perfume rose from her clothing. He closed his eyes, fighting the urge to break down the bathroom door, to drink the water from her skin, to taste the honey between her legs.

Lost in hot reverie, he didn't even hear the water stop running. It took a moment for him to process the new silence. He cursed, throwing her clothes back down onto the floor. He had to get out of there before she saw him. But he just couldn't get around the bed in time.

Mariah walked out of the bathroom, head bent over as she toweled out her hair. She was completely naked just as he'd been envisioning. She was phenomenal. He had seen her naked at *Silver Twilight*, but up close and personal was so much better. Stephan swallowed hard. He was caught.

Mariah flipped her damp hair back over her shoulder and froze as she registered him standing just feet from her. Her eyes flickered between surprise and desire as she stood there, towel hanging from her right hand to the ground, not disrupting his view in the slightest. She kept still for a moment, sizing him up, before she continued on to the bed.

"So, you didn't have anywhere else to be?" She set the towel on the bed, and picked up the T-shirt he had laid out for her earlier. He couldn't get his brain to function as he watched her lift his T-shirt. Everything seemed to be moving in slow motion as she lifted her arms up, slowly sliding the shirt over her head, giving him a perfect view of her breasts and tight, erect nipples, before she slid his shirt home. The shirt settled and hung down, barely covering the curve of her ass. His shirt had never looked that good before.

Stephan took a deep breath, knowing she had asked him a question and that he should probably respond, but not remembering anything but her...naked...wet. What was he supposed to say?

Mariah was shaking. She was trying so hard to remain cool and collected, but her stomach was Jell-O and she had no idea what to do next. Should she just jump him and get it over with? He was there, did that mean he wanted her? At least she had some clothing on now, some type of barrier so he couldn't immediately notice how her nipples were reaching out and begging to be touched by him, how her pussy ached to be fucked and moisture slid down her legs. She squeezed her thighs together and tried to keep from moaning at the pressure building inside. It didn't help that the shirt smelled just like him and teased against her nipples, making them almost hurt with the need for relief.

"How was your shower?"

Mariah felt her face burning and knew that she was blushing ten different shades of red. Did he know what she'd been fantasizing about?

"Um...great...just fine. Nice. Yeah. Nice." She wanted to jump under the bed covers and hide until he went away. She couldn't even hold a decent conversation with the man. She just wanted him so badly she couldn't even think straight. He had to be laughing at her. She shot a glance in his direction. He wasn't laughing, he wasn't even smiling. He was looking at her like she was an ice-cream cone that he wanted to lick all over, slowly, up and down and all around. She squeaked at the imagery that brought to mind.

Stephan swallowed a moan. "That's good." *I was wishing I could've helped.* "You look refreshed."

She nodded, then her eyes lowered, focusing on the bulge in his pants. Her nipples beaded even tighter under the shirt he'd loaned her. She wanted him as badly as he wanted her.

His feet felt glued to the floor as his mind and body raged in battle. He was the reason she was in such grave danger, but that was all the more reason he had to have her. He knew that it would strengthen his desire to keep her safe. There was no way he was leaving this room tonight unless she forcefully threw him out. And even then, he wasn't sure he could resist.

He wanted to make everything all right, to learn every inch of her and drive her higher than she'd ever thought possible. The guys were taking care of business tonight, he just wanted to take care of Mariah.

Stephan picked up the discarded towel and walked behind her. With his right hand, he gently gathered up her damp hair and began massaging her scalp and hair with the towel. A tremble rippled through her body. She smelled of soap and woman and sex. God, he could smell her arousal rising off her in perfumed waves. He had to calm himself down now or he was going to come before he even got inside of her. And he was going to be inside of her. He was certain of that now.

"I couldn't let you go to bed with wet hair." His hands continued their massage. "I wouldn't want you to get sick or anything."

"Th-that's very thoughtful of you."

Stephan dropped the towel to the floor, and smoothed her hair back over her right shoulder so it draped over her breast.

His hands slid down the gentle slopes of her arms as he closed in behind her. Her skin was fine and soft, not like anything his hands were used to touching. He resisted the temptation to pick her up and lay her on the bed so he could immediately go to work. This had to be perfect.

His lips found the sweet spot where her neck met her shoulders and he settled in. A soft moan welled from her lips and she swayed back into him. He kept kissing her neck, his tongue gently flicking against her skin, forever burning the taste of her into his mind.

His hands slid from her arms to her hips and pulled her deeply into his body. The exquisite pleasure/pain of her ass against his cock almost drove him to animalistic behavior. But he knew that it was time to be gentle. It wouldn't be right to take her hard and fast like he wanted to do. He had plenty of time to make everything perfect. She made him feel things he'd never felt before. Maybe he could make her feel the same by rocking her world harder and longer than it had ever been rocked.

Mariah couldn't think, couldn't breathe, caught up in a whirlwind of sensation, fire, heat, pleasure. It was all there, a direct line from her neck to her cunt. She was trembling but she couldn't stop. If he stopped now, if he left her alone, she would lose her mind. No vigorous masturbation fantasies were going to help her now. She had to have cock—his cock.

Stephan's hands slid past her hips and slowly lifted up the T-shirt. Settling his hands back on her naked skin, he skimmed them up her body, gently caressing her curves, before settling both hands below her breasts, his thumbs gently rubbing each erect nipple. The calluses on his large hands made her skin tingle, and she arched in to meet his touch more completely. His lips moved to her ear where he whispered, "I'm gonna take you now."

A fresh wave of wetness pooled between her legs. "God, yes. Now. Please..." Her voice was raspy. She nodded to make sure he understood her. His hands slid the rest of the way up her body and removed the T-shirt, throwing it to the floor.

He turned her to face him. Any remaining doubts flew out of her head when she looked into his eyes. Trust, safety, desire. He was everything she'd always wanted and never believed existed.

She stepped toward him, wrapping her arms around his neck, pushing herself flush against his body. She could feel his cock against her belly and she smiled. "Yes. Take me now." His lips stole the words from her mouth as his tongue entered and began to devour.

Was it minutes? Hours? She had no way to determine time and she didn't care. All thought was about him and how he made her feel.

God, he knew how to kiss. She wanted him so badly, her body ached for him, but she could just stand there and get kissed by him all night and still walk away the next morning believing that her time with him had been the most erotic experience she'd ever had.

He made love to her lips. His hands cupped her face, his fingers ran through her hair and along the back of her neck. She relaxed under his touch.

She rubbed against him, reminding herself that he was still fully clothed and in need of a remedy to that situation. Her hands shifted to his waist and tugged at his T-shirt, desperately wanting to rub her nipples against his bare skin. He broke the kiss and smiled at her as she ripped his T-shirt off over his head. She paused as she stared at the wounds on his chest, still pink and raw, but mostly healed. Her fingers shook as she lightly traced the claw marks. "How? I saw you get hurt...I saw the blood."

Stephan took her hand and kissed her fingertips. "Fiero healed me. Just as he healed you."

"What? When? Who's Fiero?" Mariah tried to focus on the questions, but her mind was full of Stephan and his body. She wanted answers, but she wanted Stephan more.

"The night we met. I brought you back here. Your head was bleeding. You were dying and Fiero—"

"I was dying?"

"I couldn't let that happen." Stephan leaned down and kissed Mariah again. "Fiero's our healer. He took care of you and—" Stephan motioned to his chest "— these. I'm mortal. I can die. Fiero helps us stay alive."

"Do they hurt?" Mariah's fingers resumed lightly tracing the scars.

"No, but if you keep touching me like that other parts of me are gonna keep hurting."

Mariah felt the heat rising to her cheeks, but the knowledge that he was feeling the same way she was feeling was a heady experience. She pressed her lips to his chest, and lightly ran her tongue along the pattern of the scar. Stephan moaned and crushed her to him. His hands grabbed her ass roughly, grinding her against his jutting cock. The denim abraded her pussy but she didn't care.

Stephan's and Mariah's hands tangled as they both tried to remove his jeans. He was still wearing heavy, black leather boots. "Fuck!" He sat down on the edge of the bed trying to untie them. His fingers fumbled and the knots tightened. Reaching into his pocket, he pulled out a switchblade and within moments sliced through the laces and tossed his boots and blade to the floor. His socks, jeans and briefs quickly followed.

Mariah swallowed. He was magnificent. He wasn't overly muscular, but every part of him was tight and well-defined. He was lean and sharp and so stunning he took her breath away. She looked down at his cock and swallowed again. He was large and thick and God she had to have him now or she was going to die.

Stephan picked her up and carried her the last few steps to the bed. He laid her down on the comforter and reclined next to her. He placed his hand on her stomach, caressing in ever widening circles, his fingers lightly brushing over her clit.

Mariah moaned and arched into his touch. He replaced his hand with his lips and kissed her stomach, working his way down. The smell of her musk drove him wild. He didn't know how long he could make this last.

She had only a small patch of neatly trimmed hair. The rest of her was completely smooth and hairless. He ran his hands over her mound, marveling at every inch of her. He shifted position and knelt between her legs. His thumb stroked over her clit and then lowered, parting the swollen folds of her pussy. He breathed moist air on her cunt and felt her squirm beneath his hands. He glanced at Mariah's face. Her eyes were closed, mouth open, neck tilted back, her chest rising and falling rapidly to match her panted breathing. Her hands were fisted around the comforter beneath her, twisting and grasping as she ground against his hand.

Almost overcome with need, he lowered his face to her cunt and deeply inhaled. He wanted to burn the sweet honeyed scent of her arousal into his memory. She mewled and trembled beneath him.

His cock was hard enough to drill through steel, yet he forced himself to move slowly. He wanted her to remember this night, in case it was the only one they shared. So he would taste her first, sup on the elixir she so readily offered. Match the taste of her to the scent he relished.

Mariah practically jumped out of her skin with the first caress of his tongue against her clit. She squeezed her hands tighter in the blanket, trying to hold back the scream building inside. His tongue continued to explore, coaxing more feelings from her and she couldn't hold back the moans. She felt wild and free and she thrust her cunt into his mouth, wanting more, always more. She wanted him, all of him, not just his cock, but his essence. His soul. She'd never felt this way before. God, what did it mean?

He continued to taste her, delving deep inside, fucking her with his tongue. His hands held her ass against his mouth. Every stroke of his tongue was magic against her moist folds. Tension coiled deep inside, winding tighter and tighter until she felt the pressure of her impending orgasm throughout every cell in her body.

Her scream echoed in the room around her as her orgasm finally hit her, rocketing through her body in sharp waves. She soared with the pleasure as it took her over, her body only vaguely aware of its physical surroundings. She returned to earth as Stephan made his way back up her body. He brushed her hair out of her face then paused when he saw her tear-filled eyes.

"Whoa, baby, did I hurt you?"

"God, no!" She quickly wiped away the tears. "I can't—I mean, I've never felt like that before."

"So, you're okay? You're sure?" He continued to stroke her face, his eyes searching hers for the answers he sought.

She smiled up at him and winked trying to reassure him. "Let's do it one more time just to make sure."

He laughed and she kissed him, tasting herself on his tongue. A wicked thrill shot through her. She wrapped her arms around his body, pulling him down onto her, crushing their bodies together. For tonight, he was all hers.

She continued to kiss him as she shifted her body underneath his, trying to align herself with him. She wanted him inside of her now, wanted that completion. His cock nudged her pussy and she spread her legs wide, desperately needing him to thrust inside of her. One small shift and the head of his cock slipped inside her channel. She moaned into his mouth. He felt so good, so right. He pulled out of her quickly and she cried out at the loss of his presence.

"Baby, I can't, not yet. Just a sec." He reached over to the nightstand and fumbled through the drawer. He swore under his breath as socks, weapons and other strange items fell out of the drawer. Finally, he removed an unopened box of condoms, a look of triumph crossing his face. He ripped at the top of the box and removed a condom.

"Stephan, wait."

Every muscle in his body tensed, poised over her, rigid as steel. Sweat beaded on his temple and one drip slid down his jaw, falling on her breast. His face lowered and her heart stopped at the dual emotions flashing through his eyes. Desire. And fear.

He took a deep breath, then swallowed deeply. "Do you want me to stop?"

"NO! Please, no. But you don't need to use a condom if you don't want to. I'm clean, and I'm assuming you are?"

"Yes. Completely. But pregnancy?"

"It's okay. I won't. I can't. Don't worry about it…please, I want to feel you inside of me. All of you. I don't want any barriers. God, you have no idea how badly I need this." Mariah closed her eyes on that last admission, almost embarrassed by how much she wanted him.

"Open your eyes. Look at me."

Mariah did and her breath caught. He was so unbelievably gorgeous. She trusted him. She even thought she might love him, and that he might love her in return. God, that scared her.

Stephan moved back over her, his cock nudging her entrance. He slowly filled her, stretching her, owning her. Every inch of cock he sank into her cunt broke through a mental barrier she'd held up for to long.

"God, you're so tight. So hot and tight wrapped around me. You feel so good."

Stephan's words took her even higher. Every movement he made brought her new waves of pleasure. She didn't know how long she could take this. She felt like she'd been made to be pleasured by this man alone.

When he was completely seated inside of her they both stopped, lost in the moment and what it might mean. Mariah's hand reached up and stroked his face. She pulled his head to hers and kissed him, before she could swear her undying love for him. She couldn't do that. Not now. Not like this.

Stephan pulled away from the kiss and stared into her eyes, slowly pumping in and out of her. His eyes radiated the same heat as their bodies, and she stared deeply into him, lost in a trance of desire. As he thrust all the way inside, he spoke, his voice thick and heavy with passionate intensity. "You really are mine now. Mine."

His words of ownership didn't scare her. She wanted to be his. She broke their stare, leaned forward and ran her tongue up his neck and to his ear. Her hands ran over his back and his muscles rippled in response to her touch. "I'm yours and you're mine." He growled in agreement and found her mouth, ramming his tongue inside. Their bodies dueled, tongues tangling and seeking. Stephan's cock continued to thrust and she clenched him tight inside her hot cunt. They were one.

They stayed that way for what felt like hours. They fucked slowly, intensely, drawing each pleasure out, riding the wave up, then slowly cresting down, neither of them ready to completely let it end. His hands touched her everywhere, learning every inch of her body. He kissed her face, eyelids, neck and shoulders. His tongue laved each of her nipples, keeping them taut and erect. And through it all he continued to fuck her.

Mariah couldn't handle it any longer. She locked her ankles behind his ass and forced him balls deep inside of her. He moaned around one nipple. Knotting her fingers in his hair, she lifted his head from her breast to meet her eyes before she said, "I want you to fuck me hard now. I need to feel you come deep inside of me. I can't wait any longer."

Stephan growled his response as he began to gradually speed up his fucking. Mariah felt the burn inside rage up to inferno status. Every muscle in her cunt clutched his cock with every thrust. In...out...in...out...faster, harder. She was coming again and couldn't control the rapid tremors rocketing through her body. She screamed out her orgasm as Stephan slid home and released, his moan mingling with her scream. Every throb of his cock as his seed filled her completed her in a way she didn't understand. His mouth found hers and their tongues danced as they both rode the pleasure to its end. Then he slowly removed his cock and slid down her body until his head found her chest.

She caressed his neck and back, loving the feel of slick, hot skin beneath her hands. His weight sprawled over her was comforting. Mariah couldn't imagine ever wanting the magic of this night to end. She closed her eyes and slept, overwhelmed with the feelings of complete safety and the possibility of love.

Chapter Seven

Voices awakened Twyla from her uncomfortable sleep. They were muffled, but she could hear them through the door. Holding her breath, she tried to make out what the men were saying. She swallowed hard when she heard the deeper voice declare that Mariah would be bait to catch Stephan. The other voice, Freeze's voice, inquired about Twyla but she just tuned it out. She didn't want to hear what they would do to her.

The door opened, the light turned on and in walked Freeze and another man, the one she thought was probably in charge.

"You put a blanket over her?" Whoever this beautiful, dark-haired man was glared at her with soulless eyes. She couldn't repress the involuntary shiver that ran through her. He was gorgeous, but clearly capable of much evil.

"That was when you gave a damn." Freeze walked closer to her. She scrutinized her cell, trying to think of a way to just get herself out of there. She had to get to Mariah to warn her. No matter what it took, she had to escape.

"Get her up!" The soulless one grabbed a corner of the blanket and whisked it off of her like a magician doing the tablecloth trick. He stood completely motionless as Freeze effortlessly picked up the cot with Twyla on it and leaned it against a wall. The concrete floor was cold against her feet as she stood there both bound and leaning.

"What, you wanted a better look at me? Like you've never seen a girl before. Will you cover me back up?" Twyla was astonished at her own words. She just didn't want to start shivering again.

The scary one wearing all black with a red collar walked over to her and brazenly looked her up and down as if devouring her every curve. She'd seen that look on many a man.

And she would have liked it if it came from just about any other man. Creepy, soulless man was indeed beautiful, but the impenetrable blackness in his eyes made Twyla just as uneasy as she was cold.

"What happened to her shoulder wound?" he coldly questioned Freeze.

"You said I could do whatever I wanted with her." Freeze crossed his arms.

"Oh yes, that's right..." He turned to face Freeze directly, his voice rising in intensity. "Next time you do something like that, you okay it with me." He forcefully approached Freeze, who stepped back while meeting his superior's eyes.

"Hello? My shoulder feels a lot better, can we just get on with all of this? Thank you." Twyla didn't want the crazy guy to follow through on what he seemed to be implying in his minor furor toward Freeze. How could she hate a man who'd brought out her own courage and magical strength? Her shoulder felt better now than it ever had.

"A particular group of men are prowling more than usual." The dark one waved his hand slowly as though to draw information from her. She felt an odd sort of pull within her chest. She strained against it as the pulling tightened inside of her. It was as if her insides were being drawn toward the soulless man.

"Okay...that narrows it down. A lot of men 'prowl' around me. I don't even notice it anymore." Twyla rolled her eyes, trying to pretend that what he was doing wasn't bothering her. "Y'know, I'm not even talking until you cover me up." Maybe he was talking about the guys Mariah had mentioned to her the night before she was kidnapped. The very hot guys who owned the import store on the pier. She hadn't actually met them although they had been fodder for many a daydream. But what could this man want with them?

"C'mon, Craze, her high beams are on." So that was the soulless one's name. She bit her lip to keep from laughing at the appropriateness of it. The pull inside of her relaxed with Craze's matching movement. He had to be doing something to her with magic. It was almost as though he was a magnet that drew her insides toward him every time he waved his hand. Her heart, lungs and abdomen were being manipulated as if he'd thrown a rope around them, tightened the noose and pulled, making her body stretch out like a bow being readied to shoot an arrow. More magic indeed. She wondered who was more powerful, Freeze or Craze.

Freeze approached her with the blanket. A shiver went down her spine and she wasn't sure if that was because of Freeze or because she was freezing. She could've sworn that Freeze was trying to communicate something to her.

"Don't you dare." Craze's tone stopped Freeze in his tracks. "I want to watch every inch of her squirm when I tell her what will happen to her best friend if she doesn't tell me everything she knows about those men." Craze's cool grin washed over Twyla with a dark intensity.

"I'm sure I already know. I've heard it all before. Torture, death...oh hurt me you bad, bad man..." Twyla shifted her weight onto one foot just to get her other off the cold ground. "You don't scare me. I have nothing to tell you because I don't know anything, you idiot!" The pull tightened fiercely as he extended his hand and drew it back toward his body. She gasped and strained against her binding. Craze was making it rather difficult for her to stand up. The pain was not entirely unbearable. It was more of a shock to her system. She knew she could hold her ground, but Craze's magic was quite potent.

On the up side, at least all of the tugging seemed to have loosened her ankles and wrists just a bit. Craze had created more slack by magically tugging at her body so hard. Then again, even if she wiggled for another few hours and got free, where could she go?

Don't think like that. Get yourself free. Figure out the rest after that.

Although Craze didn't otherwise move, she could tell she'd angered him. His eyes actually got blacker and what appeared to be sparks shot and shimmered off his body in every direction. He gracefully shifted, as though every action had been planned and executed many times before, no movement made that wasn't necessary. He got right in her face and was just about to say something, but paused while Twyla spoke with heated intensity. "That's it, come closer. Come a little closer. Come on, Craze. Show me just how crazy you are."

Twyla could feel his rage mounting as the sparks shooting off his body increased in range and number. They lit up the room like fireworks, cascading down at every angle. Magenta, teal, gold, crimson, the cell was awash with color. She found it odd that for all the display, there was no heat from the sparks. In fact, they were like tiny shards of ice that melted upon contact with her skin. Craze's pull on her relaxed in intensity as he lowered his hand. Freeze moved in right next to him. Calculatingly, Craze scrutinized her eyes then lowered his head to her face and the pull subsided completely.

Twyla leaned forward and licked Craze's cheek.

He slapped her.

"I just wanted to taste a man who couldn't get what he wanted from me. It's never happened before."

Twyla knew she had probably just signed her own death certificate, but she didn't care. Her cheek stung, but at least Craze had stepped away from her. She saw a quick grin cross Freeze's face before he disguised his humor behind a mask of calm control.

In a swift maneuver, Craze was back in her face, taking her head in his hands to administer a rape of a kiss combined with what had to be a magically induced blinding light in her mind's eye. It was as though he was trying to make her pass out. She fought as hard as she could to keep from fainting. Her mind reeled. He was quite forceful, but she refused to let him have complete power over her. She'd sooner die than let a man have any kind of mastery.

Craze broke away from her and headed for the door. He paused and glanced back at Freeze. "She's not lying. She knows nothing about the Shadow Walkers. Kill her however you would like. And take your time. No one disrespects a Dread Lord without paying for it." He faced Twyla and smiled a purely evil grin. He bowed down, a quick, yet graceful maneuver. "Thank you, my lady, for a purely unique experience. I will never forget it." He turned and walked out, closing the door behind him.

"That was amazing." Freeze grinned at her. "You've got quite a tongue on you." He removed a dagger from his boot as he spoke.

"You want a taste as well?" Twyla said as she shivered, staring at the dagger, wondering if the end would be quick or slow.

"I just might."

"Bring it on. I've got nothing to lose. I know I'm not leaving this room." Twyla shifted her weight back to her other foot. Freeze's closeness made her warmer for some reason. Perhaps it was just his hair, his chest. No, it was the eyes. They challenged her somehow.

"I might play for a little while." Oh great. It was going to be slow. Freeze tossed the dagger from one hand to the other. His eyes smiled, but his mouth was firm. Why on earth did facing her death make her so hot? "Dread Lords don't take kindly to insult. He's right. You should pay."

"Then take it out of my flesh. I dare you. Wouldn't you rather me be more useful?" Goodwill wasn't generally extended to prisoners yet this man had surprised her with his tender generosity. She hoped she was right, that there was more behind those eyes than just a ruthless killer's soul. Because if not, she was already dead.

Although, maybe she could make a deal with his more generous side. "I don't much like the guys that Mariah's shacking up with," she lied. "You let me out of here and you can have all their heads on platters."

Freeze laughed. "You think you could take them out?"

"I think I can lead you to them. I don't wanna get my hands bloody." Something clicked behind those blue eyes of his—some type of realization. She continued forcing her point. "Just stay away from Mariah."

"How bad do you want it?"

"How bad do I want what?" She matched his intensity as yet another shiver racked through her body.

"This blanket." He tossed it in the air and twirled it around with a wicked grin.

"All right. Kill me now. Just end it. That's what Craze wanted you to do. You dare disobey a Dread Lord?" She tried to hit that button. Apparently, she missed.

"I've never disobeyed anyone I thought worthy of obedience."

"Cover me with that blanket?" She had to try before her nipples froze off. She'd been turned on many times before and still her nipples hadn't been as hard as they were at that moment.

Freeze just laughed. "Okay...you got me on that one. But not because you're worthy of obedience." He grabbed the cot and set it back on the floor. She settled back on its uncomfortable length and he covered her with the blanket once more.

"You got a heater while you're at it?" She was starting to tire of the antics, but for some reason she enjoyed his company. It kept her situation from really terrifying her. She wanted to die just so it would be over with.

Then he lay on the cot next to her. Her mind reeled. He traced the dagger down her wrist to her elbow, never breaking her skin. It was hard to believe the blade was so much colder than her flesh. All of her senses were nearing overload.

The cot wasn't quite big enough for two so he was on his side. Those ice blue eyes were clearly amused.

"Just take me then. If you're into bondage, looks like I'm ready to go. Shall I start panting now or wait a little while?" *How could she be enjoying this?* The heat. His warmth. She must have been blinded by delirium from the cold.

He slid the blade down her upper arm to her collarbone. He was silent as he moved it across her just above the edge of the blanket and underneath her chin along her neck. He seemed to be drawing something. She didn't feel any pain or wetness other than what was between her thighs so she assumed he wasn't actually tearing her skin. Her whole body tingled as the heat coursed through her veins. Wondering just how deranged he was, she tried to read his eyes, but his face was too close to hers.

"Don't speak. You wouldn't want me to lose my concentration now, would you?" Freeze brought the dagger over the blanket and circled her breasts. She swallowed hard as the blanket fell away from her skin. The dagger was indeed sharp. It took a generously talented hand to expertly slice through a thin layer of blanket without wounding the flesh underneath. "That's what I thought."

She tried to imagine herself seeing Mariah again, or standing on the pier or being anywhere but where she was right now. But for some reason, she couldn't seem to focus on her best friend. All she could focus on was the cold metal blade teasing her stomach and tracing her hourglass curves. As her body regained warmth, she could feel the extra heat from his cock against her hip. She wondered if she should enjoy this kind of torture. One moment she wanted him to fuck her because she knew there was no tomorrow and the next moment she just wanted to break free.

Then the dagger found her clit.

The icy cold of the blade felt amazing against the heat her cunt was generating. She had to remind herself that arching into it would be a very bad idea. It remained there as she gasped in both pleasure and fear.

"Remember this moment," he said roughly.

She vigorously shook her head yes. Too many thoughts crashed through her mind to really think straight. She closed her eyes tightly.

"For you never know where life might take you next." The dagger slid back up to her stomach and lingered in slow circles. "One moment you think you know what you want and the next you find you are horribly mistaken."

The dagger fell sideways as it slid from her stomach. Her breath remained quick. She knew what he was talking about and was intrigued by it. For once, she felt challenged. Men had fucked their way in and out of her life without her ever really paying much attention to more than the easy orgasms.

She couldn't recall a time when she'd even had a conversation this long with a man while lying down...and he was doing most of the talking. Usually, once the guy found out that not only could she not get pregnant, thanks to a lovely genetic problem, but that she'd never wanted to anyway, all dialogue ended and the fuckfest began. Her thoughts ceased as she heard the dagger clank onto the floor.

"Are you getting warm yet?" His breath caressed her neck while his cock increased in both warmth and size against her hip, setting it on fire as much as her inner thighs.

"No. Not yet. Maybe you should get under the blanket. I could share your body heat more directly." She faked teeth chattering...or maybe it was just an extension of the tingle that rippled through her body at the thought?

"Oh...aren't we brazen?" He lifted himself up a bit to peer more directly into her eyes.

"Why, yes. Good of you to notice. Why don't you just take off your jacket and your shirt as well?" If her mind and her cunt were fighting before, they had certainly come into agreement once she'd realized that she wanted the dagger he'd held to her clit to be his cock instead.

He removed his jacket without effort and then smiled. He pulled off his gray T-shirt and she met his eyes squarely with her own. From experience, she knew the look of desire in a man's eyes. Freeze, she was certain, had that look. He coupled it with something more, but she couldn't figure out what that something else was. His eyes were clouded with passion and she grinned slightly as she realized they mirrored her own. She then took in his tight chest. Freeze was not overly muscled, but a man of pure, lean strength. His tight chest muscles rippled as he leaned back down next to her.

"What's your problem? Afraid to get under the blanket with me? I'm tied up. I can't hurt you." Twyla smiled at him and put her desire for his warmth in her eyes so he could not misread it.

He pulled the tattered blanket from beneath him and placed it over the two of them. Twyla inhaled his scent and moaned breathily as the blanket floated back down. She'd been with many men. None ever caught her fancy for more than a night. They were all so concerned about getting their rocks off that she soon forgot about them.

She had a sex drive that was stronger than the average male. It was good to be a borderline nymphomaniac who couldn't get pregnant. But she wasn't the type to fuck just any man. She chose them based upon which ones were pleasing to the eye and appeared to be inventive. There was nothing worse than a hard cock without an imagination to go with it.

"You're right. You can't hurt me. I can hurt you, though," he whispered sensually in her ear.

"Are you kidding? You've put the dagger down, what else have you got that could possibly hurt me? I don't think you have anything big enough to cause any real pain." She couldn't find more challenging words.

His chuckle let her know just what he thought of her. "You better watch out or I'll have to prove you wrong."

"Just fuck me, Freeze. Okay? Can you do that?" She couldn't help but let her true colors show. He was the bad guy, but there was just something so good about him as he breathed against her neck...as his hand caressed her thigh...as his tongue slid along her neck to her jaw.

"You want me to fuck you? But I'm supposed to torture you and then kill you." His fingers nimbly undid the front hook of her bra. Her breasts sprang forth as she arched her back as high as she could. She knew how to put on a show to make a guy fuck her. It was actually pretty easy.

He took the bait as he slid on top of her, his weight forcing her flat against the cot, his mouth owning hers for a powerful moment. Now she was certain he had magical power beyond the healing he'd done. Her entire body was on fire with passion. He was a sly devil and it turned her on even more as she furiously fought against her binding. As she twisted, she could feel a little give on the ties that bound her ankles.

"Where is that damn dagger?" she half shouted. "Get me out of this!"

"No, no, no." He licked her cheek and grinned. "I'm not allowed to let you out of here."

"That's not what I meant!"

Her ankles had been held together with one piece of strapping which was cleverly knotted around each ankle, but not tied to the cot as her wrists were. All that stretching Craze had done to her had weakened one of the knots on her ankles and she managed to break one free, which in turn allowed her to wrap her strong legs around him and pull him tightly to her. She grinned at the surprise in his eyes.

"You gonna show me what else you got in your pants or what?" She ran one leg up his back as high as she could get it. "I like a little control. What can I say?" She quickly released him by spreading her legs wide and using all of her strength to shuffle him to the side of her. She had always been flexible. She'd gained her strength from running along the beach as well as hard sex.

He fought with his jeans, but at last he was freed of their confines. His cock was quite hard and long. She wished she could have tasted it, but he was busy sliding her thong down her legs. His hands took their time.

"Freeze?" She felt a sparkle of pleasure run from his fingertips as they toyed with her clit. There was the usual sensation of a man's fingertip touching her, but there was also something more. Something so much more pleasurable than the heaven brought on by a man's touch in that sweetly sensitive area. She studied his eyes, desperate to read them. All she saw was mischief and pleasure. This man was magically inclined in such a good way. He healed her, he pleased her. Perhaps it wasn't so bad to be at his mercy.

"Yes, Twyla?" The melody of her name rolled from his lips once more. Why on earth was she enjoying this so much?

"Kiss me."

Leaning down, he tasted the wet folds between her legs for just a torturous moment. She gasped and moaned in answer. Then, his fingers wandered between her thighs, one finger intimately tracing where his tongue had been. Another finger followed and the pleasure sparks multiplied, sailing faster throughout her body causing her to thrash against the cot as her cunt spasmed.

Dammit! She wanted to watch what he was doing to her. Nothing had ever felt this good before. Straining against her bindings, she lifted her head and peered over her breasts at the pleasuring mischief-maker between her legs. Inquisitively, he shifted his hand to her abdomen and she felt a sort of exploring tingle shoot through her. If he really was as magically inclined as he seemed to be, he was searching for answers.

"I'm clean, Freeze. Nothing works down there, either." She laid her head back on the cot.

"I'm clean as well and there are a few things that work just fine down here..." He sent further sparks through her clit. They seemed to echo in every nook and cranny of her body and soul. She spread her legs wide as he climbed between them.

Closing her eyes, she lost track of her body and just let herself indulge in pure sensation. He was more imaginative than any other man she'd been with.

Freeze shifted on the cot and she opened her eyes just in time to see the fire in his own before his lips set about claiming hers. His tongue darted into her mouth to mate with hers. She completely welcomed him with all her being. As if she didn't think she could get any higher, she felt sparkles and tingles from every place where his skin touched hers. She had never been this aroused in her entire life. Not one man had ever made her feel like this. And she doubted any other man could.

He had been supporting his weight above her with his arms. She couldn't stand it anymore. She wrapped her legs around him and forced him to enter her. He immediately responded. Twyla's entire body felt like a giant orgasm was taking hold, but she knew she hadn't reached its climax. If this was the way she was going to die, then she was going to die willingly.

Their thrusts met each other's in perfect rhythm. She had taught herself how to escalate to match a man's passion. She knew how to manage an orgasm from a three-stroke wonder. But Freeze, well, she didn't have to work at all to get off. He was doing it all for her. He seemed to know exactly what she wanted. He gave it to her again and again until she was sure this was her death. Or maybe she had surpassed death and gone straight to heaven.

Among the pleasure sparks, sweet little orgasms exploded within her. He escalated them. She wanted desperately to give some back to him. She opened her eyes and met his. Her cunt tightened on his full length as she neared her threshold. He plunged as deep as he could reach and brought them both home. She wrenched her legs tighter around his ass while her body shook with each hard tremor of passion.

Breathing heavily, he fell limp against her. She was near tears at the pleasure she'd just experienced. Even without the addition of magic, this was the best she'd ever had.

Slowly, he raised his weight off of her and met her gaze. She swallowed hard at the raw emotion he was showing her. "Some torture there, Freeze."

"Yeah," he said between quick breaths. She closed her eyes, wallowing in the continued tingles surging through her body.

Moments later, she felt her wrists free from their binding and she quickly opened her eyes. He sat on the edge of the cot, pulling on his pants and boots then sheathing the dagger. His hands shook as he grabbed his shirt and laid it over her breasts. She gasped at the way his shirt felt against her. He'd left her with residual pleasure sparkles that screamed louder in her erogenous zones.

She brought her arms down trying to get some good circulation back through them. The rest of her blood was flowing like it never had before. He picked his jacket up from the floor and put it on. He clenched his hands into fists, which still shook as he looked at them in surprise.

He stuttered gently, "You will return…wh-whatever you get about th-the men…or…I'll…"

"Yes, Freeze." It was her turn to be obedient for just a brief moment. She refastened her bra and put his shirt on as he opened a secret door on the wall opposite the regular door. He turned back as if he wanted to say something, but no words passed his lips. His eyes spoke volumes however. Desire was there, but also…surprise?

She opened her mouth to inquire but before she could, he turned rapidly and walked through the doorway he'd created. His shoulder slammed into the archway and she heard a mumbled, "Fuck!" under his breath before he disappeared into the darkness, leaving the doorway open behind him.

Twyla shook her head. Freeze was as overwhelmed and disoriented as she was. His scent was so fresh and intoxicating all over her body. She stood up. His shirt was just long enough to cover everything important. She found her thong on the edge of the cot and slid it on. Her legs were weak from holding onto him so tightly.

She knew there was no forgetting what had just happened. And she also knew that every man she'd have from now on would end up being compared to Freeze and would most likely fall far short of him. She figured she'd decide if that was a bad thing or not when the sparks Freeze had sent through her subsided. She was so satisfied, but just inhaling his scent from his shirt kept her hot. There was no relief from the tingling as she came down from the highest high she'd ever experienced. Each spark exploded and dissipated. One by one. Leaving her trembling with mini-orgasms. If she hadn't been standing alone in the room, she'd swear she was still fucking him.

Twyla sighed deeply as she continued to gather her wits, then headed through the doorway that Freeze had left for her. She had no idea how much time had passed or how to get out of there, let alone find some clothing that didn't keep her near mini-orgasm, but she had to find Mariah and take them both away somewhere safe, somewhere that they wouldn't be found. She cursed herself for not staying as focused as she should have been. But she surely didn't curse the fuck that had set her free.

Chapter Eight

Stephan woke up underneath Mariah, her body relaxed around him in sleep. He knew she had to be tired. They'd made love several times last night.

Made love. Didn't he mean fucked? He cursed himself as he lightly stroked his hand through her hair and down her body. Who was he trying to fool? What they had done was a lot more than just sex. She snuggled against him in her sleep and his cock immediately jumped to action, ready to go again.

He had to get away from her before he did something he'd regret. He was becoming too attached to her…the smell of her, the taste of her. The way she moaned when he thrust himself deep inside. How tight her cunt was around his cock. The look in her eyes when she came. The way she made him feel…. He closed his eyes, trying to block out the images that were forever burned in his mind after last night.

He knew he couldn't have it. That after all was said and done, for her own safety, he'd have to let her go. Shit! He had never hated his life more than he did at this very moment.

Slowly, so as not to disturb her sleep, he slid out from underneath her. He bit his tongue to keep from moaning when his cock brushed against her hand. Even after their marathon night together, he wanted more.

He slipped into his clothes and picked up his boots, reminding himself he'd need a new pair of laces. He glanced over his shoulder one last time before he left the room. Her hair was tussled around her, its dark length a stark contrast to the creamy white of her bare skin. The black jersey sheet was tangled around her, showing more of her naked body than it covered. Her perfectly rounded ass was visible, and his cock twitched and hardened even more at the thought of taking her again while she slept...of hearing her impassioned moans when she woke with him already deep inside of her.

He turned his head back around and stepped through the door. She was beautiful and she was his...and he had to let her go.

Shutting the door quietly behind him with a sigh, he walked away and headed for Dusty's room. He needed a shower. A cold shower. He needed ice cubes to rain down over his too hot body. Everything was just too hot for him. His memories of the night, the scent of her on him. She was everywhere for him.

He looked at his boots as he set them down inside the door. The frayed cut laces just made him think of the heat all over again. Pulling off his shirt, he headed into Dusty's bathroom, thankful that Dusty wasn't there to question him. Stephan wasn't ready to explain his actions or to debate what he should do next to make things right.

Stephan tried to gather his wits as the warm water splashed against him. Fucking her was so much better than he'd imagined it would be. And it went way beyond just fucking. "No more!" he said under his breath as he finished scrubbing himself off. He was determined to find something else to keep his mind occupied. There was no way he could go back to his room with her lying there. He'd just end up making love to her until the end of time. He turned the water to as cold as it would go and stood there waiting for it to steal away all of his heat.

Just before he was going to give up and admit defeat, he felt a shiver rage through his body and his cock actually went into hiding. It was time to get out. He concentrated on toweling off and getting his clothes back on. From there, he focused his thoughts on the need to straighten out business.

What business? Oh, yes, *Rare and Unusual Imports*. It had been awhile since he'd squared away the inventory reports. Yes. That's what he needed to do. Square inventory. That would involve counting and working with a computer. Simple yet necessary tasks that would take his focus off of Mariah.

Lover's Talisman

Mariah...lying naked in his bed. No! He had to think of numbers...hmmm...the number of times he'd fucked her last night.

God, this had to stop. He stole laces from an old pair of Dusty's boots and installed them in his own before he headed upstairs into the back room.

The computer was always on, but left locked. He quickly typed in the password as he sat down. Opening the desk drawer, he removed a pair of glasses, then went over to the kitchenette and filled a glass with water.

He put on the glasses, grabbed the water and sat down at the computer. Simple tasks, one step at a time. He could do this. Now numbers. He needed to square the numbers. The inventory system was a mess. He took a deep breath as the spreadsheet materialized on the screen. He could smell the woman. His cock jumped right back to attention, forgetting the punishment he'd inflicted on it so recently in the shower. Mariah's scent seemed to be all over him. But he'd tried to wash it all away. He had to be imagining it.

He ran a hand through his damp hair. Focus. He needed to focus.

There were five cartons of Kool-Aid in the system, but none on the shelf across the room where it was supposed to be. Jake had mentioned something yesterday about some demons coming for the Kool-Aid. That was right before Stephan had almost fucked Mariah against the back wall of her house.

Shit! How was it that no matter what tactic he used, he could not get her out of his head?

She consumed his every thought. His cock strained against his jeans. The woman would be the death of him. He was sure of that. If he couldn't get his mind back on the inventory, he'd be out of business and then where would he be? Living with Mariah in a shack in a bad area of town. There'd be four children to feed and he wouldn't even be able to bring them any Kool-Aid for a treat.

"This has got to stop..." Although if the old adage were true, "like father, like son," he'd probably make a terrible father. His biological dad had been one of his mother's many one-night stands and his arrogant stepfather—Marlin's father—hadn't wanted to raise anyone else's bastard. Then he'd been sent to foster care, where he'd been on the receiving end of his foster father's fists while protecting his foster sister Lisa. At least that asshole had taught him how to take a punch. Dismissing his memories without a second thought, Stephan searched through the spreadsheet for any other discrepancies. There had to be more. He absorbed himself in it. A significant amount of time passed before he got Mariah out of the forefront of his mind, but it finally happened as one by one, he squared each line of inventory.

It seemed as though for that hour, everything related to Mariah in some way, but at least he'd gotten his mind off fucking her. He wondered what kind of toothpaste she used and whether or not she would like one of the fountains he'd brought in from the water dimension. He wondered about everything in relation to her.

Rare and Unusual Imports was the place to go for indeed, the rare and unusual. What the general public did not know was that such rarities came from several other dimensions. Stephan had come up with this highly profitable idea after playing tour guide to so many different demons who wanted simple things like Kool-Aid, Cheerios and even cacti. He was known inter-dimensionally for always having the best merchandise. The best way to acquire dimensional imports was to barter for them. He smiled as he wondered if Mariah would like it if he bartered Kenny Rogers CDs for some filmy fabric similar to what she wore at *Silver Twilight*.

"Glasses, huh? I'll bet you can't see straight..." Stephan hadn't even heard Marlin enter the room.

"What?"

"Was it good?" Marlin inquired as he pulled a chair around. He straddled it backward and sat down.

"How'd you—" Stephan swallowed hard.

"Sounded like you rocked her world." So that was what this was about. Marlin must have really wanted a piece of the action. Well, there was no way that would happen now. Stephan would all out brawl with his brother before he'd let him anywhere near Mariah in bed.

"I gotta get this done." Stephan turned his attention back to the spreadsheet and pretended to ignore Marlin. He didn't want him to know that he really was falling for the woman.

"You're gonna wreck your life…and ours too. Don't get messed up with her." Marlin's voice was intense.

"It's not about her. I gotta make this right." Stephan turned to fully face his brother, hoping that by convincing Marlin, he could convince himself.

"I'm with ya, but when the shit hits the fan, don't come crying to me." Marlin shook his head.

"You came crying to me after Judy. Lay off, man. I'll make sure nothing happens to Mariah." He turned back to the desk, hoping to find something to distract him. There was a pile of unopened mail that caught his attention.

"Like I made sure nothing would happen to Judy. Let Mariah go now. Before you get too deep, bro."

Stephan knew Marlin was right, but he didn't want to talk about this anymore. Twinges of pain tugged at his heart as he thought of losing Mariah the way Marlin had lost Judy those years ago. He mindlessly searched through the mail. There was a postcard, which he read quickly in hopes of a diversion from his current conversation. Luck was on his side.

"Look. Another postcard from Lisa. She's studying at Oxford now." He smiled at the thought of his sister. They weren't actually siblings. Stephan had been fostered by Lisa's parents. He loved her as a sister and used to protect her from her drunken father. When he'd become a Shadow Walker, he hadn't wanted any demons to take their rage out on her, so he'd sent her away to school. He heard from her via postcard and phone calls on occasion, and he couldn't have been more proud of her.

"You sent her away so nothing would happen to her. It looks like it worked." Marlin was ruthless. Stephan glared at him for a moment before Marlin continued.

"Don't fuck her again. She'll fuck your mind up until you can't think about anything *but* fucking her."

"Look, Marlin. I know what you're doing. It's not like that. She's just a fuck. She'll be gone soon." It pained him to lie like that knowing he would have to force himself to believe it was true. What happened to Marlin couldn't happen to him.

"Don't give me that bullshit. It's too late, isn't it? You've gone and fucked her and now you can't think about anything else, can you? It's 6AM and not only are you awake after a romp like that, you're working! I've never seen you so diligent, either. Stephan, you're wearing your glasses! You only wear your glasses when you both literally and figuratively can't see straight." Marlin stood up. "Y'know. There's nothing I can do now. It's all over. We're gonna have to deal with you daydreaming about fucking Mariah all the while trying to make sure we don't get our asses kicked by whatever this new force in town is.

"There wasn't anything new at the house. I came back early because all of the tracks have been covered. And what did I hear through the door? The ride of your life and hers too, I'm sure! I'm glad my room isn't next to yours or you two would have kept me up all night! Dammit, Stephan! Don't fuck her anymore!" Marlin shot away from his chair.

"Get out." Stephan couldn't admit his brother was right. He just couldn't do it. And more than that, his brother would not dictate to him how to live. Marlin's problems happened years ago and things had changed drastically since then. Why couldn't he see that?

"Gladly. Call me when you wanna meet—and can think about something other than Mariah. I'm gonna pack up the online sales so I can open the store later, since it seems I'm the only one who got any sleep last night." He shook his head as he stalked away from Stephan.

Stephan's breath caught in his throat. He had a lot of thinking to do. A lot of planning to do as well. But how could he plan if he didn't have the full story? What he really wanted to do was crawl back into the nice warm bed with Mariah. He knew she could make it all better. She could take him places he'd never known existed. The sound of her throaty moans could lead him anywhere. He took off his glasses and nearly crushed them in his hand. He sighed deeply and scratched his head. Spreadsheet. Got to study the spreadsheet. He put his glasses back on again.

"I'm glad you're up. I got some answers." Ryan closed the door from the back alley entrance and strode straight for Stephan.

Tension shot down Stephan's spine. This couldn't be good.

Ryan stopped and narrowed his eyes. "You okay? One of the other guys tell you already? You're lookin' like hell."

"I'm fine. What did you find out?"

"I hooked up with those freaks. *Silver Twilight*. The joint was kind of quiet. Some guys said that one of the regular girls wasn't performing."

He'd used the word "regular." Mariah was far from regular. She was perfection. Sweet utter perfection.

"Anyway, I uh…charmed them into talking." Ryan deftly drew a switchblade from one of his pockets, released the blade and expertly folded it back in. The entire movement took less time than Stephan needed to clear his mind of seeing Mariah dance at *Silver Twilight*.

"The old flick of the switchblade. That always works best for you, doesn't it?"

"It's all in the style. And these guys spilled what they knew."

Ryan shook his head and took a deep breath. A chill crossed the back of Stephan's neck. Whatever Ryan was about to say was going to change things. And not for the better.

"It's the Dread Lords, Stephan. They finally made it to Talisman Bay."

Stephan grimaced. "Fuckin' Dread Lords, man. I knew it was just a matter of time before they got here. Hell, they might even give us a run for our money."

Stephan shook his head. They'd all known it would happen someday. The Sacred Order had been battling the Dread Lords since the dawn of time. They had created the Shadow Walkers to fight the Dread Lords, to watch over the dimensional portals, and to keep the control on the side of good. It was easy to determine which towns the Dread Lords controlled. Wherever high instances of crime took place, wherever murders outnumbered births, that was where Dread Lords ruled.

But they'd avoided Talisman Bay, until now. Smaller bands of rogue demons had tried to take Talisman Bay over the years, but they had never succeeded. And neither would the Dread Lords.

"But, now that I know who we're facing, I can plan our attack. You kicked ass, Ryan. Go get some sleep now while you have a chance. I'll wake you out of your favorite pastime when I need you back here."

"Cool. I'll catch you later. Don't work too hard, man. This is just another annoyance we'll put behind us." Ryan nodded his head for emphasis before he went downstairs.

So, the Dread Lords thought they could win? Thought that by threatening their women the Shadow Walkers would just walk away? Not fucking likely. Just recently, Talisman Bay had been named one of the safest cities to live in. He and the guys were proud of what they'd accomplished. He'd often wondered what would happen if he decided to start a family. He wanted Talisman Bay to be a safe place to raise his children. Now, that

Lover's Talisman

thought had the potential to be reality. That is, of course, if the Shadow Walkers could get the Dread Lords out of Talisman Bay.

Stephan turned back to the computer screen. He couldn't ask Mariah to stay while the Dread Lords threatened, but he couldn't let her go either. There weren't any options at all. He wanted her as badly as he needed her to stay away for her own safety. And to top it off, he knew he had to keep her near him because he had endangered her. Even knowing that the strongest men in town would all be on her side, how could he ask her to join the insanity of his world? He pounded a fist on the desk. His water glass teetered but he caught it before it fell over.

"Hey man. You okay? Frustration doesn't suit you too well. Maybe you should go to see your Pleasure goddess and relax a little."

Stephan turned and glared at Jake.

"I'm fine, Jake. You don't need to sneak everywhere you go, do you?"

"Isn't that what you sent me out to do? I don't have much for you, though." Jake paused and cocked his head to the side, like he was trying to understand Stephan. "You should really take it easy. You look like you've been through hell."

"What have you got for me?" Stephan leaned back in his chair, quickly changing the subject.

Jake turned the chair around that Marlin had sat in earlier and climbed on it. He sat on the top and put his feet on the seat. "You need to talk?" Stephan just glared at him. "Naw, I'm serious, man. Something's a lot different since last night when I left. What's going on? Did we lose somebody or something?"

"Yeah, well, I'm gonna lose somebody, but there's nothing I can do about it. You gonna tell me what you learned or should I try to rope you into helping me with inventory?" Stephan wanted to spill his guts. Jake wasn't the one to tell it all to, though. Jake would announce everything to the whole world and then he'd never be able to keep Mariah safe.

"I see how it is…I ain't pushin' it. Just don't end up like Marlin. Okay? That's all I gotta say, right?"

"Yeah, that's it. Now tell me what you learned so I can see if it matches up with what Ryan found out."

Jake raised one eyebrow questioningly, but started talking. "Okay. I found this sort of mysterious group of buildings in the older area of town. They have regular doors for all the people who live in the apartments to go in and out, but in two of the alleys between them, some guys just materialize like they're coming out of the walls. Like there are secret doors there or something. I dunno. I tried to get in, but they're protected. I was thinking maybe I needed some kind of key or something. It was really weird.

"I've never seen anything like it and I never knew there was anything weird about those buildings. They probably have a dimensional fissure kind of complex like we do. But it's nothing we've mapped out before. I mean I crawled all over that building because my gut was telling me that what's her name, Twyla, could have been taken there. I know all the other haunts around this place. I'd've figured it out if she was in any of those. But these buildings, man, they're really weird." Jake readjusted his position on top of the chair.

Stephan smiled. Things were looking better already. "I'll have to check that out. Sounds like you found the Dread Lord compound."

Jake let out a low whistle. "Damn. They finally made it to Talisman Bay."

Stephan just nodded and continued. "So it doesn't surprise me that there's some heavy magic involved at their compound. I dunno why these guys chose to come now, but they're going down. One way or another." Stephan was glad for the diversion. At last he had something more to think about than a beautiful naked woman sleeping alone in his bed.

"I'm gonna catch a few winks. Sounds like we have one hell of a battle ahead of us." Jake grinned. "Hell, I'm lookin' forward to it. Click-in if you wanna meet or something. I need to refuel on a little sleep. I'll catch you later." With that, Jake gracefully jumped from the chair and headed through the door to the compound below.

He turned back to the computer screen and read a few more lines. If his mind hadn't been reeling before, it certainly was now. He'd gotten more information, but certainly not enough. And Mariah still danced about in his head as well. It felt like a carousel of problems spinning and going up and down all at the same time. He would have to let something go just so he could keep track of everything else. The safety of the city was most important. The Dread Lords must go down.

"Well, you didn't send me on the fox hunt tonight, but I got the fox anyway." With an unsure look on his face, Dusty held out a paper shopping bag. "I talked to old Milty at the pawn shop. He didn't want to say anything at first, but when I reminded him that we know he's a demon in hiding, amazingly, he had something to say, as well as this bag to hand over."

Stephan frowned and took the bag.

"You okay? Been staring at the screen for too long or something? You even got your glasses on." Dusty pulled a chair closer to Stephan and sat down.

"I've just got a lot on my mind. This'll make it worse, huh?" He held up the bag and inspected the outside of it for anything unusual. It was just a plain shopping bag. Carefully, he reached in and pulled out shredded and tattered women's clothing: a shirt, a skirt and some stiletto heels. Something else rustled in the bottom of the bag. He reached in to retrieve a beaded necklace. "Twyla."

"Milty said the guy who dropped this stuff off was new in town. He could tell by the look of innocence on the kid's face. Then he said something about the same thing would happen to this girl's best friend if we didn't cooperate. I dunno." Dusty ran his hands through his hair. "This is pretty serious, isn't it?"

"Yeah. It's very serious, man. This is the work of the Dread Lords. And they're not messin' around. This isn't what I wanted to tell Mariah. How do I tell her that I can't bring her friend back because she's dead?"

Dusty nodded slowly. "Yeah. Dread Lords. Makes sense." Then he crossed his arms over his chest and glared at Stephan. "Wait. What the fuck, Stephan? We don't know that Twyla's dead. Where's your brain? There's no blood on the clothing, except for a minor bit on the shoulder of the blouse. I checked it out. There's no reason to assume she was wearing these when they were thrashed. It's a warning, nothing more, until we know better. This girl's just the bargaining chip. Trust me, she ain't dead."

"I'm just a little too close to the whole thing, I guess. It's just been so long since there was real action in this town. I'd forgotten what it was like. I always knew the day would come, I just wish it wasn't now." Then again, without the Dread Lords showing up, Mariah might never have come into his life. Talk about a sick twist of fate.

Stephan inspected the clothing and necklace as he set them on the desk. If Twyla really was dead, there'd be no way he could face Mariah after assuring her that he would get Twyla back for her. "Why did you wait so long to bring this back here?"

"Well...I uh...had to make up the date with Jeneane."

"Bullshit! You went to her and then to the pawn shop, didn't you?" Stephan just grinned and shook his head. He couldn't lay it on too thick because he was guilty of fucking around too.

"Hey, I'm not a complete asshole. I went to the shop first and Milty wasn't there—it was late y'know and he wasn't around. I thought I'd cruise the streets, and a few of Milty's haunts, and I ran into Jeneane. She thought I'd looked her up to apologize and I couldn't turn her down. But I left her at the crack of dawn to corner Milty before he opened. So, maybe I fucked up, but at least I brought back good stuff." Dusty stopped in his excuses and gave Stephan the once over. "Shit! You didn't go out at all either, did you? I'll bet you were shackin', too, huh? She must be getting good sleep now if you're up here."

"I was protecting her." The excuse jumped off Stephan's tongue before he could stop it. Dusty just laughed.

"Protecting yourself right into her bed. Nice..." Stephan attempted to give him the cold shoulder, but he knew Dusty was right. Dusty continued with a grin, "I'm going downstairs. Do you want anything?" Dusty raised his eyebrows and stood up to head for the compound.

"Naw, I think I'll be just fine." Stephan was in agony. He had to find a way to let Mariah go.

"Sure, you will. I recognize that look on your face. You and your brother, man. As much as you guys are completely different, you're totally the same. Hey, that's why I won't fall for Jeneane. There's no reason I can't fuck her, though. And she doesn't want anything more than that anyway. Hey, ya want me to check on your girl for you?"

"No. Let her sleep. I gotta figure out what I'm gonna tell her about Twyla." Stephan choose to ignore the "your girl" comment.

"All right, I'm gettin' an hour of sleep now. Maybe you should, too."

"Yeah. Thanks." Stephan crumpled some junk mail and tossed it in the trash as Dusty headed through the secret door. Mariah had to only be a fuck. There was no other choice. No more pretending there could be more...because with the Dread Lords in town, there never would be.

Chapter Nine

Mariah stretched as she woke, enjoying the lingering muscle pain and tenderness in her cunt. Last night was going on record as one of the best of her life, hands down, dampened only by the fact that she couldn't immediately share it with her best friend. Hell, living vicariously through Twyla's rather imaginative and vigorous sex life was the closest she'd come to getting laid in over five years. Twyla'd want to know details of the night that had broken the fuck-free streak, and Mariah longed to share them with her.

She really should be more tired than she was, since she'd hardly slept at all. They'd both woken each other up so many times, and done so many different things to each other...she couldn't help but blush at the memories. The positions Twyla had told her about in her many adventures had been put to good use. She'd wanted to do everything with and to him, and she'd packed as much fucking into last night as she could. Her body still felt like one giant raw nerve ending. She'd lost count of the amount of orgasms she'd had somewhere around six. Not a bad way to break a celibacy streak that was for sure.

It was too bad Stephan had left her a few hours earlier. She'd heard the door click shut sometime around 5A.M., much earlier than her brain functioned. She knew he had work to do, but it hadn't stopped her from wishing he could stay with her, so they could wake each other up in pleasant, overly distracting ways.

Her world would be perfect if only Twyla was found. Twyla had been telling her for years not to treat every man as though he was Michael. And she had finally found someone worth opening up to, and she couldn't even share it with her best friend. It made this moment bittersweet.

But she couldn't think this way. She would get Twyla back. Twyla was strong enough and smart enough to stay alive under most any circumstance. And Twyla would be pissed at her if she continued to mope around and didn't enjoy her newfound sex life to the fullest. With Stephan's help, and the rest of the Shadow Walkers, her best friend would be brought home safe and sound. Mariah forced herself not to think of any other possibilities.

Her feet found the floor and she slowly stood up, truly discovering that she was one giant pleasure ache. A shower was also very necessary — the stickiness that coated her inner thighs attested that both of them had very much enjoyed last night. Sex was fun — more than fun, it was amazing — but could never be described as clean.

One hot shower later — just standing there under the multiple shower heads sent residual orgasmic tremors through her body — and she felt ready to go search out a cup of coffee and something to fill the empty hole in her stomach. Stephan had fed her part of a sandwich at some point last night, but her tongue had enjoyed licking his fingers more than the food. Then she'd decided that she wanted to taste the rest of him. Boy, did he satisfy every craving. The rest of the sandwich had been very much forgotten.

She needed something to wear before she prowled around. A bundle on the floor showed interesting promise, but upon closer inspection a peach nightgown just wasn't going to cut it for daytime wear. So that was what Stephan had used to tie her hands together to the bed post during one interesting game. He must have brought it to her last night. He was so thoughtful. And it had come in handy quite well last night, just not as he had probably originally intended…or maybe he had? She knew she grinned like an idiot with every thought of him, but she couldn't help it. He made her happy.

Her shirt from yesterday was pretty dirty, but her jeans were salvageable. She'd have to forego the panties since they'd seen a bit too much action yesterday as well. Maybe she should hint that very thing the next time she saw Stephan. Perhaps a quickie was in order.

The shirt Stephan had loaned her last night to sleep in—how long had that lasted?—was on the floor. She picked it up and shook it out. It'd do fine. She quickly dressed, knotting his shirt under her breasts. She couldn't help but think that he'd probably like that.

With a spring to her step she hadn't had in awhile, she headed for the kitchen. The whole living area was quiet. An empty coffee pot sat on the counter and a quick check through the cupboards found the grounds and filter. In ten minutes she'd be in coffee heaven.

Mariah's curiosity got the better of her and she began exploring. The entertainment center beckoned and she couldn't resist. She approached the massive CD changer with caution. It was huge! It had to hold at least five hundred CDs and had so many buttons and knobs that she didn't know where to start.

Humming to herself, she pressed a few buttons then jumped when loud music poured forth all around her. She quickly turned down the volume so as not to wake anyone who might still be sleeping.

The CD playing had a great beat and she vaguely recognized the song. Music and dance fed her soul and was how she dealt with pretty much everything in her life. The deep bass guided her on, as well as the sexy, raspy voice of the male singer, and she began to move and sway her hips, dancing and swinging to the music, as she waited for her drug of choice to be ready. A new dance routine was already forming in her mind and she let the vision guide her. For the first time in awhile, her dancing came from a place of happiness inside of her, rather than the pain of betrayal she'd carried with her for so long.

Thinking of Stephan brought out a new sexuality to her moves. As an exotic dancer, her moves were, of course, always sexual, but now she reveled in the feeling that burned through her veins as she accepted the rhythm of the music into her body. Her hands were Stephan's hands as she caressed her body. She wondered what Stephan would think of her being a stripper, if it would bother him to know that she showed her all every night, or if he would get off on it. She'd have to tell him, maybe by giving him an exclusive one on one show...that thought made her body heat up faster than any coffee ever could.

Caught up with thoughts of a private show with Stephan, her hands cupped her breasts, and slowly slid down her body. The male voice on the song became Stephan's voice and it coaxed her along. With her legs widespread, she slid her arms down to her feet and looked between her legs, spying a pair of jean-clad legs, light gray T-shirted chest, and an unknown male face staring appreciatively back at her. Her heart stopped and she quickly jumped up and turned around, casting herself against the stereo behind her. The beat continued to throb through her, accelerating her already rapidly beating pulse.

"Hey. Sorry I scared you. Feel free to keep going." His mouth formed a grin as he watched her sheepishly. "I was really enjoying the view. Sorry. I'm Dusty. You must be Mariah." Dusty held out a large paw of a hand for her to shake. She studied his hand for a moment, trying to get her mind to work again after that scare, then took his hand, amazed at how it completely swallowed hers. He was not someone she'd want to meet in a dark alley...well, actually it would depend on why she was meeting him. She swallowed a grin. She'd definitely indulged in too much sex if she was sizing up every guy she met.

She forced herself to calm down from the almost heart attack Dusty had given her, taking deep breaths as she let her gaze wander over his body. Although not as handsome as Stephan, Dusty was ruggedly good looking. He was larger than Stephan in his body mass and could probably take someone out with one good punch. His hair was dirty blond and was longer and more unkempt than Stephan's. But Twyla was right. All of the guys she'd seen around here were ones you wouldn't kick out of bed. And the twinkle in his eyes led her to believe that she was completely safe around him.

She realized she'd been staring at him and not talking. His smile had turned into a knowing grin and Mariah felt a blush creeping over her features. "Oh, sorry. Yeah, I'm Mariah." She pulled her hand from his. "Next time you let me know you're there, okay? Before I make a fool out of myself."

Dusty's eyes lit up with mischief. "I can't promise anything. I mean, what guy in his right mind would want you to stop? It's kinda against our natural, basic instinct."

Mariah crossed her arms over her chest, trying to give him a stern look. She really just wanted to laugh out loud. A grin cracked over her face and Dusty laughed in response. "All right. All right. You win this time. I'll just have to be more careful where I dance. It serves me right to get so into it when just anybody could walk in." Mariah turned and headed back into the kitchen. Dusty's voice followed behind her.

"Oh, now don't do that. Where's the fun?"

"I just made a fresh pot of coffee. Can I get you some?"

"All right. Sounds good. I don't usually drink coffee around here because Ryan makes it so thick you have to eat it with a spoon. He swears he does it right, but I really don't think the grounds are supposed to land in the cup." Dusty laughed at his story, and Mariah couldn't help but join in.

She dug through the cupboards and found two mugs, which she poured full of coffee, then turned and handed one to him, returning his smile. "Fresh coffee. No grounds included."

He took a sip and his eyes widened. "This is heaven. Such pure heaven. Will you marry me?"

Mariah almost snorted the coffee she was drinking as the laughter overtook her once again.

"No, I'm really serious. Marry me and make me coffee like this everyday and I'll keep you happy. I promise. Jewelry, flowers, whatever you want. Just brew me this manna from heaven every morning and the world is yours."

"Wow. What an offer. Let me think about it, will ya?" Mariah smiled up at Dusty over her coffee cup. "So, you mentioned Ryan. I haven't met him yet. How many of you are there?"

"How many of who? You mean guys who own this shop?" He smiled at her, but his eyebrows rose questioningly.

"Well, sure. Or Shadow Walkers."

It was Dusty's turn to snort his coffee. "Shadow Walkers? How did you know?"

"Stephan told me last night. He just didn't give me details. I know his brother Marlin is one, and of course Stephan, and someone named Fiero is a healer, but that's all I really know. I'm assuming you're one as well since you're down here in this other dimension..." Mariah was surprised by how easy this conversation was to have. Twenty-four hours earlier she didn't know anything, but for some reason it all made sense now.

Dusty remained quiet for a moment, just watching her. He seemed to be trying to gather his thoughts. "Well...okay.... You know Stephan, Marlin, Fiero and now me. There's also Jake and Ryan. That's it locally."

"Locally?"

"Well, yeah...there are Shadow Walkers everywhere, all over the world. Y'know, I dunno how much I should be telling you so let's just leave it at that. I kinda forget what I should and shouldn't be saying when I'm around a beautiful woman."

Mariah smiled at his remark, though her tone got serious. "Um...you wouldn't happen to have any information on my friend Twyla, would you?"

Dusty's face showed his concern. "Not exactly. Well, I can't really say, but I can tell you this. We don't lose. We'll get her back for you."

Mariah nodded, her stomach sinking. She just wanted everything to be okay, now. "I know. I just keep hoping—"

"Soon, okay? Keep smilin'." Dusty reached a hand out and cupped her face, lifting her chin and wiping away the few tears that had slipped free. There was something unreadable in his eyes, a yearning maybe? "I promise...it'll be okay."

Mariah smiled up at Dusty as he dropped his hand. He continued to watch her closely, the unknown look still visible in his eyes. "Thank you. And thanks for sharing conversation—"

"And coffee. And don't forget my offer. The world is yours if you say yes." Dusty's eyes resumed their sparkle as he turned to go.

"Hey! Have you seen Stephan?" Mariah hoped she didn't sound too eager, too happy or too horny.

"Oh, man! Stephan? I should go kick his ass. Lucky guy. Drinking your coffee." Mariah just grinned at him. "All right. All right. Yeah, he's upstairs, crunching numbers or somethin'. You need me to get him for you?"

"No, that's okay. Thanks. I'm just going to get some breakfast." Mariah smiled again at Dusty as a thought began percolating in her head. She could make breakfast for Stephan. She wasn't Ms. Domestic or anything, but she could manage to throw together a decent breakfast.

"Okay, I'll see ya around." Dusty left the room and Mariah got started. The cupboards had revealed some stale crackers, and cans of soup and not much else when she'd searched earlier for the coffee. It was pretty obvious that these guys didn't make meals very often. *Typical bachelors, they'd starve to death without fast food and take-out.*

The fridge contained some cheese—lacking mold, always a good sign—a half carton of eggs and some bread, butter and jam. Enough for a decent breakfast, just nothing to win her any Martha Stewart awards. Oh hell, Martha Stewart was not someone she aspired to be...the woman had to be possessed. That was it! Martha Stewart was a demon—suddenly everything about her made sense.

Mariah dug through a few more cupboards and found a skillet then went to work. She whipped up the eggs, added cheese and folded them, making a semi-decent omelet. She toasted the bread, lightly buttered it and added some strawberry jam. The jam made her blush as she reminisced about licking some off of Stephan's fingers last night when he was feeding her the sandwich. He'd taken some of the jam and smeared it on her nipples, feasting on her for a while. Her pussy came roaring back to life. She added the jam to the tray she'd found. Maybe they could use it later.

Two cups of coffee, some sugar, napkins and forks and she was ready to go find Stephan. *The way to a man's heart is through his stomach...* She shook her head to remove those thoughts. One step at a time...

She picked up the tray and carefully balanced it as she walked slowly up the stairs. The sound of voices leaked through the partially open door. Stopping when she heard Stephan say her name, she leaned on the wall next to the door. She ignored her inner voice when it told her that eavesdropping could only lead to disappointment.

"...Oh...So Mariah's awake?" She could tell that was Stephan. He sounded tired, but that wasn't surprising.

"Yeah...awake and moving that fine ass of hers all over the compound." Mariah blushed at Dusty's words. "I got my own private show before she realized I was there. You called her Mariah, but I didn't get it until I saw her. That was Mariah, *Silver Twilight's* main attraction, up close and personal." Her stomach clenched. Dusty had recognized her! What would Stephan think? She should have told him earlier. When Stephan started to talk she focused back in on the conversation.

"Yeah, she knows how to do one hell of a show, huh? I saw her the other night at *Silver Twilight*. That night you all were fighting about who was gonna go there. There was something about her that really..." He paused and Mariah held her breath. "Well, I got more than I ever imagined."

Mariah's thoughts spiraled through her mind like a tornado bent on destruction. What was Stephan saying? Did he care for her? Was it just sex? She didn't know what she was expecting but she waited, barely breathing, for Stephan to say something that would clear her mind, make her believe that what they'd shared was more than just a great night together. He hadn't promised more, and she hadn't expected more, really. But last night had changed something inside of her, given her the spark of hope that there was someone out there for her. Someone who would care for her, love her, keep her safe. Dusty's voice interrupted her thoughts.

"So wait a minute, you actually fucked her? Damn, man! She's the ice queen of *Silver Twilight*! She'll take your money for a dance, but she'd never let a guy in. God, there're even bets that she's a lesbian, which made her even more impossible. What the hell did you do to get the special treatment?"

"She's *not* a lesbian." Stephan let out a small laugh and Mariah's heart broke a little. "Hey man, I just rescued her from Asfar. Right place, right time, you know how it goes. And when I stupidly told Asfar that she was mine...well, now the Dread Lords are after her so I gotta keep her close. I've never enjoyed having to keep a woman close quite so much." The sound of male laughter and hands slapping backs broke Mariah's remaining hope into a million tiny pieces. Stephan didn't care for her. She was just a warm body he'd rescued. And worse, he was the reason she was in danger in the first place. She couldn't think anymore, she could only feel...and she hurt.

She slammed the door open with the tray and both guys jumped to their feet, seemingly prepared to fight whatever was coming at them. Stephan's face showed concern as he quickly approached Mariah.

"Whoa...what's wrong?"

"You fucking asshole." The words came out on a whisper. Hurt, anger and pain filled her every thought as she desperately tried to hold back the tears. "You asshole! You're enjoying me? Enjoying the fact that you have the ice queen in your bed? Well, don't fucking count on it ever happening again."

Stephan's face went carefully blank and he stopped a few feet from her. His calm demeanor just made her madder and she threw the tray of food at his feet. He jumped backward, narrowly missing getting splashed by the hot coffee. "You bastard! My best friend is missing and you're using this as a chance to get your dick wet! My best friend is missing because of *you*! Something you obviously forgot to mention to me because you knew you wouldn't get any if I knew. You used me, you fucker..." Dusty cautiously maneuvered around her and slunk down the stairs, out of the room. Mariah noticed, but Stephan was the one who deserved her wrath.

Stephan's eyes flashed red. He clenched his jaw and remained quiet. His posture was as rigid as a steel bar. Mariah's anger grew and grew. Tears blurred her vision but she wiped them away.

"I'm leaving. Now. Don't follow me. Don't look for me. I don't ever want to see you again."

"No." His eyes went from red to black in an instant, and Mariah shivered at the darkness she saw reflected there.

"Yes. I am. I'll be safer away from you."

One second he was feet from her, the next he had her pressed against the wall, his arms blocking her in. "No. I can't let you leave."

"Can't...or won't?" Mariah struggled against his arms but he held his body against hers to stifle her movements. His erection found her pussy and she struggled harder, ignoring the automatic throbbing reaction of her cunt. Damn body hadn't caught up with what was going on yet. "You can't hold me against my will. I want away from you. You're the reason I'm being stalked, you're the reason my best friend is missing. When I'm away from you, I'll be safe again."

"No." His voice was little more than a growl. "You're staying here. I'm not gonna chase you around town trying to protect you. You got no idea what these Dread Lords are capable of...what they'll do to you if they get their hands on you." His voice and eyes both softened for a moment. "I'll make it better, I promise." His eyes flashed red once more. "And if you think I'm bad? I'm nothin' compared to what they would do to you." He leaned into her and nuzzled her neck, his tongue laving her skin to her ear. He whispered, "And right now, I'm all you've got."

"Bastard," she whispered back at him. She stiffened against his assault on her senses and pushed him away. This time he let her. She slapped him, but he continued to stare her down, his only noticeable movement that of his jaw tightening. She turned her face away as the tears blurred her vision again, and she wiped her neck and ear where he'd tasted her.

Out of the corner of her eye, she saw him start toward her again, but then he stopped. "Get back downstairs. Now. You're not safe up here. And you're not going anywhere else, either." Stephan's voice was ice cold. "Look, I don't have time to deal with you and get your friend back. Go." He pointed toward the door.

Mariah turned back to face him, her anger and pain overflowing. "You still think you're the hero? What a joke. You're the reason Twyla is missing. You're the reason I'm in danger. You damn well better bring her back! The losers who give me money to dance for them are more heroic than you are." His eyes flashed something but in her rage she couldn't figure out what. "They know their place and they know where the fantasy ends. And since you obviously don't, I'll make it very clear for you. Your fantasy just ended. I'll go back downstairs, not because you told me to, but because I don't want you wasting time following me when you should be finding Twyla. I'll wait for you to bring her back to me and then it's over. You've received your payment in full."

As she turned to leave, she saw Twyla's favorite good luck outfit in a heap next to the computer on the desk. She walked the few feet toward the clothes in a pained daze. They were shredded nearly beyond recognition. Her stomach dropped and blood rushed to her head. Dizziness overwhelmed her. Twyla was dead. She had to be dead. Mariah held onto the desk to keep from collapsing. "What the hell did you do to my best friend?" Tears welled in her eyes in spite of herself. She bit her lip and forced the tears back. She would not cry again in front of this worthless creep of a man. Twyla was dead…was she next?

"I didn't do a damn thing to her. I'm trying to find her."

Lover's Talisman

"Yeah, fucking me is the best way to go out and look for a person. She's dead anyway, isn't she?"

Stephan's voice was little more than a growl. He stood close to the wall, his hands tightly fisted at his sides in barely restrained fury. "Just because her clothes are wasted, doesn't mean she is, okay? You have no idea. No fucking idea everything I'm doing for you. Go back downstairs. I'll bring her to you when I get her."

Her hands clasped the tattered remains of Twyla's clothes. There was something wrapped inside them. She pulled out the blue and silver bead necklace Twyla had made for her, the same necklace that had been missing since the night she was attacked…the night Stephan said he'd saved her. Rage exploded inside of her.

"Why the fuck do you have this? Did you keep it that night? As some sort of trophy? What the fuck did you do and what does it have to do with Twyla?" She clenched the necklace to her chest, hating the man she'd only one hour ago thought she might love.

He pushed himself away from the wall and approached her, anger evident in every move. Mariah actually thought he might want to strike her. She held herself still, but she was afraid. He stopped several feet from her, his breathing ragged. It was obvious he was barely restraining himself. The distance between them pulsed with angry energy.

Stephan's voice was loud and harsh as he spoke. "Trophy? Hey, it was with her clothes. Mariah, don't you get it? It was supposed to be you! They wanted you. They wanted to take you out to break me down, but they grabbed the wrong girl. They obviously know they've got the wrong girl and that's why you aren't safe up here. So, get your ass back downstairs where you belong. I already promised I'd get Twyla back. What more do you want from me?"

There was a lot she'd wanted from him, but obviously she'd been very mistaken. Mariah's hands shook as she picked the necklace up and put it on. "Twyla made this necklace, put a protection spell on it to keep me safe from all the assholes in the world. I lost it when I met you, which is obviously when I needed it most. Bring her back to me..." She took a deep breath and stared hard into his eyes, letting her disdain show. "If she is dead, I will kill you. I don't care who you are or what you think you stand for. If Twyla isn't brought back to me safe and unharmed, I'll destroy you." She bit her tongue before she could say anything worse. If he really was going to bring Twyla to her, she couldn't let him hear what she really thought of him.

He charged toward her, closing the distance between them, harsh determination on his face. She didn't give him the chance to forcibly push her back downstairs. She turned and walked back down the stairs, visually cool and composed...but inside she was dying. She'd known better than to even think about falling in love but her heart hadn't listened. Men were all the same, they just wanted to get their dick wet. She'd stick with the ones that paid her for their fantasies. Money may not be a warm bedmate, but neither was a broken heart.

Chapter Ten

Stephan watched Mariah walk down the stairs, taking his heart with him. His chest was tight and the pain was almost unbearable. He couldn't recollect the last time he'd felt quite as lost. Her words rang in his ears seemingly louder than she'd screamed them at him. There was nothing like having the woman you love tell you off to make you realize you can't live without her. He took off his glasses with a sigh.

Stephan stopped himself from following Mariah down the stairs. Stopped himself from begging her forgiveness, picking her up, and kissing and loving her until she realized that they belonged together. It was what he wanted to do, but he had to prove himself to her first. She'd pointed out all the stuff he knew he'd done wrong. Boy did she know how to go for the gut. And surprisingly, she was worth the agony.

Stephan clicked-in to Jake.

Sorry man, time to wake up. I need you to watch Mariah.

Whaaa-t? Jake's voice was groggy and Stephan almost felt guilty for waking him up. But someone had to watch Mariah, and it couldn't be himself.

Watch Mariah. Downstairs. Make sure she doesn't leave. She's not happy, but she can't go anywhere.

Yeah, okay, got it.

She can't leave. Understood?

I said 'Got it,' didn't I? I may be asleep, but I ain't deaf. What the hell crawled outta your ass this morning?

Just keep her down there. Stephan clicked-out.

He looked at the floor and the food that covered it. Coffee mixed with egg and toast to form a large, wet mess. She'd made him breakfast...and included the jam they'd both so much enjoyed last night. He hurriedly scooped up the mess and deposited it into the sink. She loved him back, or had loved him until she'd overheard his stupid comments to Dusty. That would teach him to try to make light of something that was so obviously not. Why'd he try to convince himself it wasn't love? He couldn't even remember now. Well, it didn't matter. She was his. And everything in his being wanted to make things right. He'd be the hero she once thought he was.

He should have told Mariah the truth about Asfar immediately. Well, he couldn't change his mistakes now. But he would make them up to her, starting by getting Twyla back. After that, he'd make sure Mariah was completely safe and secure—preferably in his arms every night.

He grabbed his leather jacket and checked to make sure that all his assorted weaponry was stored in the secretly concealed pockets. He had a battle ahead, and not just with the Dread Lords. The real battle would happen when he told the guys he was going to marry Mariah, if she'd have him. He already knew the havoc that would wreak. But he didn't care. It didn't matter. She was his and he couldn't live without her. She had awakened him in so many different ways. He'd forgotten what it was like to feel something other than hate and disdain.

He pushed through the small door that separated the backroom from the main room of the import store. Marlin stood up from the counter and faced him.

"So, you did it. It's over with her. Good for you."

"Not quite. I'll make it right." Stephan kept walking toward the front door. He had places to go, a girl to rescue and his woman to win back. It was going to be a busy day.

"Wait...excuse me? You 'not quite' ended it? What the hell's that supposed to mean? That's not what it sounded like to me."

"Did you love Judy?" Stephan turned to face Marlin. He had to hear the words directly from his brother.

"Yeah, of course I did."

"So, you know the magic you felt with her...this same craziness that I can't get outta my head—"

"Yeah. It's called love and it doesn't go away."

"I don't want it to go away. And I'm not gonna let anything make it go away. We're older and have our shit more together now than we did then. We can deal with it now. I'm not livin' without her. End of discussion."

Marlin's eyes widened. "Oh, bullshit, end of discussion. Yeah, we got our shit together more now, but that doesn't change the worst of it. The fucking Dread Lords are in town. Ryan clicked-in and told me. Your life is in worse danger than it was before. And Mariah will be in that constant danger, too. Let her go."

"Mariah will be in constant danger only because I love her. I'd rather be by her side protecting her from that constant danger than let it take her away. I know we love each other. I know we'll make it work."

"Oh that's just bloody, fuckin' great. You're spouting love and poetry and we're all gonna die because you got caught up in a great fuck."

Stephan's rage mounted. He crossed to the counter and leaned over into Marlin's face. His brother stared back, his eyes mirror images of Stephan's rage. "She's going to be your fucking sister-in-law and you're gonna treat her with the respect she deserves. Y'know, if she was really just a fuck, would I be this pissed off? Would I give a shit about how she felt or what she thought of me? Would I care if she was just some piece of ass? No! She isn't a fuck, she's everything I care about." Stephan paused to take a breath. "Look, Marlin, I know you loved Judy, and I know that you regret that part of your life because you lost her. But I can't live my life without Mariah because of what happened to you. Now, I'm gonna go find Twyla, bring her back here, and go about proving to Mariah that we should be together."

"You don't wanna do this."

"Yes, I do. It's the first thing I've wanted in a very long time."

Stephan turned and exited the shop, his stride long and determined. This was going to be a good day. He wouldn't let it end any other way.

Marlin watched Stephan walk out of the shop. Shit. This was going to get so much worse before it got better...if it got better. Stephan had no idea the pain he was opening himself up for. There was nothing that could take that pain away. Nothing.

He wanted to hit something, kick something, preferably Stephan, to knock some sense into his love-fucked brain. He'd been there, hell, he was still there. Judy still haunted him, everyday, every night. Every woman he fucked was the woman he was with because he'd let Judy die. That would never go away.

God, he hoped Mariah was worth it.

* * * * *

Mariah stood just inside the doorway to the stairs. Where was she supposed to go? What was she supposed to do? She didn't want to be here anymore. Everything about this place reminded her of Stephan, about the night they'd shared, and about the fool he'd made of her.

She leaned against the wall next to the door, and sighed. Why did she let herself fall for guys who were dangerous? What was wrong with her? She wiped the tears from her eyes. Fucking Michael...fucking Stephan. Why did the bastards pick her?

It had to be genetic. Growing up, her mom had always told her that to give of your heart was the biggest mistake you could make. Yet her mom hadn't been able to follow her own advice.

Three marriages, dozens of live-in boyfriends...and she'd never been happy. Oh, she'd go on for awhile with each of them, thinking they were the one, then one after another, the men would show their true nature, and out the door they'd go…usually taking money, jewelry and anything else they could get their hands on—one of them even took the toilet seat. Mariah had learned not to think of any of them as more than passing through, and to keep hidden away anything she didn't want to disappear with them.

Mariah had never even known her father. He'd disappeared from her mother's life a few months before she was born. Mariah's mom had never really seemed to get over him. She wouldn't talk of him, but there was a look in her eyes when he was mentioned…a look Mariah had never forgotten. Her mom had been desperately in love with him, and seemed to spend the rest of her life searching for the same thing with someone else, just never finding it.

The last one of them all could claim the serious bastard prize though—Bruce. He'd actually been around the longest, almost one full year, when her mom had died of a heart attack— Mariah figured her heart had finally just stopped, tired of searching for the elusive "one" that didn't exist.

Mariah was just out of high school, a few weeks past her eighteenth birthday, and suddenly alone in the world. Hours after her mother's sparsely attended funeral, she'd curled up in bed and cried herself to sleep, still dressed in her white blouse and black denim skirt—the closest thing she'd had to a mourning outfit.

A short time later she was awakened to a shifting of the bed next to her, then a hand slid up her arm and clamped down hard on her shoulder. Sticky warm, stale beer breath wafted over her, almost knocking her out with its powerful odor. Bruce's voice, crackled and rough with the abuse of smoking, sent a chill down her spine. "You're so pretty lying there, just like your mother." The hand not holding her pinned to the bed started on the buttons at the bottom of her blouse. "I've watched you both in your sleep so many times. The inviting way you move and sigh…you knew I was watching you. You were just waiting…we don't have to wait anymore."

She'd lain there, almost frozen in fear, until he'd undone the last button and slid the blouse open to reveal her lacy bra. She had seen a sickness in his eyes, a desire for her, and she'd panicked. Grabbing the small lamp she kept next to her bed, she slammed him repeatedly…first on the side of his head, and then over and over, wherever she could reach, until she was sure he wasn't going to come after her.

The last thing she'd seen as she ran from the room was his blood staining her white floral sheets. She later learned he hadn't died…which seemed almost a pity. If only she'd hit him harder.

Just a few days later she met Michael, and spent two years believing she'd met the man she'd spend forever with. She'd been happy and in love…

Until he tried to kill her.

Mariah shook her head. She sure knew how to pick 'em.

Her thoughts flew back to the present as a strange man entered the living room area, from the hallway. She quickly wiped away the tears she hadn't been aware were flowing freely down her face. This man didn't need to see her cry.

He sauntered over to her, his hair mussed, eyes half closed with sleep. "I'm Jake. I'll be your baby-sitter today." He yawned and stretched. "I'm usually a lotta fun to be around, so work with me. I'll wake up and entertain you…or somethin'." He rubbed his hand over his face and looked at her, his striking, deep blue eyes almost pleading. "You wouldn't happen to know if there's any coffee, would you?"

She wanted to hate him. Wanted to put him in the same barrel with the rest of the stinky fish around here. He was holding her against her will. It was too bad he looked like an overgrown kid in desperate need of a haircut to tame the random curls springing up into his mop of a "hairdon't." It made him harder to hate.

"I made coffee earlier. There should be some left in the kitchen."

Lover's Talisman

"And if I go get it, you gonna try to scat?"

Mariah just glared at him, refusing to honor that with an answer.

"Yeah, that's what I thought. Come on. Don't fight. I'm really, really too tired to fight." Jake turned and headed for the kitchen. For half a second she was tempted to try to escape, but ignored that idea, knowing she couldn't get away when he was so close, and not wanting to ruin future escape attempts by pissing him off now and getting herself tied up or otherwise incapacitated.

An hour later she was still waiting for a chance to get away. Jake was crashed out on the couch, with her on the recliner, and they were watching some bad 80's movie that she was pretending to enjoy. She kept waiting for him to nod off, but he managed to keep one eye on her, and one eye on the movie.

During the obligatory movie love scene, the exaggerated moans and sighs from the actors shook Mariah straight to her core. Stephan had been an amazing lover, dammit! He'd really seemed to care about her, about what she wanted. When she'd looked into his eyes, she'd seen more than just desire...she would have sworn there had been something in him worth betting her future on.

This morning he'd seemed almost shocked by her words, and pained by her reactions. Before he'd closed himself off...and ripped into her like it was all her fault. *Asshole*.

He'd been wearing wire-rimmed glasses and looked damn good in them. It was strange the things she could remember now. When he'd jumped up and approached her as she barreled through the door, in that brief moment, she'd seen love in his gaze. She shook her head. He was a lying bastard who bragged about getting her into his bed. He wasn't worth any more thought. She just needed to get out of there, find Twyla, and then get the hell out of town for awhile, until things calmed down.

She glanced over at Jake. His eyes were closed and his chest rose and fell in the rhythm of sleep. Quietly, she lifted herself out of the recliner, thankful that the expensive leather didn't creak when she stood. Her bare feet padded silently over the plush carpet. She didn't have shoes, but she'd find something once she got out of there. Nothing else mattered, she just needed to get free.

She snuck a quick glance back at Jake, who hadn't moved. He obviously hadn't thought she was really a flight risk. Well, she'd show them. She turned back around and placed her hand on the doorknob and squealed as she was lifted up from behind.

"Damn it, Mariah. I told you I was tired. Why couldn't you have just watched the movie? It's a good movie." Jake carried her back to the couch and put her down, seating himself right next to her. Mariah stood up. Jake reached up, grabbed her and pulled her back down again.

She turned toward him and put on her "evil-eye" stare. Jake shrugged his shoulders. "Look. I don't know what's up with you and Stephan. He's been acting like a bear with a thorn in his paw since I first saw him earlier this morning. But, whatever happened between the two of you, he asked me to keep you safe, and I gotta do that. So, please, don't fight me on this. You won't win and wouldn't it be better if we just spent some nice time together watching a movie? We can talk…I'll talk about anything. It's up to you." Jake sat back on the couch.

Mariah watched Jake for a moment, and then sat back into her corner of the couch. She didn't want to talk about Stephan. She needed to try to get him out of her mind…and her heart. But sitting here watching a bad movie wasn't going to free her mind of its battle. *Oh, what the hell?* She might as well learn something about what these guys supposedly did to protect the world.

"Okay. Tell me about being a Shadow Walker."

"You wanna hear about life as a Shadow Walker…hmmm…okay." Jake grinned. "Bein' a Shadow Walker is a big pain in the ass, but it's better than what I used to do."

"What did you use to do?"

Jake's grin widened. "I used to get into a lot of fights and get my ass kicked. It sucked pretty hard. Now I still get in fights, but at least I know I'm doing some good."

"Born troublemaker. Okay, I get it." Mariah smiled up at him. She didn't want to be enjoying herself so much, but Jake was sweet and cute and nothing to look at next to Stephan—but she wasn't going to think about that now. Jake's eyes sparkled mischievously while he talked, unlike Stephan who's eyes flared with passion. *Oh hell!* Jake's eyes would probably flare with passion too if they had sex—flaring passionate eyes did not mean love! She tried to shove her thoughts of Stephan into her mental trashcan. Men were not worth wasting precious brain reserves.

Must ask more questions. "So, how'd it happen? Being a Shadow Walker, I mean. Is it, like, genetic or something?" Mariah laughed at the amused expression on Jake's face. "Sorry for all the questions, but if I'm forced to stay here, I might as well learn something about this strange existence I've never heard of before."

"Nah, that's cool. Well, it kinda just happened abruptly. Like, either die, or fight the forces of darkness. I can't really tell outsiders too much, but if Stephan even brought you down here, I guess I can say some stuff to you. You haven't freaked out too much yet."

"No more than any woman being held against her will by a group of rich bachelor businessmen claiming to be heroes fighting paranormal activity, would freak out, right?" Saying it out loud made her realize that most women would kill to be in her place, even if this place was reminiscent of the Twilight Zone. "Hey, weren't you guys named Talisman Bay's most eligible bachelors last year or something? Didn't I read something in the paper about an auction and raising all sorts of money for charity?"

"Oh yeah. Not our finest hour. Nothing like having to take out a bunch of old matrons with larger pocketbooks than good sense. I mean, it was for a good cause, but man, the lady who got me was old enough to be my great-grandma. And she had wandering hands." Jake shuddered dramatically. "Nah, I'd prefer to fight all kinds of demons before going through that again." He laughed and shook his head.

"But, I think Marlin got the worst raw deal. All the ladies wanted him so they auctioned him off near the end. Y'know he was all smiley and kooky and stuff and these women were just goin' higher and higher until it got down to a war between this real hot young chick and her grandma. Yeah, grandma...she was like ninety years old or something. And apparently she had the bigger checkbook! Yeah, Marlin won't talk about Gertrude too much. She must have traumatized him or somethin', I dunno. Hell, maybe she rocked his world." Jake grinned and winked.

"Anyway, that hot young chick bid on Stephan. I figured something would come of it, but he flat out said that blondes don't do anything for him. He likes brunettes. Yeah, with real boobs, too." Jake paused and a blush lit up his features as he eyed her chest before quickly turning away. "Yeah, um...Stephan doesn't like any of those built up chicks. He likes the real deal or nothing at all. That's one of the reasons he doesn't really date. He..." Jake paused again, then continued in a stumbling rush. "Uh actually he thinks it's more important to keep the city safe."

Jake trailed off but Mariah was still lost in what he'd said. Stephan liked real breasts, which would explain why he'd practically worshipped hers last night. She was one of the few dancers at *Silver Twilight* who was still au naturale. She shook her head and her hair flew in her face. Her brunette hair. She scowled. It didn't matter. She cleared her mind and smiled up at Jake again.

"So, tell me what's in that big cabinet over there." She pointed toward the gleaming cherry wood cabinet that had tempted her curiosity since she'd first noticed it yesterday. "It must be important if you keep a lock on it, even down here."

Lover's Talisman

"Just fightin' gear. Nothing special. We gotta have all sorts of toys if we're playing with demons and stuff. I mean, most of it I don't even know what it's called. I just grab what looks like what I'll need if I know what kind of bad thing I'm gonna fight. We keep it locked just in case. 'Sides, we wouldn't want Dusty to wander home drunk and start playing with stuff again. He hasn't done that for a while, but last time, he accidentally shot off this harpoon thing and if Stephan hadn't been so quick on his feet, he'd've lost them. We just learned it's a good thing to keep it locked in any case. But you probably really want me to tell you some kind of story, right? Do you want tales from the dark side, or what?"

"Yeah. Doesn't matter. Tell me a good story." *Preferably about Stephan…No! No! No! I don't like him anymore. Moving on…moving on…brain, dammit, start moving on!*

"Okay. Have you heard the one about the water demon?" Jake kicked his feet up onto the coffee table, locked his hands behind his head, and settled in for his story.

She shook her head no, trying to shake out all remaining thoughts of Stephan at the same time. As time went on, it was getting harder to hate him for his actions. She was still mad, and still hurt, but maybe…. Jake's story interrupted her inner diatribe.

"Well, this was a long time ago. Almost ten years ago now. We didn't know what we were doing yet, but we knew that the thing was bad. I was crawlin' around on the buildings. Marlin was going down alleys and stuff in the shadows. Ryan and Dusty were just walkin' in plain sight.

"I was the one who called for back-up. Those were the days when we didn't patrol by ourselves all the time. Anyway, I saw a big ol' puddle of water shift into something more human-shaped so the guys were gonna check it out with me. So, the thing attacks Dusty and Ryan. But it's like water so what can you do? It made a mess of them. Marlin shot right through it. He'd've wasted its brain if it had one. Damn, he was always a good shot. I tried to jump down on it, but I fell right through it.

So, here all four of us are, totally soaking wet and trying to fight something that can't be fought and losing horribly because it was suffocating us like we'd jumped into the ocean without taking a big breath first.

"So Stephan shows up and annihilates it in like two seconds. We'd've died if he hadn't figured out that water would take the shape of whatever container it was in. The darn thing had so much space what with covering all four of us that Stephan grabbed one of those big fifty gallon garbage cans and fitted it over the top of the thing while he shouted for us to just drop to the ground and roll away. So we all did that and there Stephan stood looking at this upside down garbage can with a perplexed look on his face. I mean, he got us out, but we still had to get rid of the thing.

"He clicked-in to see what Fiero knew about water demons. Turns out, chlorine will kill them so Stephan grabbed a lid and we lifted the edge up so he could get the lid under it. We all carried it down the street to the community pool and just dumped it in and it died. We all looked at each other all soaking wet except Stephan and just started bustin' up because that was the weirdest thing we'd seen yet. It was kind of like an initiation into the super duper weird shit and if Stephan hadn't been usin' his brain, we'd've totally been dead.

"He does that kind of shit all the time. I mean, Marlin'll save the day a lot. Dusty kicks a lot of ass, but Stephan, man…he's got to be the biggest hero kind of guy. He'll go runnin' right into a fight without even taking into consideration how big the demon is. And he always wins, too. 'Cuz he's smart. Me, I just snoop around and look for stuff. I try not to fight too much with my hands. I'm more inclined to use little things like knives or throwing stars or stuff like that. Stephan uses everything he's got. I mean, he'll use a gun if he's packin'. He'll use knives. Whatever. And he fights dirty, too. I've seen him kick a guy in the balls to save this chick that was gonna be raped. Man, he's dirty, but he gets the job done when it comes to stuff he really cares about." Jake paused in his lengthy storytelling. "What's that look on your face?"

"Nothing...nothing. I think I'm just going to watch this movie after all. It looks like it's going to get better." She turned away from Jake's perplexed expression, pulled her knees to her chest and pretended to get involved in the movie.

She hadn't understood much of what Jake had said. Clicking-in? Water demons? But she'd understood that the rest of the guys admired Stephan, just by the look in Jake's eyes and the awe in his voice when he spoke of him. What did it all mean? Was she wrong in her accusations and anger toward him? But he had lied to her...he'd admitted as much to Dusty. And he had used her for sex, hadn't he? But dammit, it wasn't as though she'd have fought it. She'd wanted him, even if it was just for the one night. Truthfully, she'd used him too.

She laid her head down on her knees and closed her eyes. Her hands clasped the necklace Twyla had made for her, her fingers rubbing the beads around her neck as though it was a rosary. Twyla had made the necklace for her, as a talisman against evil. Too bad it hadn't worked. So much had gone wrong. Mariah swallowed a sob. She just wanted Twyla back. Once she was back, it would all be over and she could try to figure out the rest of the mess inside of her head.

She chose to ignore the pain in her heart that told her life would never be the same again.

Chapter Eleven

It seemed like forever to get out of that God-forsaken maze, but Twyla managed to escape its twists and turns. She let her instinct tell her when to zig and when to zag and when to duck out of sight of the enemy.

Her frozen bare feet pounded the boards of the pier as she headed for the import store. Mariah had to be there with those hot men. And getting closer to any kind of heat enticed her just that much more. Freeze's shirt helped a little, but all it really seemed to do was make her tingle with the cold as much as the pleasure.

Rare and Unusual Imports. That was the place. She pushed open the door and charged right in. There, behind the counter, stood one of the most amazingly gorgeous men she'd ever seen. His chocolate brown eyes widened as a crooked grin brightened his face. Twyla just plowed right for the counter.

"Damn, you're a hot one even up close. Where's Mariah?" Twyla searched the store for another exit behind the counter. Freeze's tingly shirt was relentless. And this man certainly wouldn't be kicked out of Twyla's bed without a great romp or two or three or four. He grabbed a black silk kimono-like robe from a rack behind the counter and handed it to her like she should cover up or something. "Hell, I've worn less than this to the grocery store. Where the fuck is Mariah? Is she here, Prettyboy?"

"Actually, you just look cold. Uh…Twyla?" His voice was like velvet. With bedroom eyes plus that smooth voice, Twyla safely assumed he'd be a great lay if the situation ever arose. She took a mental note to work on that.

"Yeah." Was he dense? "Why else would I come here?"

"Are you okay? Where were you? How'd you...?" Prettyboy still didn't move. Did he not sense the urgency? His eyes were on the door behind her.

"I'm tired. I'm cold. I've had it. Where's Mariah? Is she here? Hello? Can't a girl rescue herself when there's no hero to be found?" Twyla put on the kimono robe. The dragons on the back and sleeves were a nice touch.

"Ouch. Hey, my name's Marlin, not Prettyboy." He walked over to the door and flipped over a sign that read "Back in 10 Minutes."

"Whatever." Twyla followed him into the back room.

"I'll take you down there." Those damn pleasure tingles and the sight of Marlin's perfect masculine body from behind as he swaggered into the back room made Twyla even more impatient to find Mariah and get out of there.

"Wait, did you say downstairs? As in below the pier, swimming in the ocean, downstairs?"

"Yeah, you're quick. It's...um...kinda hard to explain."

"Ya know what? It doesn't matter. I've seen enough crazy shit in the last twenty-four hours. Just take me to Mariah so we can get the hell outta here."

Marlin unlocked a door and held it open for her, bowing gallantly and holding his arm out to show the way. "Ladies first."

"Just so you can watch my ass, huh, Prettyboy? I'll even shake it a little extra for ya." She heard Marlin stifle a laugh as she seductively walked down the stairs. Hell yeah, she'd play his game, especially if she could get him in bed someday.

The stairs ended at another closed door and she swung it open. She didn't have time for another show of gallantry from Marlin. She marched through the door and froze, spying Mariah fast asleep on the couch, in the arms of an equally sleeping man. "Well this place must be hell frozen over, because I never thought I'd see Mariah snoozing in the arms of a *man*. And even then, he really doesn't look like her type."

"Wh—Stephan came back?" Marlin stepped through the door behind her. "Oh, shit. Jake, wake up man."

Stunning blue eyes opened quickly, and Twyla's stomach dropped. For just one moment she'd seen ice blue eyes—Freeze's eyes. The pleasure tingles rippled through her body once again. She couldn't control the resulting shiver.

The man behind the eyes smiled up at her and began to rise, then seemed to realize that he had someone attached to him. "Well, hell. No wonder I was sleeping so good. Nothin' like the warmth of a beautiful woman to help you sleep. Mariah, wake up. You got company." He smiled up at Twyla again. "I take it you're the woman all the hubbub's been about?"

"Yeah. Sure. Mariah, wake your ass up. We gotta get outta here."

Mariah's eyes slowly opened and she blinked up in her direction. She gasped, eyes widening as she focused on Twyla. Jumping up, she threw her arms around Twyla. "I never thought I was going to see you again!"

"You should know I'm not that easy to get rid of." She squeezed Mariah back and swallowed the tears that threatened. Now was not the time to get mushy. It had to be the damn pleasure tingles still arcing from the shirt, weakening her constitution. Nothing to do with the fact that she'd doubted for a while she'd see Mariah again either.

Mariah stepped back, tears filling her eyes. "God, I've turned into a damn sprinkler system since you disappeared. Don't do that to me again! How'd you…" Mariah's eyes focused behind her. "Marlin? You brought her back to me?" Mariah stepped behind Twyla and threw her arms around Marlin. "Thank you! I could just kiss you!"

Twyla grinned, as Marlin actually appeared to struggle with what to do with the woman whose arms squeezed him tightly. His hands wandered over her back, as if he was afraid to actually touch her. "Um…Mariah—"

"Mariah, sweetie, as nice as Marlin's body must be to fondle, you should know by now I don't need a man to come riding to my rescue. I saved myself."

Mariah sprang free of Marlin's embrace and turned a blushing face back to Twyla. "Oh. Of course." Marlin just chuckled while raising a quick eyebrow at the guy still sitting on the couch. Hmmm...was Mariah having a fling with Mr. Blue Eyes? It was about time she got some action.

"C'mon, I'll explain all later. We've gotta get outta town for awhile. Get anything you've got here and let's get going."

"Sorry ladies. You're not going anywhere." Marlin sternly watched them both, back against the exit, arms crossed over his chest—which was nicely defined by the navy blue T-shirt he was wearing, she noticed.

"No time for games, Prettyboy—"

"I'm not playing games. You can't go anywhere. It's not safe for either of you out there."

"No shit. But it's definitely not safe with you guys either. That's why we're *leaving*." Twyla bounced from foot to foot, the pleasure tingles growing stronger the more agitated she got. She reached a hand back and grabbed Mariah's hand. "C'mon Mariah, let's go."

"I don't think—" Mariah started.

Marlin interrupted. "I'm sorry. I really am. As much as I'd like to, I can't in good conscience let you two leave here until I know it's safe. Now, just sit down and relax. We'll take good care of you. I promise."

Twyla was pissed. Why was everyone trying to take her control away? She could take care of herself, and Mariah if she had to. She stormed forward, pulling Mariah behind her, adrenaline pumping as the pleasure tingles practically took over her body with new force. "Damn it, Prettyboy, just get the hell outta my way!" With her free hand she pushed against Marlin's chest.

Twyla gasped, Marlin's eyes bugged and Mariah squeaked as a current of sexual electricity raced through them. Twyla bit her lip to keep from shouting as an amazing climax rocketed through her body. Marlin's eyes closed on a moan and she heard a whimper from behind her as Mariah squeezed her hand in a death grip. Holy shit! What had she done?

Marlin's eyes blinked open—oh yeah, he definitely had bedroom eyes. Using his right hand, he removed her hand from his chest and dropped it, stepping back and away. Distancing himself. "Yeah…thanks…I think. I gotta go back…reopen the shop. You two stay here. Jake…?" Marlin stumbled backward through the door and closed it after him. The sound of the door shutting brought Twyla out of her after sex, or at least after climax, stupor.

"What the hell did I miss out on here?" Jake's voice from behind awakened Twyla even further and she spun around to face him. She spotted Mariah out of the corner of her eye, still quivering from the after effects of her orgasm. Hell, poor girl, it was probably the first orgasm she'd had with a man around in years. Or maybe not if she was having a fling with Ol' Blue Eyes. She definitely needed to get that story out of Mariah in private, and find out exactly what was going on.

"You gotta room, Blue Eyes? Someplace Mariah and I can sit and talk and do girlie things without your watching eyes?" She needed to regroup, to plan, to figure out how the hell they could get out of there. And she needed to figure out what the hell she was capable of doing…

Mariah's voice whispered huskily, "My stuff, it's in a room down the hall. We can go there, right?" Twyla wanted to smile. She had never heard Mariah sound like a phone sex operator before. Mariah definitely needed to orgasm more often.

"Yeah, go ahead," Jake replied. "But I'll be out here if you need me." The fact that he'd be watching the door, watching their escape route, remained unspoken, but Twyla heard the warning in his words all the same.

Chapter Twelve

"What the hell did you do? And how the hell did you do it?" Mariah closed the door behind them both, and slid in a boneless heap to the floor. Her eyes focused past Twyla, and onto the unmade bed, and she shivered with the immediate flood of sensual memories. God, she'd had more orgasms in the last twelve hours than she'd probably had in the last couple of years combined.

Twyla sat down on the edge of the bed and raised an eyebrow at Mariah. "So, you gonna tell me or do I have to pry it out of you?"

"Tell you what?"

Twyla smirked. "Oh, please. I walk in down here, you're cuddled up asleep in some hot guy's arms and you're wearing a man's T-shirt. Now, I gotta admit, I'm surprised, because he really didn't look like your type—"

"Wait. Hold it! Jake? No! Not Jake."

"Well, it wasn't Marlin. I could tell by the way he held you when you threw yourself at him—which, by the way, smart move on your part. Feeling up those goods. Yum. Next time, grab his ass, though. I wanna know if it feels as hot as it looks." Twyla grinned and licked her lips. Mariah couldn't help but laugh.

"Yes, he's very nice to look at and touch. But, you're changing the subject. What did you do out there to us?" Wait, was that a blush shadowing Twyla's cheeks? Good, get the focus off of her confusing sex life and onto Twyla's interesting new ability.

"Girl, if you can't figure out what an orgasm is, I don't think I can be of any help to you." Twyla fidgeted and for once, didn't meet her eyes.

"Oh, don't you try that with me. I *know* what an orgasm is! But how did you do that?"

Twyla began to pick at imaginary lint on the kimono robe. "Well, that's a harder question to answer. I dunno."

"You 'don't know' how with one touch you managed to take all three of us on a sexual roller coaster? I didn't think I could handle any more orgasms…" Mariah froze and peeked at Twyla, hoping her last admission would go unnoticed. No such luck. Twyla's eyes lit up and a grin covered her face.

"Well, shit! You *did* get laid. I was guessing, but you just confirmed it. Why didn't you tell me the second we walked in here? Hello! I'm your best friend. I need all the dirty little details. I gotta know how long. I mean, was he a real man, or just a boy? And was it, like, three minutes or three hours? And how many times, how many positions, and if you were really, really naughty, how many men? So, spill it!"

"You're changing the subject again."

"Oh, no. That's not gonna work this time. Your new and improved sex life is much more important than my accidental orgasm zap."

Mariah swallowed. Then swallowed again. Then she sighed. "It was wonderful. Knock me off my feet, world spinning, life altering sex." She sighed again. "But it was a one time deal. And it shouldn't have happened. I wasn't thinking straight. Hell, I wasn't thinking at all. At least not with my brain." She forced a smile, trying to make her heart stop hurting with every thought that she would never be in Stephan's arms again. She still wanted to be mad at him for what he'd said earlier, and for not telling her the truth about Twyla's disappearance, but with Twyla back and safe, it was getting harder and harder to stay angry with him. He'd tried to protect her. How could she fault him for that?

Twyla stood up from the bed, came over and slid down the wall next to Mariah. "Hey, I've been telling you to get laid, nothing more. Honey, why'd you go and get your heart involved? You silly girl. And don't try to deny it. I see that look in your eyes."

Mariah leaned her head on Twyla's shoulder. "There's just something about him. I can't explain it. He—"

"Okay, not meaning to interrupt, but I'd like to put a face to who you're talking about here. Who'd you fuck? Although I bet I can guess. Stephan, right? The tallest one...dark brown hair, hazel eyes. Uh huh. I've seen him. Darkly intense...serious...but fucking hot!"

"Yeah...Stephan." Just saying his name aloud brought a pain to her chest. "Yesterday, I spent the whole day looking for you. I was worried out of my mind, going crazy. The police didn't help. They explained away the damage to your car saying you did it yourself."

"Wait, did you say my car was," she swallowed hard, "damaged? Oh God, please don't tell me my baby is hurt?"

"Hey, shut up, I'm getting deep here. Your car just needs a new convertible top, no biggie, okay? We have bigger things to worry about."

Twyla shrugged and then patted Mariah's leg. "Yeah, okay. Sorry, continue."

"So, Stephan offered to help. He was the first person all day yesterday who took charge, and I actually felt that with him, I'd have a chance at getting you back." Mariah took a deep breath and then continued. "We went to the house, so I could show him where I found your stuff, and your car. While we were there we were attacked by a werewolf—"

"Shit. That's probably the thing that attacked me that morning. Big, ugly, hairy thing, right? Long, drippy fangs...red eyes?"

"That's it. Stephan fought it...I mean, God, he protected me. The thing had grabbed me and was carrying me off, and he jumped right in and wrestled the thing so I could get away. He—he's a Shadow Walker. I guess it's some type of secret organization that fights against all these paranormal things that try to take over. All the guys are. In fact, this place we're in now is actually some other dimension."

Twyla nodded. "That makes sense. I always knew there was more out there. Too much weird stuff happens that no one can explain rationally."

"It's just hard to take it all in. I mean, I believe it, I have to, I've seen too much with my own eyes. But when I start to really think about it, it blows my mind." She stopped for a moment and took another deep breath. "Anyway, there was something between Stephan and I before the attack, and afterward, well, I came on to him pretty strong, and in no uncertain terms I let him know that I wanted him."

"Good girl. That's the way to do it."

"Yeah, well, we had an amazing night. It was an unbelievable way to end my celibacy streak. He's an incredible lover…attentive, and boy does the man have stamina." Mariah shared Twyla's grin. "But I really thought there was more to it. It was so intense. Being with him shook me to my core." Mariah stopped. She didn't want to share the fight, to relive the moment when her dream night had become just sex.

"Honey, good sex is awesome, you know that, I know that. Don't hurt yourself by wanting more. Keep your heart out of it." Twyla's hand squeezed her knee.

"I overheard him talking to another one of the guys this morning. Stephan knew I was a dancer, and had wanted me from the first moment he saw me on stage. He rescued me that first night, but I guess something he said put me in danger. Somebody's after me now, thinking they can get to Stephan and the Shadow Walkers through me. So, truthfully, it's Stephan's fault that you and I are in trouble." Mariah paused again, the pain eating her up inside. "I fought with him. Told him I wanted nothing to do with him because of what I'd overheard. But now I can't decide whether I did the right thing. I'm mad at myself, I'm mad at him." Her voice wavered as she finally spoke her feelings out loud. "I think I fell a little bit in love with him."

"It can happen, especially after a good romp. But, be careful, okay? Now is not the time to discover love." Twyla sighed. "And you're right. Someone is after you, I got that much from the guys who took me."

"Oh, God, Twyla! I'm horrible. I'm bitching about a disappointment in my love life when you just escaped. You're okay, right?" She was failing miserably with her friendship and with her sex life. She needed to get herself back together.

"Yeah, I'm fine. But there's a whole group of creeps after you. They wanna bring down the Shadow Walkers and probably kill you, too. We need to get you away from all of this." Twyla quickly stood up and rapidly paced around the room. Mariah watched her, almost smiling at how her dear friend was going to take over and make everything all right again.

"I don't know how we can get out of here. Jake will watch that door like a hawk. I tried to leave earlier while he was sleeping, and he still managed to keep me from escaping. I don't think a normal distraction will work. And anyway, don't you think we're safe down here?"

Twyla shook her head. "I dunno. All I know is that getting away from everyone around here seems like a good idea." She continued pacing. Then she glanced down and stopped dead in her tracks. "I gotta get me some pants! Our escape may require running and this thing'll trip me." She laughed as she swirled the billowing loose kimono robe.

"Yeah, and if you land on your ass, I'll probably end up on top of you. There's got to be something here you can wear." Mariah stood up and walked to the dresser and began rummaging through the drawers. Stephan's smell, his essence, wafted up from the clothing and she couldn't help but inhale it in deeply, settling it into her memory. Twyla may have been convinced that Mariah was just in lust, but the pain inside wasn't going away. Maybe it was just a crush, but she wished that she could have had more time to explore it.

She kept flashing back to the look in his eyes when she'd first confronted him. At any other time she would have thought that he felt more for her, too. But she was a lousy judge of character and should just stop thinking about that.

She pulled a pair of silk boxers from the back of the drawer. They still had tags attached. Turning, she tossed them to Twyla. "Here, try these. I don't think he'll miss them."

"Oh, you've got to be joking?" Twyla held up the boxers, emblazoned with happy faces.

"No, sorry. That's all I could find." Mariah laughed. "Besides, I think they'll look quite nice on you, and it's not like you haven't worn less."

Twyla grumbled as she pulled off the robe, exposing the man's dark gray T-shirt she was wearing underneath.

"Where'd you get the shirt? Stephan has your good luck outfit upstairs. I guess your kidnappers must have shredded it."

Twyla turned to face her as she stepped into the boxers. "Bummer. I loved that get up. Oh well, I'll get another one." She grinned at Mariah and winked. "I fucked one of my kidnappers and he gave me this shirt."

Mariah's jaw dropped. "What? You fucked a guy for a T-shirt? Did he force you?"

"No, in fact it was the best lay of my life." Twyla grinned and her eyes sparkled mischievously. "There was something about that guy. I dunno. Here. Try this thing on."

She easily pulled the shirt off over her head and threw it at Mariah. "What? Why do you want me to try it on?"

Twyla raised an eyebrow. "Just humor me, okay?"

Mariah shrugged and pulled off Stephan's T-shirt, and put on the other one. "Okay, what now?"

Twyla looked at Mariah, hands on her hips. "So, do you feel anything...anything unusual?"

"Um...no? Did you hit your head or something? You're acting weird."

"Well, hell, give it back to me then if it doesn't work for you." Twyla sighed happily as she pulled the T-shirt back over her head after Mariah handed it to her. Mariah put Stephan's T-shirt back on. She had to admit that she liked having that little bit of him close against her skin.

"So, what was that about? Why did you want me to try on that shirt?"

Twyla smiled at Mariah. "Freeze, the guy who I fucked and whose shirt I'm wearing, knows magic. He did something to this shirt, something that has caused it to give me these incredible pleasure tingles when I have it on. And since it didn't do anything for you, it means he probably did the spell specific to me." Twyla's grin widened. "God, he was an amazing fuck. It's too bad he's one of the bad guys. Anyway, I think this shirt had something to do with what I did out there. I think I somehow transferred the tingles when I touched both you and Marlin. Hell, I don't really know, but this shirt just might come in handy. I can already think of several uses for it on my own."

Mariah laughed and shook her head. "So, I was worried about you, and you were fucking the bad guy and enjoying it. You amaze me."

A serious expression crossed Twyla's face. "Honey, the bad guys really are after you. Just because I fucked my way through the situation doesn't mean you aren't in trouble. We have to get you somewhere safe. And I guess this is as inconspicuous as I'm gonna get." Twyla gave Mariah a quick hug. "We're going to be okay. I promise."

Mariah squeezed Twyla back. "You're back and you're safe. Things are already okay."

Twyla pulled away and Mariah saw tears welling in her eyes. But Twyla never cried, and Mariah watched the tears disappear as quickly as they had appeared. Twyla reached her hand out and lifted the necklace from Mariah's neck, confusion flickering in her eyes. "I thought you lost this when you were attacked. I overheard the kidnappers say that they located us through the scents on a necklace."

"It was with your bag of shredded clothes. Apparently, this was a part of the message they sent." Mariah shrugged. "I figured maybe the spell of protection would work better the second time around...and I just wanted something of yours to bring you closer to me."

Twyla closed her eyes, but kept her grasp on the necklace. Words quietly fell from her tongue, so whispered that Mariah couldn't catch their meaning before they were gone. The moment passed quickly and Twyla opened her eyes again, dropped her hand, and grinned. "Well, let's see if that spell works better this time."

Mariah wanted to ask her what she'd done to the necklace, but voices coming from the hall quieted them both. They both stepped up to the door and leaned against it, waiting to see what would happen.

Jake's voice came through loud and clear.

"I can't believe you're back, Ana. You look amazing. But why now?"

A woman's voice responded and Mariah strained to hear what she was saying. "It was time. Themonius actually came and got me, told me that it was time to fulfill my duties. Jake, something's started, something big. I don't know what it is, but this might not be something we can walk away from."

"We never walk away."

"No, I know that. I mean, this might not be something we can survive."

"Dread Lords have finally come to Talisman Bay. Personally, I'm not quakin' in my boots just yet, but I know they never give up. Once they get started, it's all over. I just know we can handle it."

"But it's not that simple. Themonius has never demanded I return before. I think it's bigger than this. I don't know... But I've been traveling for thirty-six hours straight to get here. I need a shower..." The voices were cut off as the door across the hall closed.

Twyla met her eyes. "Whoa, this is our window of opportunity. Jake's occupied. Let's go."

Mariah grabbed her purse and quickly glanced back at the bed. Her stomach dropped. She didn't want to leave like this. But Twyla knew what she was doing, and they needed to get away, to be safe. She followed Twyla through the open door and quietly closed it behind her. They ran down the hall, both of them barefoot, Mariah carrying her sandals in her hand since she hadn't had time to put them on.

None of the guys jumped out to stop them as they opened the door to the stairwell that would lead them to freedom. Mariah closed it behind her as Twyla climbed the stairs. Twyla opened the door at the top and peeked out. She turned, mouthing "all clear" and gestured for Mariah to run through.

Marlin could be heard making a sale in the front of the store. Mariah gestured to the back entrance and she and Twyla ran toward it. Mariah kept expecting someone to jump out, to stop them, but no one showed up. The door opened silently and they stepped out into freedom. Twyla grinned up at her. "Told ya I'd get us out of there. Now, let's get to the bus station and outta town for awhile."

She grabbed Twyla's hand as they ran down the back alley, away from Stephan, away from danger. God, she hoped they were doing the right thing.

* * * * *

Hey man, Twyla's here. She got away from the Dread Lords by herself. Damn, what a fox, too. I'll take a piece of that pie any day. Stephan nearly stopped in his tracks when Marlin clicked-in. It was a relief and a surprise that Twyla was resourceful enough to escape.

You got her there at the shop? Don't let her leave.

I took her down to Jake. He was already babysitting Mariah. You should see this girl. Wow! **Marlin laughed.** *She's fine. And she knows sex magic. Hot damn! She touched me and I came.*

Is that all you ever think about? Stephan headed for the flower shop where he'd wrestled and killed the L'Fail demon. He wanted to make sure everything was okay there before returning to the import store…and Mariah. From the sound of it, Marlin would make sure Twyla stayed. Women couldn't resist him.

Yeah. Usually. But I'm serious. She touched me, and Twyla, Mariah and I all came, just like that. I haven't come in my jeans since I first hit puberty. I don't think she meant it to happen, but hell, it was fuckin' amazing even though it was so weird.

Mariah? Stephan couldn't stop the jealousy that shot through him when he thought of Marlin witnessing Mariah climaxing. That visual should be his only.

Yeah, Mariah. Mariah and Twyla and me. Hell, my first ménage where we all remained fully clothed. Marlin chuckled and Stephan sent a blast of raw rage through their connection. Marlin just laughed louder. *All right, I'll stop talking 'bout it. I got the shop open and stuff, too. Get any good leads?*

Stephan went straight to business. *I scoped out entry into the Dread Lord compound. It's magically protected. Wait. You said Twyla got out?*

Yeah. By herself. Why? Marlin seemed to be planning as well.

That just answered my remaining question of which door to enter through once the magic is extinguished. Okay, I won't go in alone, but we'll storm these bastards. Take them down so hard they won't fuck with Talisman Bay again.

I'll be here. Marlin clicked-out.

Stephan smiled. Everything was going to work out.

But something still bothered him. Why did the Dread Lords show up after he'd claimed Mariah as his? It was almost like they'd been waiting…waiting for Stephan to make the first move. And what did that have to do with Mariah? Why would that have set them off?

Well, fuck them. Mariah was more important. Once he made things right with her, he'd work on eradicating those bastards.

Stephan walked into the flower shop after doing a quick inspection of the outside. No trace of demon. His men had done well once again.

"Hi Stephan! What can I help you with today? I haven't seen you since the last Chamber of Commerce meeting…" The clerk bubbled over with enthusiasm as she came around the counter to greet him.

"Yeah, I've been busy with the store." He smiled at the woman who was glowing at him. *What was her name?* He slyly glanced at her nametag. "Jill, I heard your window got busted in the other night. Was anything taken?" Stephan nonchalantly inspected the floor where he'd killed the demon. Still not a trace.

"That was the strangest thing. I checked the safe and all my nice pots and equipment. Everything was still here. I'm just counting my blessings that the broken window only damaged a few flowers." She wiped her hands on her apron, her smile still shining brightly. "Have you had any problems over at your store?"

"No. That's why I was curious about yours. I'm just hoping it was an accident and whoever did it was too afraid to stick around and pay up. Talisman Bay doesn't need any vandals trying to cause problems." Stephan put on his best fellow business owner smile.

Truthfully, he wanted to celebrate. Just two nights ago, he'd grumbled about love and roses and how it could never happen to him. Yet here he was, back in that same shop, and all he wanted to do was buy some flowers for the woman he'd so quickly fallen in love with.

Jill brought him out of his love musings with her reply. "Oh. Well. No one saw anything, unfortunately." She paused, giving him a knowing look. Her smile grew even wider. "I don't think you came here just to check up on me though, did you? I know that confused guy look anywhere."

"Am I that obvious?" If Jill could tell, he figured the whole world must know by now.

"I've seen the look is all." She winked as she slid closer to him. "So, how long have you known her? Is she just a friend or do you want something that says a little more than that?"

"Well, um...I don't really know." Jill was going to think him a fool if he couldn't even answer her simple question. "How about these?" He picked up some white flowers, hoping that whatever they were, they were appropriate for sharing his feelings.

"Wouldn't you rather have a pretty bouquet?" She led him to a refrigerated area with bouquets in water. He had no idea that shopping for flowers could be this complicated. There were reds and pinks and yellows and on and on and on. He just wanted to grab something, anything, and get out of there.

"This may sound crazy, but what about one of each of all of these?" He pointed to a section of flowers in a wide variety of colors. He recognized some roses, but that was about it. He really had no idea what he was doing. Hopefully Mariah wouldn't be able to tell that he was clueless.

"You must really have a thing for her, huh?" Jill immediately began to gather together the best flowers of each bunch.

"With each moment that passes, I do believe my thing for her is blooming as plentifully and as colorfully as these flowers."

Oh God. Did he just say that out loud? Marlin was right. Love had turned him into a stupid fuck. If his *blooming* speech got out, he'd never be taken seriously again. He could hear the snickers now from everyone else on the board of the Chamber of Commerce. And if the guys heard about this...Stephan barely repressed a groan. The only hope he had was if Jill kept his sappy little outburst to herself. Although watching Jill as she properly wrapped the flowers, his hope waned. She looked ready to burst with glee over what he'd said to her. His heart sank...but at least Mariah would know how he felt about her. Nothing like a little humiliation to put things into perspective.

"I'm sure she will cherish these for a long time." Jill winked and Stephan wished she would go a little faster. He had to get out of there before he said anything else stupid. Not to mention he was ready to go back to *Rare and Unusual Imports* to make things right with Mariah and to set a future with her in motion. Slowly but surely, things were getting better. He'd figure out what to do about the Dread Lords and the rest of the horrors later.

"I certainly hope so. Thank you very much." Stephan walked out of the store with a spring in his step and a smile on his face. Both of which lasted all the way back to the import store.

Marlin was behind the counter. "Ana's back. What's with the flowers?"

"Ana's here? What the hell is going on? I never thought we'd see her again. How is she? Did she say why she came back? Is it because of the Dread Lords?" He chose not to respond to the flower question, but the reappearance of Ana was not a topic he'd let slide.

"I hope you're not trying to get Mariah back, man." Marlin stepped aside as Stephan headed for the back room.

"Maybe I haven't learned a damn thing from your experience, but I'd like to try a few things a little differently. Did you talk to Ana at all? What does she know? Is everything okay?"

"I dunno. She just got here a little while ago. She looked good. She's definitely grown up." Marlin stayed in the back room as Stephan rushed down to the lower compound. Obviously, he'd have to talk to Ana himself to find out exactly what was going on, and why she'd come back now.

Jake sat on the couch watching television. He appeared rather tired, but awake nonetheless.

"Hey. Marlin said Ana's here? What's up with that? Did she say?"

"She's takin' a shower now. Themonius told her she had to get back here to fulfill her duties or something. She's pretty tired so she didn't explain in detail. What's with the flowers?" Jake shifted positions as he rubbed his tired eyes.

"Where's Mariah?" Stephan totally ignored Jake's inquiry about the flowers. He knew he'd end up enduring significant criticism from all the guys, but they could wait. He wanted to win her back first.

"She's in your room with Twyla." He pointed down the hall.

Stephan didn't waste a moment. He strode directly to his room. This would be where it would all begin. He'd tell her everything she wanted to know. He'd make her understand that he would give his life to keep her safe no matter what the Dread Lords, or anyone else, threw at them.

Fiero appeared right in Stephan's path. "Whoa. Sorry."

"That's okay." He tried to continue past Fiero, but he grabbed his arm and stopped him cold. "What's up, man?"

"I just need to talk to you for a second."

"Can it wait? I gotta go do something."

"No. Now. Sorry. I sort of screwed up I guess." Fiero looked quite uneasy, which was odd, unless he was bringing bad news from The Order.

"What is it?"

"I should have told you sooner, but the truth is, I wasn't really sure. I had to make sure before I said anything. Then again, it probably doesn't really matter anyway. I don't know." He took a deep breath. "I've been thinking about Mariah."

Stephan scowled. "And what have you been thinking?" Was Fiero going to start lecturing him about Mariah now? But Stephan immediately knew that wasn't it. Just looking at Fiero, he knew this was something bigger.

"Okay. When I was searching to see if she was harmed in any way, I discovered something about her." Fiero led Stephan down the hall out of earshot of Jake. "She had something brutal happen to her. She had horrible damage internally, lots of scar tissue.... Essentially, she couldn't have children."

Stephan's heart broke for Mariah. "Why are you telling me this? I'm sure she would've told me in time. Although, yeah, it's not exactly somethin' that would be brought up in regular conversation."

"Well, I wasn't gonna say anything, except that when I set the healing spell to heal all, I realized that it had healed something else as well. The lights paused and flared over her abdomen. I just wasn't thinking. I should have at least asked her first."

Stephan's heart began to pound a rapid crescendo. "Fiero, what are you trying to tell me? You healed her, right?" If she was healed, she could be pregnant. He actually smiled at the thought. Mariah large with his child. But she didn't know. Wouldn't have known. How was he going to explain *this* to her. *Oh sorry, Fiero healed you and I could have impregnated you last night, but please don't mind that and marry me and I'll take care of you and our children and make you happy....*

"I healed her completely. She can have children. I just thought you might want to know that in case—"

"I gotta go talk to her. Thanks, man." He walked away before Fiero could tell him anything else that would make life more difficult.

He went to knock on his bedroom door, but discovered that the door wasn't closed all the way so he lightly eased it open. If she was sleeping he didn't want to wake her. There was nothing worse than a grumpy woman being awakened from a good dream.

The room was empty. He tossed the flowers on the bed. "Jake! You said she was in here? Where is she? And Twyla?" Maybe they had just gone into another room. Jake arrived and looked around, his eyes widening.

"They were both in here. I swear it. Girl talkin' and stuff." He followed Stephan as he searched down the hall.

"Jake! What the fuck is going on here? This isn't like you, man? Where are they?"

"I'm sorry. When Ana got here, I had to show her where the towels were. I swear I was only gone for two seconds. Fuck!"

"No. No. This can't be happening." Stephan's mind reeled. His life had gone from the possibility of greatness, to shit in a matter of moments. Jake never screwed up like this. Maybe Twyla had done something. She obviously was good enough to get herself out of the Dread Lord's magically fortified compound. Now the women could be anywhere.

His mind continued to spin but then a thought had him pausing in horror. Why the hell hadn't he realized this before? His love-fucked mind had clouded his judgment and Mariah was going to pay for his mistake. The Dread Lords were not some fly by night organization. There was no way that Twyla would have been able to casually walk out of their compound. It had to be a set up. Which meant they had his woman...

His theory was unfortunately confirmed when Marlin blasted down the stairs and nearly plowed over his brother. He looked like he'd seen a ghost. "The Dread Lords have Mariah and Twyla. And if you wanna see Mariah again, you gotta turn yourself over. Only you. And they left this as a warning."

Stephan took a dagger from Marlin's outstretched hand. His heart stopped cold. The silver and blue beaded necklace that Mariah had put on during their fight was wrapped haphazardly around the base of the blade. One free end dangled over the hilt, the sound of the beads hitting the leather wrapped hilt as he turned the dagger over, almost musical in their distraction. Blood streaked the blade from the tip to the necklace, and drops of crimson shone amongst the varied beads.

As if Stephan's day could get any worse.

"They want me? They can have me." Shoving past Marlin, Stephan bolted out of the safety of the compound, his rage knowing no worthy adversary.

Chapter Thirteen

Twyla awoke and remembered that her world was spinning out of control again. She tried to open her eyes, but she was blindfolded. She would have cursed in frustration, but she was gagged as well. If she hadn't been tied to a bed spread eagle, she would have remedied her situation. Tugging on her bonds, she gasped as a bolt of pain shot through her left wrist. She wiggled her fingers just to make sure they were still there.

That fucking asshole, Freeze, must have sold her out and followed her right to Mariah. If her best friend was going to die, then surely she would, too. Perhaps Freeze would attempt his special brand of torture again. Then she'd bite his dick off.

The scent of fine incense filled the air as though it was burned hours earlier but had long since been extinguished. She took further inventory of herself. She was wearing clothes at least. That was a good start. Freeze's pleasure shirt was dulling with time. It kept her adrenaline higher than normal, though. Luckily the bed was much more comfortable than that cot, the sheets soft against her legs. And the room was much warmer, absolutely still and felt completely devoid of anyone other than herself.

"Just as you said, I got her here. She's in there. And no one else knows." A young voice could be heard through a wall or door.

"For your trouble." That was Freeze. Paper crinkled. Was he paying someone?

"I tied her up tight. She's a fighter. Actually almost took me out a few times. I had to tranq her. Sorry about her wrist, too."

"You hurt her?" Freeze's voice rose and was full of the same cold intensity as the first time Twyla had heard him speak, when he'd offered to kill her. He was such an enigma.

"I'm sorry." The kid's voice weakened. "I-I'm r-really sorry. S-she fought so hard. She even bit me."

"I told you to bring her back unharmed. Give me that back and get outta here." A doorknob turned. Twyla froze, not wanting to give away that she was awake.

"But I got her here. If you don't gimme back that money, I'll tell Craze she's not dead and she's with you."

Twyla heard a scuffle, a crash and then a gurgling sound. Freeze's voice, low and menacing, carried through the door. "You tell anyone and you're out. Dead. Gone. You are nobody and would never be missed." The next sound was of a body dropping to the floor and someone gasping for breath. "Get out of here. Now. Before I change my mind and smash your fucking head in." Footsteps scrambled away in one direction and another set moved toward her as the door closed. Twyla calmed her breathing and relaxed her body, faking sleep.

He stopped at the edge of the bed and even with her eyes shrouded, she knew he was staring at her. Heat washed through her body but she kept herself from outwardly reacting. He took several deep breaths, then crossed the room. The sound of glass clinking was followed by the flicking of a lighter. "Ah yes. Sleeping beauty." He paused on the right side of the bed. "You don't mind my dark side, do you? Too bad it's the only side left of me that feels comfortable."

She could feel his breath on her face. He smelled of mint, like he had just sucked on a Tic Tac. His footsteps rounded the bed once more. The lighter clicked again. The scent of sandalwood and some sort of berry filled the air, and Twyla assumed he must be lighting candles. He tugged at her pillow. "I have you at my mercy again. And oh how I like that. Believe me, I want to have you. Do you want to have me, too?"

His words hit her face like a caress, and each syllable struck an aching chord in her cunt. Her body wanted him again. It obviously didn't understand that he was dark, evil…dangerous. He stepped away from the bed. "Surely you do. Or at least you did."

Twyla considered letting him know that she was awake, but decided against it. He clearly had no problem talking to her if he thought she was asleep. Maybe he'd end up selling himself out like he'd sold her out. She could hear him pacing the room. His voice was a strong whisper.

"Well, y'know, this is just great. I didn't sign up for this shit. I am not supposed to be here like this. It shouldn't be happening. But if Craze finds out, it's all over. How on earth am I to kill a woman? An innocent one, no less?"

He thought she was innocent? Twyla always fancied herself more on the naughty side.

She hoped he would be even further loose-lipped. She wanted to know where Mariah was so she could get out of there and find her...again.

"Such a beautiful, small woman. Craze eats ones like you for breakfast. But they don't fight much. Not like you do. You're a hot one." His breath washed across her cheek then left her feeling cold and empty when he stepped away. "I hope Mariah will be strong enough to fight. She should be, considering who her father was. Then again, I suppose Craze's plans are more in depth than just eating her."

He sat on the edge of the bed. "And yet again, what concern of that is mine? My concern is all right here. Right here in my bed."

Great. This was his bed. He was going to keep her tied here like his little sex slave. How nice. He was going to feed Mariah to Craze and keep Twyla in chains. But what was it he'd said about Mariah's father? Mariah didn't know her father...never had. What did he mean? It was getting increasingly difficult to stay still. *All right, mister, what have you got for me now? Shall I give up now and resign myself to being your sex slave? It wouldn't be too bad. I mean, how could I face Mariah again anyway after you tricked me into selling her out? That is, of course, if she's alive. I should have known you wouldn't just let me leave like that.*

"You're even still wearing my shirt, aren't you? You like what I did to it?" It was everything Twyla could do not to gasp as he placed his hand on her chest and re-energized the shirt. Her nipples had already been taut and with his touch, they tightened to full erection. "You do that to me, Twyla. Betcha didn't know that. You're a mean one, aren't you?"

Twyla cursed what she'd felt for Freeze. Now her body was totally on fire again. But it wasn't a burning fire; it was rapturous, her own nirvana. Why hadn't she asked Mariah for one of Stephan's shirts?

He circled the bed as he spoke barely above a whisper. "That's okay. I can't expect a woman in your position to even remotely be nice to me anymore. Not like this. Not now. Things could change someday. But for now, your hatred is certainly acceptable. I'm sure that's all I deserve."

Freeze stopped moving and talking. She couldn't figure out what he was doing or exactly where he was. Twyla focused on recounting the details of how she had gotten taken again. She'd run out into the back alley behind the import store with Mariah close behind and then a tearing pain in her wrist as she and Mariah were wrenched violently apart. And she knew Mariah had been terrified. Twyla would be haunted by the echo of her muffled screams for the rest of her life. It was her fault Mariah was captured. She'd never forgive herself for that.

Twyla felt his presence return mere moments before he spoke. "Let's see what happened to you here." His warm hand traced along her left arm from elbow to wrist. His touch was just as gentle as always. Damn him for that. Her body couldn't tell the difference between a good man and a bad man. It only knew what it felt like to be touched. And it wanted Freeze to be the one doing the touching. Her skin came alive as his hand slid over hers.

"That fucking goon boy." Freeze fiddled with the tie that bound her injured wrist and soon it was free. "What am I gonna do with you, Twyla? If I keep you here, you'll kill me. If I let you go, Craze will kill me and you as well." He touched her hand as though it was a fragile little doll as he traced each finger with his own.

"Craze is such an idiot sometimes. He knows just enough to be dangerous on this one. And I can't tell him what's really going on. I don't want to be here anymore. He still wants to use Mariah like she's just another pawn. Revenge and power...he thrives on it. Then again, I'm sure she'll wish she were dead before Craze gets through with her. He just never gives up. No matter who ends up dead."

Twyla wanted to scream. Did that mean that Craze would just start taking everyone out until he got what he wanted? Well, whatever it was that he actually wanted... Freeze's hand shifted and picked up her wrist. The severe pain had her fighting to remain limp. He brought her arm down to her side. His touch was so assuredly gentle. Every little touch from his hands confused her more. She had to focus on the facts. Freeze knew something that Craze didn't know. Maybe he could be used to keep Mariah alive. His shirt combined with his touch certainly kept the rest of her body alive.

"Hey, those are silly boxers." He chuckled as he tugged lightly at the fabric. "You never struck me as the smiley face type. Nor the type who'd wear men's boxers as a fashion statement. Then again, what do I know of you? Only the fire in your eyes and perhaps the fire in your heart. It mingles with the magic that is your strength. I wish I could show you how to use it. My constitution has weakened so much, though. I doubt I stand a chance. I would be too weak. And then where would we be?"

Such profundity. From a male no less. Twyla cursed her cunt for heating up, her mind for wanting to trust and believe him and all out hating him for putting her in this situation. She liked bad boys. But usually they were about as smart as a bedpost. Not intriguing like Freeze.

He slid one hand below hers on the bed and placed his other hand over her wrist. There was something about his touch that felt like he could reach clear to her soul if he really wanted to. What a creep. She hated him for that.

"At least I can take this away for you. This is easy. You don't have to fight me anymore, Twyla. I know. You led us right to Mariah. Craze was pissed off enough. He'd've had me kill you as he said. But we'd planned before we entered the room. Planned for you to lead us to her, bring her out where we could attack. And then things got out of hand." Well, that was an understatement. Twyla's whole world had gotten out of hand.

"You were much more of a woman than I knew how to deal with and I really let myself go. That has never happened to me, Twyla. Never." His voice shook. "Maybe that magic you hold deep within does come out from time to time. You just bewitched me. Next thing I know, you'll seduce me again only to chop my dick off."

How right he was! But what else was he saying? His voice sounded so tortured. Like he was talking from somewhere deep within himself. Somewhere that he rarely opened up and shared.

"That should be better." He rotated her wrist. It felt good as new. Then he started to remove her gag. "I bet you'll wail if I take this off. We wouldn't want to cause a commotion. Maybe I should just leave this on." His actions belied his words and the gag was fully removed. Her blood raced. Everything was making her tingle all over. But he still hadn't told her where Mariah was. *Hold on, girl. Just get your body turned back off again. Please!*

He gently kissed her lips. She swore she was going to cry if she had to stay motionless any longer. It was like a mini-orgasm every time he touched her. What a creep! She wanted that kind of power over him, not the other way around!

"I hope you wake up soon. I need your help to get me out of this. I can't get you out of here until it's safe. Until Craze decides what he's going to do. But he never backs down. Reinventing himself is an art form for him. He doesn't know I have you. And he doesn't know I even care. I told him if I ever saw you again, I'd finish you. I didn't tell him what happened. Hell, I'm still trying to get myself to believe what happened." He paused for a moment with a sigh. "What a strange mess I've gotten myself into. I'm not sure I want out anymore. From here, it's hard to tell. It's nice to be powerful like this."

He caressed Twyla's face, then began to remove her blindfold. Now that her wrist was healed and she could see him, she couldn't hold her rage in any longer.

"Bastard!" Twyla spat fury as she punched him squarely in the cheek with her freed fist. She hit him so hard, she figured she'd broken her whole hand this time.

* * * * *

Mariah was scared.

And pissed.

Stephan had been right. She'd been in danger. Even more danger than she could possibly have imagined. She tugged and pulled at the ropes binding her wrists behind her. Nothing. She couldn't budge at all. At least her feet weren't tied. Her mouth ached from the gag tied tightly around her, and she desperately wanted a drink of anything to get rid of the foul flavor.

Pain burned down the side of her neck. Just from the feel of it, she thought she must have gotten cut somehow during the attack. She didn't remember anything beyond being wrenched away from Twyla, a rough hand covering her mouth as she screamed, and then a stabbing pain in her arm as her assailant jammed a needle in deep. *It better have been a clean needle*, she mused. *The last thing I need is to catch something from these bastards. Then again, that's assuming they even let me live.*

She wasn't blindfolded, but it didn't matter because the room was pitch black. When she'd first awakened, she'd tried crawling around the room, hoping to find something, anything to rub the ropes binding her wrists against, like she'd seen done so many times in the movies. Or even a door to escape through. Well, the door was not surprisingly locked, and either the movies made it look easier than it was, or she just wasn't very good at saving herself because she hadn't found anything that would fray the ropes even a bit.

The room was small, no bigger than her walk-in closet at home. Rough wood planking covered the walls and floor. And there was nothing else in the room. She'd shimmied and scooted herself over every available inch, desperate for anything at all. During her expedition she'd managed to break a few nails and scratch the hell out of her arms, though. *A side effect of being an unwilling victim*, she sarcastically thought.

The floor rocked slowly back and forth beneath her again. She'd figured out earlier, just by the continuous sway of the room, that she must be on a boat. It reminded her of the time she and Twyla had rented a sailboat and gone out for a day of sun and fun a few miles off the Talisman Bay coast. They'd both come back sunburned, drunk, and very relaxed. It was a great memory. She struggled against her bonds again. Damn it, she refused to let that memory be all she had left to hang on to!

She wasn't sure how much time had passed since she'd woken up, or how long she'd been unconscious. No one had come by, and she hadn't heard anything at all. *Were they just planning on leaving her here to rot?* That wasn't the most pleasant thought. *And where the hell had they taken Twyla? Was she somewhere on this boat as well?*

Mariah jumped, or she would have if she'd been standing, when the door slammed open. The bright light from outside blinded her, and she barely made out the profile of a figure standing in the doorway. *Oh please, let this be a rescuer...Stephan?* She blinked and mentally cried out when the man grabbed her and roughly pulled her up by her hair. Definitely not Stephan. Her eyes teared up and she wanted to fight, but the gun in the bastard's hands kept her from struggling. Not now. She'd have to wait.

The man threw her against the wall and stepped back, eyeing her up and down. A slow, sick grin covered his face as he began to fondle himself through his baggy pants. His other hand kept the gun aimed at her chest. She tried to hide the fear that welled up inside as his cock grew inside his pants, but the vicious grin crossing his face let her know that she hadn't hidden it well enough. She'd rather die than let this bastard rape her.

He stopped fondling himself just long enough to lower his zipper, freeing his small, ugly cock from the confines of his pants. She shuddered and closed her eyes, not wanting to see that thing, or her captor, or what he was going to do to her. She tried to think of Stephan, of the safety she'd felt in his arms, of how amazing he'd made her feel in bed…anything but the ugly bastard masturbating just feet from her.

"Open your eyes, bitch, or I'll kill you now. Watch me. You'll be next." She opened her eyes, forcing back the tears that had welled up with his threat. She stared at him, unblinkingly, refusing to let him see the sheer terror that had turned her blood to ice. Fuck him. With all the shit that had happened to her over the last few days, she'd be damned if this bastard would see her cry.

Besides, he had a tiny cock. She should be laughing, not crying. She'd be laughing in his face if she weren't gagged. If he were going to kill her, she'd at least humiliate the bastard first.

So instead she glared at him, letting all her hatred for every man who'd ever betrayed her show in her eyes. He pumped his cock and leered at her as she continued to stare, not blinking, showing him in the only way she could that he was nothing to her, that no matter what he did to her, he wouldn't win. Her eyes burned, whether from the pain of not blinking, or from the hatred she felt, she wasn't sure. His eyes watched hers, and a flash of fear crossed his features. His cock withered in his grasp, disappearing back into his pants.

Surprise, and then rage, filled his face. He stepped toward her. "What the hell did you do to me, you bitch?" He punched her cheek and her head slammed back into the wall she was leaning against. Stars blurred her vision as she fell to the floor. He kicked her in the ribs twice, quickly, and she curled up, trying to protect herself. She flashed back to another time, another place, when she'd crumpled beneath blows, waiting to die. Twyla had saved her then, but somehow, she didn't think that was going to happen this time.

Her attacker hunched down next to her, his breath hot and fetid on her face. "You will die, Shadow Walker bitch, and I will have you. I don't mind fucking your corpse. A hole's a hole. And then I'll tell your lover the details of how I fucked you before I kill him too." He spat on her, stood up quickly, kicked her again, and walked out of the room.

This time, she allowed herself to cry. She cried for Twyla, who was probably suffering the same type of torture. She cried for the life she'd always wanted to live and for the children she'd never have.

And she cried for Stephan. For the love he'd shown her during their one night together. For the chance at love that they just maybe could have had. And because she'd never get to tell him she was sorry and that she did think of him as a hero. He'd tried to protect her and she had chosen not to listen.

She cried until she couldn't cry anymore. The tears dried up and anger replaced them.

Then she started to plan. She wasn't going to die crying — she'd die fighting.

* * * * *

"What the hell?" Freeze landed squarely on his ass then rubbed his cheek where Twyla'd clocked him. Glaring at him, her adrenaline mounted. He looked at her with wide eyes. "How much did you hear?" He actually seemed worried.

"I heard enough." She answered nonchalantly. There was no way in hell she would give him the luxury of a clear answer.

"No, really. When did you wake up?" He scrambled to his feet. He seemed a bit overly concerned as he stood just barely out of her reach. She shook her head and then grinned wickedly.

"Hmmm…something about enjoying having power over me." Twyla flicked her hand and wiggled her fingers. They were slow to respond. That was bad. If he came anywhere near her, she wanted to hit him again. Or at least grab his balls and squeeze.

"What? That's not what I meant. I mean, yeah, you're tied up and stuff." He rubbed his cheek one more time. There was something else in his eyes though. Unfortunately, she couldn't read minds.

"You sold me out, Freeze. You fuckin' sold me out. Damn you!" It really tore her up. She had never screwed up like that before. She'd done a few stupid things in her life. Dated quite a few stupid men, but nothing ripped her apart like what Freeze had made her do. He had completely duped her.

"Well, I am the bad guy." She wanted to be infuriated further. But for some reason, she wasn't. He was absolutely right. She looked him straight in the eye and changed her tactic.

"No, Freeze, you're not. Bad guys don't heal people they kidnap and…uh torture." Studying his eyes revealed the possibility that their thoughts paralleled about his hot, amazing torture of her. It pissed her off so much that he could feel the same, she wanted to clear both their minds of those traitorous thoughts as fast as possible. "What happened to Mariah? Is she here somewhere?"

His eyes broke from hers, turning toward one of the many candles that were lit. "Actually, I don't know. I'm assuming that she's not here. It's out of my hands now."

She held her tongue to keep from screaming at him and instead took the time to size up the room. It was obvious no woman had seen the place in years. Clothes were strewn about near his dresser. Most were just as dark gray as the shirt he'd hexed for her. Since he recharged it, she figured her cunt would never stop dripping until she got the shirt off.

None of the furniture matched. It was all antique and interesting in its own right, but not one piece matched another.

Lacy spider webs connected several pieces and lit candles cluttered the flat spaces. She was tied to a gorgeous ironwork four-poster bed that under better circumstances would have been enjoyed as a sexual jungle gym.

Daggers, swords and other various blades and weapons were just lying around. A huge crystal ball sat next to a pile of tarot cards on a desk, which was more like a workbench covered with so many candle remnants burned into oblivion and various colored crystals strewn across its surface. It was all rather creepy. Aside from the spider webs, nearly everything appeared completely clean—messy, but dirt and dust free nonetheless.

One closed door seemed to be her only chance of escape, and even without testing, she knew it had to be locked. She would have to convince Freeze to help her escape.

"Then untie me and let me go. Craze won't find out." Twyla bit her tongue. Maybe he wouldn't notice her slip.

"You said you didn't hear me until the end. Fuck!" He rushed to her side, his voice like venom. "What did you learn about the Shadow Walkers? Is Mariah already pregnant?"

"I didn't learn a damn thing and what makes you think I'd tell you even if I did. You're so smart and supposedly know more than Craze. Why don't you tell me about the Shadow Walkers, huh?" She wanted to ask him about Mariah, what he meant by his question, but she didn't want to share Mariah's history with Freeze either. Who knew what he might do with that knowledge?

"Bullshit. You heard everything, didn't you? You heard everything I had to say about everything. Great. That's just fuckin' great." He continued to pace and incessantly ran his fingers through his hair.

Twyla enjoyed watching his frustration intensify. It was nice to make him feel so infuriated, a simple payback for what he did to her. It was too bad she was tied up and beyond the physical ability to annihilate him for the emotional whirlwind he'd put her in. She'd have to stick with verbal. "Well, hey, you wouldn't've been talking if you didn't want me to hear you." She chuckled as he stopped dead in his tracks and faced her. "Now the power's in my hands. I got you by the balls and I'm not afraid to squeeze." She grinned wickedly.

"Unless, of course, I kill you."

"Freeze, get real. I'm *innocent* and *powerful* and you couldn't even find it within yourself to kill a woman, huh? I heard it all, Freeze. I know you want me. But you fucking sold me out! You set me up to get my best friend killed. Y'know, I've already dragged her away from her death once. You had me set her up to die for real this time. You fucking bastard!" Twyla couldn't help the tears in her eyes. She gritted her teeth hard and willed them to just go away. The ball was finally in her court and she would not lose it.

"It's not me! It's Craze! It's all him." He threw his hands out palms up as he sighed deeply. So he was just going to pass the buck, was he?

"You just do his bidding, right? Well, you told me once that you only obey people who are worthy of obedience. You've already ripped my heart out enough for the day, don't you think? The least you could do is untie me. It's not like I can kill you with my bare hands." Her tears faded as she saw his eyes soften.

"True, but I know you'd try." He was right. But she'd have a lot of figuring out to do first. She'd have to find a way out of that room. There weren't any windows and the door didn't appear to have a lock so a spell probably kept it closed. Somehow, she didn't think grabbing its handle and giving it an orgasm would be enough to break whatever magic he'd used on it.

"Come on, Freeze. What have you got to lose? If I come at you and try to kill you, then you have that option you were looking for. You could kill me and you wouldn't be upset about it."

"I'd be upset."

The heat in his eyes provoked a mysterious and undeniable response within her. Did he know what he was doing to her? She wanted to gulp, but didn't want to show that he'd moved her.

Freeze pulled his gaze from hers and started to loosen the bindings around her ankles. "You said you'd already saved Mariah once. What happened?" Twyla breathed a huge sigh of relief. Not only was she being freed, he was changing the subject. All she had to do was steer the conversation without letting on too much. She couldn't do that to Mariah again.

"Well, she fell in love with someone who wasn't who she thought he was. It wasn't a good situation. I came along, kicked some ass and then kicked her ass back in the game. She was finally getting over everything and now she's gonna die."

He paused after he got one ankle free. "We don't know that. It all depends on Craze. And I don't do all his bidding. Only what I choose. No one owns me." His eyes were serious. And deeper than she cared to mention. By prodding him, she hoped he would let slide a word or two about who he was and what kind of power he had so maybe she could manipulate him right into the palm of her hand.

"How did you get to be a Dread Lord?"

"I'd prefer not to say." He averted his eyes. There was obviously something more there, but his tone really made her uneasy about questioning him further. She took a mental note to push that button later if necessary.

"Why do the Dread Lords want my best friend?" She watched him closely in an effort to pick up every possible nuance of his actions. As her eyes followed him, his shirt kept her body throbbing and hot. It was hard not to think of his actions the last time they were in the same room together. As he untied her other ankle, his hands brushed against her skin quite a few times making her wish she had a change of panties. Between the shirt and his touch, her body was reaching a level of stimulation she'd never before experienced. It was the best foreplay she'd ever had.

"They want her because of the Shadow Walkers."

She came out of her daydream in a flash.

"What the hell are you talking about? She just met them. And don't even tell me the Shadow Walkers wanna rub her out. I know that's not the case at all." *Dammit, Twyla, bite your tongue!*

"Whoa. You really do know too much about everything now." He paused for a moment as he slid up the bed to her other bound wrist.

She was at last free enough to turn toward him. It felt good to bend her stiff legs and she shifted the rest of herself closer to the side of the bed. He watched her in a way that told her he was prepared if she tried to punch him again. There was a red mark on his cheek where she'd decked him. She almost felt bad. *Twyla, he's evil. What the hell has gotten into you?*

"How about Mariah's father? She never knew him. What did you mean that Mariah should be strong enough to fight because of who her father is—was?" She waited for him to reply, but he remained silent. "C'mon, Freeze. I wouldn't knowingly sell someone out, especially my best friend. I just want to know what is so damn important about kidnapping or killing Mariah that you'd take me twice just to get to her." She placed her free hand on his shoulder.

Freeze studied her face before replying. "I-I really can't say." He quickly looked back down to his work. "And please don't ask." Her wrist was free a second later. His entire body tensed and radiated consternation. That was clearly another topic to revisit if she ever got the chance.

She stretched and shook out her arm as she grabbed a pillow and leaned against it and the headboard. He sat on the edge of the bed with his head down, playing with a lighter he'd picked up from the nightstand. The flame from the lighter reflected in his eyes and it made her shiver. There was no doubt in her mind that he watched her out of the corner of his eye. She shifted positions, arching her back and thrusting out her chest. He definitely showed interest, which was exactly how she wanted him. "Well, then at least tell me how you knew my name before I even said it."

"Ask me another day. Maybe I'll tell you. Maybe not." He sighed. There was something hidden in that as well. And damn him for just teasing her with it.

"All right. Then can you at least tell me something about those damn pleasure tingle thingies you put on this shirt? What are those about?"

"I thought you'd like them." He fiddled with the lighter. "You have the ability to do them, too, you know." He smirked, but didn't look up.

"Yeah, and I accidentally climaxed two other people along with me." His head shot up and he laughed, a deep, beautiful sound that rocked her down to her now curling toes. She bit her lip to keep from moaning at the spasms coursing through her.

His eyebrows arched crookedly. "Actually, that wasn't the only time." Freeze exhaled deeply and looked away with a lopsided grin.

Twyla didn't know what he meant, but that wasn't important. If she was going to use that power again, she had to get to know how to control it. "What's the deal? How can I use that? I don't even wanna know where I get it from. Just show me something about it. Preferably something that'll get me out of here faster."

Freeze turned back to her and arched an eyebrow. His cheeks were slightly redder than the last time he'd faced her. He remained quiet for a long moment, just watching her. Twyla barely avoided squirming under his steady gaze. Then he finally broke the silence. "Well, there's really not a whole lot I can actually show you. I mean, you already know it all, it's just about harnessing it. You have to find it within yourself. And concentrate. Just make it happen. It's not easy. And you'll be really haphazard or weak when you first start, but it gets better through time. You just have to be careful when you use it. Otherwise, you could hurt yourself or someone else."

Then everything clicked. "Wait. Did you say that I can already do those tingles to you? I think I heard that." Memories of last night bubbled over in her mind. Coupled with her tingling body, she was ready to climax. She had to stop herself from grabbing Freeze's hand and jamming it between her legs so she could find the release she desperately craved. She rationalized that she would use him so her mind would be clear, then she'd be able to figure out the quickest escape.

"Umm. Yeah."

He looked at her like she was some kind of idiot. But hearing that made her want to harness her power so she could fuck his brains out again. It made her want to really torture him for making her turn over Mariah. Slowly but surely, she was gaining enough leverage over him that perhaps she really could engineer her escape from there. Well, okay, so she really just wanted to fuck his brains out so she could get out of that damn tingly shirt, then she'd kick the shit out of him. "So like, if I wanted to, I could just reach out and *zap!* You'd climax?"

"If all of your energy was in line, yeah, something like that." He amusedly sized her up. She reached out her hand toward him.

"Really? Okay, so I can just reach out and touch you and—"

Twyla's jaw dropped as Freeze completely disappeared.

Chapter Fourteen

As the door opened, the light once again blinded Mariah. She quickly stood up and faced the bastard who'd come for her earlier. Her body, especially her ribs, screamed at her for standing, but she would not let him kick her again while she was down. She thought that at least a few of her ribs were probably cracked, and her cheek throbbed where he'd punched her. But truthfully, those were the least of her worries. They would heal. She just needed to keep herself alive.

He growled at her as he approached. "The boss wants to see you now, bitch." He roughly grabbed her breasts and pinched her nipples hard through her T-shirt. Automatic reaction had her kicking out with her right leg, catching his knee. He didn't even flinch. He kept one hand tight on her breast and with the other backhanded her.

Lights flared behind her eyes as she fought the pain, refusing to pass out. "Dirty Shadow Walker whore!" He spat into her face as he grabbed her arm and dragged her from the room.

The world was spinning, Mariah could barely tell up from down, but she kept moving, trying to figure out what to do next. She tasted blood in her mouth from the last time he'd hit her. She wouldn't let them kill her, she couldn't. If given the chance she'd jump off the boat and surrender herself to the ocean. She doubted she'd be able to swim anywhere with her hands tied behind her back, a gag shoved deep in her mouth and her body throbbing with intense pain, but she'd rather the ocean take her peacefully, than let these bastards have their way with her.

As she was roughly yanked up the stairs, she discovered that the boat was larger than she'd originally thought. It appeared to be a luxury yacht or something of a similar nature.

So whoever wanted her dead liked living it up. Nice... Not like it mattered. Dead was dead.

The setting sun cast its colors onto the ocean, making the water a fiery temptress. A slight breeze ruffled her hair and Mariah inhaled the fresh ocean air, letting it calm her rapidly beating heart. A wave of peace washed over her body just in time for her to be thrown to the ground, her nose touching a pair of shiny black combat boots.

Mariah rocked back awkwardly, trying to get her balance so she could get to her feet. Her whole body ached and she wondered how much more it could take before it would shut down. She quickly pushed that thought from her mind. Giving up was not an option.

Her eyes moved up the body in front of her. Deep black jeans met the perfectly polished boots. The jeans were such a pure black Mariah wouldn't be surprised if they still had the tags on them. Her path continued upward as she made it to her knees in front of the man. She almost choked. The jeans were a perfect fit, outlining an extremely generous cock that was very, very erect. Mariah felt like she should scoot backwards to avoid being poked and prodded by the entrancing package at her eye level. Even through the jeans he was magnificent.

A black shirt was perfectly tucked into the jeans. The body beneath the shirt was just as impressive as the rest of him, each muscle visible underneath the tight fabric. A splash of red on the shoulders of his shirt marred the deep blackness of his outfit, but rather than detract from his appearance, it added to his stunning flawlessness. Mariah's eyes finally moved up to her captor's face. Perfect jaw, perfect cheekbones, perfect everything. This man was absolutely one of the most beautiful men she'd ever seen. Every inch of him, from his perfectly sculpted hair to his perfectly polished boots, was fantasy material.

For that one moment she wasn't afraid. How could she be afraid of something that stunning? Then she focused on his eyes, and her heart filled with absolute, pure, unadulterated terror.

They were evil eyes. Eyes that loved to deliver pain. Eyes as black as pure night. Eyes with no reflection. Eyes without a soul.

She wanted to run, to jump into the ocean and sink to the bottom. She had to get away from this man. Death was preferable to what might happen at his hands. Quickly she brought up her leg, trying to get off her knees and to her feet. In her haste she lost her balance and felt herself falling toward the one man she had to get away from. She tried to twist, to change the direction of her fall, anything to avoid touching the black hole of a man in front of her.

Strong hands grabbed her shoulders, steadying her fall, and pulled her to her feet. A shiver wracked through her body. His touch was so cold. Was he even human? She wanted to scream but the gag was still wedged tightly into her mouth. A smile appeared on his face, showing perfect white teeth. His smile scared her even more.

"Hello, Mariah. It's quite the honor to finally meet you. I am Craze." His voice was smooth as velvet, dark as night and cold as ice. She shivered again. She tried to put anger and hatred into her eyes, anything but the fear she felt. But he just smiled wider. He ran his hands from her shoulders up her neck to cup her cheeks. "Tsk, tsk. What did my boys do to you?" One finger traced the cut on her neck and Mariah flinched. He traced it harder until Mariah could feel blood leaking from the wound again. The gag helped her hold back the moans and whimpers she wanted to let forth. Fear raced through her and it was all she could do to keep from dropping to her knees she shook so badly.

"What did you do to our guest, Dwayne? Why is she injured?" Craze's hands traced the bruising on her face as he asked the question. His voice was smooth and controlled, demanding respect and fear.

The bastard who had assaulted her earlier answered Craze. "Look, the bitch just got what she deserved. She put a spell on me or did something with her eyes. I just returned the favor." *What the hell was he talking about? A spell? I glared at him, gave him the evil eye, nothing magical about that!*

Dwayne glared at her from behind Craze. He spat on the ground. "She's just a Shadow Walker whore—"

His sentence would forever remain unfinished. Craze pulled a gun, turned around and rapidly fired two rounds into Dwayne's skull. Mariah screamed into her gag and threw herself backward, slamming into a table. Pain spiraled through her again. Blood pooled on the surface of the deck, catching and reflecting the lights from the yacht. Mariah couldn't take her eyes off the blood as the puddle grew in size.

Craze turned back to her and placed the gun at the small of his back in his jeans. He held out his hand and laughed, bringing another shudder to Mariah's terrified body. "I offer my hand to you, yet you cannot take it." He smiled as he gently pulled her to her feet, one hand clutching her arm. "Dwayne needed to learn that his behavior was not acceptable. I value the comfort of my guests." He stroked her face and hair, tucking a loose strand behind her ear. "He won't bother you again."

Mariah's eyes sought out the body. The bloodstain continued to grow. No, he would not be bothering her again. But she'd gone from being tortured by a demon to being wooed by the devil himself. Things had just gotten much worse.

Voices echoed on the water behind her, and she could hear the sound of a smaller craft knocking against the yacht. She broke free of Craze's hold and turned toward the sounds, hoping and praying for a miracle. Three men were helping another man onto the yacht. Like a scene from a thirties noir classic, the man was bound, hands behind his back and what appeared to be a burlap bag over his head. But it didn't matter, Mariah knew in her soul, knew from the way the man stood proud and strong even though he was at such a disadvantage, that Stephan had come to her.

She tried to run to Stephan but hands surrounded her from behind, arms crossing her stomach in a lover's embrace. Her own hands, still tied behind her back, were shoved against Craze's cock, and she could feel excitement pulsating through him. She tried to pull away, move her hands, anything, but

Lover's Talisman

Craze just tightened his hold. His mouth found her ear, his tongue circling and exploring. Every muscle fought against his closeness, but there was nowhere to escape to. Mariah just kept her eyes on Stephan and tried to block out everything else.

As Stephan was jerked closer, Craze whispered into her ear, "The game of chess has so many possibilities." He lowered his mouth back down to her neck and his tongue laved the cut he had reopened. Mariah moaned but her gag swallowed the sound. Craze returned to her ear. "All of the Pawns are in line for me to be the ultimate Master." He nuzzled her ear, almost loving and romantic in his gesture. "You feel so perfect in my possession. Stephan's Queen—" he dipped his tongue into her ear and tasted her before continuing "—and I have captured you. Out of play—mine forever." One of his hands slid from her stomach and cupped her breast. He grasped her nipple between his thumb and forefinger and gradually tightened his hold, twisting and pinching the now erect nub. Mariah whimpered.

Stephan was shoved to his knees a few feet from where they stood. He knelt there, so proud and strong in front of them, his head still covered, and Mariah wanted to cry out to him, to warn him. Why had she screwed up so badly? Why hadn't she listened to him?

Craze continued caressing Mariah's breast and she could feel his smile against her neck. As the cover was pulled from Stephan's head and Mariah's eyes met his, Craze simply whispered, "Checkmate."

* * * * *

Even though the surprise regarding Freeze's disappearance was still strong, Twyla didn't waste any time heading to the door. As she suspected, no amount of pulling or shoving would get it to come open. Just for kicks, she tried to give it an orgasm and it still wouldn't budge. And she couldn't give herself an orgasm either. What the hell was that about? This was one of those times when she could really use an orgasm. Not just one of those little ones like she got from sitting on the washing machine, either. She rubbed the shirt and tried again. Nothing. Damn! Had she already lost that power? Oh well. There was nothing she could do at the moment but wait.

She frowned, taking in the room once more. So this was where Freeze spent his most private moments. She could see that he spent most of his time either in bed or at his worktable desk. Otherwise, nothing else appeared used. She spotted a doorway she hadn't noticed before and ran toward it.

It was just a bathroom—without a door no less. And it was huge. She searched the walls in hopes of a window. None. She even tried pushing on some tiles and banging on the walls hunting for a secret escape, although she was careful not to make too much noise so as not to attract any unwanted attention. Again, nothing. She sighed and returned to the main room.

She hadn't thought touching him would make him disappear. She had wished he would, but it was too hard to believe that it had actually happened. As she surveyed the room, his shirt continued to make her simmer. It was everything she could do not to just flop back down on his bed and polish her pearl until she found the release she so desperately wanted. The relentless pleasure was tiresome without an orgasm to follow it. Her eye caught on his dresser, and immediately she went in search of another more suitable shirt.

A blue one, a red one, a green one, a black one. Every one of them tingled when she put it on. They all seemed to be the same. And it wasn't like they were as well worn as the gray one he'd given her. She had hoped that maybe if he hadn't worn the shirts very much, they wouldn't affect her, but that just wasn't the case. No matter if it had buttons or zippers or if it was just a T-shirt, it kept her near climax. She started to wish he were there in the room just so she could turn him on and get herself off. She didn't really care anymore. She just needed release and using Freeze for it was sounding so much better than using her fingers. He would take her so much higher just by touching him.

Lover's Talisman

Dammit. Never mind. That asshole had set her up. Whether or not it was his intention to kill her and Mariah, he was still a creep.

Twyla scrutinized the room one more time. There had to be something she could use to claw her way out of there and find Mariah. She tried to pick up a dagger, but it burned her. Each throwing star froze her hand. She couldn't even go anywhere near a sword without it electrifying her already electrified pleasure shirt. Freeze had to be awfully powerful to be able to do all of that.

She cursed him and the shirt one more time as she flopped down on the bed. Her body ached for his touch, hell, anyone's touch. She needed release or she was going to die of pleasure.

"All right, Freeze. I see how it is. I got what I asked for and now it's not really what I want. Let me out of here! Or at least give me a better shirt...one that doesn't make me so damn horny." She went back to his dresser and searched one more time. "Fuck it." The room was warm enough. There were blankets on the bed. She took off the shirt, hoping she could breathe a sigh of relief, but she was too aroused. The silk of the smiley face boxers wasn't helping either. It just inflamed her even further. She took those off, too and grumbled at her soaking wet thong. "Why the hell do I bother?" That, and her bra, were added to the pile of clothing on the floor.

Naked, she slid under the covers on the bed, letting out a moan when the cool, crisp, soft sheets rasped against her heated skin. Her tight nipples ached for a hot mouth to bring them comfort. Yanking the covers over her head, she grumbled in frustration. The sheets smelled freshly laundered. With fabric softener, too. *Dammit Freeze. You would have to be civilized for a rogue, wouldn't you? I can't just get on with this and forget about you even for a moment!*

The scents of the candles had been mixing in the room for quite some time now, making her glad for the tranquility they offered. Too bad turmoil overruled the light and fragrance.

Jerking back the sheet, she reached over to the nightstand and tried to open the drawer. Hot damn. It actually slid open, but the only thing in the drawer was a pack of incense sticks for the burner that lay on top. She pulled out a stick and smelled it. Kinda flowery for a guy, but now it was her new favorite scent. Setting it smoking with the lighter he'd left, she placed the stick in the holder. *Relax, Twyla. Just relax. Clear your head. Think a little. Argh! I just want a fucking orgasm!*

Grunting her resolve, she surveyed the room again for good measure. No way in hell she'd polish her pearl in front of anyone whether or not it turned them on. It was usually so easy to find a hot man with a long enough schlong that her vibrator had started to collect dust.

Satisfied that there were no peeping toms, she reached between her legs and fingered her clit, just wanting to get the job done. There were more important matters at hand. But instead of instant gratification, she became more frustrated. It was like she forgot how to please herself without a real male cock around. Something she could just jump onto that would fill her enough to get her rocks off. At this point, she'd pretty much settle for anything.

"What is my world coming to?" Twyla chuckled as she got out of bed and went into the bathroom in search of something...anything that could make her experience more interesting. She opened cabinets and drawers and came up empty-handed. Freeze was apparently too masculine. Then a grin crossed her face as she opened an ornate box innocently perched by the bathtub. Score! Two unopened bottles of massage oil. Whoa. Both were rose scented. She swallowed hard. That was her favorite.

The scent of roses filled the air as she opened a bottle. This was the good stuff. She closed her eyes and inhaled its essence, then nearly fell over as her knees got weak. Too much pleasure. Way too much tingling. She no longer had clothing on and her body was still on fire. It was almost like when Freeze had touched her body last night. The pleasure sparked everywhere like pyrotechnics.

Twyla came back to reality for a moment and noticed that while thinking of Freeze she had been caressing her breast and teasing her nipple. She grinned. At this point, whatever worked!

She skipped back to the bed and dove into the massage oil, smearing it all over her body while pretending Freeze's hands were doing it for her. She was determined to end her need. Rubbing the massage oil onto her inner thighs, she could feel the heat emanating from her so wet pussy. Closing her eyes and imagining Freeze's body so close to hers, she took herself back to the night before. The surprise in his eyes when she'd trapped him with her legs. The way sparks flew through her wherever he touched her. She traced her fingers everywhere that he had touched, trying her hardest to replicate the pleasure tingles he had shot through her.

Those tingles reappeared once more. Hot damn, she hadn't lost them after all! She searched for ways to control them. She laid an oily hand on each breast and played with shooting sparks across from hand to hand. She wasn't touching anywhere near her clit but she could feel sparks down there mingling in harmony with the ones she was creating above. The sparks shot through her clit and bounced around everywhere. She was finally starting to get into the whole thing. She slid her hands down to her stomach, arching her back as she focused on bouncing the sparks she'd created within her breasts to mingle with the ones she was bouncing from hip to hip. Soon, she found that rhythm and began to grind in circles against the sparks.

She moaned as she desperately sought her release. As her hands wandered and her fingers slid inside the wet folds between her legs, she tried to control the tingles. She shot them from head to toe and made them bounce. She sent them from her fingertips as deep within her cunt as she could reach. Already hypersensitive, she continued to force the tingles throughout her body. She was actually starting to understand what Freeze had been talking about, that it was all within her, she just needed to learn how to control it. It was quite empowering that she could control the tiny little orgasms. But her body needed the earth to move. She wanted to go beyond the heavens. Instead, she used the tingles to bring about a happy medium. A small orgasm was better than no orgasm at all. It hit her harder than she was expecting and her body quaked as she gasped.

But then the tingles kept going seemingly of their own accord. She rubbed her clit with one hand while her fingers continued to slide in and out of her pussy. The tingles just started shooting everywhere. They were absolutely relentless. She was sure she would pass out. Both of her hands found her breasts as she found a sweet climax once more. But it still wasn't enough. Her body still wanted more.

"Freeze..." she breathily moaned as she closed her eyes. "Dammit! Where are you? I need you to come...to...me..." Her world was spinning and bursting coming down from the high. She wasn't completely satisfied, but it would have to do. Her breathing was so hard and heavy, she swore it had never been like that before. Hell, this was better than half of the guys she'd fucked. Her mind was definitely changed as far as this whole masturbation thing was concerned. She still wanted Freeze, though. Every corner of her being ached for him.

"I've been here the whole time, Twyla." Freeze's voice was barely more than a whisper. Her eyes shot open. She was still alone in the room.

* * * * *

"I'll get you out of this, okay?" What else could he say? Stephan wanted to stand up and rip her from the arms of the asshole who held her so close. He watched Mariah nod, one lone tear rolling down her bruised cheek and landing in her gag. Her neck was lightly bleeding from what appeared to be a knife wound. Probably from when they'd removed her necklace. But why the hell was it still bleeding? What the hell had these bastards done to her?

His heart pulled tight in his chest, making it difficult to breathe. Her fear radiated off of her, hitting him like a punch in the gut. He had to help her, had to make this right. But he knew he was at a disadvantage, and he had to make the right moves at the right times or he would lose.

Stephan took in the scene before him, needing every ounce of information available in order to calculate his moves properly. He was on a yacht and his trip out there had been of reasonable length. He had not yet heard the other vessel leave the side of this one—first possible escape, although slow going.

If he got himself and Mariah into the water, it would be a long swim, but certainly not longer than he had swam before. Through her injuries, her eyes remained strong. She clearly wouldn't give up easily, so if she were physically able, he knew he could count on her. He'd make these bastards pay for whatever they had done to her. It broke his heart that all this had happened because of him. He knew it wasn't going to be as simple as turning himself over in exchange for Mariah's life, but this was quite a bit more than he'd expected. Why hadn't he thought it all the way through? It was the Dread Lords, not just some ordinary inter-dimensional punks.

The body of a man lay reasonably near Mariah. The blood beneath the body swayed with the motion of the ship, but the pool was not growing in mass so the man must have died before Stephan had arrived. He pieced together those details in his mind. Judging from the amount of hands that had prodded and grabbed him and the amount of voices he had heard, there were three men in the smaller boat with him when he was being transported.

He recalled surrendering his weapons at the pier and there were six men at that point so three must have stayed behind. Only one man had led him off the boat, but he'd heard all three disembark. None of them were within sight at the moment, however.

The ropes binding his wrists were tight, but he'd immediately begun loosening them. He knew some tricks, but he had to go slow so as to be unnoticeable. It took patience and was not easy by any stretch of the imagination. He wasn't about to give up no matter what it took to free himself and Mariah. He would ride off into the sunset with her and no one was going to stop him.

Stephan met Mariah's eyes, trying to convey that he'd make everything all right, but all he could see from her was fear and anger tinged with sorrow. Her spark was not completely extinguished, though. Even faced with this, she had not yet given up. She truly would make a perfect Shadow Walker wife.

The man holding her brought one hand up from her stomach to her jaw, tilting her head back toward him. Stephan could see Mariah flinch as the man licked the path of her tear, then kissed both of her eyes. Mariah visibly shuddered. The man's other hand roamed possessively over her breasts and stomach, claiming as his own what Stephan would never willingly share. Stephan's blood boiled, he saw red, and he took a deep breath, calming himself before he lost it and caused the death of them both.

Talk to me, Bro. What the fuck is goin' on out there? We got a hungry mob outside. I know we can take 'em, but what's up, Bro? Marlin clicked-in and Stephan nearly fell over. Thank goodness for the diversion or he might have done something stupid.

Big trouble. Don't mess around there with anybody. Stay tight. If I don't make it out in two hours, do not, I repeat, do not *come find me. Gather all forces and annihilate the Dread Lord compound. Jake knows where it is. Just get the job done and stay focused. They will return, but that'll set them back a step.*

Okay. Got it. Kick ass, Bro. Don't go down in vain. And, we'll be here when you get out. Marlin quickly clicked-out.

Stephan looked up into the man's black eyes of hell. His whole world shifted around him and his imagination conjured up the smell of smoke, the crackling of burning wood and thoughts of impending death. The man in front of him, holding Stephan's woman in his arms, was not an unknown. This man had drastically altered the path of his life once. Stephan was not going to let it happen again.

"David." Stephan tried his best not to spit out his name with vulgar intensity. "I see the rumors of your death were greatly exaggerated."

Stephan quickly clicked-back-in to Marlin. *Their leader is David.* That was the kind of information that Marlin would know exactly how to process without a second guess considering the circumstances.

And you're our leader, man. Marlin clicked-out. Stephan knew that if he didn't make it off that boat, Marlin could hold onto Talisman Bay. The fact that David appeared to have lived and learned quite a lot since the last time they'd met in conflict meant that there was a strong chance Stephan wouldn't make it off that yacht alive. His idea of trading his life for Mariah's, while well-founded, was essentially proven preposterous by this point. He was certain David would kill them both while keeping a smile on his face.

Stephan regrouped his thoughts. There had to be some kind of weakness. David was a creature of opportunity. He got lucky when he'd trapped Stephan and his friends in that house those years ago—they hadn't been prepared for his deception. This time, the circumstances were different, and Stephan was determined to make David's luck completely run out.

David laughed and for a moment the blackness in his eyes lit up with a reddish glow. His teeth flashed white in the fading light of day as he grinned, an expression of pure triumph. *And that was his weakness, because he thought he'd already won.* Stephan returned David's smile with one of his own.

"Did you ever wonder why I tried to kill you? Why I stood outside smiling while watching you burn?"

Stephan snarled. "Because you're a crazy bastard who didn't deserve our friendship." He felt the rope around his wrists give; he was minutes from freeing himself. His hands itched to punch the smile clean off David's face, to finish what he'd started so many years ago. But the stakes were bigger now. He had to protect Mariah. David would pay, but Mariah's safety came first.

David laughed again and Mariah's eyes grew even wider. Stephan wanted to reassure her but couldn't take any chances that David would think him prepared to fight.

David rocked Mariah against him as he continued. "I go by Craze now. I felt it appropriate since your cursing and calling me crazy were the last words I heard from you...before you should have died. But there is a reason for everything. And you not dying then made all of this possible now."

Red sparks shimmered around Craze, briefly lighting up the encroaching darkness with a small pyrotechnic display. Stephan used the distraction to free his wrists from the rope with a quick twist, but returned his body to the restrained position, not wanting to give himself away until the perfect moment. He could tell that David, or Craze, was fully enjoying his moment in the spotlight, so Stephan would give it to him, and then take him down when he least expected it.

Craze continued. "Life always comes full circle. You may have been destined to be a Shadow Walker, but I was destined to be the Dread Lord who would bring you down. My need for revenge is playing out in front of a larger audience, and for bigger stakes. Little did I know when I sought you out so many years ago, the world I was stepping into."

Stephan's mind swirled with the information Craze was giving him. What was the hidden message in all of this? As insane as Craze was, there was reason to his madness.

Craze cocked his head, eyeing Stephan up and down. "You still don't understand, do you?" Craze shook his head in mock pity. "The Dread Lords fostered my hate for you, for your men, and gave me a bigger reason to bring you down. They trained me, aided me and gave me resources to match yours. And when I uncovered the prophecy of a Shadow Walker and his woman —" Craze's smile intensified "— I knew it was time for me to step forward. Because, you see," Craze cradled his hand over

Mariah's stomach, "I could never allow a Shadow Walker to bring a child into this world. Not under my watch. And not in Talisman Bay. And especially not with a woman who has Shadow Walker blood running through her veins."

Stephan froze. "What the hell are you talking about?" He almost cursed himself for showing his surprise, but he had to know more. Prophecy? Shadow Walker blood in her veins? And did that mean Mariah was already pregnant with his child? An even stronger urge to protect her whipped through him. She was his, and after their unbelievable night together, she certainly could be carrying his child. He would not let her die.

Mariah struggled in Craze's grasp and made noises through her gag. Craze ignored Stephan's question and turned Mariah to face him. "Shhhh..." Craze brushed her hair off her face, winding strands of it through his fingers. "Do you want to speak, little one?" He reached both hands behind her head and unknotted the gag.

The next moment was a blur of action. As the gag was fully removed, Mariah brought one knee up to attack Craze. He shifted his body to avoid her attack and Stephan launched himself at the two of them.

A bolt of lightning flashed from Craze's fingertips and through Stephan, striking him in mid-air and knocking him to the ground. He couldn't move, couldn't breathe, couldn't see, could only feel the pain of electricity arcing through his body. He could hear struggles coming from the direction of Craze and Mariah, but he couldn't do anything about it. He was completely helpless.

The struggling ceased. "You fucking bastard," Mariah choked out. "You killed him. You killed him." Her voice cracked and she sobbed, choking and coughing.

Craze's voice rose over her sobs. "No little one. I didn't kill him. Not yet. But I will. And then maybe I'll kill you as well."

* * * * *

"Where the fuck are you Freeze?"

Twyla was pissed. Yeah, she'd just gotten off, and had a good time doing it, but the fact that Freeze was playing some type of mind game with her was not amusing. Not now. Not like this. Now that she wasn't full of unsatisfied sexual energy—well at least not as much as before—she could think. It was past time to get the hell out of there, find Mariah, and figure out how she could destroy every man who used them as a pawn in their games.

"You didn't think I was just gonna leave you there all hot and bothered by yourself, did you?" Freeze appeared out of thin air.

"Freeze!" She glared at him through her surprise. Then again, with all the magic she'd seen lately, her surprise at his reappearance was minimal.

"See, you figured out how to use those magic tingles." A grin spread across his face. "You have more power than that, too. Do you understand my dilemma?"

"What I understand is that you are a kidnapper, a torturer, some kind of high powered magic user and a voyeur." She spat her words, glaring at him through narrowed eyes.

"Just moments ago, you were wishing I was with you." Freeze crossed his arms over his chest, a smug expression on his face.

"Yeah, well like I usually do when no man is around to help me, I took care of the problem myself." She ruffled her hair and tried to flatten out the sheets a bit. She was glad he'd reappeared because she needed to use him to get out of that room, but that was the end of it. Everything else about him being there was a source of infuriation. Her body was still tormented by residual pleasure tingles. She scowled as she realized that in every aspect of her life right now she was somehow trapped beyond her own control.

"I like that in a woman."

Twyla got out of bed and stalked toward him. "First, you make me miss what was probably the most important meeting of my life. Next, you scare the shit out of me. You fuck me like there really is no tomorrow. You make me sell out my dearest friend. You trap me again and watch my most private of moments! Damn you Freeze! Go fuck yourself this time!" Sparks crackled all around her as her venomous words flew forth. She felt as though she wore her pleasure tingles on the outside of her body this time.

"Whoa. Hey. Calm down..." Freeze took a step back. Strong concern showed in his eyes as he put his hands up defensively.

"Calm down? How can I? You hexed a shirt for me that has me riled beyond comprehension and you want me to calm down? I'd sooner rip your balls off and feed them to you! No more, Freeze! Get me out of here!" A clanging sound drew her attention and she noticed that all of the weapons in the room were standing on end. Each seemed prepared for battle, as though some invisible army was ready to go to war on her behalf. She knew she should be scared, but she wasn't. The power was within her, and *she* was in control now.

"Twyla, please." Every time he said her name it was a melody. *Damn him!* "Look if you don't calm down, this entire room is gonna erupt weaponry and I'll bet most of it's gonna hit me." He sighed, but then met her intensity. "If you take me out, you can't get out of this room. The spell is my own concoction. Do you see how you are controlling everything? It's all you. Use your strength." He grabbed her shoulders and she gasped at his touch. Her body hadn't been finished completely. He kissed her and she provoked all of the weapons to fling themselves into a whirlwind around them.

She pulled away before she would let her body win. "Tell me about the Dread Lords and perhaps I'll let you keep all your fingers."

"You know I'm stronger than you are." He remained close and just as intense. Her mind was in the same kind of whirlwind as all of the weapons flying around them.

"I know, but you said I'd either be haphazard or weak with my powers. So, if I were to aim, say, a dagger to remove your pinky finger, what are the odds it'll remove your heart instead?" *Get him, girl. Keep the weapon tornado going. He actually looks a little scared.*

Freeze frowned and put some distance between the two of them. "I swear it. I can't tell you anything." A throwing star whizzed by his ear close enough to remove a lock of his hair. "Okay…all right. The Dread Lords are not a new organization. Craze is the local leader and organizer. But it's not just about the Dread Lords." Freeze took a deep breath. "Although he's strong, Craze is new to his power. He's not as experienced. Not like I am." He swallowed hard.

"So, you want to be him, do you?"

"No."

"You don't even have it in you, Freeze."

He grabbed her and administered a more passionate kiss. He waved one hand and the weapon tornado ceased its activity. She desperately fought to keep the tornado going and a few of the throwing stars whizzed past him and stuck in the wooden dresser. Her cunt yearned for him. He had a certain way of kissing her that affected her throughout her entire body and soul. And that infuriated her even further. His hands traced from her shoulders to caress her breasts. She saw her chance and stepped away before he could go any further.

"No, Freeze." Her breath was ragged. *Keep your head, girl. Ignore your cunt. Keep your head!* "You've got my life in such a fucked up place. I can't do this anymore. Stop this!" A sword stood on end and the throwing stars popped out of the wood of the dresser and began the deadly tornado once again.

"You're the captured one, not me."

There had to be an ounce of control she could gain for herself somehow, somewhere, some way. "Get me out of here, you evil bastard." With all her might, she tried to send every sharp piece of metal at him.

Blood splattered in her eyes just before she shut them.

Chapter Fifteen

"Fucking bastard!"

Mariah glared at Craze before turning her attention to Stephan. She couldn't stop the tears from falling as she looked over at him lying flat on the deck of the ship. Electricity still arced from his body, which jerked with each spark that flew from him.

Craze had her pinned to the deck of the ship with his body. His weight against her damaged ribs was excruciating. She struggled for breath, closing her eyes, focusing every thought on just getting enough air to stay alive, stay conscious.

She shouldn't have tried to hurt Craze, had known it would probably be fruitless, but the need to inflict pain on this bastard was overwhelming. Of course, he didn't suffer for it, Stephan did.

She needed to get to Stephan, to make sure he really was still alive. Her entire body ached with the need to just be close to him, to tell him how sorry she was for putting him in this situation. Mariah opened her eyes and stared at Stephan's inert body. The sparks had dissipated, but she couldn't see any rise and fall of his chest.

Craze shifted off her in one fluid motion, standing up and walking away. Mariah took a deep breath and immediately started choking and coughing. The pain wracked through her ribcage again. Her vision blurred around the edges and a roaring filled her ears. God, she couldn't pass out now!

A hand sought to give comfort but instead a chill ripped through Mariah's already victimized body.

"Drink this."

She sought to focus her vision. Craze was holding an open bottle of water to her parched lips. "You should drink something. I'm sure your mouth is dry."

He was right. She should drink something. Her tongue felt strangely huge and swollen in her mouth. But she didn't trust him. Who knew what he'd put in that water.

Craze grinned at her. It was obvious he knew what she was thinking. He tilted back his head and drank from the open bottle, then held it to her lips. "Drink. Deeply. And have no worries. If I do kill you, it won't be by deceptive means."

The last thing she wanted to do was place her lips where his had been, but she had to have something to drink. He tilted the bottle against her lips and she drank, keeping her eyes on Craze the whole time. The water was cool and refreshing and made her feel surprisingly better.

When she was finished with the bottle, Craze patted her on the head, caressed her face, then turned and walked away. He sat down at the table Mariah had crashed into after he'd killed Dwayne, and almost instantly several men showed up, laying plates of exquisite looking foods in front of him. Mariah's stomach growled, but she'd be damned before she'd share a meal with this bastard.

Craze waved a hand at Dwayne's body and a few men picked him up, weighted him down and threw him overboard, while another few cleaned up the blood, before all of them disappeared back into the depths of the ship. All of this seemed to happen in a matter of seconds.

As Craze dug into his food, Mariah wasted no time rising to her knees and crawling over to Stephan. Craze seemed to be ignoring her, although she could feel his eyes on her back as she scurried over to Stephan. Mariah knew her time was limited, and being close to Stephan was the only thing that mattered to her anymore. As she approached him, his chest slowly moved up and down and his eyes blinked open. A wave of relief washed over her. He was alive…for now.

Mariah's eyes met Stephan's and she remembered why she'd thought she could fall in love with him. His eyes were tender and loving, protective and fierce, and shone with determination. A part of her started to believe that just maybe they'd make it off this boat together, and she could work on making the rest of her dreams come true.

"I'm so sorry," Mariah whispered. Stephan's eyes registered confusion and concern. "This is my fault. I should have listened to you. I shouldn't have tried to get away from you." She felt her tears bubbling to the surface again but she willed them away. They wouldn't help her now. She knelt closer to him, trying desperately to maintain her balance. She wanted to touch him, to kiss him, to show him what he meant to her. Her ribs screamed and her breath hissed out between her tightly gritted teeth in a pained rush.

"You'll be okay. I'll get us out." Stephan's words were barely more than a mumble.

"What?" Mariah could hardly believe him. He looked like he was almost dead, but he still wanted to be the hero.

"I can barely move." Now Mariah understood why he was mumbling. His lips weren't moving as he spoke. "I'm just starting to get feeling back."

"I'm so sorry."

"No. I am. Hush, sweetheart. This is not over yet."

Mariah could see the pain in his eyes and she desperately wanted to touch him, to run her hands over his face, across his chest, through his hair. Her fingertips ached to feel his skin, but there was no freeing herself from the ropes binding her. She couldn't kneel over him without her ribs screaming at her.

She sat down next to him and stretched her body out in a semi-reclined position, facing him. Her ribs still screamed, but the pain was worth it to feel him against her. Her lips were inches from his, and the warmth of his breath washed over her face. She met his eyes again, so caring and warm, and she leaned into him, placing her lips against his.

His lips were soft and smooth against hers. She flicked out her tongue, running it along the crease of his lips, and felt his response in his quick exhale. She breathed him in, knowing that this could be her last intimate moment with him. His lips tasted salty from the ocean air. She delved deeper and his tongue came to life against hers, mingling and loving in return. She moaned into his mouth as her body lit up, the yearning to have more time with him, a lifetime, and not just the few minutes they probably had left.

Mariah pulled back, breathing heavily. She peered into the deep hazel of his eyes and knew that no matter how tonight ended, she'd never regret what had happened between the two of them. Stephan had brought her back to life again, and her brief time with him was worth more than living a long life without him.

"Mariah...?" His lips moved this time, but his voice was still barely above a whisper.

"Yes?" The inches that separated their faces seemed too far, and she placed her face back against his, brushing her lips over his cheek and jaw and down his neck. She inhaled deeply of his masculine scent. God, he was perfect.

"You're driving me crazy," he rasped throatily. Was she hurting him? "There's a crazy bastard not ten feet away from us, and all I can think about is thrusting my cock deep inside you again. Of listening to you moan as you come."

His coarse words brought her pussy roaring to life and she could feel the dampness begin between her legs. God she wanted this man. She didn't even care that they had an audience. Heat flashed through her and Mariah couldn't help it, she laughed. "This is insane, isn't it?" She kissed her way back to his lips. "But I can't help it..."

This time his tongue explored her mouth, her lips. Mariah still felt Craze's gaze on them, but she refused to care. She was where she belonged.

"I love you, Mariah."

Mariah's world stopped. The words had been spoken almost fiercely—confidently—directly into her mouth, and it took a second for her to realize exactly what he had said. A continuous warmth flooded her from the top of her head to the bottoms of her feet, and her aches and pains seemed to disappear. She pulled herself back so she could look into his eyes again. They radiated sincere love and the promise of so much more.

It was like a light came on inside of her, awakening her to all that she had believed impossible. She smiled as her world came amazingly, stunningly alive with the knowledge that she was in love and loved in return. "I love you, too. Since the first moment you held me and told me you'd make everything okay, you've had my heart. I tried to deny it, tried to make it go away, but I don't want to. I can't live without you."

Determination crossed his face. "You won't."

And then he kissed her again. She pushed herself closer to him, almost laying on top of him, her breasts smashed against his chest, her legs on the deck parallel to his. His hand flexed against her side, a slight almost unnoticeable movement.

He ran his mouth over her face, kissing her eyes, her forehead, her cheeks and nose. He touched every part of her he could reach. She leaned down to kiss his neck and his mouth found her ear. His voice whispered and even though he spoke directly into her ear, she had to strain to hear him he spoke so quietly. "In a minute I want you to turn your back to me and face Craze." He kissed her between words, obviously trying to disguise that he was talking to her. "Place your wrists next to my hand and I'll untie you." His tongue entered her ear for a moment and she shivered, her cunt pulsing with need, even through the fear and excitement that coursed through her at the thought that they might be able to escape.

Stephan continued. "Distract him. Ask him questions. Get him talking." He nuzzled her again. "Can you swim?"

Mariah moaned loudly, playing it up for Craze's benefit. "Oh, God, yes..."

Lover's Talisman

Stephan chuckled. "You're good. When you're untied, keep up the farce. I'm going to get us out of here. Now, kiss me..."

She did. She put all the passion, all the love, every bit of her soul into that kiss. As she pulled away from him, she smiled softly. "No matter what happens, I love you."

"You are mine, always."

"You are mine, now."

Both Craze and Stephan spoke the words at the same time, pulling Mariah back to reality, to the world that she might be leaving any moment. She might be Craze's now, but she would definitely be Stephan's for always. No matter what this bastard did to them now, he couldn't destroy their love for each other.

Mariah turned to Craze, shifting her body so her wrists rested against Stephan's hand. He immediately went to work on the knots. Craze was still calmly sitting at the candlelit table, although his eyes practically impaled her with his glare. Mariah returned his stare with one of her own. "I'll never be yours. You may have captured me, and you may be prepared to kill me, but that does not make me yours."

Craze laughed. "In the capture, you became mine. That's how the game is played." He smiled at her as she continued to stare daggers at him, and lifted a full crystal goblet in her direction. "To the dancer and the Shadow Walker, for making it so easy to win." He smiled again and downed the fluid in one long drink, then threw the goblet hard on the deck a foot from where they lay. It shattered and Mariah couldn't stifle the scream as shards of it rained down upon them.

Mariah forced her heart to slow to normal. She had to keep her wits, and she needed to keep Craze from deciding to kill them right now. She searched her mind for anything to say. *Of course!*

"You're wrong about me, you know. I'm not a Shadow Walker. And I can't carry a child. So your little prophecy — or whatever — has some serious flaws."

Craze studied her coldly through narrowed eyes. Mariah shivered. Maybe pushing his buttons and antagonizing him was not the smartest thing for her to do.

"You *are* a Shadow Walker." Craze rose from his chair, and leaned back against the table facing her, his long legs crossed at the ankle, his arms crossed over his chest. He appeared relaxed, but Mariah could see a muscle twitching in his jaw and his teeth were clenched. "Don't you ever wonder about the father you never knew? And why he disappeared from your mother's life?"

"Not really." *What was he saying?* Her stomach rolled and she spit out her reply. "My mother didn't exactly have the best taste in men. He left her, just like every other guy did."

Craze grinned, obviously enjoying himself. "He left your mother because he was captured and killed by a demon horde. But your mother didn't know that, did she? He kept that side of himself from her. And he didn't let any other Shadow Walkers know of her existence. He led two separate lives, just like your esteemed Talisman Bay Shadow Walkers."

Mariah's mind spun in a whirlwind of disillusionment. Her whole world had been turned topsy-turvy. Her poor mom. She had loved a man she'd never really known. "How do you know this?"

He laughed. "That's easy. The prophecy *'or whatever'* spoke of your existence. It took me almost no time to trace your parentage. Your absentee father's name was on your birth certificate. And yes, he was a Shadow Walker." He nonchalantly waved his hand for emphasis as his eyes remained intent upon hers.

"No, no, no." Something, somehow, had her life figured out before she even lived it? She refused to believe it.

"And you, dear Mariah. Don't you wonder why you attract such a following at *Silver Twilight*? Why those poor simple-minded men empty their pocketbooks for nothing more than a glimpse of your assets? You may be beautiful, but no one else inspires that type of devotion." Craze paused, drawing out

Mariah's fearful anticipation. "It's the Shadow Walker in you. The power you employ. You enthrall them with your eyes. They can't resist. They give you exactly what you desire...money...and then they leave you alone. You're little better than a thief who preys upon the souls of weak men."

Oh God. She wanted to deny everything he'd said, throw something back into his face, but she knew he was right. She'd never understood why she made so much more money than any of the other dancers, and had just assumed that she was finally getting her recompense for the shit her life had thrown at her. But if she had power in her eyes to get what she desired, could she use it against Craze? She summoned up all her angry energy and glared at him, wishing that he'd let them go, that he'd burst into a ball of flame, or hell, that he'd turn into a ballerina during the final scene of Swan Lake.

Craze laughed. "Only on the souls of weak men, Mariah. Your power doesn't work on me."

Of course not. She couldn't have a power that would do her good when she was in danger.

Mariah felt a swift pull on her wrists and then the ropes loosened. She was free! She kept her fingers wrapped around the ropes so at a glance it appeared she was still tied.

She wracked her brain for something else to say. She needed to give Stephan more time to get the feeling back in his body. "Okay. So I'm a Shadow Walker. Big deal. The rest of your prophecy is still wrong. I can't have kids."

Craze's eyes narrowed to slits of pure black. "Why do you lie to me? It doesn't change the outcome."

"I'm not lying!" The heat of rage burned across her cheeks. "I was in an...accident. I can't have children...not anymore."

Red flashed from the darkness of his eyes. "Nothing's impossible. But that's irrelevant. It's time for Stephan to die. I'm going to keep you around for a while. You're quite entertaining." Craze stood up from his reclined position, and the men from earlier appeared at his side, carrying a length of thick, impossibly heavy looking chain.

The blood froze in her veins. She had to stall. They needed more time.

"Where's Twyla? What did you do with her?"

Craze's grin widened and his eyes lit up with dark humor. He pulled her abruptly to her feet and up against him. Mariah struggled to keep the ropes wrapped around her wrist as he pressed a kiss to her forehead. "Hmmm...where do bitches go when they die?"

"You asshole! She didn't do anything!" Mariah wanted to scream, to hit and punch Craze, to make him feel just a small percentage of the pain she felt. But she couldn't. If she wanted to survive, she had to pretend she was weak. But no matter what happened, she'd make sure this bastard would pay.

The clank of chain sounded from behind her and Mariah strained her neck, twisting in Craze's grip to see what was happening. The other men had pulled Stephan to his feet. He leaned heavily against one man, and although his eyes were sharp, he didn't look like he had the strength to fight. They wrapped the thick length of chain around him, pinning his arms to his sides.

"No..." Mariah moaned and struggled against Craze's grip. She could feel his excitement at his victory, his cock hard and throbbing against her stomach.

Craze turned her around and shoved his cock against her hands. She could feel its heat through his jeans. "You don't want to miss this," he whispered silkily into her ear. His voice got louder as he addressed Stephan. "Fire didn't kill you before, so this time I'm using water. And to avoid any possibility of your escape this time, a bullet to the brain should finish you off."

Mariah couldn't take her eyes off Stephan, her heart in her throat, as he was led to the edge of the ship just a few feet from where she stood. The weighted chains scraped against the deck, the sound a death toll echoing in her mind. When Stephan was turned to face her and Craze, his eyes sought out hers. "I love you, Mariah. Always…" Stephan's eyes darkened as he lifted his eyes to Craze's. "This is not the end. Soon, you will be nothing but dust beneath my feet."

Craze shoved Mariah away from him and pulled his gun out from the small of his back. "Such big words, with no way to back them up. Good night, Shadow Walker."

The sound of the gun exploding and Mariah's angry scream filled the still ocean air around them. Everything blurred as she dove toward Stephan, her only thought to protect him from the bullet. She heard Stephan yell, "Mariah, no!" as pain ripped through her shoulder. She kept moving forward, her feet unable to grasp purchase on the deck. She slammed into Stephan, propelling them both into the cold, dark ocean depths.

Chapter Sixteen

"Ow! Dammit!"

Freeze's curses surprised Twyla and she quickly opened her eyes. She'd assumed he would be dead. He was recoiling his hand from just in front of her forehead. All of the throwing stars were stuck in the chair she had been standing next to. Well, all but one. The remaining one was stuck in Freeze's hand. "What did I tell you about being careful? If I hadn't been paying attention, you could have hurt both of us!" He cursed under his breath as he grabbed the wrist of his injured hand. The pain was clearly visible in his eyes. He strode into the bathroom.

"I just wanna get out of here, Freeze." The words didn't come out as forcefully as she'd hoped they would. Twyla was torn. As much as she'd wanted to scare him, watching him bleed made her realize that she really didn't want to hurt him. Ultimately, she wanted to get out of there and find Mariah. Now that she knew she could evoke weaponry, she figured she had a better chance at rescuing her. Hopefully, there'd be lots of weaponry wherever Mariah was being held seeing as how that was the only thing Twyla was even remotely confident about using—next to pleasure tingles, and she didn't think they would work well in a rescue situation.

In the bathroom, Freeze grunted in pain. There was the sound of a small metal disc as it clanked against tile. She winced and rewound the situation in her head. She could tell something had been flying toward her, but it was too fast to see exactly what it was. She remembered him reaching up with lightning speed. Had he actually caught the throwing star instead of letting it hurt her? Those blades were incredibly sharp. She could have been dead. "Freeze. Why'd you do that?"

"Nice of you to notice." His voice strained through a tight throat. Boy, did he sound irritated.

Lover's Talisman

"No. Seriously. Why didn't you just let it kill me and be done with me?" Twyla's mind spun. This was not something a purely evil man would do.

He appeared in the doorway with a bloody towel wrapped around his hand.

"I told you. I'd be upset if you were dead."

She was speechless. There just wasn't any kind of snappy comeback arriving in her whirlwind brain. Pain, anger—and was that lust?—shone from his eyes. This was just too much for her to comprehend.

"Let me show you something. I know you can't do it. But I can and I have to before this thing gets any worse." He unwrapped his hand. Twyla swallowed hard. It wasn't that his hand looked really bad, it was that she'd done it to him. *Twyla, hello? This is your brain calling! Wake up! This man has you trapped here, remember? You have to get out and rescue Mariah. Make your cunt stop dripping and stop caring that this bad guy is hurt!*

He spoke quickly. "Hey, it's not that bad. I've had much worse. Okay. Healing. There's a few different ways to do it. You'll learn which ones are the best for each situation. Right now, I just gotta get this thing closed up before I lose too much blood. I'm fightin' shock already. A gentle touch is always best. Tap into your inner strength. I think you might be able to use your pleasure tingle strength for this. A healing light or spark will appear. In a quick burst of thought, tell it what to do and launch it." He appeared to follow his own instructions. His shoulders relaxed as a blue spark swirled around his hand, flashed and then disappeared. All that remained of his wound was a bit of redness where the skin had closed. "You'll figure it out for yourself, someday. It's different for everybody. But that's how it works for me. It'll make you a little tired, but it goes away." He paused, giving her a concerned look. "Are you okay?"

While watching him heal his hand, she'd taken serious inventory of her life and just about everything in it was overwhelming. Her head was spinning. She just wanted to run away. Anywhere but where she was. "Freeze, I need to get out of here." She pushed past him to the door.

"Twyla." She swallowed a moan as he said her name. She desperately wanted to get her head back in order. Here was a beautiful but far too dangerous man alone with her. He made her contradict herself. He made her forget about everything in her life. It was as though he caused her to focus only on herself and her own needs and just forget about everyone else in her life. But that wasn't the person she wanted to be...not now. She couldn't forget that she had to get to Mariah. It was all just too much.

She grabbed the door handle. It didn't budge. She tried to hurl a sword at the door, anything to get free, but Freeze caught it before it found its mark.

"Watch it! I'm not gonna hurt you." He put down the sword and slowly approached as Twyla continued to fiddle with the door. "Please. It's okay."

"Why are you holding me here?" She paused and leaned against the door. Her voice was distant as she calculated just how much power she could muster. "And why are you still here with me?" Maybe she could blow up the door. Anything. Escape. *Yes! Escape is good!* She could not admit to herself or anyone else that Freeze had any kind of power over her whatsoever.

After losing her virginity to a rapist when she was sixteen, she swore she would never let a man have any kind of power over her ever again. She never allowed her experience to degrade her and make her feel as though she was used goods. In fact, she turned it around and made the best of it instead. She'd wanted to save herself for her wedding night, but since that option was ripped from her, she vowed she would always maintain the upper hand. Funny how no man was ever interested in anything more than a fuck after she'd turned her misfortune into her strength. It seemed they were all too afraid.

She furiously tried to hide just how much her body wanted him. Her nipples were erect, desperately seeking the attention of his mouth or hands. Her chest rose and fell with each ragged breath. But most importantly, now that he had come closer, she didn't want to move away from him. He stirred her to life and she was not about to step away. True, she didn't need him. But oh, how she wanted him.

"Well, I'm sorry, but I just can't say why I won't walk away from you." He stepped closer to her, and she cursed herself for not knowing how to read minds. His eyes were so expressive, yet she couldn't quite place the emotions he displayed. Taking a deep breath, she inhaled his scent deep into her body. Every sense was filled with Freeze. Her heart buzzed and her thoughts swirled. This was almost too much.

He gathered her into his arms and as much as she wanted to fight it, she gave in and rested her head on his shoulder. She couldn't help it. In such close proximity, he could probably make her do anything. *Damn him.* Freeze spoke quietly against her hair. "I just can't tell you everything. But right now, this is the safest place for you to be."

"Trapped against my will while my only true friend is in trouble. I might as well be dead." She tried to gather her wits, but her entire being was clouded with passion. His body was so warm against hers. The heat from his erect cock was mere kindling for her own inner fire.

"Twyla, have you ever wondered if there's something bigger than the world we see around us?"

"Yeah. All the time."

His eyes studied hers and then flashed something unrecognizable before he spoke in barely a whisper. "I...Wow. Um...you have dark circles under your eyes. Maybe you should get some sleep." Her mind was made up in that very instant.

"You know damn well that I am not gonna lay down in that bed without you, Freeze." His eyes darkened with lust as she continued with a mischievous grin. "Fuck me, Freeze. Can you do that?" She chuckled at the memory of the first time she had said that to him. Although, this had to be the first time in her life that more than just her cunt was hot for a man. Her mind jumped for joy and her heart had even started beating faster. She launched herself at him and he kissed her with more passion than she'd ever known existed. She ignored the voice of her conscience blaring in her ears. This was something she had always wanted and she was not going to let her mind overrule her body this time. Any other time but this one.

Freeze picked her up, continuing to kiss her. He chuckled through a kiss and Twyla pulled back questioningly.

"If you had any idea the thoughts that went through my mind when you said that the first time."

"I'm sure my thoughts were the same. I want you, Freeze. Is that hard for you to believe?" Their eyes met intensely for a brief moment.

"Yeah, I guess it is." He took her to the bed and gently laid her down.

"You must be joking." She sat up and pulled off his shirt. "Just take me."

"I'm gonna take you. You bet I will." He kissed her as she fought to get his pants undone.

"Don't go so slow. I need you right now. I can't wait any longer. You've had me hot for you since the moment I met you."

He appeared stunned. "Really?"

"Get these damn things off!" She practically ripped off his pants.

"Take it easy." He used some quick magic to loosen his boots so he could toss them aside and step out of his pants.

"Nothing in my life is easy. Especially not now. So don't even tell me to take anything easy because believe me, if I could, I would, but it's not." She ran her tongue along his chest. "What could you possibly be waiting for?"

"You really need me?" He moved in closer, his breath ragged. Her eyes rested on his cock and she instantly wanted to taste it.

"Yes."

"You really gotta have me?" Her eyes traced their way up his body to meet his gaze.

"Yes!"

"Then, you're just gonna have to wait." He chuckled as he grabbed the rose scented massage oil and immediately teased her clit with his freshly oiled finger. Twyla was going to jump him, but she just fell back on the bed in ecstasy. "Because I want you first."

His finger slid between her folds and she arched into his touch. Every touch of his fingers against her clit and aching pussy made her want to beg him to take her now, hard. The man knew exactly how to press her buttons. Using a circular motion, he brought her higher with each revolution. Then he added a second finger and delved deep inside her pussy. His eyes narrowed with lust and Twyla felt the burn of his passion in every corner of her being. It was too much for her to even try to comprehend the feelings he evoked within her because they were so powerful and so different from any other she had ever felt with a man. It was like he was trying to touch her soul as well as her body. She reached out a hand to him. "You're too far away."

"Am I?" He removed his fingers from her pussy and she nearly cried out at the great loss. How could he be so cruel? Then, leaning down, he fluttered kisses over her stomach, hips and just above her mound. She'd never felt such heat from a man especially without him inside of her.

His hands captured her thighs and drew her open even wider for him. She lifted her head to try to see what he would do to her. Her pussy throbbed relentlessly under his heated gaze. How dare he keep her waiting! His eyes remained hot on her desperate pussy, and he licked his lips while one hand slid up to her clit. This man knew his foreplay.... Writhing in ecstasy, she moaned and thrust her pussy against his skillful hand. Each fingertip, one by one, paid homage to her clit. And oh God, Twyla liked his thumb the best.

"Maybe not." Twisting the covers with both hands, she watched him touch her. He climbed onto the bed and knelt beside her.

"You're ready to come just by lookin' at me." He had such a sweetly excited grin on his face.

"I am, Freeze. Don't you get it?"

"I guess you won't need any of these, then." Placing the palm of his hand on her clit, his fingers folded down parting her slickened folds. Gasping, she shuddered as he released a pleasure tingle that overflowed her body. She screamed out her climax while everything else in her world blurred.

When the room stopped spinning, she heard him chuckling. "Damn, you're easy. I like that."

"I'm easy, but I'm also insatiable. Is that the best you can do?" Her mind still reeled as her body continued to spasm from the waves of ecstasy he'd bestowed upon her. But she didn't want it to end.

He climbed over her and began to tease her clit with his hard cock. Each touch was another mini-orgasm, but she wasn't sure that he was using magic this time. It was too hard to tell.

"But Freeze, you're still…too…far…" She forgot what she was saying.

"You want me closer? How close? Like this?" His cock invaded her opening. She moaned out another mini-orgasm as her hips rose to meet him.

"If you don't fuck me, I'm gonna fuck you and you may not like it." She grinned mischievously. She was not at all afraid to take matters into her own hands. She could torture him as he was torturing her. But then again, it was this kind of torture that made her want him so badly in the first place.

"Try me, Twyla."

Well, that was a direct challenge. No one could accuse her of not being able to bring a man to ecstasy. She slid out from under him and forcefully yanked the arm that he was using to hold himself up. He fell onto his back and Twyla jumped on top of him. "Let's see how you like it." She slid her hands from his shoulders down to take possession of his hard length and it was his turn to moan. She worked her hands back up to his chest and then to either side of him. Leaning over, she grazed her taut nipples against his chest. Her hand found the massage oil. Oh, the possibilities. She slid it to the side for future use.

She tongued his nipples as he gasped. Then, she slid down to his erection and teased him by suckling the sides of it. His knuckles were turning white grasping the covers so tightly. She licked a circle around his width a few times, ending at the tip. Then she took him into her mouth.

"Oh, Twyla." It seemed that every time he said her name, he brought her closer to orgasm. She removed her lips from him as she opened the rose scented oil and put some in her hand. She stroked the base of his cock in her oiled hand and teased the head with her tongue. His body reacted like no other man she had ever been with. Then again, she'd never given another man this much attention with both her mouth as well as her hand.

His eyes were open, watching her. So many emotions flashed through them each time she glanced up from her work. His hand clasped her neck, holding her tight against his cock. She wanted to laugh. It wasn't like she was going anywhere. His cock throbbed in her mouth. She made sure she was paying attention to his entire length. His balls were tight against his shaft and she knew he was close to coming.

In a blur of movement he pulled his cock out of her mouth, slid her body up the length of him and rolled her over. Twyla knew he was beyond ready for mating with her. She could see the blazing urgency in his eyes and through the trembling of his body. He entered her hard and she raised her hips to meet each deep thrust with a shared urgency. She was shocked to discover just how much she wanted him to stay with her. It was like her world was spinning so fast that it appeared to be standing still. The only things that made sense were her and him.

Their gazes locked as her climax neared. The desperate need in his eyes mystified her, empowered her, intimidated her and took her right over the edge. She exploded so hard for a minute all that existed was pleasure. He came deep within her cunt and she soared even higher. It was as though they had joined their souls.

"Twyla. I..." his breath was ragged and his voice barely a whisper, "think I've fallen in love with you."

"What?" She couldn't be sure of what he'd said because her orgasm still raged loudly inside of her. And having this man admit something so powerful as love was more than her lust-fucked brain could interpret.

Freeze pulled away and seemed to float above her. His clothing materialized on him. Twyla reached out for him, trying to pull him back to her. She wasn't ready for this to end. Even though he still seemed close enough to touch, her fingers passed right through him. His eyes pleaded with her to understand something — they were caring and perhaps a bit sad. He reached out to her and she felt a warmth resonate throughout her body, then Freeze completely disappeared. "I'm sorry..." His voice echoed throughout the room then faded away.

Twyla blinked rapidly. Freeze still didn't reappear. She could still feel his sperm warm inside her pussy, and the memories of his touch on her body, but he was gone. She knew this time he wasn't playing with her. The room felt colder and truly empty of his presence. She shivered. Twyla had a horrible feeling that this time, Freeze might not be coming back. And for the first time, it actually bothered her that after sex, a man had just rolled over and disappeared out of her life.

Chapter Seventeen

The shock of cold water enveloping Stephan's body removed the remaining numbness the electricity had put into his limbs. He sank at an incredible rate and needed every ounce of energy to get the chains off of his body.

The Dread Lords who'd wrapped the chains around him hadn't had a clue...or they didn't really want him dead. The chain wasn't fastened right and they hadn't noticed that he'd held his arms slightly away from his body, therefore allowing more room to wiggle free.

As the chains fell free and continued sinking to what would have been his grave, Stephan shot to the surface and toward where they'd entered the water. He wasn't sure which he needed more: air or Mariah. Actually, there was no comparison. Without Mariah, breathing wouldn't matter. He couldn't live without her.

Mariah had taken a bullet for him. One that surely would have killed him. He'd contrived a dangerous game of dodging, but she'd done him one better. She had saved his life as well as getting them both off the boat at the same time. He had planned on faking his death, then sneaking back onto the boat to rescue her. Now, when he found her and got her to safety, he didn't know whether he should thank her or punish her. Well first, he was going to love every inch of her, then he'd make sure she never put herself in danger again.

He refused to think that she could be lying dead in the water.

Stephan broke through the surface and gasped for breath as he searched the surrounding water for Mariah. *Where was she?* The sun was almost completely down, turning the ocean into a dark and dangerous adversary. He scanned the surface of the water. She wasn't there. His heart pounded painfully in his chest. God, he couldn't lose her now!

He dove beneath the surface, unwilling to give up. No light permeated the ocean below, but he continued swimming…searching…hoping. When his lungs burned he resurfaced, then dove again. Nothing. Only minutes had passed since they'd fallen from the boat, but every moment he couldn't find her a part of him died.

Resolve hardened and darkened him. If Mariah was dead, he was going to go back on that boat and slowly torture and kill every last person on it. If he died in the process, all the better. He swam toward the yacht, his decision made.

Stephan froze as something brushed against his body, then his world righted as Mariah's head broke the surface in front of him.

"Stephan?" She choked and coughed, gasping for breath. Her eyes betrayed the pain she was in.

"Where were you shot?" Stephan ran his hands over her body. She seemed to flinch no matter where he touched her. But she was alive.

"My shoulder." She continued to gasp for breath. "I can't move my right arm."

The front of her shoulder was unmarred. He swam behind her. The wound was bleeding heavily. The bullet had entered through her back and had to still be lodged inside. He needed to get her to safety, to Fiero so he could heal her.

Mariah's eyes glazed over. Her lips and skin had a bluish tint and her teeth chattered as she spoke. "I couldn't find you. I tried to swim…tried to find you…" Her eyes drifted shut.

Shit! "Mariah! Look at—"

"They're alive. Fuck! Craze, they're alive!" The voices bounced across the water.

Mariah's eyes fluttered open. Stephan kissed her, hard and fast, before just as swiftly pulling away. She was cold to the touch. "Mariah, we have to swim. Just hold onto me. I'll get us out of this." Stephan wrapped one arm around her and began swimming with the other.

Gunshots rang out from the boat. "Big breath, Mariah!" He pulled them both under and kept swimming, pushing to get the needed distance from the Dread Lords, and toward the shore.

Stephan felt a mild burn in his calf as a bullet grazed him. It wouldn't slow him down. Getting Mariah to safety was the only thing that mattered.

The gunshots subsided and Stephan headed for the surface. He had no choice. They both needed to breathe.

Once on the surface, he checked to see if the boat followed them. He could hear voices from that direction, but it didn't seem like they were coming after them. He checked his heading and decided the cave would be the best refuge. It was another safe area like the Shadow Walker compound where Fiero could appear and heal Mariah. And they wouldn't have to deal with any Dread Lords who would be waiting outside of *Rare and Unusual Imports.*

"Just a little bit further, okay sweetheart? Then you can rest."

Mariah nodded and a small, pained smile crossed her face.

"I love you, Mariah. Hold on to me. Tight." He began to swim with her in tow. In two days she'd made his life worth living again. He'd never before believed in love at first sight. Maybe Craze was right about them being fated to be together, because Stephan knew that no matter what, they were going to make it through this and they were going to spend their lives together.

She gasped and choked on the water, but her grip on him was strong.

"I...love you...too." Her breath was warm against his ear. He could see the love in her eyes and it spurred him forward.

After what felt like an eternity of swimming, but was probably only fifteen minutes, his feet found sand. Mariah's head fell to his shoulder as he picked her up and carried her out of the water. She shook and shivered in his arms. He nestled her closer, feeling the sticky wetness of blood against his arms where he held her. A pained moan escaped through her chattering teeth. She must have more internal injuries than the bullet wound in her shoulder. Those bastards had really done a number on her. They would pay. He would make sure they all felt immeasurable pain.

Stephan clicked-in to Fiero. *I need you at the cave. Can you make it quick?*

I can do my best. You made it out of danger, I trust. Fiero sounded relieved.

Yeah. Mariah took a bullet for me. She's losing a lot of blood. I can't lose her.

I'll be right there. Fiero clicked-out.

"Stay with me, Mariah. Stay with me." Her eyes were closed, her dark eyelashes a striking contrast against her pale skin. He brushed his lips to her forehead. She was so cold. "C'mon baby, you're gonna be fine. Just stay with me."

Stephan approached the protected mouth of the cave. What appeared to be an impassable rock wall was actually the doorway to another safe dimension.

"Where'm I gonna go? I can't live without you." Her words were mumbled against his chest.

"Yeah, I can't live without you either." He kissed the top of her head as he stepped through the wall and into the cave.

"Lights."

Torches interspersed sporadically along the rock walls and a fire pit in the center of the great room burst into flame. Stephan could feel the needed heat as he stepped further into the cave.

Only the Shadow Walkers knew of the cave. They hadn't used it in the past slow demon months. It doubled as a jail, for when killing demons was not the best option. There were plenty of handcuffs, chains, manacles and assorted demon torture devices collecting cobwebs. It looked like the set of a really bad horror movie where the Set Dresser had more fun than necessary procuring appropriate scenery.

He stepped past all of that and strode deeper into the cave. A makeshift bed was set up on a natural shelf in the rock. It was secluded from the rest of the cave and had curtains to keep it private. He laid Mariah down on the mostly clean sheets.

She was soaking wet, and whatever skin he could see had a bluish tint to it. He couldn't wait for the heat to dry her clothes. She needed to be warm and dry now.

Her jeans were plastered to her body. He unzipped them and tried tugging on them. She cried out with a pained moan but her eyes remained shut. Stephan had undressed many a woman, but never in this situation. He peeled the clinging denim down and sighed in relief as he got her legs free without any further cries of pain.

She wasn't wearing underwear.

He reminded his overeager cock that now was not the time—that she was injured because of him—as he wrapped her legs in a wool blanket at the foot of the bed.

The shirt would have to go. He reached behind him for a knife and sliced through the white cotton. Raw anger rushed to the surface as her ribs came in to view. *What the fuck had those bastards done to her?*

Her stomach and ribs were black and blue, the dark colors leaching up her skin and under her bra. He'd never seen anyone alive with such extensive bruising. He wanted to hold her close and make everything better, to take away the memories of pain that she'd always carry with her. Instead he took her hand and held it to his lips.

"Mariah, you're safe now. I promise."

Her eyes stayed closed.

"Mariah, sweetheart…look at me. Open your eyes and look at me!" Stephan felt for her pulse. It was there, but weak and thready. "Please…Mariah…baby!"

Still no response.

"Fiero! Now!"

"What happened to her?" Fiero appeared and immediately went to work, mumbling his healing words and setting the lights in motion.

Stephan watched the green lights grow in number and intensity. They seemed to circle and throb over every inch of Mariah's body. "I don't know everything that happened to her. And she was conscious until just a minute ago—"

"It's probably better that she's unconscious…"

"What? What aren't you saying? What do you know?"

Fiero's hands ran the length of Mariah's body. When he pulled his hands away, the lights floated to her abdomen, flared brightly and then just hovered, encasing her stomach in a warm glow. "She's got fractured ribs, a swollen cheek, and a hole in her shoulder. Numerous scratches and bruises. It looks to me like someone used her as a punching bag. She's in a lot of pain."

"Was she raped?" The words practically caught in his throat. If she'd been violated that way, he'd lose it.

"No."

Stephan breathed a sigh of relief. *Thank God.*

"What about you? You okay?" Fiero looked him over and Stephan glanced down at his bloodstained clothing.

"Yeah. This isn't my blood." *God, so much blood from such a little thing. How could she still be alive?* Stephan didn't even feel the need to mention that a bullet had hit him. Compared to Mariah, he was doing just fine. Yet he could tell from the set of Fiero's shoulders that he hadn't told him everything.

"But…"

Fiero turned back to his patient but not before Stephan saw the concern and worry marring his usually easygoing demeanor. His heart felt like it was going to beat its way out of his chest. He watched Mariah, so pale and still under the sheet. He stepped past Fiero and knelt next to the bed, enveloping Mariah's hand in his and kissing her fingers.

Lover's Talisman

"Fiero, tell me...is she gonna be okay?"

Fiero's words were quiet, barely more than a whisper. "She's pregnant. You're gonna be a father."

Stephan's world seemed to spiral for an out of control moment. Then as the tornado unwound, it was more like a beautiful firework exploding.

"Stephan, you okay?"

"That's really...wow..." He paused to try to think a bit more clearly. He could not remember a time in his life that encompassed more joy—or fear. "But how the hell am I supposed to keep her and our child safe?"

"We'll do what we have to do, Stephan. You know that. Our life isn't easy, but we won't let anything happen to Mariah or the baby." Fiero rested his hand on Stephan's shoulder.

"No, I won't let anything happen to her." Stephan stared at *his* woman carrying *his* child. His stomach clenched as he made a silent pact. Never would he let anything or anyone hurt Mariah or their child. If he had to take them to the Order to keep them safe he'd do it. This woman represented everything to him. More than he ever expected his life could give him. But his joy was marred in anger.

"You know what, Fiero, I'm really thinking this is a load of bullshit. How the fuck did David know that Mariah would be pregnant? How's he gonna know something like that? Dammit, Fiero. There's something either you're not telling me or the Order isn't telling you. And now, more than ever, I need answers. You get Themonius here—now—so he can see how near death she is. You get him here or I'm not doing anything about the Dread Lords. I'm not gonna do anything but protect my family."

"What? What are you saying?"

"I'm saying that for once in my fucking Shadow Walker life, I finally have a taste of happiness. And if David's just gonna use that against me, then fuck him. I'd sooner hole up here in the cave just to enjoy my new family. That's something I never really had. You guys were my family. Y'know, in reality, I've always been a father. You guys would be dead without me! Hell, you already are..."

Stephan took a deep breath to try to calm his wits. "Sorry, man. This is just too close. It's too real that I could lose everything I really care about." Shadow Walking was his life and he was not yet ready to give it up. But if the Order was going to withhold information that could surely mean life or death, what was the point?

"It's okay, man. It's okay. I'll get Themonius here somehow. When he arrives, tell it just like you did now. The Order is so far removed from humanity they might not completely understand your urgency nor your frustration. Let Mariah sleep it off awhile longer. The lights will help her heal faster. I'd imagine you also have some thinking to do."

"Yeah, I do. Go get him." Stephan took yet another deep breath in an effort to calm down as Fiero disappeared. His clothes were still damp and beginning to chafe. Luckily, there were always spare clothes at the cave. He exchanged his blood soaked jeans and shirt for sweat pants and another T-shirt. As he pulled on the pants, he inspected the small scrape on his leg. A bullet had hit him in the water. It hadn't been enough to stop him from swimming and now that he could see the actual damage, he nearly chuckled aloud. It wasn't even worth a band-aid compared to what Mariah had been through.

He gently placed a hand over Mariah's stomach. This was something so amazing to him. He was really going to be a father. Despite being a Shadow Walker. Despite the danger. There was a child growing in her womb. He wondered what the rest of the guys would say.

On that thought he realized he hadn't let his brother know that he was okay. Funny, how nothing else seemed quite as important as Mariah's safety. He quickly clicked-in to Marlin.

Yeah, bro. We were just about to strike. The mob's kinda rowdy. Marlin's voice sounded quite relieved.

No. Not yet. Right now we wait. There's a lot more going on here that the Order isn't telling us about and I'm not gonna continue doing their bidding until I know everything. I'll take out David. He will go down, but not until I talk to Themonius.

You're gonna talk to Themonius? I thought you can't go directly to the Order.

I told Fiero to bring Themonius's high and mighty ass here.

You think he'll cooperate?

If he doesn't, we all quit. No more risking our own asses for the Sacred Order. Got it?

Yeah. Wouldn't that be a relief? I'll let the rest of the guys know.

Hey, bro? Stephan knew he had to tell someone about all that he'd learned.

Yeah, man. What is it?

How do you feel about being an uncle?

Well, that's never gonna happen.

It will happen. About nine months from now.

What? You? No.

Yeah. We're gonna have to do everything to keep them safe. I won't lose them.

I dunno whether to laugh or cry. I'll have to get back to you on that.

It's okay, man. We'll work all this out.

Well, we're gonna have to, aren't we?

Stephan could feel Marlin's fear for him through the connection.

Yeah. It's all good, though. Themonius will be here any minute. You round up the guys and get them ready to storm the Dread Lord compound. Do nothing until I signal.

Got it.

If plans change, I'll let you know.

Okay. And bro? Marlin paused for a brief moment. *Congratulations, man.*

Stephan could hear the mixed emotions in his brother's voice. He knew exactly what was going through his mind, but he wouldn't go there. *Thanks. I expect you to be available for babysitting sometimes.*

Yeah. I will.

Get the guys ready. Stephan clicked-out. It was time to come up with a plan of attack. Themonius wouldn't know what hit him when Stephan's furor of responsibility was through with him.

"Why is it that I have been summoned?" Themonius's thundering voice startled Stephan and he whipped around to face him.

"Keep your voice down! Don't wake her up." Stephan glowered at Themonius.

In a flurry of white flowing robes, Themonius strode toward the bed. "And how is she?"

Stephan blocked Themonius's approach. "She's fine. Tell me why the Dread Lords know more about my own destiny than I do. And don't bullshit."

Themonius frowned as he lifted his robes off the floor. "This place is filthy. I should hope you'll take better care of your woman than you do this place."

Stephan clenched his fists. He wanted to punch a hole through Themonius's chest, wipe the "better than thou" expression off his face. "I do take care of my woman. Just as I have taken care of this godforsaken town and if you won't give me the information I want, I'm out. The Talisman Bay Shadow Walkers are through."

Themonius smirked. "You can't just walk away. Your destiny has found you."

"Watch me. No more fighting, no more following the Orders' demands. How do you expect us to win this war when we don't even know why we're fighting? This is bullshit, Themonius, and you know it."

Themonius walked to a bench, swiped his hand over it and pursed his lips into a tight frown. He stepped back toward Stephan, then reclined himself in mid-air, crossing his legs at the ankle. "We cannot tell you what we do not yet know. Or tell you things you would have no reason to believe. Truth is only an interpreter, and Fate has its whimsy."

"Stop speaking in riddles. I wanna know everything you know about Mariah, and our child, and why we're being prophesied."

Themonius sighed. "You had to find love with Mariah on your own. That was not something we could control. If you had known what your life entailed, you would never have let your heart rule your decisions. Everything must be told in its time. There is reason behind what we've done."

Stephan glared at Themonius. "Well, I do love her. And I won't let that love cause her anymore pain. Don't you understand? I love her enough that I'll do anything to keep her safe, including walk away from all this."

Themonius met his eyes, and Stephan could see a wealth of knowledge steeped in ancient history, mixed with perhaps a bit of fear. Themonius sighed again. "The world is going to change. The balance between good and evil will shift. And that balance will happen in Talisman Bay, because of you..." Themonius lifted his hands in a widespread gesture, "...because of all of you."

"So, my life's already been foretold. You knew about it and didn't think it was important to tell me? I don't fucking believe this." Stephan had to calm himself in order not to throttle Themonius. "And this 'shifting balance'? Do you mean shifting in the favor of good, or bad?"

"That is unclear. Destinies shift and fates mingle. But you, your family, and the rest of the Talisman Bay Shadow Walkers have the strength to keep things on the side of right. Without you, we have already lost." Themonius's eyes were pained and sad. "And the world will become what we most fear—evil will win."

The invisible leash that always bound Stephan to his duty wrapped around him tightly, preventing his escape. He couldn't let the world collapse. He couldn't let the bad guys win. But he still had questions. "Why us? Why Mariah?"

Themonius stopped floating in air and stood tall once again. "Because you are the ones with the power to change the world." Themonius stepped to Mariah's side and placed his hand above her stomach. Mariah shifted in her sleep, one hand coming to rest protectively over the baby she still didn't know she carried.

"Mariah's father was a very powerful Shadow Walker. His name was Doyle and he took care of his city solo. He believed himself invincible." Themonius shifted his gaze back to Stephan. "But he fell in love. Knowing the danger he put Mariah's mother in, he never told her...and he started to distance himself from his duties. But you can never escape being a Shadow Walker."

A bright white light glowed from Themonius's hand and down onto Mariah. "Mariah carries Doyle's blood in her veins. Shadow Walker children are always stronger than their parents. There has never been a third generation Shadow Walker born...and never one to parents both of Shadow Walker blood. Your child is strong with life's magic, stronger than you and she both. But the child's magic will be attractive to both sides."

"So, what, you're telling me that my child is gonna be in danger all the time because of destiny? That's not good enough. I won't let my family be in danger for your cause."

Themonius stepped away from Mariah. "It's not just our cause. You don't understand. This is bigger than the Order. All of you, Marlin, Dusty, Ryan, Jake, Ana and even Fiero were chosen not just because you fight as a team, but because your destinies are all strong. You all have roles to play. This will not end tonight. The Dread Lords will stop at nothing to gain that control. Keeping Mariah safe is of high priority to the Order as well. We are already training a Shadow Watcher specifically for her and the child. A Watcher can make sure they are safe at all times."

"So, some guy's gonna follow her around for the rest of her life? This is your solution?" He wouldn't resign his family to that type of life.

"It's not like that. Shadow Watchers are specially trained. They have stronger intuition. They can sense the danger of any situation in enough time to do something about it and they don't even have to be near the intended victim. They can hone in on the person they are assigned to take care of. No one will follow her everywhere unless it is necessary."

Stephan reached out his hand in hopes of a handshake. He didn't necessarily like the information he'd been given, but he didn't doubt its reliability. Now he just needed to figure out what to do about it.

Themonius took Stephan's hand, and something passed between the two of them, a mutual understanding of sorts. They needed each other. Themonius disappeared as he walked away.

Stephan watched Mariah sleeping and could no longer deny his need to hold her. He slipped into bed and she instinctively curled into him. He wrapped his arms around her, cradling her belly, needing the completion he felt with her at his side.

Stephan didn't think he'd be able to rest; he had too much to think about and to plan for. Not only had his life changed, but his friends' lives as well. It wasn't just about Talisman Bay anymore, it was about the world. That was a heavy weight to bear.

But a few minutes of peace was all he wanted. Just a few minutes curled up with Mariah to enjoy the woman who'd changed his life. The woman he would do anything for. His thoughts waned as Mariah's warmth comforted him and he drifted into much-needed sleep.

Chapter Eighteen

Although only a dream, the colors were bright and focused, every detail sharply etched into her waking memory.

A man, gentle in nature but whose sheer presence exuded strength and courage, walked toward her through a brightly lit, crowded room. The colorfully dressed people blocking his path parted in his wake, every movement he made as he approached her, graceful and smooth. He wore all black, standing out amidst the bright colors and pastels that everyone else wore, further lending to his dangerous and intriguing aura. His face was familiar, although one she'd only before seen in photographs. His full dark brown hair was sprinkled with gray at the temples, as was his mustache. Eyes sparkled and a smile tilted up the corners of his mouth when he reached her side.

A large hand caressed her face and with her accepting nod and smile, he swooped her into his arms. "My beautiful little girl. I'm so proud of you."

Mariah clung to her father, embracing the man she'd always wanted to believe in, but through circumstance had never been able to know. She hiccupped out a sob against his chest, as his hand stroked her hair. "I missed you, Daddy."

"You are so strong little one...so strong. And so much rests on you. But you have the power inside of you, the power to change the world." He murmured the words into her hair as he continued to hold her tight. "Stephan will take care of you, love you as you deserve to be loved. With him, you will understand what your mother and I shared...what we are able to share now together."

"What?" Mariah lifted her face and met the eyes that she'd only before seen reflected in a mirror.

Lover's Talisman

"Look..." A gesture from her father and the crowd parted again. A woman, dark blonde hair tumbling over her shoulders, dressed in whispers of silk and light, walked toward them both. Her eyes glistened with tears of love and happiness.

"Mom?" Mariah ran toward her mother's outstretched arms. Her mom laughed, a joyous sound, as they met in a tight embrace.

Another set of arms surrounded them both. Mariah joyfully stared at both of her parents, for the first time together in her mind's eye.

"Be happy Mariah, and be safe. And know that your father and I have found in death what we never could have in life. Death is just another life we live, another role we play."

A sad memory flashed through her mind at her mother's words. "Twyla? Mom, dad, is Twyla here? Can I see her? Tell her I'm sorry?"

Her mother clasped Mariah's hand. "She's not here." She smiled mischievously. "In fact, she's very much alive, and safe where she is and who she is with. All will be as it should be."

Relief filled Mariah in comforting waves. "Thank you for telling me."

Her father took her other hand in his. "We love you, and the child you carry—"

"But, I can't—"

"Your world is different, your powers have been brought to your attention. The doors to things thought impossible have opened." He squeezed her hand. "Things forever broken can be fixed. And sleeping dreams are not always fantasy." His lips touched her forehead with fatherly love then he stepped back and winked.

"Wake now, Mariah. We will visit you again in time..."

As all dreams do, the edges faded and blurred until the pictures were gone, nothing but a memory hovering on the edge between sleep and wake. Mariah held herself still, eyes tightly shut, imprinting, forcing the images to remain clear and sharp. Because she knew this dream was real. It had to be.

With the images firmly etched in her mind, Mariah blinked her eyes open, trying to remember where she was and how she'd gotten there. Stephan's arms cradled her close, her back against his chest, and she could feel his breath against the back of her neck. The memories of her pre-dream world came tumbling back.

She'd been shot. Almost drowned.

And she was pregnant.

But that had been just a part of the dream, wasn't it?

Mariah knew better. Everything inside of her shouted with joy that she was pregnant, carrying Stephan's child.

She smiled wide, the happiness filling her heart and body. Everything was going to be okay. Twyla was alive. And Mariah had found her soulmate.

She snuggled deeper into Stephan and instantly realized two things. One, she was naked. And two, Stephan wasn't, but he was very aware of her presence. His cock was issuing a blatant invitation and she was of the mind to accept.

Right now.

* * * * *

The fire burned closer, smoke nearly engulfing them in its thick blackness. The roar of flame devouring dry timber masked the frantic screams and yells as they desperately sought an exit from the abandoned house on the outskirts of town. This was their place away from the world.

And now their refuge was the tomb a friend had locked them in to die. David had smiled as he shot Fiero through the barred window, smiled as he poured the gasoline, smiled as he lit the match. Smiled as he watched them burn.

Stephan sat up from where he'd been kneeling over Fiero's body, his best friend's blood still warm on his hands. The smell of burning flesh and hair filled his nostrils, gagging him with the stench. He looked at his arms and realized the smell was of his own skin burning.

Through the smoke, he searched for his friends. Dusty threw himself against the door, again and again, but the old hardwood held firm. Marlin and Ryan were at one window, Jake and Ana at another, all of them frantically clawing at the unmoving steel bars locking them in. As Stephan watched, Ana bent over coughing and choking, her body screaming for the air they were all being denied. Jake fell next to her, holding her to him, pulling her with him to the center of the room where the only air remained.

There were only seconds left. Seconds before their air would be gone, seconds before the walls and roof would collapse in on them. As though they all knew the end was near, they gathered close, wanting to go out the same way they'd spent their lives.

Together.

Blistering heat. Pain. Choking.

And then a question from the edge of death. Join us and live. Become Shadow Walkers, fight another day.

Or die.

But death was never an option.

The nightmare of that day had never dulled, still playing with unerring accuracy all the details of that grim event. Stephan could still feel the blistering heat surrounding him.

But it was a different heat surrounding him now. A warm, wet haven, suckling and loving every inch of his cock. Reaction had him thrusting deeper, wanting more. A purring laughter vibrated his length. He moaned.

Stephan awakened more fully and opened his eyes to witness heaven. Mariah, naked, her hair falling over her shoulders, taut nipples peeking through the strands, as she knelt between his legs sucking him deeply.

He moaned again. She looked up at him, eyes sparkling mischievously, then smiled around his shaft. Removing him from her mouth, she ran her tongue down his full length. She took great care, not ignoring any part of him.

Her fingers discovered his sac, and they caressed and fondled as her tongue continued its tactile observation of his cock. Then her mouth lowered and her tongue found his balls as well. She sucked first one, then the other into her welcoming mouth.

This went on for what felt like forever, as she explored, learned and tasted him. Stephan was in pain, desperately wanting to thrust himself inside of her…anywhere. Didn't matter, he just wanted to feel her tight and warm around him.

She worked her way up his body, bunching his shirt up as she moved, her nipples trailing along his bare skin. Every nerve ending screamed at him to take her now, fuck her, brand her as his forever.

"Mmmm…do you like that?"

"What do you think?" His words came out strangled, his vocal cords not wanting to do anything but moan. He wanted to come. But he didn't want it like this. He wanted to take Mariah with him.

She reached his chest, where she patiently began alternately biting and licking his nipples. Her legs straddled his thighs, her moist heat pressing right against his cock. He didn't need further invitation.

Stephan grabbed Mariah to him, holding her tight as he flipped them both over on the bed.

Well, that's what he tried to do.

Unfortunately, Mariah hadn't fully removed his sweats when she'd gone down on him while he slept. His legs, tangled in the mass of sheets and sweats, kept him off balance and he fell to the thick pile of furs on the floor next to the bed, bringing Mariah with him.

Reflexively, he flipped them in mid-air so she landed on top of him. Their eyes met and Mariah grinned, then burst into giggles.

"You okay?" Her laughter convinced him she was probably just fine, but he had to ask. The last thing he wanted to do was hurt her or their child because he was a clumsy, desperate, love-fucked idiot in bed. But he absolutely had to have her. There was no question in his mind about that.

Mariah leaned down kissing him directly on the tip of his nose. "Yes, I'm uh...fine. Although I am in need of something you can provide." The wet glide of pussy across bare flesh was explanation enough.

Thank God! He kicked his sweat pants completely off so he wouldn't encore his performance of stupidity and yanked his T-shirt over his head. "Good. Turnabout is fair play." Tilting his hips, he teased her opening with his shaft. Mariah arched her head back and moaned, baring her incredible body to him. Leaning down, he suckled a breast, pulling tight on the nipple. "These are just so damn perfect. I could suck on them for hours. You wouldn't mind, would you?"

Mariah whimpered as he rolled her tight nub around on his tongue. "God, Stephan, don't stop. Don't ever stop."

"Oh, I won't." Sliding his hands to her hips, he lifted her, then settled her solidly down on his cock until even his balls were nestled deeply between her thighs. She was all he ever needed. His fiery hot Mariah.

He ran his tongue along the curve of her neck, shoulders, breasts, tasting her everywhere. His hands guided her hips—grinding, swaying, circling, pumping his length. She closed her eyes and gasped, her mewls of desire echoing around them, making his cock surge even deeper. Claiming her mouth, he took complete ownership of her.

Studying her every move, he countered with a hand, his tongue, a thrust of his hips. Her pussy spasmed, tightening around his cock, showing him just how ready she was. He couldn't hold out any longer. But, she was his and he would take her with him.

His thrusts sped up, and he angled his hips so every stroke hit Mariah's clit. She whimpered and moaned, anchoring her fingers into his arms, screaming as she climaxed. That was all he needed to hear. He closed his eyes and came, shooting his seed deep into the body of the woman he loved. He kept coming, until he felt like he'd completely drained his body. Mariah lay limp against him, although her hips still rocked against him, slight, small movements, massaging and squeezing his cock. Stephan locked his arms around her, running his hands over her tangled strands of hair. There was no denying this love.

Sweet Mariah. His soulmate. His forever.

* * * * *

"You still okay, sweetheart?" Stephan kissed her forehead, waking her from her sex-induced coma.

Nuzzling deeper into him, she mumbled into his chest. "Not sure. Think I've lost all feeling in the lower half of my body. I might need cock to vagina resuscitation."

Stephan laughed, his hand casually stroking up and down her body. Casually, but Mariah's over stimulated neurons took it oh so seriously. Then his hand stopped on her abdomen, cradling her stomach, and she smiled. He already knew. She placed her hand over his, interlocking their fingers. "Did you have a name in mind?"

Stephan let out a deep exhale and held her tighter, then brushed a kiss across the top of her head. "So you do know. How?"

"My parents came to me and told me I was pregnant." Tears fell from her eyes as she remembered her mother's smiling face. "My parents are happy. And they're together. I know you probably think I'm crazy, believing that my parents spoke to me in my dream, but I know it's real."

"A demon, a werewolf, fate and an insane man brought us together, and you think I'd be surprised that you learned of this in a dream? You're a Shadow Walker, not much can surprise us." He wrapped his body around hers. She leaned into him, completely content.

"And you're okay with it?" Stephan asked cautiously.

"Having a baby with the man I love? Having a baby when I didn't think I could?" She lifted her head from his chest and met his eyes, not wanting him to doubt what she was saying. "Why wouldn't I be? I love you, Stephan. I can't imagine my life any other way. Even with all the craziness."

Stephan's eyes were serious. "I'll protect you. Keep you both safe. Actually, I need to get you to the import store soon. We're attacking the Dread Lords at dawn. David won't be a threat any longer. I'm ending this once and for all. He started this twelve years ago when he tried to kill us. That was the catalyst for us becoming Shadow Walkers. You actually woke me up from a recurring nightmare about that day. God, you've awakened me in so many ways."

Mariah kissed him, wishing she could take his pain away, wanting to extend the time they had together before Stephan went to battle. He growled and lifted her closer, his kisses hungry, impatient. He pulled away slightly, whispering into her mouth, "I want you again. Now."

Mariah backed away slightly, her mind whirling. She wanted to make this special, do something he'd never forget. But she needed to regain control first or she'd jump him before she even started. She scooted a bit more away from Stephan and settled herself back into the furs. He grinned, as though he knew what she was planning, and lay back down, faking repose.

Mariah took a deep, calming breath. "So do we have time?" She did her best to put on an alluring pose, but realized with her sleep-mussed, post being-held-captive-by-a-maniac hair and a white sheet wrapped around her body, she probably looked more like a drunken sorority girl after a bad toga party, than a sexy vixen. But she wasn't ready to walk out of this cave yet, to go back out into the world where too many people wanted them dead. That reality could wait.

"What did you have in mind?" Stephan's eyes narrowed and his gaze trailed the length of her body. Every nerve ending came alive under the sheer sexuality of his oh so slow perusal, as though he was reaching out, touching her, bringing her skin to life. But he didn't move closer. He just continued to lie there, resting on one elbow, for all the world a relaxed man. But he couldn't hide his very un-relaxed erection. It was as though he was proudly displaying his jutting length, making her want it even more.

Idly, he traced his free hand along the edge of the sheet tucked around her breasts. Back and forth, back and forth, his rough fingers barely skimming her flesh. Fresh wetness seeped between her legs, mixing with the earlier juice of their combined orgasms. Oh lord, he barely touched her and her entire body vibrated with violent need for him.

Before she could forget what she so badly wanted to do for him...for both of them, she spoke. "D-dance for you. I want to dance for you, Stephan." Saying the words aloud had her head spinning, the walls of her cunt flowing with frenzied desire. Her secret fantasy had been revealed. There was no backing down now.

Stephan closed in. His breath skimming her cheek, he raggedly inhaled, then charmed her with a wolfish grin. "I smell your arousal, sweetheart. You wanna dance for me? You know I'd really like that, don't you? Your pussy's already open and crying for me to thrust myself inside. It's beckoning me to slide in there while your hot sweet juices rain all over my throbbing cock. Waiting for me to fuck you. And I will. I'll fuck you until you scream." Stephan licked his lips, emanating carnal desire as he continued. "But not yet. First, you'll dance for me. I want you alone dancing. For my eyes only. Showing me how beautiful you are. Always for me only."

His words surrounded her, consumed her, filled her with the most desperate longing she could possibly imagine. *Oh lord, it was his fantasy, too.*

Dipping his head, he latched his mouth around the rapid pulse point of her neck. He drew against the skin, suckling it into his mouth, tasting her, marking her. Mariah's neck tilted back on a moan. Hands freely roamed her body, barely skimming her skin just as he had done earlier, the feathery touch arousing her to a fevered pitch. Pure sublime torture. Her body screamed out for fulfillment. For the mouth bruising her neck to move down her body, to bite her nipples, to suck on her cunt. Dammit! Didn't he know what he was doing to her?

Then everything stopped. Stephan's breath panted hot over her neck as he pulled away. "Dance now, Mariah. While you still cream for my touch. While your clit still aches for my tongue to lick it…while your pussy still craves the stroking of my cock. I want you, Mariah. And I want you to show me how much you want me too."

On shaking knees, she stood, dragging the sheet with her. She held it loosely over her breasts, the small barricade her only help in keeping her rapidly dwindling hold on sanity. Could you lose your mind from overwhelming desire? From loving a man so much your body boils over with need? Well, if she was going down, she was taking Stephan with her.

Stepping to a clear section of floor, she dropped the sheet, then turned her back on Stephan and took deep calming breaths. Or at least she tried. Her insides quivered nervously, her skin ached to be touched, and her brain was screaming, *Fantasy, shmantasy, I just wanna be fucked.* Mariah shut everything out, listened to the music in her soul and started to dance.

The first moves were always the hardest for her, before she fully sank into the role she was playing and began performing in earnest. But she'd never danced for someone she loved either. Surprisingly, that made it more of a challenge because her attention was divided. Even though she hadn't looked at Stephan since she'd dropped the sheet and turned around, she could feel the heat of his stare. Her skin felt stretched tight over her body, hypersensitive to every single temperature flux in the room. And it was just getting hotter.

Her feet moved almost without provocation, translating her emotions into a rhythm of love and desire. Then she turned to face him, meeting his eyes, and the beat became deeper, more primitive. The air between them throbbed in time with the music of her soul. This was her man, she was his woman, and nothing and no one could come between them.

Stephan remained stretched on the furs, but absent of any covering. His cock had grown impossibly longer, the shaft an angry red, the head swollen and purple, glistening with pre-ejaculate. As she continued to move for him, she let her gaze devour his toned body, the lean hips, tightly muscled abdomen and chest, the light pink scars from his earlier battles. All hers.

Her dancing brought her to the edge of the furs, and she knelt in front of him, still rhythmically twisting and swaying. She placed herself barely out of his reach, just enough to keep up the pretense of a show, and to avoid lunging for him and impaling herself on his cock. Spreading open her legs, wetness seeped from her pussy, sliding down to coat her thighs. Her offering to him.

A low growl warned her that he couldn't take much more. She quickly met his narrow eyed stare. "I wanna watch you...I want to watch you fuck yourself now. I wanna see you thrust your fingers inside your creaming pussy working your body while your man watches you. Show me your heat...how you want to be fucked by me. Show me how you ache for me."

Mariah nodded and licked her lips, locking her gaze with Stephan's before sliding her hands up her body from where they rested on her thighs. The desire in his gaze made her stomach clench in pleasured agony. Cupping her breasts with both hands, she used her thumb and forefingers to squeeze her overly erect nubs, whimpering at the pleasure/pain. Stephan didn't even blink. Electric desire coursed from her nipples to her cunt, shattering her resolve to go slow.

Moaning, she trailed one hand from her breast, avoiding her supersensitive clit, and parted her labia. She dipped a finger inside her saturated pussy and moved it in and out, in and out, arching into her touch. And still Stephan didn't move.

Pulling out her dripping fingers, she traced her nipples with the moisture, then cupped her breasts, holding them up for his approval. His breathing came faster but he still didn't accept her unspoken invitation.

She stuck one finger in her mouth and began to suck. Stephan didn't move, but his knuckles turned white where he grasped the furs beneath him. *Ha! Finally a response.* Mimicking her earlier thrusting, she moaned around her finger, then removed it with a small pop. "I can taste us both. Jealous?"

He growled and lunged for her nipple, practically swallowing it. His other hand dove between her open thighs, and thrust two fingers deep into her pussy. Mariah's whole world swirled as she rocked into his thrusting fingers. Locking her fingers in his silky hair, she let him feast for a moment, then yanked him away. Her other hand caught the wrist pumping between her thighs. "No." She shook her head when he growled. "You can't touch. Not yet. I'm not done letting you watch."

In defiance, he leaned in, licked one final swipe across her nipple, then twisted his fingers inside of her, lightly scraping the walls of her channel before pulling out. Biting her tongue to keep from begging him for more, she waited until he settled back down, before continuing. "Where was I? Oh…I remember." Returning one finger to her mouth, she got it wet, then trailed it down her body, between her breasts, over her stomach, and began circling her clit. Oh lord, she wouldn't last if she kept this up. But then again, she doubted Stephan would either.

Circling her clit faster and faster, Mariah's orgasm built inside her like a dam waiting to burst. Meeting Stephan's eyes, she saw the love and desire he felt for her, the deep, eternal connection binding them together. This was what looking into forever felt like.

Then it became too much, the pleasure conquering her, taking over. She screamed, "Stephan!" as she came. He climbed over her and in one quick thrust was deep inside, his cock pressed against her womb. His teeth found her nipples and he bit the already erect nubs. He bit her shoulders, her neck, everywhere he could reach while still fucking her, leaving light red marks in his wake. She cried out as he thrust hard and fast. It was exactly what she wanted. She needed him to mark her, to make her his in a primal way. The room spun around her as she cried out another orgasm, but he still didn't stop thrusting.

"Say you're mine," he growled.

"I'm yours! Always…"

"…and forever." His pulsing climax took her over the edge again and they soared, their souls and bodies united as one.

Time stood still as the world waited for them to recover.

Chapter Nineteen

"The beach is beautiful at night, don't you think?"

Mariah interrupted Stephan's thoughts of the battle ahead of him. He looked at her, sweetly smiling up at him, their hands linked tightly as they walked the mile down the beach toward *Rare and Unusual Imports*. The moonlight caressed her body in silver, and even wearing an old pair of sweats he'd procured for her in the cave, she looked like a goddess. His goddess, he smugly thought to himself. The love bite he'd left on her neck visible proof of her status.

"You're beautiful." His voice almost caught as she graced him with an even wider smile. Damn, he wanted her again. Making love to her tonight was the smartest thing he could have done before going into battle. He'd never felt so relaxed and completely prepared to defend Mariah until his last breath.

Which wasn't going to happen. He wouldn't let it.

Turning quickly, he pulled Mariah into his arms, tangling his hands into her hair and tilting her head back so he could feast on her again. She moaned into his mouth and ground herself against him.

Dammit, Stephan, we need you here, now, man. The Dread Lords are here in full force. We're fucking surrounded. Leave Mariah at the cave and get your ass here. Marlin's voice shouting in Stephan's head instantly chilled his desire. The battle had arrived on his very doorstep. He flashed back to the first refuge where David had attacked. He should have known the bastard would do it again. David liked to make it personal.

Too late. We're almost there. Fuck! I don't wanna bring Mariah into this!

Just get here quick, all right? We're seriously outnumbered. Marlin clicked-out.

Stephan grudgingly separated himself from Mariah. Her lust-filled eyes blinked up at him. "Sweetheart, I'm sorry. The guys are in trouble. Serious trouble. The Dread Lords have attacked the shop. I gotta get there, but I just can't take you into that hell." He increased his pace, one hand clamped on her elbow, the other tucked in his jacket pocket, holding a gun.

"I'm going with you."

"No. They'll capture you, Mariah. And they want the rest of us dead. I gotta keep you in a safe place."

"I'm safest with you. We both know that."

Stephan stopped and grabbed Mariah, pulling her to him. He wanted to shake her, make her understand the danger she would always be in. But her simply spoken words were correct. She would be safer by his side, because he'd do anything to keep her alive. "You're mine now. I have to protect you. I can't—I won't lose you."

Mariah smiled up at him, and she moved her hands to his face, cupping his cheeks before she stood up on tiptoe and kissed him. It was the most tender moment of his life.

Mariah pulled away. "You won't lose me, but I can't lose you either. I need to do this. This is my fight, too."

Stephan wanted to argue. But he didn't have time. If Marlin was asking for help, he *really* needed help. It had been years since any of them had needed backup during a battle, so Stephan knew this was serious.

"Can you fight?"

"I took self-defense classes with Twyla. I was pretty good."

"Pretty good isn't gonna cut it. Do you know how to shoot or fight with a weapon at all?"

"I can shoot. I just don't like to."

Stephan took Mariah's hand and pulled her with him. She had to run to keep up with him.

He reached into his jacket and pulled out a gun small enough for her to handle, yet not so small that it would be ineffective, a stiletto, and some pepper spray. "Use the gun first. Shoot to kill. If something bad comes closer, use the pepper spray. Hide the blade on you somewhere for a last resort. If you have to use it, remember that flesh can be very tough to stab through. You'll have to use all your strength, but aim for eyes or groin or somewhere that'll immobilize the attacker as fast as possible. Don't think you can kill him with one slash. But let's hope I kill them all before you have to fire a single bullet.

"Remember, it'll recoil so keep your face away from just behind it. You already know what to do with the pepper spray, right? Do you think you can handle all of this?"

Mariah gave him a proud, fierce stare. "Nothing will stand in my way."

He didn't want to think of the danger she would be in, but from the seriousness in her eyes, he knew that she wouldn't go down without a fight either. And with the rest of the Shadow Walkers there to help protect her, he convinced himself that she would be just fine.

"All right. But you stay with me. And listen to what I say. If I tell you to run, do it, okay?"

Mariah nodded and they ran down the pier toward *Rare and Unusual Imports*. Bulky figures battled in the shadows. Moonlight bounced off weaponry. The sounds of death moans echoed on the breeze. He shivered. He was leading Mariah straight into hell.

* * * * *

My own private, fucking hell. I swear I'm gonna kick Freeze's ass for putting me in this situation.

Yet Twyla couldn't help but think about his claim that he'd fallen in love with her. She'd taken a bath to try to wash away everything, including her damning thoughts, but even that wasn't enough. A skirmish had happened outside the room while she was bathing and she'd cursed herself for thinking that if the door came down, Freeze would've rushed in like Superman to rescue her. In defiance, she'd stayed in the tub and scrubbed her skin nearly raw, hoping to cleanse him completely from her system.

But it hadn't worked. And Freeze hadn't returned. The jerk had probably forgotten about her.

Rummaging through dresser drawers, she found another of his T-shirts. Luckily this navy blue one didn't arouse her as much as that damn gray one had. Adding flannel pants with a drawstring waistband wrenched down to fit her plus a pair of socks, she was more than ready to get that godforsaken door to come open.

Startled by a brilliant violet gleam, Twyla turned toward Freeze's worktable. Pushing aside various crystals and rocks, she discovered an amethyst the size of a chocolate truffle. It seemed to beckon her with its luscious orchid hue. Picking it up, she opened her mind. There had to be some sort of her own magic that she could evoke. Her chaotic whirlwind of emotions materialized as another weapon tornado. She smiled, figuring that if she threw enough blades against the wooden door it would have to splinter like a tree being chopped by an axe.

The weapons spun faster and faster, reaching a velocity where she could barely see them spinning around her. It was such a feeling of power, knowing that she had created the deadly force surrounding her. Arms out, she twirled her body in the peaceful core of the deadly tornado, preparing to hurl all the blades.

The door crashed open and she dropped her hands in confusion. A cacophony of metallic clanging assailed her ears as the tornado fell to the floor. Had Superman come for her after all?

"I have to get you out of here," Freeze hoarsely growled as he staggered into the room.

Time slowed down as she took in the sight before her. Just about every square inch of his clothing was soaked in blood and…guts, perhaps? One pant leg was completely mutilated and the skin beneath had multiple deep lacerations. His shirt was missing completely and that beautiful chest of his was marred with bruises and gore. Blood still oozed from a deep gash in his shoulder. Tattered remnants of coarse rope clung about his wrists. Nasty reddened abrasions swelled beneath the malicious bindings. Blood dripped down his face from a cut somewhere above his hairline.

His eyes, however, were strong. Very strong. Almost knocking Twyla over. He charged toward her as though he wasn't injured in the slightest, then belied that conclusion by losing his footing and flinching painfully when she caught him.

He spoke in whispering gasps. "Craze knows that Stephan and Mariah aren't dead and he's comin' after me. If he finds you…. Shit. I can't let anything happen to you. I gotta get you to the Shadow Walkers."

"Freeze, you already look like *you're* gonna die. Everyone else is okay, but you're not. What the hell is going on?" Twyla couldn't reach the towel she'd thrown onto the bed without fear that Freeze would collapse if she didn't hold him up. She pocketed the amethyst in order to get a better hold on him as he closed his eyes and swayed into her further. He was clearly fighting shock again and she had absolutely no idea what to do about anything. Sure the doggone door was open now, but she wasn't about to go through it without Freeze.

She wasn't even sure if he'd heard her question. Every breath he took seemed to take more energy than he had, but he continued. "He summoned me to help take care of them, but I tricked him using a spell that made it look like they were floating dead in the water. You were so concerned about her…Shit. Not now. There's no time to explain. Twyla, you need to stay with the Shadow Walkers. I'm almost out of energy."

"Well, shit, that's obvious. Freeze, I—" Her words ceased as he wrapped his arms around her, infusing his body with hers, kissing her with such urgency it seemed his very survival may have depended upon it.

She wanted to help him somehow. Maybe share some of her energy with him. If that was even possible. She closed her eyes, opening her mind like when she'd evoked the weapon tornado, and offered herself to Freeze. His tongue induced rapture as it twisted with hers. His hands squeezed and stroked and swept along her body, as though he needed to touch all of her at once, uniting their bodies as one. All of her senses were on overload and her mind's eye lost sight. It was as though he was reaching within her or pushing her away or both, but their bodies couldn't get any closer without melting into one another.

Upon regaining sight, she was in front of the import store with him. She felt woozy and incomplete, like he really had taken something from her. All around them were the sounds of battle. Screams, mayhem, death. But she couldn't take her eyes away from the torture in her lover's eyes.

Freeze slid his hands onto her shoulders. "You're gonna have to be strong, Twyla. Use your powers. You have a lot more within you than you think…and I meant what I said before I left you earlier."

"What?" A strong arm grabbed her around her waist and she turned her head, prepared to fight. Marlin held her close, a gun pointed toward Freeze, a fierce look in his eyes. Glancing back at Freeze, her jaw dropped. He had disappeared.

And she'd been right. He'd taken a piece of her heart with him.

* * * * *

Mariah gagged with every breath she took, the pungent stench of demon death permeating the air around her. Chaos assailed her ears, the moans of the dying, the screams of the wounded, and the sound of Stephan meting punishment on the creatures attacking him. He fought like he did everything else, with complete focus, yet Mariah could tell he knew exactly where she was at all times. And nothing made it past him.

Mariah remained amazingly unscathed. He'd promised to keep her safe, and she knew he'd keep that promise.

Moonlight and scattered streetlamps melded, providing the only light, but shadows overtook their efforts. Mariah knew that not seeing the horrors afoot was probably preferable to viewing the carnage. She stayed as close to Stephan as she could, afraid if they got separated in the melee, she wouldn't be able to find him again.

The demons kept coming. No matter how quickly they were dispatched, there was always another...and another...and another to continue the fight. Stephan never faltered, his movements so fast and furious Mariah could only watch as the bodies hit the ground, some disintegrating, some melting, some lying in bloodied lumps.

Adrenaline flooded her system, her only thoughts: staying alive, keeping her baby safe, and helping Stephan fight if she could. Her inner rationality dueled with her emotions. She knew she had to stay out of the way, but she wanted to help, anything more than just stand at Stephan's back.

Something warm and wet splashed across her face. Turning her head, she saw Dusty fighting on her right. Mariah swiped her hand across her face and shuddered as it came away covered in thick green mucus.

Dusty growled as he punched his fist clear through a tall hairy creature. Ripping his hand back out, the demon fell at his feet and was quickly kicked to the side.

His eyes quickly met hers. "You okay?"

Mariah frantically nodded as Dusty turned and jumped back into the fight.

Glass shattered as a scaly creature jumped through the front window of *Rare and Unusual Imports*. A well-muscled man Mariah didn't recognize—maybe Ryan?—followed him and within seconds the bloodied demon was thrown back outside...in pieces. The man jumped back through the window, blades flashing as he took on several more creatures.

Jake stood on the roof of the import store, throwing some type of metal discs into the battle below. Whatever he was using seemed to work as Mariah could see bodies falling wherever he aimed.

Stephan grunted and slammed back into her, his hand reaching behind him as though to protect her from himself. She scattered backward, her bare feet slipping in demon slime although she somehow managed to stay upright. He hit the ground and immediately four demons converged on him.

"No!!!" Rage ripped through her and she screamed, raising the gun, rapidly firing into the onslaught of beasts. They fell like dominoes, knocking over two other demons, then crumbling to dust as they hit the ground. Stephan was already back on his feet, brawling with something else.

Only a few minutes had passed since they'd arrived on the pier...a few minutes that felt like hours.

Stephan prevented the demons from getting close enough for her to fight hand to hand, but with heightened senses, she was always moving, always watching. A fire raged nearby, and a woman with long red hair seemed to control the flames, manipulating creatures into the blaze and to their death. Thankful for both the death of demons and for the light provided by the inferno, Mariah took a solitary deep breath. It looked like the demons were lessening.

Then, through the crowd, she spotted Twyla. Firelight glinted off discarded blades as she picked them up. Thank God she was still alive! Marlin shadowed her every move as she slashed at whatever creatures approached. Holding a gun in each hand, he continuously fired into the beasts around him.

A shout breached Mariah's concentration and she turned her head in time to see Jake being thrown from the roof into a group of hellions below. Dusty disappeared into the crowd after him.

Slam! The next thing Mariah knew, she was on the ground staring up at the night sky. She rolled to her feet, searching for

Stephan, but only seeing a crowd of demons where he had been. Then a demon fell in the mass and she saw Stephan locked in battle, claws wrapped around his neck. Fear had her surging forward, emptying her gun at the demons surrounding Stephan, but as though multiplying at death, they instantly replaced themselves. Numbness took over, and in a blind rage she attacked with the pepper spray and the butt of the gun, spraying and slamming at anything that came near.

"Dammit, Mariah, run!" Stephan shouted but her feet wouldn't listen and she stepped up her attack. She couldn't leave him here, wouldn't leave him alone.

Stephan shouted again, but this time in pain as a claw pierced his shoulder.

"Somebody help!" Mariah screamed. She stole a moment to look around, hoping someone was near. The man she thought was Ryan raced toward her, dodging weapons as he approached. His eyes widened and he fell, a weird skewer sticking out off his ribs. His attacker pounced on him, but met a shredding death. Dusty knocked his way through the unholy chaos, his eyes flashing between Ryan, Stephan and herself. His roar filled the night and he fell as a short, squatty demon bit down on his calf, removing a chunk before scurrying away.

Three of the Shadow Walkers were down. Mariah wanted to scream—what the hell could she do? Her can of pepper spray long since emptied, she threw it to the ground. Somehow she'd lost her gun, so she began attacking with her bare hands. The demons surrounding Stephan acted like they didn't even notice her, not even bothering to shrug her off or prevent her attack.

Incredibly, Stephan was holding his own although he'd sustained some cuts and bruises. Through the melee, his eyes met Mariah's for a brief second, full of pain, fear and love. She remembered his fight with the werewolf the other night and what Marlin had said about his fighting prowess, about all of their abilities. She hoped they weren't outnumbered this time.

"Mariah! Run!" She heard Twyla's scream and looked up from her fighting to see a terror struck Twyla hurtling toward her through the battle. But then Twyla went out of view as Mariah was jerked off her feet by a pair of strong arms and rapidly pulled away from the battle. She assumed Marlin was trying to help, but then the man spoke.

"You are mine."

Craze's voice instantly curdled her blood. In a frenzy, she clawed at the arms entrapping her, fighting against his overwhelming strength. He just laughed and spun her around, kissing her so deeply she lost sight.

His kiss was a brutal rape on her senses. Struggling against the blindness, she managed to pull her mouth away. Craze chuckled and ran his tongue down her face. One arm held her tight against him in a punishing grip. He waved his free hand, and like earlier on the yacht, electricity arced from him. But this time, the electricity seemed to burn the very air.

Mariah stared, torn between fascination and horror. Where before there had been nothing, now stood a doorway—no, a portal—into what looked to be a paradise. Like a picture of heaven, vivid blue sky, bright sun, lush greenery, flowers, and a gentle river, beckoned to her, an escape from the butchering and havoc. But she teetered on the edge with a madman, and paradise with him would be true hell.

"Our sanctuary, Mariah." Craze spun her around, facing the skirmish, his arms now wrapped around her from behind. "Stephan will die. Just watch this fray."

"No, I'd prefer to participate." With lightning speed, Mariah drew the stiletto Stephan had given her and slammed it into Craze's thigh as hard as she could. She waited for him to roar in pain, to drop his arm and let her go.

All he did was hold her tighter. "Mmmm...I am really going to relish mastering you." He latched his lips onto her neck and sucked hard.

Oh, God.... Mariah's blood ran cold. He must have seen the love mark Stephan had left on her earlier and was trying to mark her as well. "You fucking asshole."

He laughed, then pulled the stiletto from his thigh as though nothing had happened. "Look at all the Pawns, Mariah. I believe we are at Check right now. The Queen is mine and all of the Pawns will be removed from play. There will be no trading for the Queen today. Not one will survive to cross this board." Using the stiletto, he gestured across the battlefield. He didn't even seem to notice his own disgusting blood dripping from it. "Besides, I want you all to myself. Your fire. The hotter, the better."

If he wanted to talk in riddles, she could play that game. "Haven't you heard? I'm the ice queen of *Silver Twilight*. I don't burn."

"Everything has a combustion point, Mariah." He placed his hand over her stomach, small sparks arcing between his fingertips and the bloody stiletto's length. "And I can make you burn…"

* * * * *

Where the hell was Mariah? Stephan kicked something off his leg, and threw another demon to the side. He rolled to his feet, searching for her. Had she run like he'd told her to? His instincts screamed of danger, but that was obvious.

Something slashed his back diagonally from shoulder to waist, the excruciating pain nearly bringing him to his knees. Wetness immediately poured from the wound. Whipping about, he decimated the ghastly perpetrator with a quick stab to the heart, twisting the blade for good measure. The bloody sword it carried clattered to rest on the gore-soaked wood of the pier.

Blinking back the newfound burning agony, he took in the destruction before him. Some of his men were down, but still fighting. And Mariah wasn't with any of them. He turned in a full circle, taking in all the carnage, fighting off demons as he desperately searched for her.

His heart nearly stopped when he finally located Mariah. Wrapped in Craze's embrace, she wanted to fight, but the bastard had one hand over her stomach, the stiletto ready to pierce her womb. They were standing in front of a dimensional portal—one step back and his family would be gone. The same way Marlin had lost Judy.

Stephan open-clicked to the Shadow Walkers. *Craze has Mariah so don't do anything stupid. No fast tricks. Protect the injured. Remember, no one goes down in vain.* He clicked-out. Jake immediately appeared at his side, stepping in to the clash, giving Stephan the escape he needed. He stalked toward Craze and Mariah, throwing demons to the side, not letting anything stop him from reaching her.

The whirring of a great wind took Stephan aback. Turning toward the sound, he saw a small dark-haired woman he assumed must be Twyla. She stood defiantly with arms raised to the sky. Metal clanged as weapons took to the air, spinning like a deadly tornado around her. Demon weaponry, Shadow Walker weaponry, any and all menacing devices took to the air. Even the stiletto that Craze was holding joined the whirlwind.

Aghast, Stephan threw himself to the pier, barely avoiding beheading by more than one blade. As the wind increased, all of the weapons in his jacket emptied into the twister. He quickly surveyed the danger. All Shadow Walkers remained alive, though battered.

But Mariah remained threatened.

The tempest raged with fury taking the demons by surprise, murdering around half of them. With such show of decimation, many more actually retreated.

Using the chaos of the cyclone, Stephan snaked his way toward Mariah and her captor. It looked as though Craze enjoyed the show of Twyla's power. With one arm outstretched, he motioned in her direction. Losing her balance, she dropped her arms and slid toward him against her will. The weapons crashed to the pier, imbedding in wood and flesh. Stephan rolled to avoid being turned into a shish kabob, grabbing weapons and pocketing them as he moved.

When Stephan was only a few feet from Mariah, a blond haired man appeared directly between Twyla and Craze, breaking whatever spell Craze had placed on her. Twyla stumbled to a halt, falling backward. Although the man was battered and bruised, Stephan hadn't seen him engaged in the battle thus far.

"Traitorous ways are not becoming, Freeze," Craze taunted, lowering his hand as though changing tactics. But the blond man countered his move, drawing one fist back and pointing his other hand at the portal behind Craze. Flames burst forth, licking the edges of the portal as it morphed and twisted, turning into a hell. Damn. Stephan just hoped the man was one of the good guys.

"I shoulda done this a long time ago." The man hurled his fist, making solid contact with Craze's jaw as Mariah ducked the impact.

Whoever that man was, Stephan was thankful for the distraction. He charged in, ripping Mariah from Craze's grasp.

Shoving her behind him to keep her as far away from that bastard as possible, he turned his attention to Craze. This had to end tonight.

With flames licking around his body, Craze stood calmly on the edge of the portal, watching Stephan. With all of his remaining strength, Stephan lunged, forcing the whoreson deeper into the portal. "Die, you fucking bastard!"

Craze hovered as the flames twisted around him, a knowing grin wide across his face. "Who's the bastard, brother of mine?"

Craze calmly fell into the portal. Stephan wasn't even sure if he pushed Craze hard enough or the monster just fell.

His brother.

Stephan backed away and quickly turned to find Mariah. When he saw that she was safely behind him, he reached for her, but an explosion had him ripping his head back around as a fireball blasted out of the portal toward him.

He dove for Mariah, throwing her to the ground and covering her with his body. He watched as Twyla raised her arm, shooting a purple spark, knocking the fireball off course. The spark ricocheted, slamming the blond man into the portal as the fireball shot off into the night sky.

"Freeze!" Twyla shouted in anguish as she rushed toward the portal. It shimmered vibrantly then closed. She sank to the ground, her whole body shaking.

Stephan winced as he wearily lifted himself off Mariah. The painful wounds tormenting his shoulder and back were finally beginning to drain his strength as the adrenaline slowly left his bloodstream.

He glanced around the area, making sure no danger remained. Every last demon had either died or retreated. Marlin had his arms wrapped tightly around Twyla. She still knelt in front of where the portal had been, rocking back and forth in his arms. Jake and Ana were helping Ryan and Dusty into the import store. Everyone was in need of Fiero's services tonight.

It was over. At least for now. But, he didn't harbor the belief that all was won.

Helping Mariah to her feet, he smoothed her hair from her face and wiped a smear of blood off her cheek. She smiled up at him and his heart melted. "You okay, sweetheart?"

She simply nodded and stood on tiptoe, placing her lips against his. He kissed her hard and long, unable to deny himself the connection he so desperately sought. His hands roamed her body, needing the reassurance that she really was okay.

When he was satisfied Mariah was unscathed, he slowly pulled away and met her loving eyes. Tenderly she ran a hand over his face, skimming over the cuts and bruises he'd sustained. She lowered her hand to his shoulder, cringing as she pulled the shredded remnants of his jacket apart, examining the wound beneath. "Let's take care of you," she whispered quietly.

He took her hand, limping toward the shop. He looked at his friends, his family, and the battlefield the pier had been turned into. It would take awhile to get *Rare and Unusual Imports* back in shape again, but it was a small price to pay. Clearly, the battle had been won. But a war of tremendous magnitude and complexity had just begun. Thankfully, he knew he wouldn't face it alone.

Epilogue

One week later

Mariah danced into the living room area of her new home beneath the import store. Her world had changed so significantly in the past week, but she couldn't imagine it any other way.

Twyla sat cross-legged on the floor next to the couch, piles of beads surrounding her as she worked on a new necklace. She'd moved into the Shadow Walker compound as well. It was getting rather crowded down there, with all the guys, Ana, and Mariah and Twyla moving in.

And even though Twyla wouldn't admit it, she was suffering aftershocks from her captivity. Mariah could sense that something had happened to Twyla that she hadn't yet shared. But Mariah would be there for her when she was ready to talk about it.

Talisman Bay had been remarkably quiet since David had disappeared into another dimension. Without their leader, the Dread Lords had quietly disappeared back into whatever hellhole they'd crawled out of, although no one fostered hope that it was going to end that simply. *Rare and Unusual Imports* had taken quite a beating during the attack, but the local police had chalked it up to the same vandals that had hit the flower shop. The import store was open for business within a day and the locals quickly forgot about it.

Stephan had used a few of his resources and learned that David had been telling the truth about their relationship. They did share a father, and a lineage that Stephan wanted no part of. Mariah and their baby were his family.

Lover's Talisman

Twyla glanced up at Mariah and smiled as she danced over, though her eyes remained sad. "Still the happy new love bird. I told you ya just needed to get laid."

Mariah laughed. "Well, you were half right. Getting laid has definitely improved my outlook on life, but it wouldn't have mattered if I didn't love Stephan so much."

Twyla sighed and looked back down at the necklace clenched in her hand. Mariah couldn't remain quiet.

"You know, you can talk to me about anything."

"Yeah, I know." Twyla remained silent. "So…did you call Monte?"

So, she wanted to change the subject. Okay…. "Yeah. I did. And you won't believe it. I've been so afraid to tell Monte that I'm never coming back to *Silver Twilight*, and when I finally work up the nerve to tell him, he tells me that he's leaving as well."

Twyla looked up, her brown eyes questioning.

"Yeah, Lewis auditioned for a role in a soap opera last month, and he got the part. It's a recurring role, with the possibility of becoming a major character. So Monte and Lewis are moving to Los Angeles."

"Good for Lewis. I always liked him," Twyla said, her voice genuinely sounding happy.

"But the best part is that Monte sold *Silver Twilight* to Diesel. I think he'll make a great new owner."

"Diesel's the hot bouncer guy, right? Bald, muscular, bad-assed…" A mild note of interest crept into Twyla's voice. "The one you dated?"

"Yeah, that's him. And it was only one date." Mariah shrugged.

"Well, it sucks that he's losing the biggest money draw before he even takes over."

"Well, he'll have to manage because no one is seeing my woman naked anymore but me." Stephan stepped through the stairway door and Mariah's body lit up just at the sight of him. She knew that they'd spend the next hour in bed as had become usual during his daily lunch breaks.

Mariah dodged the furniture and ran to him. When she reached him, he swept her up and kissed her, practically knocking her senseless. God how she loved this man.

"Hello, gorgeous. Ready for lunch?" He wiggled his eyebrows and grinned.

She kissed him again. "Is that answer enough for you?"

"And how's the baby?"

"Not a problem…but it has only been a week. Most normal people wouldn't even know they were pregnant yet."

Stephan's hazel eyes sparkled with love as he knelt down and kissed her still flat stomach. "Hello, baby. You keep being good to your mommy."

Mariah's heart swelled with pride. He was so tender, so caring kneeling there in front of her. He would make an amazing father. Just like her father would have if he'd been given the chance.

Mariah ran her fingers through Stephan's thick dark hair and he looked up at her and smiled. He slid up her body and kissed her nose. "Let's go to bed."

The door behind them opened and Dusty lumbered through. He still had a limp from the demon bite he'd sustained during the Dread Lord battle. Fiero had chastised him for taking too long to get healed. The poison from the bite had infected the muscles and tendons in his calf, and even with Fiero's magic would probably never fully heal. But Dusty didn't seem to notice. Mariah had learned that nothing slowed down the Shadow Walkers.

"Oh, there you are. Jake and I just finished our sweep of the old Dread Lord compound. It's still quiet. We haven't been able to open a few doors in the place, but Fiero's working with The Order on some spells so we can make sure they aren't hiding anything important behind them."

Twyla's voice sounded out from the corner of the room. "When you open the doors, I wanna be there."

Mariah saw a look pass between Dusty and Stephan. Stephan spoke up. "We'll make sure you're there."

Stephan grasped Mariah's hand in his. "Dusty, we're eating lunch now—"

Dusty grinned. "I'd like to 'eat lunch' like you do everyday." He laughed as Stephan scowled at him. "Have fun." Dusty shuffled to his room, his laughter echoing behind him.

Twyla stood up from the floor and made her way toward the both of them. Mariah could feel Stephan's desperation to get her alone, but she also knew that her friend needed her.

Twyla stopped in front of Stephan and crossed her arms in front of her chest. "I'll kill you if you hurt her."

Mariah's jaw dropped as she looked between her friend and her lover. "He wouldn't—"

"You can kill me if I ever hurt her. But I never will. I promise you." Stephan placed one arm protectively around Mariah and reached his other hand out to Twyla. She looked him over and then nodded, taking his hand and shaking it.

"Um...hello? Standing right here!"

Twyla held out her clenched hand and gestured for Mariah to do the same. She held out her hand as Twyla dropped a necklace into it.

"You fixed it!" Mariah held up the silver blue necklace that had been ripped from her neck when the Dread Lords had kidnapped her. "Now I can wear it when I go out so it can protect me."

"I protect you," Stephan reminded her. Mariah laughed and began to put on the necklace. Stephan took it from her and fastened it around her neck.

"There isn't a protection spell on it," Twyla said nonchalantly.

"Oh? Did the spell wear off? Doesn't matter. I'll wear it anyway." Mariah happily patted it. The necklace felt *right*.

"Actually, I never put a protection spell on it."

Mariah looked at her in astonishment. "What? Why?"

Twyla grinned, but her eyes still held a hint of sadness. For a moment Mariah forgot what she was talking about and just wished Twyla would confide in her.

"I just wanted you to be happy. You'd been alone for too long. So, I put a spell on it for you to find your heart's greatest desire. It wasn't a protector's talisman, it was a lover's talisman."

Twyla's grin widened as Mariah's jaw dropped open yet again. Mariah glanced at Stephan, who stared at her with the same look of wonder.

"Thanks aren't necessary. The look on both of your faces is enough...not to mention the sounds you two make all night long."

Twyla turned around and headed back to where she'd been sitting earlier.

Mariah looked into the eyes of her greatest desire and smiled. Twyla had been right all along.

Stephan returned her smile and took her hand, guiding her to their bedroom. She went with him willingly, knowing she wouldn't have it any other way.

As the two lovebirds disappeared down the hallway together, Twyla resumed her position on the floor. She held the necklace she'd just finished making that morning, the warmth of the beads burning her hands that had been unnaturally cold for the last week—since she'd accidentally sent Freeze along with Craze to the hell dimension and then sealed his fate by closing the portal. She murmured the spell again, the spell she'd used on Mariah's necklace that had brought her love to her. For the last week she'd tried everything she knew, everything she was learning, to bring Freeze back to her. She had even tried to gather his essence from the amethyst crystal she'd grabbed from his worktable.

But he was gone. The void she felt inside attested to that.

Twyla tried to ignore the fear that had become a constant companion. But she couldn't. The magic Freeze had told her she carried inside grew stronger by the day. And with that magic came a knowledge, a knowledge she wished she didn't have.

All of them were still in danger.

And Craze was very much alive.

The fight was far from over. In fact, it had barely just begun.

The End

Coming Soon

An innocent woman's life is forever altered by the evil determined to destroy the Shadow Walkers. With no knowledge of who she is or where she came from, she takes solace in the arms of the man who is determined to keep her safe. But will their search for the truth of who she really is destroy them both? Watch for *Forsaken Talisman*, coming soon...

About the author:

Sometimes two people meet, become good friends, and share a lot in common. When you're really lucky, you meet someone who understands you, who thinks like you, can finish your sentences and together, the both of you can create whole new worlds. Ashleigh Raine is the pen name for two best friends, Jennifer and Lisa, who share a passion for strong alpha males that succumb to the women they fall in love with. Both of them are married to their soul mates, who are the best support and inspiration. As Ashleigh Raine, this duo has many stories to tell, as their collective mind never stops creating fantasies that must be written down. They write larger than life stories, with adventures, hot sex, peril, hot sex, mystery, and more hot sex...but most assuredly they have a happy ending, usually with hot sex. Watch for many titles coming soon from this duo who are glad to have found their niche in writing erotic romances.

Ashleigh Raine welcomes mail from readers. You can write to her c/o Ellora's Cave Publishing at P.O. Box 787, Hudson, Ohio 44236-0787.

Also by ASHLEIGH RAINE:

- Acting On Impulse

Why an electronic book?

We live in the Information Age—an exciting time in the history of human civilization in which technology rules supreme and continues to progress in leaps and bounds every minute of every hour of every day. For a multitude of reasons, more and more avid literary fans are opting to purchase e-books instead of paperbacks. The question to those not yet initiated to the world of electronic reading is simply: *why?*

1. *Price.* An electronic title at Ellora's Cave Publishing runs anywhere from 40-75% less than the cover price of the <u>exact same title</u> in paperback format. Why? Cold mathematics. It is less expensive to publish an e-book than it is to publish a paperback, so the savings are passed along to the consumer.
2. *Space.* Running out of room to house your paperback books? That is one worry you will never have with electronic novels. For a low one-time cost, you can purchase a handheld computer designed specifically for e-reading purposes. Many e-readers are larger than the average handheld, giving you plenty of screen room. Better yet, hundreds of titles can be stored within your new library—a single microchip. (Please note that Ellora's Cave does not endorse any specific brands. You can check our website at www.ellorascave.com for customer recommendations we make available to new consumers.)

3. *Mobility.* Because your new library now consists of only a microchip, your entire cache of books can be taken with you wherever you go.
4. *Personal preferences are accounted for.* Are the words you are currently reading too small? Too large? Too...**ANNOYING**? Paperback books cannot be modified according to personal preferences, but e-books can.
5. *Innovation.* The way you read a book is not the only advancement the Information Age has gifted the literary community with. There is also the factor of what you can read. Ellora's Cave Publishing will be introducing a new line of interactive titles that are available in e-book format only.
6. *Instant gratification.* Is it the middle of the night and all the bookstores are closed? Are you tired of waiting days—sometimes weeks—for online and offline bookstores to ship the novels you bought? Ellora's Cave Publishing sells instantaneous downloads 24 hours a day, 7 days a week, 365 days a year. Our e-book delivery system is 100% automated, meaning your order is filled as soon as you pay for it.

Those are a few of the top reasons why electronic novels are displacing paperbacks for many an avid reader. As always, Ellora's Cave Publishing welcomes your questions and comments. We invite you to email us at service@ellorascave.com or write to us directly at: P.O. Box 787, Hudson, Ohio 44236-0787.

Printed in the United States
1500800001B/71